Equinox

EQUINOX

The Second Book of Ascension

Dirk Strasser

Chimaera Publications

First published by Pan Macmillan Australia in 1996
Macmillan Momentum eBook editions published in 2013
This edition published in 2014 by Chimaera Publications

Chimaera Publications / Aurealis Books
www.aurealis.com.au
PO Box 2164, Mt Waverley Vic 3149, Australia

National Library of Australia Cataloguing-in-Publication entry: (hardback)
Creator: Strasser, Dirk, author.
Title: Equinox: the second book of ascension / Dirk Strasser.
ISBN: 9781922031846 (hardback)
Series: Books of ascension; 2.
Subjects: Fantasy fiction.
Dewey Number: A823.3

National Library of Australia Cataloguing-in-Publication entry: (paperback)
Creator: Strasser, Dirk, author.
Title: Equinox: the second book of ascension / Dirk Strasser.
ISBN: 9781922031815 (paperback)
Series: Books of ascension; 2.
Subjects: Fantasy fiction.
Dewey Number: A823.3

For my brother Volker, even if you don't like fantasy

I write this for the generations of Maelir to come so that they may learn of the great Mountain which is the axis of the universe, its spirit the heart of the world. And as with any heart, when it is broken it cries in pain for what has been lost, and when it is mended it cries in joy for what has been regained.

–The Book of Maelur

Praise for Equinox and the Books of Ascension

'*Zenith* was a great book... *Equinox* is even better in virtually every regard... it's an engrossing story that touches on serious issues.'
  –Van Ikin

'*Equinox* has sword fights, adventure, intrigue, wars, characters who fall in love and get laid, yet behind it all there is a sense of political realism, of integrity, of imagination, that is unusual in modern fantasy.'
  –Bill Congreve, *Aurealis*

'Strasser... delivers meaningful character and plot development while continuing the same high standard of world-building, adventure, and wonder which make *Zenith* so enjoyable. Highly recommended to fans of *Zenith*, and a worthy lead-up to *Eclipse*.'
  –Alex Stevenson

'*Equinox* delivers! I was drawn in immediately as I continued the story from the first book... This series is unfolding into a complex tale that reminds me of why I have a deep rooted love for epic fantasies. Again, fans of fantasy, you will not be disappointed with Strasser's Books of Ascension series!'
  –Pretty Little Pages

'*Equinox* by Dirk Strasser builds on the foundation of book one, *Zenith*, maintaining the same atmospheric quality and intensely spellbinding plot, this time ratcheting up the tension... This is truly epic fantasy that comes to life in your mind and can be read and re-read with ease.'
  –Tome Tender

'Dirk Strasser's *Zenith*... is on my list of all-time worldwide Top Ten fantasy novels... It does what all good quest novels do, and does it better than almost any of them – that is, it creates wonders.'
    –Richard Harland, author of *Worldshaker*

'*Zenith* deserves to sell as many copies as all the other best-selling quest fantasy novels which fill our bookstores, if only because it does what they do as well as (if not better than) they do it. *Zenith* is enjoyable, entertaining and, in the end, a satisfying read. What more can I ask for?'
    –*Eidolon*

'More of this please... a real story, real characters with believable backgrounds... a colossal canvas... and a good story.'
    –*Australian Realms*

'*Zenith* moves along at a good pace and has a strong central character. Strasser handles the elements of mysticism with insight and still keeps an entertaining flow... a mind-blowing metaphysical experience.'
    –*The Courier-Mail*

'At last in the world of letters we have a novel where women approach a patriarchal religion with the appropriate attitude... *Zenith* is a good read; it is also both original and intellectually stimulating.'
    –*The Mentor*

Strasser's unique blend of adventure, esotericism, Eastern mysticism, and fantasy makes for compelling reading... Strasser has not just written down a legend, rather, he has crafted one.'
    –Amazon review

'These books have shown me why I appreciate and love fantasy so much. All of the parts of this trilogy blend so effortlessly... This series is one that fantasy fans will adore and fly through. If you

haven't discovered Dirk Strasser's Books of Ascension series, do yourself a favor and pick them up. You'll not be disappointed.'
    –Pretty Little Pages

'With great writing, characters who go through such steady development readers can easily follow along on their journey, and an epic, engaging world, Dirk Strasser has weaved an intriguing fantasy series that is a must-read for all fans of epic fantasy.'
    –I Heart Reading

'When I finished this last book in the trilogy, I was sad to leave Atreu's world... When a reader becomes that engrossed, that connected to the tale and its people that is the sign of masterful writing!'
    –Tome Tender

'Strasser's descriptive writing style made me feel like I was actually watching this on the big screen... I recommend this series to science-fiction and fantasy lovers. In particular those who like stories centered around epic journeys like *The Lord of the Rings*.'
    –Readers and Writers Connect

'This one will set the heart aflutter for the true fantasy reader... and with a dose of spiritualism and action tossed in the mix, it's bound to attract the attention of several genres.'
    –For the Love of Books

'The world Dirk Strasser has created is genuinely original and fascinating... with characters so engaging that I really found it hard to stop reading. In fact, this was one of those books that I began to lament ending. The book is packed full of ideas that could spawn books in their own right.'
    –Shane M Brown, author of *Plaza*

Also by Dirk Strasser

Zenith: The First Book of Ascension

Eclipse: The Lost Book of Ascension

Stories of the Sand

Graffiti

Aurealis Duo: Transalienation

Aurealis: The Collectors' Edition (co-editor)

The Aurealis Mega Oz SF Anthology (co-editor)

Aurealis – Australian Fantasy & Science Fiction (co-editor)

Acknowledgements

How can one person create a world? Thank you to Lucy, who gave it colour and depth, and to the others who helped *Equinox* see the light of day: Eugen Strasser, Erika Strasser, Michael Pryor, Stephen Higgins, Mark Dusting, Greg Hill, Malcolm Parsons, Geoff Phillips, Kim McKillop, Megan Burke, Van Ikin, Madonna Duffy and Catherine Gibson.

The Second Book

The old Reader closed the book and turned to his silent companion.

'So you see, my young friend, as always the end is the beginning and the beginning is the end.' He was used to the age-cracked edge in his own voice, and had long ago given up wondering how it sounded to others.

The Reader stood up slowly, his joints groaning like ancient wood, and he shuffled towards the shelves of books which lined the walls of his room. He ran his finger across the lettering embossed on the rich leather cover of the book he had just been reading.

'As you now know,' he said, inclining his head slightly in the direction of his silent companion, but without actually looking at him, 'the last page is always the first and so we begin again.'

There was no reply, but the old man nodded his head wisely as if he had heard a comment he had expected.

'Yes, of course you are right, my young friend. It is never exactly the same, because we have grown in knowledge in the reading.'

He slowly slid the book back into its place on the shelf. 'We grow in the telling just as the tale does. How perceptive of you.'

His fingers trembled slightly as he touched the next book on the shelf. He drew a deep breath.

'It is always the same with a new one. You don't have to tell me – I know your hand shakes as does mine and your breath quickens as does mine. We just never know how the next one will change us, do we?' He pulled the book out and stared at the cover for a moment.

'And I hope, my silent young friend, that you learnt your lesson from the last one. We are all a tale within a tale within a tale. And who knows, at this very moment, someone in some far-distant land may be reading about us.'

The Reader laughed softly to himself as if he had just become aware of a joke. 'Now, there's a thought.'

He looked at the title on the cover and the laughter caught in his throat like a fishbone.

'I'm afraid,' he said, 'the darkness may grow in this one.' His fingers traced a path along the book's edge. 'Although you never can tell, can you? You just never can tell.'

For a moment, it was as if his silent companion was about to speak.

'No,' he said quickly, motioning to stop the words, 'now is not the time. We are about to embark on another journey. Whether this one will be an Ascent or a Descent, I do not yet know. Nor do I want to know. Perhaps, as with the last one, it will be both.'

He opened to the first page. 'And, my young friend, you must promise me, as you did the last time, not to look.' He hesitated. 'Can you promise me that?'

The Reader turned towards his silent companion, but there was no-one there.

He smiled and turned back to the book to begin reading.

Prologue

Alone girl made her way through the maze of giant granite boulders. She was grateful that the eve-wind masked the sound of her footfalls. The deep red ringlets of her hair almost straightened as warm gusts of wind hit her face and shot past. She laughed to herself. This will be easy, she thought, perhaps even easier than the others had been. She knew that the villagers would suspect nothing – they had been too engrossed in their preparations for Harvest Night. The celebrations would, no doubt, be well under way, the wine and ale flowing as swiftly as the River Maelstrom. How fitting that this was to be the night.

Her eyes scanned the ground for signs of impermanence. She knew it was the only thing she wouldn't be able to control, the only thing beyond anyone's control. There had been no indication of cracks or fissures, but although few had her eye for the signs, she could never be certain. Still, it would have to be a major upheaval to stop the raid that had been planned.

A knowing smile twisted her otherwise fair young face. The Watching gave her a sense of power over the destinies of the Maelir, and with each of the nine days of Zenith, the power had seemed to grow. Safely hidden from view, she felt it course through her strong, lithe body: the feeling that she could choose who would survive and who would die. Of course, she knew the feeling was still elusive. The heat of battle often brought its own unexpected results, and she had as yet no control over the other members of the coveyn. She did know, however, that despite her tender years, her stature grew with every victory.

As the rocks around her increased to massive heights, the gusts of wind lost much of their force. Although she thought it unlikely that any villager would be this far from the celebrations, her hand never left the handle of her sheathstone knife. She had already learned never to be too certain of anything in life. Her path forked constantly, but she quickened her pace, trusting her uncanny eye for detail to lead her in the right direction. Turning a final corner, she saw the coveyn encampment. It was a mass of frantic activity as her sisters prepared for battle.

'Valkyra, tell us your news.' The coveyn leader, Rhea, directed the order at her immediately.

'The villagers are only going through the motions of having vigils for the night,' said Valkyra. 'It won't be long before the vigils join in the celebrations as well. If we choose the early morning, there won't be many Maelir in fit a state to resist us.'

'So you offer battle plans as well, Valkyra? You may be tall for your age, but you are still many years away from the experience needed to give counsel. Stick to your talents as a Watcher.'

Valkyra glared at the coveyn leader. 'I thought I was stating the obvious, Rhea. Surely the morning is the best time.'

Rhea's gaze burned back brightly. The young girl's arrogance was growing daily, and if she was already openly defiant as a nine-year-old, then she would present a real threat to Rhea's leadership in the future. 'Your counsel will be treated with the respect it deserves.' She raised her voice as she gave the command to the others. 'Make ready for battle! We move under the cover of night, as always.'

Valkyra clenched her teeth and turned away. This was not the time for any stand. She knew Rhea was threatened by her, and the leader was letting it affect her judgement. But it didn't really matter – Valkyra knew she already had the ear of many of the younger members of the coveyn. Time was on her side.

'Come, help us with the brimstones. Don't think your Watching duties spare you from all the other tasks.' The call came from Ahrai, one of the older girls standing on the small rise in a far corner of the clearing.

Valkyra joined the group of five who were busy removing the top layer of soil from a shallow pit. On her hands and knees she sifted through the dirt until she came upon one of the small deep red stones they were looking for. As always, she marvelled at the coolness that belied its violent red heart. She carefully placed it on the small pile with the others. In the gathering darkness she could see the brimstones burning with a redness that almost matched her hair. 'How long have these been buried?' she asked.

'Since our encampment,' said one of the others.

'Nine Zeniths? No wonder their flames are so bright. The village and all its ripe grain is going to burn like a giant torch.' Valkyra laughed. 'I hope the Maelir enjoy their celebrations.'

'Tell us about the Faelen in the village,' asked Ahrai, still busily sifting for brimstones as she spoke.

Valkyra stopped and directed an icy glare in Ahrai's direction. 'Hold your tongue, Ahrai. I don't want to hear that word.'

'Valkyra, you talk sometimes as if you lead the coveyn instead of being just a Watcher. I'll use any word I wish in your presence. I use *Faelen* to mean what the Faemir have always taken it to mean: the unfree, the fallen ones. There's nothing wrong with saying the word. It's *being* a Faelen that's the problem.'

Valkyra's lithe body tensed – Ahrai's barb had stung her. She had little choice but to suffer humiliation at the hands of Rhea, but this was another matter entirely.

'Who was your Birthmother?' continued Ahrai, clearly revelling in the effect she was having on Valkyra. 'I know mine.'

This was too much for Valkyra. She sprang from her crouched position onto Ahrai, clawing furiously at her tormentor's face as she pinned her to the ground.

Ahrai writhed underneath her and tried to push her off. Then Valkyra felt a knee in the small of her back, and she winced as Ahrai flung her to the ground. They both jumped to their feet, and Valkyra grimaced slightly as she felt the pain shoot down her back and into her leg.

The two stared at each other silently. Valkyra felt the heat flush her cheeks – she was aware her face now reflected the deep flame colour of her hair. The battle preparations had ceased as the coveyn crowded around the two combatants. Rhea was the only one who could stop the confrontation, but Valkyra was certain she would let it run its course.

Valkyra felt her muscles tense, her chest heaving with each breath. She had never tested her combat skills against a girl so much older. Her instincts told her she was Ahrai's match in an equal contest, but she had also already learnt that few contests were equal. One thing was certain: neither of them was going to back down. Without warning Ahrai dived, arm outstretched, towards the pile of brimstones.

Valkyra quickly realised her intention and lunged after her. She was a fraction too late – Ahrai already held one of the stones in her hand. Using her considerable strength, Valkyra grasped the older girl's wrist tightly and tried to shake it to make her release the brimstone. But it was to no avail – Ahrai held the stone firm.

Then a faint smile crossed Valkyra's lips. Releasing her grip of Ahrai's wrist, she grasped the fist that enclosed the brimstone and applied all the pressure she could muster. There was a look of confusion on Ahrai's face, but this soon turned to horrific recognition. She began to struggle furiously to break the hold. With her free arm and feet she battered her opponent – yet Valkyra's grip did not loosen.

The pressure on the stone soon began to take effect. Ahrai felt its tingling warmth rapidly burgeon into an unbearable fire. A burning ache gnawed at her palm and she screamed. Valkyra could feel Ahrai's efforts to break free become more frantic, yet she held on. The stench of burning flesh filled the air and Ahrai's strength was ebbing, but Valkyra clasped even tighter. A foul-smelling smoke began to emerge from between Ahrai's fingers, and Valkyra sensed that her opponent was about to lose consciousness.

Why doesn't Rhea order me to stop? thought Valkyra. Then it became clear to her. She wants me to show weakness in front of the others, damn her. We would both be saved if she intervened.

Ahrai's eyes were no longer focusing.

Damn you, Rhea! With a cry, Valkyra released her hold. She carefully unclenched Ahrai's fist, turned her hand over, and allowed the brimstone to fall to the ground from the hole in the flesh in which it had embedded itself.

'Quick, get some salve,' she called as she examined the deep wound which had been burned into Ahrai's hand.

There seemed to be a faint look of surprise on Ahrai's face. 'You'll live,' said Valkyra as she signalled to one of the onlookers to dress the wound.

Valkyra trembled slightly as she turned to face the still-silent Rhea. More weakness, she thought, and they can all see it.

'On with the preparations,' ordered Rhea. 'We will have to fight with even greater valour now that two of our number are no longer fit for battle.'

Valkyra opened her mouth in protest.

'Don't speak, Valkyra,' commanded Rhea. 'You've shown mercy and that makes you unfit for battle. Stay here with the feeble, the sick and the young – it's where you belong. Perhaps we'll bring back some Faelen captives to keep you company.'

Valkyra felt the quiver in her voice as she spoke. 'But ...' I ...'

'Silence. Go tend to the hearth with the old women.'

There were mutterings from many corners, but nothing was said outright. Valkyra knew she had allowed herself to be ensnared by Rhea. The strange fury that had always stood her in such good stead in battle had worked against her this time. Now that her head was clear, she could think of a dozen ways of besting

Ahrai without putting herself in the position of having to show mercy. But it was too late. None of her allies or admirers would now speak for her. Perhaps she was weak. Perhaps she had no right to aspire to the coveyn leadership.

As she walked towards where the hearth fires burned, none of the old women spoke. One of them simply motioned her towards some trivial task. Tears of rage and self-pity welled up in her eyes as she watched her sisters prepare for the raid.

She watched the tension in the camp build as the time for battle approached. Many of the Faemir fidgeted nervously, making endless minor adjustments to their battle garb. Others compulsively touched or rubbed their weapons, almost as if they were reassuring themselves of their existence. A few talked incessantly, with only the occasional forced laugh betraying what they were feeling. One or two sat in isolation and stared at the sky.

As the hour approached, a heavy darkness, punctured only by the fires of the hearth, oppressed the encampment.

When the call finally came, the tension broke. 'We move now!' ordered Rhea.

There was a collective sigh of relief. Knives and swords were sheathed, axes slung over shoulders, and the water-soaked bags carrying the brimstones were checked one last time.

Valkyra watched, trembling, as Rhea led the hundred-strong band into the narrow passage leading through the steep cliffs.

Damn her! She'll pay for this humiliation.

Shrugging off one of the toothless old women who tried to comfort her, Valkyra walked away from the hearth. Without the smell of battle, she had nothing. It was all she had ever known in her short lifetime – save for those first few months after birth. Damn. Why hadn't she been born free? Rhea and Ahrai were both right. She had been born a Faelen, and if it wasn't for the coveyn raid nine years ago, she would have lived her life as a Faelen, forever under the yoke of the Maelir.

She walked towards a pile of battle swords which had been left behind and crouched down to run her hand along the handle of one. It was cool and hard. It cried out for battle. Suddenly a violent wave of resolve washed over her. She was not quite sure what she would do, but she would not remain behind. Glancing at Ahrai who lay against a rock, Valkyra clenched her teeth. Then she grabbed the sword and dashed towards the passage to follow the others. This was to be her fight.

*

Valkyra's footfalls were silent and deliberate. Although the band had moved with haste, Valkyra knew that she could easily overtake them if she wanted to. Not only did she have the advantage of travelling alone, but she also had trodden the path many times during her Watching. She knew the way well, however she had no desire to catch up with the others.

Her course of action was only gradually forming in her mind. The rage had dissipated as quickly as it had been born. In its place grew a coldness. There was something inevitable about what she now felt. Rhea was both ruthless and shrewd – she had simply waited for the right opportunity to throw Valkyra into disgrace. Rhea had used Valkyra's strength, her battle fury, and had turned it against her. Valkyra had destroyed herself. And as usual, Rhea had used others to get what she wanted. Had the barb about Faelen been thrown first by Rhea and not Ahrai, the conflict would have been out in the open. Valkyra was unsure what the outcome would have been, but at least she would have known where she stood. Unfortunately, Rhea was too devious. Valkyra would have to learn from that.

The night seemed strangely silent. Valkyra knew that the eve-wind never blew for long after dark on this part of the Mountain, yet the air was rarely as deathly still as this. The sheer cliff faces on either side were no longer high enough to block out sound but, despite this, nothing reached her ears. She strained to discern a noise – anything that would break the stillness.

Then her heart missed a beat. A faint sound echoed from

some indeterminate place, a sound barely audible above the over-bearing silence. Where was its source? Surely the band would not be so careless or overconfident that she could hear them? Perhaps the celebrations of the villagers had reached some fever pitch? But that, too, was impossible. There was no way a sound could travel so far, even on a still summer's night.

Realisation slowly set in. Perhaps that element over which she had no control had suddenly become active again. That was it! She tried to reproduce the sound in her head to confirm it. Yes, she was almost certain. It was the early warning sign of instability in the surface of the Mountain. The outbreak could be days away – or mere moments. No-one could predict it, not even someone of Valkyra's talent. What she did know, however, was that once the rumblings started, the outbreak was inevitable.

It suddenly struck her that she could use even this to her advantage. No-one would be prepared for the instability. She had only heard it because she had been straining to listen at the precise moment when it occurred. She doubted if any of the band would have thoughts other than those of the imminent battle on their minds. And the villagers would be too engrossed in the spirit of the Harvest Night by now. Valkyra was unsure what her new-found knowledge would mean, but a hint of a smile crossed her lips.

She was now almost out in the open. She sought the path that would lead to the large boulders where she had watched the village for the past seven days. Valkyra knew Rhea would be leading the band to the pocket of forest adjacent to the village. The Watch was well hidden, but it was too far from the village to launch an effective attack. Valkyra grinned wryly at the thought that she had been the one who had identified the forest as the best place from which to launch the onslaught, yet Rhea, as leader, had once again taken the credit.

Valkyra increased her pace as the bright lights of the village started to come into view. A wave of hatred for the Maelir overcame her, as it did every time she saw one of their settlements.

Her hand unconsciously stroked the cool hardness of the sword. These accursed men even robbed her people of their *will* to be free. Valkyra never forgot why the Faemir raided their villages and stole the young Faelen. And she knew the feeling was different for her, more intense. The other coveyn members often seemed to be going through the motions because they knew nothing else. The raids had been etched into the Faemir psyche as a way of life, yet Valkyra wanted it to be more. She knew she could instil her sense of passion into the others, if she had the chance. And it was here that she felt her advantage over Rhea lay. Strong leader though she was, Rhea's actions were not fuelled by a festering hatred. She would never be able to fan the fury that smouldered in the hearts of the Faemir.

Valkyra reached the Watch and sat down against one of the boulders. The sounds of minstrels and laughing voices echoed up the terraced hillside to her. The clear night air allowed her to distinguish individual voices, many of them unmistakably female – the Faelen, the fallen sisters. A strange mixture of anger and pity welled up inside her. Many Faelen would die along with the Maelir – there was no other way.

It was then that the sky exploded. Had the attack begun so soon? No, the band was still moving into position through the woodland pocket. Valkyra stared into the sky as a series of high-pitched sounds were followed by a splash of riotous colour. Her heart raced as she tried to make sense of what she saw. The answer came to her as another shower of sparks fell from above. Of course. The fabled fireworks. They must be part of the Harvest Night celebrations. She now stared in awe. The burst of sound brought her memories of the violence of battle, yet here, strangely, they were mixed with laughter.

Something awoke within her, a feeling akin to battle euphoria, yet fundamentally different. As the explosions increased, creating pockets of day-like light on the hillside, she was overcome by a breathlessness. She leaned back on her hands. Her gaze followed a shower of red and gold to her left ...

She'd almost forgotten. Her sisters were still preparing for battle. Valkyra managed to gain control over herself. These fireworks would not be good for the attack. The unexpected was never welcome, and even from this distance she could sense an air of hesitancy and confusion in the band. Every time the hill lit up, they were in danger of being detected by the villagers below. Rhea's timing could not have been worse as it turned out, and Valkyra's own counsel to attack at daybreak was looking increasingly sound.

Valkyra watched as the band was coerced back into order. There was a flurry of activity, and at first it was unclear what was happening. The fireworks still danced in the night sky, and the laughter and cheering continued unabated. But then she realised what Rhea's course of action was. Several fires were now visible in the mounds of the newly harvested grain that had been ceremoniously placed around the village. Rhea had once again demonstrated just how shrewd she really could be. She was using the unanticipated fireworks to her advantage. She had timed the first volley of brimstones so that they were catapulted into the grain at precisely the moment the sky was alight. The chances were that the villagers would be so engrossed with the display that they would not notice anything until the fires had taken hold.

The first scream was the catalyst. The music stopped abruptly. Valkyra watched in fascination as the scene rapidly transformed from one of joyous merriment to one of tumult. Despite the initial confusion, it quickly became clear that for many of the villagers the drink had not yet dulled their judgement. Small groups were rapidly organised to put out the fires with a combination of large dampeners and buckets of water. It was with disgust that Valkyra noticed many Faelen appeared to be at the front line of the activity. The villagers weren't quite the rabble she had believed them to be – the band might be in for a real battle.

High above the village, the fireworks still splashed into the sky as the brimstone flames ignited them one by one on the ground. The effect was now a grotesque parody of the celebrations. With a sudden rush, the sky burst into mock daylight. Screams of terror echoed across the hillside as the villagers' eyes turned upwards to where the approaching band was exposed. Now there will be a contest, thought Valkyra. Rhea always relied on the cover of dark for her battle plans, and for once the element of stealth was denied her.

There was now only one choice for the band, and it came as no surprise to Valkyra when the signal for a full charge was given. Unlike previous charges though, the band still had some distance to run, and the villagers had a little more time to prepare. Already the warning horn was blowing, and the Maelir were dropping their buckets of water and grabbing weapons. A chill tore through Valkyra as the battle wail of the Faemir pierced the night air. Never had she heard that most soul-destroying of cries – she had always been too engrossed by the battle euphoria herself. But now, at this distance, she could feel the wail's effect.

The time of contact had almost arrived. The Maelir had clearly decided to concentrate their defences in one long formation. It was unusual for villagers to possess such battle sense, thought Valkyra. In all the victories she had been part of, the Maelir had been scattered and confused. Rhea would have to be thinking on the run now. Various strategies sprang to Valkyra's mind, but she knew that under pressure it wouldn't be that easy.

The first clash of stone was tumultuous. Rhea herself had led the charge, but was repulsed almost immediately. The villagers' formation had proved simple but effective. More sparks flashed as the combatants stood toe to toe, swords and axes ringing across the hillside. This was not the way the Faemir were used to fighting. It was not on their terms – with the activity so concentrated, there was little room for them to use their finely honed battle skills.

Rhea had already changed tactics and was directing the warriors to fan out. A clever manoeuvre, thought Valkyra, with a mixture of envy and loathing. Rhea was trying to envelop the formation, searching for the weakness that would cause the breach.

The clashes were becoming increasingly furious, yet the Faemir were no closer to victory. The formation was simply too long to encircle fully, and sporadic attacks from the few villagers still fighting the fires made the strategy ineffective.

Both sides were suffering casualties but the balance wasn't changing. Valkyra could sense it was almost a stalemate. The Faemir would expose themselves if they retreated now. They had no other option except to persist and hopefully wear down the villagers. The Maelir were caught in a similar position. Theirs was a purely defensive formation and any attempt to convert it into attack would clearly leave an unprotected weakness for the Faemir to exploit.

Valkyra's attention was deflected momentarily. There was a distinct undertone to the battle cries. She shuddered. The sounds of instability were unmistakable. She could feel the impermanence brooding beneath her feet like a caged animal. Tiny surface cracks began to appear not far from where she sat. Her heart beat faster. Strangely, she did not fear for her own safety – a fascination captured her instead. She knew that a new element was about to be introduced into the battle below.

Then the ground began to shake under her. She went to stand up, but before she could get to her feet, a huge wedge of rock emerged and lifted her skyward. She screamed as she struggled to keep her balance.

She glanced around as pillars erupted from the ground all about her. Then the wedge on which she stood started to move down the hillside towards the village, cutting through the ground like a knife. She looked down at the combatants. Both Faemir and Maelir had stopped in mid battle and were staring at her as she raced towards them.

Use the moment, she thought as the air rushed past her ears. Spreading her legs a little wider for balance, she drew her sword and raised it into the air. With a chilling cry that could be heard above the groans of the Mountain, she rode the wedge straight into the battle melee.

Some of the Maelir made a half-hearted attempt to continue the fight, but for most, their spirit was broken. They turned and ran down the hill, deserting their village.

The wedge had sunk further into the ground and Valkyra jumped off. 'The young Faelen,' she cried, 'don't let them get away.'

Rhea looked around in dismay when she realised the band were quickly following Valkyra's orders.

'Get out of my way,' said Valkyra, as she pushed past the woman who was no longer her leader and joined in the hunt for Faelen.

The ground still shook underfoot as she rounded one of the outer buildings of the village. Suddenly, someone jumped her, pushing her to the ground. With almost ridiculous ease she swung her assailant around and climbed on top.

To her surprise it was a young Faelen of her size and build, her long ringlets covering her face. Valkyra held the sword to her throat.

'Tell me why you shouldn't die, Faelen,' she said.

The girl shook her head violently and the hair fell away to reveal her face.

Valkyra gasped. The face she was looking into was her own.

Chapter One

Nine years later ...

The wind bit with the needle sharpness of the teeth of a Dusk-rat. Atreu felt it stinging his eyes as he stepped outside. Yet strangely, there was no sound, no rush of air past his ears, no beat of his heart, no proof of his own breathing.

What had happened?

It was as if a dense webbing hung across his thoughts and he was struggling to push through it to see to the other side. He could have been the only one left on the Mountain. There was no sign of any of the other Ascenders who had completed their last Zenith. He was vaguely aware that the Holy Men had disappeared before the end. And Micah had vanished with them. But now his brother Teyth too was nowhere to be found.

After closing his Book, Atreu had fallen into a soft, dreamless sleep. He had no idea how much time had passed, although it seemed to him it could have been a mere moment. On awakening, he had searched for Teyth, first in the cell in which he had left him, and then in the room they had shared during the time of Zenith. Both their beds were unmade, and there was no sign that he had been there recently. The candles had long ago burnt their full length, and the wax was hard and cold.

Atreu had wandered through the corridors and rooms, but had found no-one. Not that it was easy to tell, for darkness had invaded the labyrinth. Not a single candle burned, and if it were not for the glimmerstones, Atreu would have been blundering like a blind man.

And now he was outside, scanning the slopes for signs of life.

He opened his mouth to cry his brother's name, but just as the word escaped his lips, the Mountain shook and he lost his footing and fell sprawling into the snow.

He shivered as he realised he hadn't heard the sound of his own voice. It was as if it had been sucked away to some unknown place.

Atreu got to his feet slowly and lifted his hands to his mouth to try to call for his brother again. But before anything could come out, the Mountain lurched and bucked under him like a giant beast, and he found himself lying in the snow again.

Damn this, he thought, climbing to his feet. He brushed the dry white powder from his broadcloth and looked around. The mists of the summit were beginning to swirl again – white on white on white. He could make out the occasional dark rocky out-crop, but even these sharp contours were slowly fading to an all-pervasive whiteness.

What was he going to do now? What happens after the Ascent? What happens if you can't go any higher? He was at the Summit, the whole Mountain was at his feet, but now, as the mists closed in around him, his view was more limited than it had ever been.

He reached down and scooped up a handful of snow. I cannot speak, I cannot hear, he thought, but at least I can feel. He closed his eyes and pressed the snow onto his eyelids. At first he felt nothing because the wind had numbed all his exposed skin, but gradually a deeper cold burgeoned. It seeped through into his eyes and then behind them and into his head.

He felt the cold bury itself into his skull like a worm, but as it did, he called forth the R'angkur to do battle with it. Thankfully, the skill had not deserted him. The point of his heat, once summoned, quickly sought out its icy brother, called to it, and finally enveloped it. And the cold was transformed and became its opposite.

Atreu lowered his hand and opened his eyes. After taking a moment to focus, he could see the snow had melted and he was holding water.

The deep blue eyes of his reflection peered back at him. He smiled. The R'angkur was one Ritual whose results were tangible.

Slowly, he let the water trickle to the ground. No more, he thought, no more. A feeling of power surged within him. Too many things had just *happened* to him and around him. He had been led along paths rather than walking along those of his own choosing. He had followed Rituals mindlessly when he should have demanded their meaning. He had been given information not when he required it, but when others chose to give it to him.

No more, he thought, no more.

He had questioned so little. He, who as a boy had always questioned everything. He, who had always threatened to stare into the sun at Zenith. What had happened? He had just accepted that was how it was. He had accepted others were in control of his destiny.

No more, he thought, no more.

He stared at the snow-covered ground with the heat of the R'angkur still burning inside his head. Then slowly and deliberately he said the name, 'Teyth.'

The ground shook, but he kept his footing.

'Teyth,' he said again, this time a little louder, and the Mountain side shook with greater force. He relaxed his knees so they didn't buckle underneath him, and eventually the shaking subsided.

'Teyth.' This time it was a whisper and the Mountain trembled slightly.

And again. 'Teyth.' Louder this time.

And another. 'Teyth,' louder still.

The ground heaved and groaned, but Atreu rode with it, refusing to fall to the ground.

Now he leant back slightly and drew a deep breath. He felt the tiny point of the R'angkur being sucked into the back of his throat, and with all the power he could muster, he let out a cry that could have been heard in the Lower Reaches.

'Teyth!'

An entire hill of snow crashed to the ground as the Mountain convulsed like a madman. Screaming, roaring, bellowing, crying. Pillars shot up at insane angles, chasms opened and shut again in the blink of an eye. Hillsides rippled like waves and then crashed into each other, foaming with snow and churning like the waters of the Maelstrom.

And still Atreu stood.

One moment he was rushing skyward on a pillar with the speed of the wind and the next he was sinking into the deepest chasm.

And still Atreu stood.

Nothing could knock him from his feet. He teetered but never toppled over, always keeping his balance. He gritted his teeth and drew sharp breaths. He screamed at his limbs for control. He drew on everything he had been taught and everything he had learned and some things he wasn't aware he knew.

And as the convulsions slowly subsided and the Mountain side returned to calm, Atreu was standing, his legs planted firmly apart and his hands on his hips.

'Now listen to me,' he cried – to the Mountain, to the sky, to the air, to anyone who could hear – 'I will no longer follow blind Rituals. I must know their meaning. I must know.'

For a moment there was nothing. Then, as if in reply, he heard the familiar wail of the Zenith horn. With the mists eddying around him, he began to walk in its direction.

*

In front of him was what looked like a sheer cliff wall of ice, the top of which was lost in the clouds. The wail of the Zenith horn was fading into its last dying notes, but Atreu no longer had any need of it. He knew it was coming from the top of the cliff.

He ran his hand along its smooth surface. How was he going to get up there? He started walking to find some way of climbing to the top. Silence still filled the air around him, and all he could hear was the soft squelching of his footsteps in the snow. The Mountain had now subsided and was calm.

Verlinden's face formed itself in his mind. It was funny that his first impulse was to find his brother, and not the Faemir with whom he had shared the final Zenith. She, of course, was safe now, back with her own people. She would tell them. She had experienced Zenith, the first Faemir ever to do so, and she would tell them. The war would be over. She would tell them ...

Atreu closed his eyes as he continued to walk along the cliff, and as he walked, he trailed his hand along its smooth surface.

She would tell them: Zenith belonged to both Maelir and Faemir. The killing and fighting would stop.

Atreu opened his eyes again. I've been a fool, he thought. Every step of the way up the Mountain I've been a naive fool. I've blundered all along, and even after the final Zenith I just let her go back to her people. Just like that.

He stared up the wall of the cliff, but again couldn't see past the bank of clouds. Who was up there? Perhaps a lone horn blower was all that remained of the Holy Orders at the Summit. There was no doubt, judging by the silence, that the fighting downslope had stopped – but what did that mean?

He had seen the handiwork of the Faemir first-hand at Crosanct. He shuddered at the thought of the five bloodied figures in the snow. If they could slaughter Ascenders who were simply meditating, they could be capable of anything. Verlinden was different – but was she the only one?

And what of his revelation at Zenith about the Dusk People? He knew he was right. Another, even greater threat, was invading the Mountain. Atreu laughed a cold laugh. He had been such a fool. His Ascent had been his only concern; he had rejoiced in his own insights, revelled in his own successes. But now he saw that they were nothing. He had been thinking like a boy. Ha! Close your eyes and no-one can see you. You are the world. Believe the Summit is a giant glistening city of silver spires, and that's what it shall be. Reach it in time for Zenith and all will be well.

All could be dead.

He had been walking for what seemed like half the afternoon – if indeed it was afternoon for he had no way of telling – when he noticed footsteps in the snow in front of him.

There was someone else.

Judging by the direction of the prints, the person was also walking along the cliff, no doubt trying to find a way up. Atreu continued more carefully, straining through the strands of mist to see whoever it was in front of him.

He estimated he was now a long way from where he had heard the horn, but there was simply no choice but to go forward. This was the longest cliff face he had ever seen. His legs were now growing weary – he had done very little walking since he had arrived at the Summit, and it was beginning to show.

He stopped now and then and cupped his hand to his ear to listen for the sounds of the person up ahead, but there was nothing. Perhaps it was Verlinden in front of him, just keeping out of reach. Somehow he doubted it because the footprints were too large. Then again, he knew prints in the snow sometimes were misleading. Perhaps it was one of the other Ascenders, or Micah ... or Teyth.

Teyth.

Of course. He placed his foot carefully inside the next print. It was a perfect fit!

'Teyth,' he called out loud and the Mountain shook once more.

He started running as soon as he regained his balance. 'Teyth.'

And Atreu was thrown, crashing into the cliff wall. He got up and started running again. He was about to call out his twin's name a third time but stopped himself.

He ran as fast as the powder snow would allow. He ran until his legs screamed for rest. He ran until his lungs rasped desperately at the thin, cold air. He ran shouting his brother's name inside his head with every step.

Where are you? Damn you, Teyth. We were always so evenly matched, I could never catch you. I always had to wait for you to stumble. And that happened so rarely.

Then he stopped.

Tears welled up in his eyes as he stared at the second set of footprints which had suddenly appeared in front of him. You are still a fool, Atreu, he thought to himself. Despite your Ascent, despite your Zenith, you are still a fool.

The footprints were his own.

He looked around. He was back where he had started. It wasn't a real cliff after all, but something like a giant pillar jutting out from the Mountain.

His body heaved as he raked in one deep breath after the other. He leant against the smooth surface of the pillar and slowly allowed himself to slide down into a sitting position.

Perhaps the horn was some strange echo from the last Zenith. Perhaps it had been created by the wind blowing through a narrow gap in a rock formation. Perhaps he was the only Maelir left at the Summit.

Then, as if to mock him, the wail of the Zenith horn floated through the air again. He got up slowly and faced the wall.

'This is Atreu,' he cried. 'I need to get up there.'

The ground convulsed but he managed to stay on his feet.

'I said, *This is Atreu*. Please help me.'

He thought back to the time when he had sought entry to the Monastery at Lhorong. It all seemed like a game then, so long ago. The Felsen had waited for the agitation in his mind to subside.

He pounded the wall with his fist.

'Don't you play games with me now.'

The wind seemed to shift slightly but, apart from that, nothing changed. The Mountain, too, seemed to have given up reacting to his voice.

Atreu slowly sat down. He shook his head – he was no man of action. What would Teyth do in his position? He laughed. He would probably take out his battle-axe and hammer at the pillar until someone came down to stop him or until the whole thing collapsed.

His Book! Where was it? Had he left it in the cave? He couldn't remember seeing it after he had woken up. Surely he would have picked it up instinctively if it had been there? How could he have been so confused? Well, no matter, he knew the story, and his Ascent was over now.

Darkness was turning the white mists grey when the wind again began to shift. Atreu sensed a shadow hovering just out of his view. Then it landed, like the gentle lap of water in a lake, and a dark figure stood in front of him.

'We meet once again in strange circumstances,' said the deep voice.

Atreu tried to clear his vision. The details of the person standing in front of him were hard to make out, but there was no need. He knew who it was.

'The windrider from Crosanct.' Atreu smiled.

'Well, not really *from* Crosanct, Atreu, but I know what you mean.'

'You know my name, but I don't remember introducing myself.'

The windrider stepped closer, and Atreu's eyes followed the woodwork and almost transparent material of his wings, finally resting on his face.

'I don't think our last meeting was one for formal introductions, Atreu, but I always make it my business to find out the names of those whose lives I save.'

'And I make it my business to discover the names of those who save me from Faemir arrows.'

'I am Riell,' said the windrider, his wings creaking as he bowed awkwardly. 'At your service.'

'It should be *me* who is at *your* service. I am indebted to you for rescuing me – and my Book.'

'We all perform our duty and do what we can.'

'I have come across some strange duties in my Ascent, Riell, some which I doubt the value of, but I am forever grateful for your sense of it.'

Riell smiled. 'I believe you want access to the Keep.'

'The Keep?'

'Yes.' He indicated the top of the wall. 'This mountain on top of the Mountain.'

'Is that where they all are?'

'I don't know about all of them. We lost too many Ascenders and Holy Men on the way to the Summit to say they are all up there, but yes, the Inner Sanctum is up there.'

'That's another term I've never heard before. The Inner Sanctum. What is it?'

'Something you would never have known about if you hadn't completed Zenith. The Holy Orders are filled with secrets. The Keep and the Inner Sanctum are two such secrets.'

'Should you be revealing these things to me?'

'Of course, Atreu, of course. You have as much right to know these things as I do – probably more. They are waiting for you up there. It is my task to take you to them.'

'I see,' said Atreu, slowly getting to his feet. 'You wouldn't want to offend the Inner Sanctum, would you?'

'Indeed not.' Riell laughed. 'Now do you remember how this is done?'

'Yes ... I think so. I just hang on for dear life and hope none of the arrows hit me.' Atreu smiled at the windrider.

'Something like that. We might try this harness here this time.

You should find it a lot easier. Sorry, but somehow I just didn't have the time to tell you about it in Crosanct.'

Riell helped Atreu with the leather straps and buckles.

'Tell me one thing,' said Atreu. 'Why did you take so long to come and get me?'

Riell laughed. 'You wouldn't stand still for long enough.'

'Very funny.'

'No, Atreu, we heard your call so we knew you were down here. Visibility is very poor and the wind changes are less than helpful, so it wasn't the easiest thing in the world to find you. The two sets of footprints confused me after a while. I had to be more careful because I thought you were being followed.'

'So it would have been better if I had simply stayed where I was?'

'I think so.'

'And done nothing.'

Riell nodded. 'Sometimes the best course of action is inaction.'

Atreu laughed out loud. 'That sounds like something a Holy Man would say.'

Riell's smile suddenly turned into a frown. 'Don't mock me, my friend. Please don't mock me.'

The windrider arched back slightly, allowing the gust of air to whip up at the material that was stretched tightly across the wooden frame of his wings. Silently, as if it were the most natural thing in the world, Atreu felt his feet lift up off the ground.

*

The Keep was much higher than he anticipated, and the giant pillar seemed to widen as they ascended. Atreu's flight was not as exhilarating as his first one. Riell's strange silence made it seem like an eternity. At times the sporadic winds buffeted them so close to the smooth rock that Atreu was sure they would be crushed, but Riell's skill was such that he managed to avoid any damage. Occasionally he would be so close to the wall that he had to kick off, but he did it with such precise timing that Atreu soon ceased worrying about it.

He watched the mists wrap their tendrils along his arms and legs, only to release their hold as the two flew higher. Now and then small particles of ice would prick his face and he would have to close his eyes, but he couldn't keep them shut for long. He wanted to see all he could.

The ground had disappeared quickly in a swirl of white below them. Atreu looked up, trying to will the mists to part so that the top of the pillar would be revealed, but they refused to oblige.

And Riell spoke not a word to him.

This has happened before, thought Atreu. My Ascent was riddled with silence, people not telling me things. I am sick of this. Perhaps I have blundered somehow, but I need to find out where I have erred.

'You speak of the secrets of the Holy Orders,' said Atreu.

Riell didn't answer.

Atreu continued. 'Yet you are keeping something from me yourself.'

There was a slight shift in Riell's flight path.

'You windriders serve the Holy Orders – that is correct isn't it, Riell?'

'Yes and no,' said Riell finally.

'There's a Holy Order type answer.'

'Nothing is that simple.'

Then Atreu recalled what Micah had said after his first sighting of the windriders. 'You cannot serve the Holy Orders and *be* a Holy Order at the same time, can you?'

Riell seemed to draw a breath. 'It could be argued that it is possible to do both.'

Atreu nodded. 'I remember Micah saying some windriders believe there could be a middle way. Between the rock and the light blows the wind.'

'Your sage said that?' They were suddenly thrown towards the wall of the Keep, but Riell kicked away.

'Do you believe there is a middle way, Riell?'

For a while Atreu heard only silence behind the whistling of the wind. Finally, Riell spoke. 'I'm afraid I'll have to answer your question with another question. Look at my garb – what do you see?'

'I ... I ...'

'What colour is it?'

'Well ... it's ...'

'This isn't a trick Liche question. Is it one of the earth-colours of the Felsen Order?'

'Well ... no, of course not.'

'Is it the purple or crimson of the Liche Order?'

'Why are you asking me this, Riell? It's obvious that the colour you are wearing is a grey-green.'

'Yes, Atreu, which is exactly my point. Anyone can see it.'

'So, what are you telling me?'

'Precisely what I've just said. I wear the colour of what I am. That's the way it is.'

Atreu felt the momentary sting of ice on his cheeks. 'You could put on crimson robes, or brown ones, if you wanted to.'

'Yes,' said Riell, 'but doing that would not make me a Holy Man ... Look, Atreu, you are touching the heart of the great dilemma for all of the windriders. You know who we are, don't you? Your sage must have told you.'

Atreu hesitated. 'You're ... most of you ... you didn't succeed in your Ascent.'

'Failed is the word, failed. We are failed Ascenders. I am a failed Ascender. We couldn't ascend in our hearts and in our minds, so we were given these wings of wood and cloth so we could at least ascend on the wind.'

'It is wonderful to ride the wind.'

'Yes, Atreu, it is. But, tell me, can you even begin to compare it with what it's like to soar with the truth of Zenith?'

'Riell ... I ...'

'No, Atreu, I know the answer. You don't have to lie to me.'

Atreu tried to shift in his harness so he could see the windrider's face. 'In my village of Valesend,' he said, 'we have a long foot-race every year. The winner is showered with glory, but there is much honour bestowed on the runners who come second and third.'

Riell shook his head. 'Atreu, I thank you for what you are trying to say, but I and the other windriders didn't come second or third or even fourth in our Ascents. We didn't finish. Tell me, Atreu, is there any honour bestowed in your race on those who do not finish?'

Atreu was silent.

'Just as I thought. There is pity, I suppose. Perhaps they tried their best but what does that matter? They failed, and their failure is necessary so that those who succeed can be valued. The failed are needed, after all, just as the windriders are needed. There is not much point to a race without a loser.'

'But what the windriders do is so important. And look what you have achieved this time. The Summit would have been over-run before Zenith was completed. We would have all been dead.'

'See, Atreu, you already speak like them. What we *do* is important, but what we *are* isn't.'

There was a sudden rush of wind pushing them upwards. Atreu tried to gather his thoughts.

'So, a windrider could never be a member of a Holy Order?'

Riell kicked away from the cliff face again. 'The Inner Sanctum would feel simply asking that question is heresy.'

'You haven't given me an answer.'

'Look, Atreu, you will have to come up with your own answer. There's not much point in me telling you what I believe. Think about what the question implies. The whole purpose of Zenith – all the Rituals, the Talismans, the Ascent of chosen twins to the Summit every year – is to decide who gains entry into the Felsen or the Liche. The nine days are celebrated in different ways on different parts of the Mountain – you must have seen that. But, the real meaning of Zenith is given by the Holy Orders to the Holy Orders. What if they allowed those who failed to enter the Felsen or Liche? What then?'

'You tell me.'

'If they allowed just one failed Ascender into a Holy Order then everything would collapse. The control over the Mountain is gone.'

'I don't see the connection.'

'You may have been given the secrets of Zenith, but the way the Orders control the Mountain is still a mystery to you. The point is, where would it stop? If failed Ascenders can enter a Holy Order, then why not anyone? Then there would be no secrets, Atreu, and it would all fall apart. The whole system of Maelir culture. Everything.'

'It seems to me that is happening anyway, thanks to the Faemir.'

'That is another matter entirely.'

'Riell, I don't think it is. It's all changed now. Things can no longer go on as they have. You see, the Maelir and the Faemir – '

'You are wrong, Atreu. We have won.'

'What?'

'Hey, don't shake the harness like that. We are getting to the most difficult part.'

'How can you say we've won? The Faemir are on the edge of the Summit. We barely completed the last Zenith.'

'But complete it we did, and now we are all safe.'

'Safe?'

'Yes, the Keep, of course. The Ascenders, the members of the Holy Orders who make up the Inner Sanctum are all up here. Safe. No-one can get up here without the aid of windriders. The Faemir will never reach them.'

'But we will starve, won't we, if we stay up here long enough?'

'No, Atreu, the windriders are the lifeline. Everything will go on as it always has done. We have a whole year until the next

Zenith. We have been caught unaware this time, but the advantage of surprise has now gone. The Maelir are marshalling forces all over the Mountain. There is no hope now for the Faemir.'

'I see.'

'Yes, don't worry, you are safe now.'

'I'm not sure it is so straightforward.'

Riell laughed. 'Well, what would I know? I'm only a windrider.' He looked up. 'Now brace yourself.'

There was a wild rushing sound and Atreu was thrown left and then right as he gripped tightly the wooden bar in front of him. A million grains of ice stung his face, and suddenly the mists seemed to clear around him.

They had reached the top.

In front of him lay what looked like a vast flat plain ringed by a halo of white cloud. Although twilight was deepening, he could see a sprawling city in the middle of the plain. On the periphery were low single-storey buildings which seemed to crouch in darkness, standing silhouetted against the sun's afterglow like an army of sentinels. And in the centre was a vast conglomeration of spiralling towers, turrets and flying buttresses. Tower after tower shone with the silvery sheen of the most exquisite gemstones, tapering into feather-like fineness as they reached for the sky.

Atreu gasped, unable to believe what he was seeing. 'The silver spires,' he whispered.

Chapter Two

'Atreu, my dear Atreu, I can't tell you how overjoyed I am to see you here.' Micah embraced him. 'It was all so chaotic down there before the last Zenith, I just didn't know what was happening.'

Atreu felt his uncle's arms encircle him, felt the beard against his face, and smelled the familiar bittersweetness of the r'lung on his breath. He sensed Micah was pleased to see him but there was something wrong – he seemed agitated in some way. His movements were jerky and his eyes seemed to be focusing in the wrong place.

'Tell me, Uncle, where is Teyth?'

Micah glanced back nervously at the tall Holy Man in crimson robes who had entered the room with him. 'I'm not supposed to tell you.'

Atreu pulled back. 'I want to see him now.'

'You can't make demands like that up here.'

Atreu bit his lip. 'Micah, my Ascent is over. I am tired of the games. I am tired of the Rituals. I would like to see my brother when I choose to see him.'

'Atreu, don't be so childish.' Micah's hand trembled slightly.

'The time for Rituals and keeping twins apart must surely be over by now. Teyth and I spent a year following the separate Paths of our Ascents. That's long enough.'

'No, the time for Rituals is never over – and you will need to follow them with even greater vigilance up here.' The voice belonged to the Holy Man with jet-black hair and dark eyes standing in the doorway. He stepped towards Atreu.

Micah straightened. 'I'm sorry, Atreu. This is Lythos. I am so overjoyed to see you.'

The tall Holy Man spoke again. His voice had an edge that Atreu didn't like. 'Micah, I think it is time you went.'

Micah looked into Atreu's eyes briefly, nodded quickly and then turned away. 'I will speak with you later.'

Atreu watched as he walked out in short broken steps. 'What is wrong with him?' he asked, after his uncle had gone.

'I'm sorry that you had to see him like that. He insisted that he greet you – he was most agitated.'

'There is something wrong.'

'Yes, well.'

'Are you going to answer me?'

Lythos glared at him. His dark eyes cast an icy stare in Atreu's direction. 'Don't demand anything of me, my young Ascender.'

'I didn't think I was still an Ascender.'

'You're not,' said Lythos, stepping closer. 'You no longer have the rights, or the privileges, or the special status of an Ascender. You are simply a twin again. In fact, as far as I'm concerned, you are nothing.' His eyes, unblinking, bored into Atreu's. 'I know what you've done,' he said slowly.

Atreu looked away, unable to match Lythos' gaze. The flickering lights of the candles which lined the walls caught his attention. The walls themselves had been carved into the most intricate pastoral scenes and the ever shifting lights of the candles seemed to bring them to life. Women worked in the fields on one side, digging into the dirt with their bare hands. Not far away, a merchant train of donkeys laden with produce made its way along a narrow track.

He looked back at Lythos to find him still staring right into him. He still could not match the dark coldness of his eyes, but he refused to turn away. It was impossible to tell the Holy Man's age, or even if he was a Lower Reacher or Mid-Reacher. His jaw-line dominated his face, giving him a look of determination and single-mindedness that Atreu had never seen before.

'If you know what I did,' said Atreu, 'then you know what I am about to say to you.'

Lythos was motionless as he spoke. 'I don't believe I want to hear this.'

'You must hear it. It is my Zenith.'

'Don't talk to me about Zenith. Your actions have shown that you have nothing but contempt for it.'

'But I understand it all now. The Maelir and the Faemir, don't you see – '

Lythos waved his hand to stop Atreu. 'I don't want to listen to your foolishness.'

'But it all fits. The union ...'

'No.' The Holy Man's voice echoed through the room.

Atreu turned and walked to one of the walls. In front of him was the carving of a group of women hunched over as they worked in a field of potatoes. He placed his hand over the figure of one of the younger women.

'If you will not listen,' he said, 'then let me speak to someone who will.'

'You will be heard – at the designated time. The Circle speaks with all those who have completed Zenith in order to judge their Ascent. But you will have your address because that has always been our way, not because you so ignorantly demand it.'

'The Circle – '

'No, you will be told no more and no less than what the others have been told. There are no special rules for you. You will have to wait your turn, and as you have been the last to arrive, your address to the Circle will be the last.'

'And when will that be?'

'You will find time has very little meaning up here.'

'That's the sort of answer I've come to expect from Holy Men,' said Atreu, his hand still covering the village woman as he looked over his shoulder at Lythos.

There was an almost imperceptible twisting at the corner of Lythos' mouth. 'Rest assured, Atreu of Valesend, I anticipate your address with much pleasure.' He turned and walked out.

Another Holy Man in the normal purple garb of the Liche Order appeared instantly in the doorway. 'Please come with me. I will take you to your room.'

'You mean my cell, don't you?' asked Atreu as he lifted his hand from the wall carving. For some reason he was a little surprised that the woman was still there.

*

Atreu leant on the windowsill of his room and looked out at the vast city of the Keep. He remembered the sense of awe he had felt when he had first seen the Mid-Reach city of Peleusar. The buildings had crowded in on each other as far as the eye could see. Towers had punctuated the sky, and arches and buttresses had filled the spaces in between.

But even that great city could not compare with what lay before him now. It was dark, but the spires shone with a multitude of tiny lights. It was breathtaking. Emerald, crimson, amber, jade – and colours he could find no name for – all glistened in exquisite clusters. Riotous. Brilliant. Eclipsing even the glorious carpet of stars that covered the sky. Lights above, lights below, and Atreu was floating somewhere in between.

He shook his head slightly, almost unable to believe what he was seeing, and the lights suddenly transformed into delicate threads dancing across his vision. Atreu laughed with pure joy. Dark and light, he thought. The threads. There's no need to close my eyes anymore. It's all here for me.

He remembered two boys playing a silly game. He remembered

darkness. He remembered the colours. He remembered spinning round and round and round. Where am I? The first thing I will see … the first thing I will see … is … me. He remembered the boy being wrong.

And the silver city was here too. Imagine that.

His attention was caught by several dark figures silhouetted against one of the towers as they flashed through the night air.

He wondered where Riell was now. The windrider had again come to his aid, and somehow he still hadn't told him the gratitude he felt for him. Where was he now? What corner of the Keep is his home? Or did his duties require him downslope? It was almost as if the windrider detested being earthbound. He had only been on the ground long enough to help Atreu undo the harness and to ensure he was delivered to the right place, and then he had, almost immediately, been airborne again.

There had been too many goodbyes since he had left Vale-send. This time, though, he sensed was not the last time he would see the windrider.

Suddenly, Atreu felt tired. He drew back from the window and looked around the room. Thank goodness he was with the Liche and not the Felsen. He didn't think he could stomach the dark austerity of the Order of the Rock just now – the tiny windows and the stark stone walls.

This was more like a room in an inn. Several paintings and a tapestry adorned the walls. His half-eaten meal of cheese, bread and fruit lay on a table in one corner. He made his way to the bed and got in. He had changed somehow since the final Zenith, he knew that. He almost couldn't believe some of the things he had demanded of Lythos. Yet, he knew he was still the same person. Perhaps, as Micah had said so long ago, he could see things more clearly now. The Rituals had served their purpose after all. He felt his eyes grow heavy and his thoughts jumble into a gentle haze.

He just managed to turn off the butter-lamp next his bed before he fell asleep …

A warm summer breeze enveloped him as he looked down at

the woman's face. He ran his fingers through the rich tangle of red hair. She smiled and pulled him closer.

With a rush of warm wind, they were both airborne. Higher, ever higher they went, until wisps of cloud touched their bare skin.

He lightly traced a line with his finger along the length of her body. He bent down and kissed her, drawing in her breaths as she drew in his. She sighed softly as their bodies merged. Gently, ever so gently, it began. The rhythm of a summer breeze. They swayed with the wind, and their movements flowed in all directions. There was no above, no below, no left, no right, no up, no down, no inhaling, no exhaling. It was all those things, all at once, and yet none of them.

He lifted his face slightly to watch her face as they rolled and turned in the breeze.

A deep yearning to speak her name overcame him.

'Verlinden,' he whispered, 'Verlinden.'

A sharp gust hit them and he felt her body stiffen.

The wind started howling around them and he could feel it ripping them apart. He tried to embrace her more tightly, but she pushed him away.

Another wild burst and they were apart. He stared at her in bewilderment and saw the venom in her eyes.

'We have both been fools,' she said, 'but you are a greater one than I.' Her ringlets almost straightened under the ferocity of the wind.

'Verlinden,' he cried, as tears welled up in his eyes.

She smiled a smile with cruelty at its corners. 'When you know who you are,' she cried, 'then come back and tell me who I am.'

He let out a cry of anguish.

Another gust rushed between them, and just as she was blown away from him, she called out, 'Farewell, Teyth.'

He looked down and saw the clouds racing by just below his feet. With a scream he felt himself falling ...

Atreu awoke with every detail of his dream etched firmly in his memory. His heart was racing and the room felt as if it was on fire. He threw off his blankets and stared through the darkness at the ceiling.

The dreams, the dreams were the key. He realised that now. He had to make sense of them. Why did Verlinden push him away? She wouldn't do that. He knew that in a way he knew no other thing. Why would she push him away?

Sweat beaded his forehead and he struggled for air.

She had said, 'When you know who you are, then come back and tell me who I am.' What did that mean, damn it?

'... tell me who I am.' He heard a voice speaking and looked up.

There floating just below the ceiling was Verlinden.

Atreu drew a sharp breath.

'Tell me who I am,' said the apparition again, a mocking smile on its face.

Then the realisation hit him. 'You're not Verlinden,' he cried. 'You're Valkyra.'

The smile only wavered slightly.

'Half right, my young Maelir, only half right.'

Atreu felt the confidence ebb from his body.

The apparition's face contorted slightly as if fighting some suppressed rage.

'All right, Atreu, I will tell you this time. But don't ever forget what I am about to say. I am both.' She laughed. 'Do you understand what that means? You cannot have Verlinden without Valkyra. You can't possess the love without the hate. I am both, Atreu, live with that.'

The apparition started to fade.

'Wait,' said Atreu, 'then who am I?'

The woman's voice already sounded as if it was speaking from a great distance. 'Only you can answer that, Atreu, only you ...'

The apparition faded to nothing and Atreu was left staring at the ceiling.

Suddenly the room was very cold. He pulled the blankets up again and fought the urge to pull them past his mouth.

*

He couldn't remember falling asleep again but it was bright daylight when he awoke. Sunlight was streaming through the open window and he rushed over to look out.

He had seen the beauty of the Keep in twilight and in darkness, but now it had transformed again. Sunlight danced around each spire, gyrating playfully along the length until it escaped into the crisp, clear sky.

He held his breath as spears of fire flew through the air, twirling and twisting like flaming dervishes, flashing with such speed that he could never focus on them fully. The Keep was alive and brilliant, and dancing before him. Glistening sparks shot from building to building, from tower to tower, from spire to spire. It was as if they were all joined by some ethereal current, the Keep was all one building, fired by the most exquisite of lights. This was the moment, thought Atreu, grasping hold of the windowsill because his legs were trembling and threatening to collapse from under him. This is what his Ascent had been leading to.

A shaft of light suddenly shot through the window and into the room. Atreu laughed as he remembered the dream he had on awakening, the first morning of his Ascent.

'Ha,' he cried, 'this time I'll get you.'

He watched the light bounce from one corner of the room to the other, zigzagging in a riotous dance.

There must be a pattern, he thought.

Then he dived just as the beam of light flashed across his bed.

Missed – but so close. He landed on the blankets and his bed creaked slightly under the impact.

The shaft raced just past his head again and he lunged for it, but again it was just too quick.

He got up, determined to try again, but the light bounced from ceiling to floor and then back out the window. Atreu tried to follow its path, but it was lost among the riot of colour and light outside.

'I'm getting closer,' said Atreu, half to himself, half to the glistening spires outside his window.

'So a successful Zenith makes you talk to yourself, does it?'

Atreu turned in the direction of the familiar voice.

'Micah,' he cried. 'How long have you been standing there?' His uncle stood in the doorway, his hands on his hips. Atreu could see a broad smile partly hidden by his grey-streaked beard.

'Long enough to see the Keep has affected your sanity.' He laughed.

Atreu frowned suddenly. 'Are you all right?'

'Indeed, yes, Atreu – why?'

'Last night ... I mean ... you seemed different. I don't know.'

Micah waved his hand as if dismissing the question. 'I've been under a good deal of strain, Atreu. It was so close, you know. The Faemir almost overran us just before the last Zenith.'

'What has happened?'

'I thought at first both of you were taken – '

'Where's Teyth? I want to see him, Micah. Our Ascents are over – you can't keep us apart anymore.'

Micah shook his head. 'No, I can't keep you apart anymore, but the Circle can do fairly much as it pleases.'

'Show me where Teyth is. I need to speak to him.' He took a step towards his uncle.

Micah again shook his head, looking wearier this time.

'I have little power here in the Keep. I no longer have any say in either of your destinies – if I ever had any. But, come Atreu, break the fast with me and I will tell you what I can.'

*

Atreu was amazed at the size of the Great Dining Hall. It was filled with long tables and the smell of food, but there the comparison with an inn ended. Huge pointed arches vaulted towards the ceiling, climbing impossibly high. Light streamed though the giant windows, bathing the entire room in the softest of yellow. Fluted colonnades stood in rows and friezes.

And all about him was the buzz and movement of Holy Men engaged in animated conversation. There was good-natured shouting and thumping on tables as he had not seen since Cluric and Edric's inn. But while those men of Teuron had all been farmers and merchants, here everyone wore the garb of the Felsen or Liche, or the Ascender's broadcloth.

'Micah,' said Atreu, tearing some soft, crusty bread from the heavily laden plate in front of him, 'I cannot believe what I am seeing here, what I have seen since last night. This must be the most wonderful place on the Mountain.'

'Some would say we are, in a way, no longer on the Mountain here, Atreu. But, yes, the Keep is a magnificent place.'

Atreu chewed slowly on the bread and was surprised as it seemed to dissolve into a sweet nothingness in his mouth. 'I have never heard of this place,' he said. 'No rumours, no whispers – even Father never spoke of it.'

Micah drew a sharp breath. 'Your father wouldn't know. No-one outside the Holy Orders does. It is one of our great secrets.'

'But the windriders know.'

'Yes, the guild has a special status. The windriders know a number of our secrets, but there are also many that they don't know.'

'So what is this place, this ... this city we are in?'

'It's the Keep, Atreu, just the Keep. All of it, from the monasts of the Felsen that encircle its Liche heart to the top of the highest spire. There is no other name that can be given to it. It is called so because it is the place where everything is kept – our secrets, our knowledge, our power.'

Atreu took a deep red fruit from a bowl and bit into it. 'It looks nothing like a monastery. The beds are soft, there are no locked doors, and the food is magnificent.'

'The Felsen, as you know, have different ideas of appropriateness for Holy Orders.'

'The darkness ...' Atreu nodded slowly.

'But they are not the Order of darkness, Atreu. They are the Order of the Rock. There is a difference.'

'And the dark buildings that rim the towers, they belong to the Felsen?'

'Yes, but the Keep is the one place on the Mountain where the Felsen and Liche mix. The opposites are brought together to form the Inner Sanctum. The Felsen reserve their monasts for meditation and sleep but, as you can see around you, they spend much of their time in the buildings of light.'

'So being here is no indication that I am to join the Liche?'

Micah hesitated. 'Well ... no. The decision is not yet made.'

'How is it to be decided – is it my choice?'

'I cannot give you a yes or no to that question.'

Atreu sighed. 'Why am I surprised at your response?'

'You must address the Circle, Atreu, but I'm sure Lythos has already told you that. Everything is decided by your responses there so, I suppose, in a way the choice is yours.'

'What are the correct things to say to the Circle?'

'There are no correct things, only the truth – and there is no doubt that it always emerges when you speak to the Circle.'

Atreu laughed. 'Which truth is that, Uncle? Human truth?'

'You remember lessons well,' cried Micah, clasping him on the arm. 'When does human truth become absolute truth? – that is the question you must ask yourself now.'

'This is too early for these sorts of discussions,' said Atreu. 'How can I see absolute truths when I'm eating?' He took another bite out of the shiny red fruit. 'Tell me, who is Lythos?'

Micah stopped chewing for a moment. 'A member of the Circle,' he said finally. 'He has the responsibility of custodianship of the Ascenders before their judgement.'

'Is he one of the leaders?'

'No,' said Micah, 'the Circle is not like the Councils that rule our villages and cities. There are no leaders and all sixty members have an equal voice, although there is a First Speaker and some say that position can provide some power if used skilfully.'

'So Lythos has the same influence as the other members?'

Micah lowered his voice so that Atreu could barely hear him. 'That is not quite what I said. Influence depends on many things. I can only say be wary of Lythos.'

Atreu swallowed slowly as he stared into his uncle's eyes.

'I don't fear him, Micah,' he said.

'I can see that, Atreu, and I don't yet know if that is a good thing or a bad thing. My help is now minimal, but please take this last piece of advice from me: if you do not fear him, then at least be wary of him.'

Atreu sat back and looked around the Hall. Many of the Holy Men had finished breaking the fast and were now leaving their tables. 'You still haven't told me about Teyth.'

'I ... I don't know exactly where he is.'

'But you could find out, Micah.'

Micah sighed. 'Things are different here, Atreu. Your Ascent is over, and I no longer have any official function in your life.'

'But you're still my uncle.'

'Yes, that is true. No-one knows that truth more than I. It has already been used against me. But, no, you have to realise I have very little influence here in the Keep. My own actions during your and Teyth's Ascent are now being questioned and assessed. I think it is safe to say we are both on shaky ground.'

'And Teyth?'

'Well ... Teyth didn't complete the last Zenith and we both know he was making little progress anyway.'

Atreu got up and grabbed Micah with both hands. 'That was my fault. My fault. No-one can blame him for missing the final Zenith.'

'Please, Atreu, sit down. You will be given a chance to state your case.'

'Micah, I don't want to *state my case*. I'm not defending anything; I just want them to act on what I tell them.'

'Yes, I know, Atreu, I know. Please sit down. Please.'

Atreu released his hold. 'I'm sorry.'

'Atreu, look at me.'

Atreu looked up and stared into Micah's grey eyes.

'Please, Atreu, tell me what I have heard about that Faemir is not true.'

'It is true – Verlinden shared the last Zenith with me.' He sat down slowly as Micah closed his eyes.

'How could you? whispered the Holy Man. 'How could you?'

'But, Micah, you must be able to see. You, who spoke of our quest to bring the twins of life together. You must remember your own words more clearly than I do; the rock and the light, the Mountain and the sun, the Felsen and the Liche – '

'Don't throw my own words back at me as if you were my teacher.'

'But why did you stop there? Did your understanding go no further?'

Micah opened his eyes again. 'I understand what I understand.'

Atreu met his uncle's gaze. 'That is the only stupid thing I have ever heard you say.'

'We cannot bring together what does not belong together.'

'But the Maelir and Faemir – we *do* belong together.'

'No, Atreu, I don't want to hear you say this. Zenith belongs to the Maelir. Look around you – you've seen what we've built here. No Faemir hands have touched the Keep; no Faemir eyes have seen a single spire. What have they done? Burned, pillaged, murdered, destroyed. They have no place here. They have no place on the Mountain. Do you know how many Holy Men they killed at Crosanct? Do you know how many Ascenders they killed during that one attack?'

Atreu ran his fingers through his hair and looked away for a moment. 'Micah, I can only tell you what I learnt during Zenith. The two belong together. Creation and destruction. Maelir and Faemir. That's my truth. That's what my whole Ascent was about.'

'I am not here to judge your Ascent. That task belongs to the Circle. Perhaps your understanding has outstripped mine and I will have to be the one to catch up.'

'Perhaps.'

Micah sighed. 'It appears as if my appetite has deserted me.'

'As has mine,' said Atreu, feeling a smile tugging at the corners of his mouth.

'Come, Atreu, there are still things I can show you, if indeed there is no longer anything I can teach you.'

'I'm sure you are not yet a spent force, Uncle.'

'Let us go, Atreu, there is one place here in the Keep that I know will be of particular interest to you.'

'Lesson over?'

'Lesson over.'

Chapter Three

The structure of the Keep proved to be like an endless lace-work of light. Each corridor was a slightly different shade to the colour of the one before. Crimson led to scarlet which led to vermilion, ultramarine to azure to ice blue, purple to violet to lilac, and important junctures always occurred when the colours shifted from one to another. Micah tried to explain the intricacies of the pattern to Atreu, but he admitted only a few of the Inner Sanctum understood all the finer details.

But, for Atreu, the most exhilarating part of his tour was when they crossed one of the many delicate bridges that led from one tower to another. He had failed to notice them at first because they were almost transparent. They hung between the spires like giant threads, only becoming visible when hit at a certain angle by a shaft of sunlight. The first time he stepped onto one, he felt as if he was walking in mid-air.

'Who needs to be a windrider?' cried Atreu as they crossed one such bridge. He looked past his feet at the ground well below them.

'Who indeed,' said Micah.

'These bridges seem so delicate, yet they bear our weight with no trouble.'

'There is nothing like them anywhere on the Mountain.'

A thought struck Atreu. 'These bridges,' he said, 'as strong as they are, they couldn't survive much instability.'

'You are right, Atreu. There is no instability here in the Keep.'

'But that's impossible. The Summit is the most unstable part of the Mountain – I saw that for myself at Zenith.'

Micah shook his head. 'Perhaps there still are some things I can teach you. The place you speak of we sometimes call the false Summit.'

'False?'

'Yes, you saw for yourself that it was constantly changing, that there was no highest point.'

'I felt a little cheated by it. It was almost as if some monstrous joke was being played on us all. All that effort and there was no real Summit.'

'I think all the Ascenders feel that, Atreu. It is a level of understanding all of us must go through. But, look around you. Here it is. The Keep is the true Summit, although there is no doubt the false Summit exists and has a value.'

'So I shouldn't feel cheated?'

'Of course not. As with all things, there is a duality. To have one, we must have both. The false Summit is the most unstable part of the Mountain; the Keep is the most stable. This is the one place never affected by instability.'

'And no-one knows about it?'

'Not outside the Holy Orders and the windriders, but there are thousands of us here, and each year more enter after their Ascent, just as you have done.'

'So the Faemir may at this very moment be overrunning the false Summit, but they have achieved nothing. And they can't get up here, even if they knew the Keep existed?'

'That's right – they would need to sprout wings.'

Atreu looked at some figures gliding through the crystal clear air in the distance. 'Or they could learn to ride the winds.'

'Impossible – the guild protect their secrets with the same care that the Orders protect theirs. And it takes years of training.'

'What if they could persuade a windrider to carry them?'

'Now you're talking nonsense, Atreu.'

'I suppose I am. It's just that for all we know, there could be an army massing below us, and everyone seems to be just sitting smugly here in the Keep.'

'If we appear smug, it is because we have prepared so well. From reports I've heard, the Faemir are pouring into the Upper Reaches in large numbers. They probably believe Crosanct fell, but in the end we chose to abandon the pass. Let them all come now. We hope the entire Faemir population reaches the false Summit. We will offer them no resistance.'

'The strategy makes little sense to me. I know it's still a year away, but how can the next Zenith be possible?'

'Atreu, although your understanding has increased, there is still much knowledge for you to gain. So far you have experienced the Upper Reaches only during the height of summer. In a few weeks it will start to grow unbearably cold, and soon after the ice storms will return. Think about it: the Hold – the rooms and caves which house the Ascenders during Zenith – will offer some protection, but the Faemir don't have the R'angkur, and how will they make fires when they are surrounded by nothing but snow and have nothing to burn?'

Atreu shuddered. 'They will all freeze to death unless they return downslope.'

'And that will not be an option for them. As you know, Crosanct is the only major pass through to the Upper Reaches on this side of the Mountain. Right now most of the Maelir armies and battalions are converging on Crosanct. We're letting the Faemir through, but they will never get back out. Atreu, do you see it now? This will be the end of the Faemir threat.'

'They will all be murdered,' said Atreu flatly.

'There are no murders in a war, Atreu – and remember it is a war that they began, so we have justice on our side.'

'Do we?' Atreu's voice was a whisper.

Micah continued talking for a while, but Atreu couldn't concentrate on what he was saying. It was as if the sounds reached his ears but had jumbled into an incomprehensible buzz.

He tried to form a picture of Verlinden in his mind as they walked, but to his dismay, he couldn't seem to get a clear focus. He chided himself again. Why *had* he sent her back to her people? He thought the two of them could solve an enmity as old as the Mountain itself. It made no sense now. Perhaps they should have stayed together. Perhaps that would have made a difference. Or was there no hope? Perhaps it didn't matter what they did. Perhaps his whole Ascent had been meaningless.

'Ah, here we are.' They were the first words to reach Atreu for some time. He shook his head as if trying to clear his thoughts. 'This is the place I wanted to show you, Atreu.'

Micah guided him through an arched doorway, and it seemed to Atreu that twilight had suddenly fallen, although he knew it was not yet midday.

'Are we with the Felsen?' asked Atreu.

'No,' said Micah, 'this place belongs to us both. It is the librum, the place of books where all of our knowledge is stored.'

'I thought knowledge was in our heads.'

Micah smiled. 'You may want to have that argument with some of the scholars here. Come, this way.'

It had taken some time for Atreu's eyes to adjust after the brightness outside. To his surprise, despite the silence around him, the room was filled with Holy Men, both Liche and Felsen, sitting at tables, some with quills in hand, but all of them with open books in front of them. The ceiling was much lower than that of the Great Dining Hall, and shelves heavily laden with books lined the entire length of every wall.

'Ah, Micah, it is good to see you.' An ancient Liche started climbing down shakily from one of the many ladders that stood near the shelves.

Atreu tried to make out the Holy Man's features through the

librum's half-light. He had little hair and his face was leathery and heavily lined, but there was keenness in his eyes and a smile tugging at the corners of his mouth.

'This is my nephew, Atreu,' said Micah. 'I haven't told him how keen you were to meet him and what you wish to show him.'

'Welcome to the librum of the Keep, Atreu. Micah is right – there is something I wish to show you,' said the ancient Liche, trembling slightly as he negotiated the final rungs. 'You look just like I did when I first arrived. There is wonder in your eyes.'

'And, Atreu, this is my friend Praether. He is the arch-librer here.'

'I am pleased to meet you.' Atreu looked around nervously as several of the monks glanced up from their books at the sound of his voice.

'Don't mind them,' said Praether. 'The Felsen always find sound an irritant and new voices in particular break their concentration.' He laughed. 'And they have no sense of humour, you know. We Liche, of course, find it hard to concentrate unless we *are* talking. Our rules here are a bit of a compromise, but the Felsen would stare you into silence if you let them.'

'I won't let them,' said Atreu, turning back towards Praether. He could see the old man even more clearly now that his eyes were adjusting to the twilight of the librum. 'What is it you wish to show – '

He froze. He had seen the old monk before. In a cave, deep under the plains of Vygird. He heard a voice echo through his head: '*The art of breathing.*' It was Metheus.

Atreu looked away. Of course it wasn't. It couldn't be. What was going on here? Was he turning mad? He started trembling.

Micah asked, 'What's wrong?'

'Come,' said Praether, 'sit down over here.'

They led him to an empty chair next to one of the tables.

Atreu felt the blood rush to his head as he struggled for control. It couldn't be Metheus, of course not. He breathed deeply, and slowly lifted his head to stare into the old Holy Man's face.

'Do I know you?' Atreu croaked.

A look of bewilderment crossed Praether's face. 'I'm afraid I don't understand your question. I feel I know much about you, but that is through what Micah has told me.' He started coughing. 'I'm sorry,' he said between coughs, 'I have problems with my lungs.'

'With your breathing?' asked Atreu.

Praether gave him a strange look, and Atreu bit his lip.

Of course, he thought, this wasn't Metheus. This was his twin. He was about to mention his time at Vygird when he sensed something that seemed to entreat him to silence. It was as if a barrier had suddenly been placed in his path.

'It looks like I'm the only healthy one here,' said Micah.

'I'm sorry,' said Praether, now that his coughing fit had subsided. 'This is not much of a welcome for an Ascender such as yourself.'

'What do you mean: *such as myself*?'

Micah sat down next to Atreu. 'Praether had high hopes for you.'

'I don't understand.'

'You see,' said Praether, 'it is so rare that a Book is chosen as a Talisman. The other librers were more than a little surprised that it happened again after so many years.'

'Believe me,' said Atreu, 'it wasn't quite what I expected either.'

'The goldsmiths here have much to be proud of,' said Praether. 'The workmanship in the many rings, pendants and other jewellery that the Ascenders carry is beyond compare, but a Book ... well that is something altogether different. I was overjoyed at the thought, but I know better than anyone of the danger as well.'

'The danger?'

'There is too much power in a book. The ideas can be too strong. But you survived, Atreu, and I am pleased you are here.'

Atreu's eyes followed the stacked shelves of books up to the ceiling. 'So I'm the only Ascender during this Ascent to have a Book?'

Praether didn't answer at first and Atreu looked down just in time to see Micah and the old Holy Man exchange a glance.

'Yes, and throughout history, there have been very few,' said Micah.

'In fact,' said Praether, 'the most recent was over twenty years ago.'

'And what happened?'

'He failed,' said Micah, looking at Atreu strangely. 'He was so close, about as close as it's possible to get. The Ascender showed a great deal of promise – you have to show promise to be given a Book in the first place – but obviously it wasn't enough. He couldn't control his Zenith in the end, an obsession overwhelmed him, and his truth was not judged worthy by the Circle.'

'Why are you looking at me like that, Micah?'

'The Ascender was your father.'

*

The chamber that Atreu had first entered proved to be the largest room in the librum. Praether led him and Micah through a series of sanctums: each one dimly lit by glimmerstones; each one smaller and dustier and more crowded than the one before; each one lined from floor to ceiling with stacks of books; and each one containing monks with heads bent in concentration, candle in one hand, or perched precariously on some rickety ladder avidly scanning leather-clad spines.

Eventually the sanctums became so small, and the piles of books so high, that the three of them had to squeeze through the gaps in single file. Praether had taken out a cloth from his pocket and was holding it in front of his nose. Atreu wished he could do the same, because the dust was beginning to irritate him.

Finally, they reached a sanctum in which there was no gap to squeeze through. Just as Praether had started to climb a large pile of books that blocked their progress, Atreu asked, 'Is this the only way?'

Praether looked back, almost losing his balance. 'I'm afraid so. We sometimes call these our true Ascents.' He chuckled. 'Most amusing, don't you think?'

Atreu and Micah exchanged glances.

'A librer joke, no doubt,' said Atreu, as he began climbing the pile. 'So, are we nearly there?'

Praether started chuckling again.

The sanctums continued to get smaller, and the piles of books blocking the way higher. Atreu was surprised the old librer had the stamina for all that climbing, because he was not finding it particularly easy going himself.

'What is in all these books?' he asked.

'Aha,' said Praether, 'the question that first time visitors to the librum always ask. I'm surprised it took you so long.'

Atreu smiled to himself as some of Metheus' words came back to him. 'A *what* question, I know. And I should have been asking a *who* or is it a *where* – I always get that mixed up.'

'What are you talking about?' asked Micah.

'Never mind,' said Atreu. 'I'm just trying to sound wise – it makes a change.'

Praether had stopped in the middle of his descent of another pile. He appeared to be nodding slowly to himself.

'What *is* in all these books?' Atreu repeated his question.

'You may as well ask what thoughts have been in a man's head since the day he was born.'

'What I mean is, are they stories or are they facts?'

'Tell me the difference.'

'Well ... stories are made up, facts are real.'

'It's that simple, is it?'

Micah interrupted. 'I think, Atreu, you are about to have an argument with Praether that many of us have been having with him for a long time.'

Praether continued his descent. 'No, Micah, I know I have had very little success with you. However, your nephew here ... well now ... he is someone who knows books.'

'How can you say that?' asked Atreu.

'Because I know you.'

'You don't, Praether, or else you would know that since my schooling in Valesend ceased, I have hardly touched a book.'

'Apart from your Talisman.'

'Yes, of course.'

'Your schoolbooks are not the sort I am talking about. I'm talking about stories of great journeys and mighty deeds.'

'Where are the books that contain these stories – there were none in Valesend as far as I could tell.'

'Of course there were. They were in your father's tales, they were in your own head, they were in your dreams.'

Atreu felt as if he had slammed against a wall. 'What are you talking about? Tales and dreams aren't books.'

Praether smiled. 'They may not yet be trapped on the page, the words may still be floating in the ether or inside someone's head, but in essence they are the same. Like water and ice.'

'But a book is something you can touch.'

'Have you never touched an idea? Have you never been touched by an idea? Is an idea not real?'

'So a book and an idea are the same thing?'

'A book and the million ideas that make up the book, yes.'

'And stories and facts are the same thing?'

Praether took away the cloth from his nose. 'I think you already know what I've been telling you. I'll use a time-honoured method of the Liche and answer your question with another question: What was in your Book, Atreu, what was in your Book?'

*

Although Atreu could not believe it was possible, the sanctums through which they walked were becoming still smaller and more crowded. None of the books were now stacked in any way, and they filled increasing portions of each room like chaotic debris. Micah and Atreu now took it in turn to lead because it was necessary to push the huge piles aside and Praether was visibly tiring. This is worse than the undergrowth of the Rimforest, thought Atreu, as he struggled through another jungle of books. And in each sanctum there was at least one Holy Man, poring over a book or rummaging through a pile. Occasionally Atreu found himself in a sanctum that appeared to be unoccupied, but at each of these times, a cough or the sound of a turning page indicated that a monk was somewhere in the room, even though the haphazard towers of books hid him.

'Are any of these rooms unoccupied?' asked Atreu, as they entered yet another sanctum.

'Possible,' said Praether. 'I couldn't tell you for sure. Researchers have been known to spend weeks on end in these hinter sanctums.'

'It's possible some might have died back here and no-one would know it.' Atreu laughed.

There was a rustling sound to his right, and the head of a monk popped out from the book pile and glared at Atreu.

'Well met, good Holy Man,' cried Atreu. 'Good to still see you're in the land of the living.'

The monk continued to glare at Atreu and the three walked past.

'No sense of humour, these Felsen,' said Praether. 'No sense of humour at all.'

The doorway to the next sanctum was partly blocked by books so it was a difficult task even entering it. The dust now lay so thickly Atreu's fingers disappeared at times as he struggled for a handhold.

'I wouldn't be surprised if there were some bones under some of these piles,' he said. 'What do you think, Micah ... Micah?'

'Sorry.'

'What were you doing?'

'I ... um ... I was just having some r'lung. Here, have some.'

'Put it away. You know I don't like the effect it has on me, the way I seem to lose myself each time I use it. Why are you having some now? There's no urgency here, is there?'

'No, Atreu, I'm struggling a little – I suppose I'm getting older.'

'It's got nothing to do with age, Micah,' said Praether, 'and you know it.'

'What are you saying?' asked Atreu.

'Micah, I've spoken to you about this ...'

'This is not the time, Praether.' Micah's voice was stern but with a surprising shrill edge.

Atreu glanced at his uncle. Sweat was beading on his brow and his eyes seemed to be following the path of a dancing beam of light. 'Micah, please tell me what's wrong with you.' He could smell the familiar bittersweetness of the r'lung on his breath.

Micah pushed past his nephew. 'Come on, we've still got quite a way to go.'

*

Atreu hadn't seen any researchers for quite some time. The sanctums were now so small it would have been possible to traverse them in four or five strides if it wasn't for the books. The piles were actually decreasing in size as they continued, but the dust was almost knee-deep in places. Micah, under the influence of the r'lung, was trying to set a more frenetic pace, but Atreu managed to hold him back to the point where Praether could keep up. The old man had the occasional brief coughing fit, but otherwise maintained the pace surprisingly well.

Eventually, though, Atreu could no longer hold Micah back without physically restraining him. The Holy Man's arms were jerking madly just as Praether began coughing again. In between coughs, Praether motioned Micah to go on.

'Go,' said Atreu. 'We'll see you there.'

Micah scrambled over a mountain of dust-laden books and disappeared.

Atreu waited for Praether to compose himself. 'It's the r'lung, isn't it?'

Praether nodded.

'It ...' Atreu struggled for the words. 'It has some sort of hold on him and it won't let go.'

'You're right, Atreu. I have seen it coming for some time.'

'Is he ... is he ... too weak?'

'I don't think that's being fair to your uncle. There are reasons which are not entirely his fault. And the r'lung can be a problem for other members of the Liche. I have always argued caution in its use. There are dangers that come with its benefits.'

'I don't like it, and I've told him that.'

'But it saved your Ascent, and probably your life, did it not?'

'Perhaps. I'd rather credit the windrider Riell with saving my life in Crosanct. As to my Ascent ... well, I don't know what will happen now that I've completed it.'

'Let us continue our little journey. I am able to continue now. Perhaps you will learn something to help you in your audience with the Circle. There may be more to your Ascent than what you think, Atreu.'

Finally, they reached a sanctum which was empty except for a fine layer of dust. Each footstep released a grey cloud into the air. On the far side of the room was a closed door. Micah was slumped up against it. His eyes were bloodshot and unfocused and his mouth drooped on one side, allowing saliva to collect on his beard.

Atreu stepped up to him and shook him. 'What is wrong with you?'

Micah's eyes seemed to clear and he focused sharply on his nephew. 'Nothing – can't a man rest? I was setting a hard pace, wasn't I? Which is more than I can say for you two snails.'

'But you took r'lung, Uncle.'

'So? That's what it's for, isn't it? To get you to places quickly. You both should have taken some as well.'

'But there is no need,' said Praether. 'We are in no particular rush.'

Atreu looked at Micah anxiously. 'Why have the effects of it worn away so soon?'

Micah shrugged as he stood up. 'They don't prepare it like they used to. I've been noticing that over the years.'

'You know that's not true,' said Praether. 'You simply need more and more.'

Micah ignored him, pointing instead to the door behind him. 'If you've forgotten your keys, Praether, I'm going to be most upset.'

Atreu and Praether exchanged glances as the old librer lifted a chain from around his neck. 'Now, I can never remember which one it is,' he said as he flicked through the hundreds of keys on the chain. 'Aha ...'

'I think that means he's found it,' said Micah, stepping aside to allow the old man to get to the lock.

Praether opened the door and they entered the room. To his dismay, Atreu realised the room was empty and there was another door on the other side. The old librer was busy searching through the keys as the three of them kicked dust clouds in the air.

They had walked through half a dozen empty chambers before Atreu realised the rooms were getting bigger. He had a sudden sinking feeling.

'Don't tell me,' he said, 'we are only just over halfway and we're going to end up in a room the size of the one we started in?'

Praether nodded. 'A lovely sense of symmetry, isn't it? And how astute of you to notice.'

'But I thought we were nearly there.' Atreu could feel the blood rushing to his face.

'Ascents are a bit like that too.' Praether chuckled. 'I don't remember saying we were nearly there.'

'But I thought because the rooms were getting smaller ... and then we reached a locked door ...'

'Ah, appearance and reality. Micah, how does our lesson on

that one go?' The old librer was still laughing softly to himself. 'Something about seeing through things.'

'You know how it goes, Praether, you were the one who told me.' There was the faintest of smiles tugging at Micah's lips.

Atreu stared at the ancient librer. 'You were Micah's sage, weren't you?'

'Well, well,' said Praether. 'I am impressed. It didn't take you long to work that out.' He patted Micah on the shoulder. 'It looks like you've done a fine job with young Atreu here ... now tell me, did you do the bit with the water in the hand?'

They both laughed and Atreu joined them.

*

Because all of the chambers were empty, they made rapid progress, the only delay being Praether's search for each key.

'Why are all these rooms empty,' asked Atreu, 'when all the others were so crammed full of books? Surely it would make more sense to spread them out and use all the space you have.'

'*Sense* – that's an interesting word,' said Praether. 'Our librum is about a lot of things, but *sense* is not one of them. Let me answer you in this way – have you noticed how no matter how much space you have, you always have exactly enough items to fill it? We could expand the librum to cover the Keep if we were allowed. In fact there *are* other librums elsewhere in the Keep, although this is the largest and the others only contain copies.'

'Do you mean all of the books we've seen are originals? Written by the author's own hand?'

'Most of them are original, yes, but often they are dictated to a scribe.'

'I can't believe that so many books have been written.'

'Believe it, Atreu. This librum contains books that have been collected since the very first Ascent by Maelur. But don't fully believe my explanation about why all these rooms are empty. I only gave you part of the reason. These locked doors are here to keep the Book we have in the very last room safe. It is the most important of all, and as arch-librer, I am entrusted with its care.'

'Please, tell me about it.'

'I don't have to – we're here.'

Praether turned the key in the last door and they entered the final chamber. Despite its size, there was a musty smell in the air. Clusters of pale glimmerstones embedded in the stone work illuminated only pockets of the room, but there was enough light to see row upon row of empty shelves lining the walls.

'It looks like there's room for more than one book here.' Atreu heard his voice echo hollowly from the far side of the chamber.

Then he noticed a book on a shelf at head height just to his right. Praether approached it reverently. He ran his fingers across the spine, touching so lightly it was as if he was afraid it would break.

A shiver raced down Atreu's back. He shot a glance at the far side of the room. 'Who's there?' he called.

Only a strange, distorted echo returned.

'Did you see something?' asked Praether. 'Tell me, what did you see?'

'Nothing. A dust mote, a shadow cast by the flicker of the glimmerstones. Nothing.'

'Did it look like an old man?'

Another shiver shot down Atreu's back. 'Yes ... I ... er ... it could have been. Is there someone here?'

Praether's voice dropped slightly. 'Sometimes I think I've seen an old man in here. He's not a Holy Man, but that's all I can say about him – I never see him for long enough.'

'Who is he?'

'I don't know. I call him the Reader.'

'Why?'

'Well, what else would he be doing in here?'

Micah's voice cut through the air. 'Let's have no more talk about ghosts and spirits. The Book is here – that's what we wanted you to see, Atreu.'

Praether smiled. 'Ah, Micah doesn't have time for such fancies. Perhaps he is not old enough, or young enough, to appreciate them. But tell me, Micah, I know we have had this discussion before, but I say it again for Atreu's benefit: does a book exist if there is no-one to read it?'

'And my answer, Praether, as always is I don't know, and most probably no-one knows, and most importantly there is no need for anyone to know.'

'Perhaps. Perhaps not ... the Book, Atreu. Here it is.'

'And this was a Talisman for an Ascent?'

'In a way, yes.'

'Either it was or it wasn't. Surely there can't be any doubt as to what it is?'

'No,' said Praether. 'Your mind is quick, but you need to have more information to come to the right conclusion. This is the Book of Maelur – the book that our great leader wrote during and after the first Ascent.'

Atreu drew a breath. 'What does it say? Tell me about it.'

'No, each person must read it for himself. I can't tell you its meaning. I don't know what its meaning is for you.'

Atreu felt a powerful sense of expectation, a tingling sensation coursed through him. 'Then let me read part of it now.'

'All right,' Praether nodded. 'Let's see what's in the Maelur chronicle for you.'

He picked it up and held it out for Atreu to open. 'You pick the page,' he said.

Atreu opened it somewhere near the start and the three of them started to read.

Chapter Four

'We still can't find anyone, Valkyra.'

'Well keep looking, damn you, everyone can't just have disappeared. There must be hidden tunnels, secret caverns – find them.'

Valkyra felt her blood heat the length of her body. She shut her eyes. *Calm yourself. Control the anger. That's how you've always won. The anger shouldn't be blind. Focus it.* They were at the Summit – the first Faemir ever to reach it. Yes, it was too late for Zenith. She felt another wave of anger course through her veins. *Focus.* Yes, they were too late, but it did not matter. They would find the monks and Ascenders and destroy them all. They would take Zenith just as they took the Summit.

'I believe it was too easy in the end, Valkyra.'

Valkyra opened her eyes to look at Rhea. 'Are you still here? Didn't I tell you to keep looking?'

'What do you think everyone is doing? They don't need another order from me.'

Valkyra nodded her head slowly.

'Did you hear what I said?' asked Rhea.

'Yes, yes, of course. You're right – it was too easy in the end. I had the same feeling about Crosanct at the time.'

'Did you? But we were attacked all the way through Crosanct and the Upper Reaches.'

'I think *harassed* is a better word. We were harassed not attacked – there was no real attempt to finish us. I felt all along that those damned windriders were simply trying to slow us down.'

'Well, they succeeded there.'

'Yes, Rhea, as you've pointed out to me several times since we arrived at the Summit, we've missed Zenith by seven days.'

'We've failed.'

Valkyra drew a sharp breath and glared at the older woman.

'But that's not the message you spread among the others, is it? You don't say *we*, do you? You say *Valkyra* failed, don't you?'

Rhea met her gaze. 'Have I ever given you anything but complete loyalty since you became leader?'

'I am only aware of what you say to my face.'

'Damn you, Valkyra. I've always supported you. I've argued for you with the other coveyns. Do you really think you gained the leadership entirely on your own? Who was it who gave you authority when you were too young to convince the others?'

'But who did you do that for? For yourself. For our coveyn perhaps. Not for me.'

'I did it for the Faemir, Valkyra. I hope that's why we've done everything that we've done.'

Valkyra clenched her teeth. 'You're right. I'm just so frustrated that we can't find anyone here.'

'Is it a trap?'

'I don't think so, Rhea. Where would they attack us from? More and more of our battalions are pouring through Crosanct. The Summit is ours.'

'But not Zenith.'

'No, not Zenith.' Valkyra's voice was a strangled whisper. She looked up as another woman entered the room. The warrior was wearing the battle garb of the Faemir; the scaled leather breastplate and shoulder pads, her sword sheathed at her side. 'Valkyra, Rhea, we've found someone – an Ascender, we believe.'

'Aha,' said Valkyra, a smile creeping onto her lips. 'Where there's one, there will be many. Where was the hidden tunnel?'

'There is no tunnel, Valkyra – we found him outside, half-covered in snow. He is barely alive.'

'Bring him here. He'll be able to tell us where the others are.'

'I don't think he can speak. He's only just conscious.'

Valkyra's smile broadened. 'Don't worry about that – I'll bring him round. Where is he?'

'Just in the next room.' The warrior turned and shouted through the open doorway. 'Bring him in.'

Two warriors carried in a deathly pale Maelir and put him on the ground in front of Valkyra.

Rhea spat on him. 'That's the broadcloth of an Ascender.'

Valkyra motioned her to be quiet.

'This was found in his hands,' said a Faemir who had just entered the room. She handed a double-sided battle-axe to Valkyra.

'What's an Ascender doing with a battle-axe?' asked Rhea.

'He is the one,' said Valkyra, suddenly banging the head of the axe on the floor and then letting it fall.

'What do you mean?' asked Rhea.

'Don't you remember the reports we were getting – from Rathsheed and Spa and elsewhere – of a warrior in the guise of an Ascender who was killing so many sisters.'

Rhea's eyes widened. 'Well, this one is quite a find.' She poked him in the stomach with her foot and he stirred slightly.

'Get him to his feet,' ordered Valkyra, and the two warriors who had brought him in lifted him to his feet, although he was still semiconscious.

Valkyra approached the Maelir as the Faemir supported him from both sides. She brought her face so close to his that she could hear his shallow breathing. Her voice was controlled. 'We have to be gentle with this one,' she said, reaching out and very gently running her hand along his ice-cold cheek. 'I have a feeling he is going to be important.'

She drew even closer, so that their faces were almost touching. She let out a breath and let the Maelir take it in. Then she traced a path down his cheek to his throat and her fingers sought the spot they knew well.

'Ever so gently,' she whispered as she began to press in.

Almost immediately, the Maelir began making a gurgling sound.

Rhea cried, 'You'll kill him.'

'But I'm so gentle,' whispered Valkyra, and while increasing her pressure, she reached up with her other hand to pull back his eyelids. The Maelir's eyes had rolled back and she could only see the whites. The gurgling sound grew louder.

'Valkyra!' Rhea was shouting now.

The Faemir leader was motionless. Her own breathing had stopped. The only sound was a sickening noise in the back of the Maelir's throat which was now like the groans of a dying animal.

Then, without warning, the Maelir's pupils rolled forward and his gaze bored into Valkyra's. A split second later, he threw off the two warriors who had been supporting him and took a step back. Rhea and the other Faemir warriors drew their swords and tensed.

Valkyra was almost motionless – a smile froze on her lips. Her only movement was a small signal for the others to stay back. The Maelir glanced quickly at the floor behind her.

'Yes,' said Valkyra in calm, measured tones, 'your axe is there – do you want it?'

Fire flamed in the young Maelir's eyes. Without warning, he dived at her throat with both arms outstretched.

Valkyra smiled as she stepped to one side, flicking up her forearm to deflect the attack. Just as she did, the Maelir's lunge changed direction and he dived towards the battle-axe. He rolled once and then jumped to his feet to face her again.

The smile left Valkyra's lips for the barest of moments. Then she drew her sword.

'I think you need to be shown how things have changed on the Mountain,' she said, slowly circling the Maelir. She could see his muscles tense.

'Take a look around, dear Ascender. The Summit is ours now. We've killed everyone.'

The Maelir's face twitched slightly.

'Yes,' Valkyra continued. 'All your Holy Men, all the Ascenders. You're the last. How does it feel to be the last of your kind?'

With a shout of rage, the Maelir ran at Valkyra swinging his battle-axe overhead. Valkyra swung her sword to meet it in mid-air. A clang resonated through the room and the walls seemed to shake.

Valkyra felt the pain of impact scream through her arms, yet she didn't flinch. She knew a sword was not the best weapon to take the full impact of a battle-axe, but she had used hers effectively in similar circumstances in the past. She was therefore surprised at the force of the Maelir's swing. This is no ordinary warrior, she thought, and that is no ordinary battle-axe.

He swung again, this time in the other direction, but she was too quick for him and her sword blocked the blow. Again the pain shot like a flame through her arms.

Damn this Ascender, he has no weak side.

She feinted to the right and then she lunged toward his stomach, forcing him on the defensive for the first time. He stepped back, swinging his axe at the sword. Valkyra felt her grip loosen for a moment, as stone met stone, before she grasped tightly at the handle.

She felt sweat beading her brow. Damn him. He uses his axe as dexterously as a sword. A battle-axe used as an effective defensive weapon – this was something new.

Valkyra double-feinted and then drove for his throat, but the Maelir had anticipated the direction and had sidestepped while swinging his axe in a wide arc at her head. Valkyra ducked but was momentarily off balance when she saw the axe start to arc back again from underneath. She swung her sword down to meet it, but, because the full weight of her body wasn't behind it, the clash wrenched the sword from her hand and it fell to the floor.

She rolled out of the way and then back onto her feet in a crouching position. He came at her but she skipped away. As he swung his axe in oscillating arcs, moving in again and again, she ducked under his guard and rammed her shoulder into his stomach. The Maelir was obviously caught by surprise and hadn't expected her to attack. His momentum faltered just long enough for her to get a grip on the handle of his axe.

They stood toe-to-toe, muscles taut as each tried to claim the battle-axe, eyes unblinking, gaze matching gaze.

When the Maelir spoke, it was from deep at the back of his throat. 'I knew you would betray us.'

Valkyra lost her composure for a split second. Then a wave of anger pulsed through her. She pushed hard at the Maelir, who hadn't expected her to push in his direction. He fell back onto the floor and his grip on the axe loosened.

Rhea quickly pounced on the axe while three other warriors pinned the Maelir to the ground.

'What are you doing?' demanded Valkyra, shaking with anger.

'It's enough,' said Rhea. 'He's too dangerous.'

'How dare you!' Her lips were tight, but the white heat was starting to fade.

'There's no point,' said Rhea. 'We don't want him dead right now.'

Valkyra nodded. 'You're right.' She sheathed her sword as the three Faemir dragged the Ascender to his feet. He was the most impressive Maelir warrior she had come across. She knew she had been at a disadvantage because she hadn't been trying to kill him. And she knew that the others could have intervened in a split second at her signal, so there was no desperation on her part – and she always fought at her best when she was desperate. Yet, in many ways, this Maelir had been a match for her.

'I've got the feeling,' she said, looking at him, 'that you will be a great deal of use to me.'

As she spoke, the strength seemed to ebb from the Maelir. His body slumped and his eyelids began to close.

'Take him away and lock him in one of the cells,' said Valkyra. 'I'll get what I want from him later.'

Rhea approached Valkyra after the others had left. 'He could be a baresark, couldn't he?' she said.

Valkyra fell silent for a moment, then said, 'I sensed something about him when they first brought him in.'

'He must have been near death in the snow outside.'

'Yes, Rhea, and I took him that little bit closer.' She ran her fingers along the line of her throat. 'And that's where he was most dangerous – at the point of death.'

'So he's like you.'

Valkyra lashed out to strike Rhea with the back of her hand but stopped herself in mid action. She lowered her arm. 'Don't compare a Maelir to me,' she said softly. 'You know there is no such thing as a Maelir baresark.'

'There are old stories – you've heard them, Valkyra.'

'Old stories – very old. If they did exist, they exist no longer.'

'You know, Valkyra, that even amongst the Faemir, baresarks occur less than one each generation. And a baresark has to be threatened with death in battle for the power to emerge.'

'Yes, yes, I understand what you're saying. A baresark can be born, live and die of old age, and never know his potential. As we've found out, the Maelir have grown soft over the generations. They have not had to fight battles. Perhaps there have been others in the past.'

'And they've simply never emerged.'

'Well, this one has emerged – and he has a weapon to match his powers.' Valkyra picked up the battle-axe, tracing the notches on the handle with her fingers. 'And we haven't seen his full potential yet.'

'How so, Valkyra? I must tell you, I was impressed with his skills.'

'He must have sensed that I wasn't going to kill him – I can always sense it – so his power wasn't at its fullest height.'

Rhea shivered slightly. 'So he is capable of more?'

Valkyra nodded.

'How much more?'

'We'll never know until we genuinely threaten his life.'

'So there is more than one reason to keep him prisoner for a while rather than to try to kill him?'

'Exactly.'

Rhea hesitated for a moment. 'But tell me, Valkyra. What did he mean when he said you had betrayed them?'

Valkyra frowned. 'I don't know ...'

'Could he have somehow known that you were born a Faelen?'

Valkyra lashed out again – this time her hand stopped just short of Rhea's cheek. 'You are the only one who I allow to say that and live.'

Rhea grimaced slightly. 'I thank you for your mercy.'

*

Valkyra heard the door shut behind her and the bolt being levered into place. She knew it would be better if they both felt trapped.

'So, my Ascender,' she said softly, 'how does it feel to be the only Maelir at the Summit?'

The Maelir sat crouched in the corner, leaning against the two walls. He had lifted his head slightly when Valkyra entered his cell, but that was the only movement he made.

'We can arrange for you to be in this cell a long time.' Valkyra took two steps towards him.

'You see, my Ascender,' she pointed to her side, 'I left my sword outside. We're even. It will have to be bare hands or nothing in here. Are you up to bare hands?'

The Maelir cocked his head to one side and appeared to focus on the floor to Valkyra's left.

'But you know I'm no mortal threat to you, don't you? Not just now, anyway. You can sense it. Am I right?' She took another step closer. 'In fact, I'm no threat at all to you just now. I don't have any weapons on me. See – nothing hidden.'

Valkyra unclipped her breastplate and removed it.

'No threat at all,' she whispered, as she removed her tunic and leggings and stood naked in front of him. She sensed a faint drawing of breath, but otherwise the Maelir sat perfectly still.

Valkyra moved closer. 'Such self-control. Ascenders are always so strong – at first. But come, if we are to be no threat to each other, we must appear to each other as equals.'

She reached down and pulled at his broadcloth. He didn't assist her, but there was no resistance either as she pulled it over his head.

Her hand ran up his bare thigh. 'Nothing hidden – am I right?' The Maelir didn't flinch. 'Ah, strength without brutishness – I like that.'

Valkyra drew still closer until their bodies and faces were all but touching. Her fingers traced a path up his stomach and chest, and finally came to rest on his throat.

'Do you remember what I can do?' She spoke softly into his ear. Her fingers pressed in slightly before she moved them back down his body again.

She lowered her head and kissed the side of his neck. 'That's not the best way to kill though, did you know that?' She nipped him gently. 'The best way is to bite into the vein just here.' Valkyra felt his heart beating, and she kissed him again as her fingers moved down past his stomach.

She smiled. 'There's always a time when self-control deserts us, isn't there?'

She drew back slightly to see the Maelir was now focusing on her, eyes wide and his face flushed.

'I think I have you now, my Ascender.' Her body shifted so that she was now astride him. Very gently, she began to move back and forth, and the Maelir closed his eyes.

She felt his strength inside her, pulsing deeper and higher.

Soon you will be mine, she thought, as she leant back to allow him to enter her further. Soon. He was succumbing like all the others. She moved faster. Yes. Soon. Then she felt his hands on the small of her back.

What was happening?

Valkyra reached back to pull his hands away, but she didn't have the strength or the will. She felt a heat grow from nowhere. No, this couldn't be. This couldn't be. Her senses blurred. He was pulling her towards him. Still deeper. It was impossible.

And then all her thoughts exploded and she felt wave, after wave, after exquisite wave. Her body crumpled momentarily into the Maelir's, only to be urged on again to greater heights. And again the waves shattered through. Stronger, higher. Impossible.

Again she collapsed, and again her body revived to greater heights. All the time the Maelir pushed further into her. Impossible. And the waves kept coming. No rest. She was drowning. Just wave on top of wave on top of wave on top of ...

When she regained consciousness, Valkyra found she was still astride the Maelir and he was still sitting, leaning against the two corner walls of the cell. She slid off, noting that he was far from a spent force, and threw up on the floor.

'Valkyra, have you finished with him?' The voice came from the other side of the locked door.

Valkyra staggered to her feet and put her battle garb on with trembling fingers.

'Valkyra, is anything wrong?' asked the voice.

'No,' she shouted back, immediately regretting the sharp edge to her voice.

'Have you finished with him?'

'Not by a long way,' she said, between gritted teeth.

She picked up the Ascender's broadcloth and threw it at his naked frame, covering his maleness. He stared back at her with a look she couldn't decipher.

She shouted, 'Open the door – I need some fresh air.' And then, softly, to the Maelir, 'I'll be back.'

She heard the bolt lift and the cell door creak open.

'Valkyra, are you all right? You look pale.'

*

The candle burnt low as Valkyra absently ran her finger back-wards and forwards across the flame.

Rhea was seated opposite her, a half-eaten meal of dry bread and cheese lay on the table in front of them. 'Another battalion arrived today. Three more are already making their way through the Upper Reaches.'

Valkyra continued to flick her finger through the candle flame.

Rhea continued. 'The news we have is that there are at least a dozen other battalions at Crosanct waiting their turn to march through. Large Maelir forces are moving upslope through the Mid-Reaches and towards the pass, but they're proceeding very slowly.'

Valkyra stopped her finger in the middle of the flame and watched it as she spoke. 'I know what they're doing. It's clear to me now. They're going to try to trap us in here for winter. They want as many of us as possible to get through Crosanct and then they're going to try and block the pass.'

'That's madness. All the Ascenders are up here, the Holy Men – '

'Yes, Rhea, but where are they? We still can't find them. No matter how many Faemir arrive, we still can't find them.'

'We've got one.'

Valkyra watched as her finger began to smoulder.

Rhea continued. 'And what use is he? You've been in there, I don't know how many times – '

'Eight.'

'Eight times then, and each time you come out more tired and exhausted than the time before. Sometimes I think he's killing you.'

The smoke was now coming from Valkyra's finger. 'He is.'

Slowly she took her finger away from the flame and held it up to her nose so she could smell the stench of her burning flesh. 'I see it now. He's killing me slowly – or at least letting me kill myself. He's draining me. There's no battle, no weapons. Just me trying to get mastery of him. And I'm failing – that's what's killing me.'

Valkyra put her finger in the cooling cup of water in front of her and continued. 'And that's what the Maelir want to do with us. They're just going to drain us. We've been so frantic in our efforts to get to the Summit that we didn't consider carefully enough what would happen once we're here.'

'That's not true, Valkyra. You know our plan was always to wipe out the Holy Orders, totally and completely.'

'And now we can't even find them.'

'There must be a tunnel somewhere – we'll find it.'

'Perhaps.'

'But, Valkyra, how can the Maelir trap us in the Upper Reaches without trapping their precious Holy Orders and Ascenders up here?'

'That's it,' said Valkyra suddenly, hitting the table with the palm of her hand. 'Wherever they are hiding, they have access to the rest of the Mountain. The windriders – don't you see – they're the key.'

'We still see them occasionally, but they're always far too high to be within arrow reach.'

'No, Rhea, we don't want to kill them just now. Choosing the right moment for a kill is very important – you should know that. We should be watching them.' Valkyra jumped out of her chair. 'That's it. We should be watching them closely. Where are they coming from? Where are they going to? There must be a pattern.'

She got up.

'Where are you going, Valkyra? It's dark outside – we can't do anything till morning.'

Valkyra looked at the burnt flesh on her finger and smiled. 'I'm going to visit our Ascender.'

She bent over and blew out the candle.

*

The familiar sound of the bolt clanged behind her. The only evidence that the Maelir had moved from his crouched position since her last visit was that most of the food on the plate had been eaten.

Valkyra smiled. 'So your appetite is returning, my Ascender? How fortunate.'

She sat down beside him so that their bodies were touching. 'I want you to speak to me tonight. I know you have a tongue.' She lifted her hand to his mouth and traced a circle around his lips before she pushed a finger into his mouth.

'There, I can feel your tongue. I knew you had one.'

The Maelir's nostrils flared slightly.

'You can bite down on my finger, if you want to,' said Valkyra. 'Go on – why don't you?'

A sliver of saliva ran down her finger, but there was no pressure from his teeth.

A wave of anger hit her. 'Damn you. You don't speak when I want you to speak. You don't bite when I want you to bite.'

Valkyra pushed her thumb into his mouth and grasped hold of his tongue. 'This is no use to you. You're better off without it.'

Suddenly she felt his teeth bite into her. She cried out and tried to pull away, but he bit deeper. The teeth had pierced her flesh, but still she couldn't get her hand out. She kicked at him, but the vice only clasped tighter.

Then, just as suddenly, she felt a calmness descend over her. She slowly reached for his eyes with her other hand. Before she had time to press into his eyeballs, he had unclamped his teeth.

Valkyra pulled out her hand and looked at the two semicircular lines of lacerated flesh.

'Finally, my Ascender, finally I know.'

Despite her injured hand, she quickly unclasped her breastplate and removed her tunic and leggings. 'It's funny how a little pain makes you see things more clearly.'

She crouched down in front of him. 'You don't know anything, do you? That was my mistake – thinking that you could give us information. You know less than I do. You really believed me when I said we had killed the others. You have no idea where they are, do you?'

'You betrayed us.' The sound of his voice chilled her.

'Ah – it speaks after all.'

The Maelir looked at her, his nostrils flared. 'I knew you would. He was wrong. He always was a dreamer. I should have trusted my instincts.'

'Ah, the Ascender speaks in riddles.'

'I knew you would betray us.'

'What are you ...' Valkyra drew a sharp breath. Now it is clear to me, she thought. She smiled as she lifted up his broadcloth and began stroking his bare skin.

'You poor confused Ascender,' she said. 'You don't even know who I am.'

There was a look in his eyes which Valkyra hadn't seen before, as she positioned herself astride him and began moving with soft rhythms.

'Now tell me,' she said, watching with satisfaction as the Maelir's face flushed and sweat appeared on his forehead, 'tell me where you last saw my sister.'

She smiled and leant back as Teyth shuddered and convulsed beneath her.

Chapter Five

Atreu's head throbbed as he read the last word of the chapter. It was as if his thoughts had been turned inside out and now hung in front of him like raw flesh. How could this be? Was he dreaming? No, this was far stranger than any dream, far more bizarre, far more unreal. He staggered back, his legs close to buckling underneath him.

'Quickly,' said Praether. 'Try to stop him from falling.'

Micah grabbed Atreu under his arms and eased him down to the floor.

Atreu felt the blackness seeking to overwhelm him. No! His face burned with a fire hotter than the hottest coals. Don't let the darkness take you again. He felt himself slipping away, but with one final effort he fought back from the brink. He stared at his feet and heaved for breath as if he had been climbing a slope for half a day.

Micah glanced from Atreu to Praether. 'What happened to him?'

'It's the Book,' said Praether.

'I don't understand,' said Micah. 'Why would the tale of Maelur's Ascent have such a powerful effect on Atreu? He must know much of the story already.'

Atreu's head jerked up. 'What are you talking about, Micah?'

'It's good to see you're all right.'

'What were you saying just then?'

'I just don't understand how the story of Maelur's Ascent – '

'Are you insane? Praether, what did we just read?'

'It was the part where Maelur talks about – '

'Are you mad as well?' cried Atreu. 'That's not what was written on these pages. Why are you doing this to me? Is this another Ritual, another test?'

'Try to calm yourself,' said Praether, putting his hand on Atreu's shoulder.

Micah looked into Atreu's eyes. 'Are you telling me you didn't read about the first Ascent just then?'

Atreu shook his head.

'You can't be well, Atreu. Perhaps your Zenith has affected your mind.'

'Micah's right, Zenith has affected you,' said Praether. 'Zenith changes your perception – we all know that is what it is supposed to do. Atreu, please tell us what was in the Book for you.'

Micah stared at the arch-librer. 'You read what was there, didn't you?'

'I read what I read,' said Praether.

'Don't treat me as if you're still my sage,' Micah exclaimed. 'I know all the games and word play as well as you. The chapter we just finished had Maelur arriving on the edges of Vygird – am I right?'

'Yes,' said Praether, 'that's what was there for me.'

'That's not what I read,' said Atreu quietly.

'Give me that book,' said Micah, grabbing it from Praether. 'This can be settled easily. Look.' He held it open in front of Atreu. 'Read the last part of the chapter again.'

Atreu felt the blood drain from his face. 'That's not what was there before. Let me have a look.' He grabbed the Book from him. 'You're showing me the wrong page.' He flicked backwards and forwards through the Book, growing increasingly frustrated. 'It's the wrong book. This is not what I was reading.'

'It's the same book, Atreu,' said Praether.

Atreu looked at the old librer in bewilderment. 'I ...'

Praether took the Book from him. 'Atreu,' he said, 'I have always believed this Book is the Maelir's most precious possession, and that books make by far the most powerful Talismans. Most of the Circle do not agree with me. They tell me that I am only saying what they would expect the arch-librer to say. But I know, and I think you are beginning to understand what I have always instinctively understood. Books aren't static, just as ideas aren't static.'

'Praether, you're an obsessive old fool,' said Micah. 'You never let it rest, do you? Do you actually believe Atreu could have read different words than the ones we all see here in front of us?'

Praether shook his head slowly. 'I wonder what is happening to you sometimes, Micah. What happened to the young Ascender who was so eager for knowledge?'

'Praether, you know books can't change.'

'But readers change. And there is no book without a reader.'

'So we're back to that again.'

'You lied to me.' Atreu's voice cut through the air and both Micah and Praether turned towards him.

'What are you talking about?' asked Micah.

'You led me to believe Teyth was safe, that he was up here in the Keep.'

'I ... I didn't actually say that. What makes you say he isn't?' Micah's voice had an edge to it.

'This ... this book that I haven't read properly.'

'What was in the chapter?' asked Praether.

Atreu ignored him. 'Why did you lie to me, Micah?'

'I ...' Micah hesitated. 'I'm sorry, Atreu, I couldn't tell you about Teyth. I can't go against our conventions. You would have been told after Equinox.'

'Equinox?' Atreu frowned. 'But that must be almost two months away. Why?'

'I can't tell you anymore. The Circle has its reasons for its decisions – they are not made lightly. It has to allow all the Ascenders to address it first and then take the time to consider them all.'

'But why Equinox?'

'Atreu, these are things I shouldn't be explaining to you. I'm no longer your sage, others will speak to you about these matters at the right time.'

'But you're still my uncle. Tell me – answer me.'

Micah sighed. 'Equinox is one of the secrets that the Holy Orders keep to themselves.'

'But we celebrate it in Valesend,' said Atreu. 'You know that.'

'Yes,' said Micah. 'As do the other villages, towns and cities on the Mountain. But it has no real importance beyond the Keep. Outside of the Holy Orders its true meaning is not known.'

'At Equinox the days and nights are of equal length – we all know that.'

'But, Atreu, that's not all. Equinox is the time of balance. Zenith is the time of power: the sun is at its highest point, the Mountain at its greatest strength. It is the force that drives us all. But pure power achieves nothing. Equinox is the time when all the power is weighed and considered. It is the time when twins are judged, when Rock and Light find their balance.'

Atreu struggled to clear his thoughts. 'So ... Equinox is the time when we know of the success or failure of our Ascents?'

'Yes.'

'But ... but ... you told me only those who are successful see the Keep. How can I be here already? And the other Ascenders are here, aren't they? There were some in the Great Dining Hall this morning.'

'Yes, Atreu, the others are here. The Faemir have interrupted our normal Rituals and we've had to make adjustments. Usually the Ascenders are housed below at the Hold until Equinox. They are flown up here blindfolded to have their audience with the Circle and then returned after their address. This time we have been forced to bring you all here.'

Atreu drew a sharp breath. 'Except for Teyth.'

'Yes.' Micah hung his head.

'Why?'

Micah didn't look up.

'Don't tell me then, Uncle. Let me tell you. He failed. There's no need to consider his Ascent because he's already failed – isn't that right?'

'It was the final Zenith. He didn't complete the final Zenith, Atreu.'

Atreu felt the tears well up in his eyes. 'It was my fault. How could I ...' Then a wave of anger hit him. 'You must tell them they're wrong. I'm here – they're still going to consider me and I missed the first Zenith. I was too late, remember?'

Micah looked up and Atreu could see there were tears in his uncle's eyes. 'I tried, Atreu, don't you think I didn't argue with them. It was no use. The final Zenith must be completed. It's one of the Circle's conventions. I tried everything I could ... why do you think I'm trying to forget?' He reached into his pocket and pulled out a small handful of r'lung. Atreu lunged forward and knocked it out of his hands.

'You don't need that. We need to think how we can get him up here safely.'

Micah crawled on the floor, searching the dust for the strands of r'lung. 'It's no use. The Faemir will have found him.'

'Stand up, Uncle. You're making me sick.'

Micah glanced over his shoulder. 'Look, Atreu, Teyth is dead. The Faemir waste little time with Ascenders. You know that as well as I do.'

'Uncle, I'm telling you he is alive.'

'Alive? How can you possibly know?'

'It was in the Book. He was there. In the Hold. The Faemir have captured him but they haven't killed him yet.'

Micah stood up and faced his nephew. 'You are insane.'

'Atreu.' Praether's tone was measured. 'Are you certain that's what you read?'

'Yes – it was Teyth.'

'Look, Praether, don't encourage him,' said Micah.

'I believe him.'

'I've no doubt he *thinks* he read about Teyth.'

'I can tell you more,' said Atreu. 'The two Faemir leaders are Valkyra and Rhea, and they've already worked out how the Maelir plan to destroy them.'

'Nonsense,' said Micah.

'Let him speak,' said Praether.

Atreu continued. 'And they're watching the windriders closely now. I think they'll work out where we are.'

Micah shook his head. 'Let me take you back. You need to rest.'

'All right then, Micah, tell me how I knew Teyth wasn't in the Keep? How did I know you had been lying to me?'

'I ... I have no idea.'

Praether ran his fingers along the Book's edge. 'What's happened to you, Micah? You used to be so open-minded. I think it's the r'lung.'

'Don't, Praether. I haven't got the energy to argue with you about that again. I don't want to give myself false hope. How can Teyth be alive? There's no way the Faemir will spare him.'

'He's not the same,' said Atreu. 'Zenith has changed him. He won't be that easy to kill.'

'What do you mean?' asked Micah.

'Well, I'm going to use one of your techniques and answer your question with another question: what's a baresark?'

Micah and Praether exchanged a glance that Atreu found hard to decipher.

*

'You could try to convince Lythos.' Micah was sitting opposite

Atreu and Praether in the Great Dining Hall. All around them, voices filled with laughter and good humour echoed from the walls and high ceiling.

'It was hard enough trying to convince *you*, Uncle.'

'Let's just keep our voices down a little,' said Praether.

'Don't worry,' said Micah. 'No-one can hear us with all the noise in here. It must be the safest place in the Keep if you don't want to be overheard.' He poured wine into the goblets on the table in front of them.

Atreu looked around. Voices echoed throughout the hall and if anything, the Holy Men seemed to be louder and more bois-terous than this morning. Only the occasional Ascender sat sub-dued. Had it been only this morning? So much had happened. And now it was only early evening, and the last rays of sunlight were being overwhelmed by the hundreds, perhaps thousands, of giant torches that flamed brightly around the hall.

Atreu sipped his wine and was immediately reminded of a small village far downslope in the Lower Reaches, and of a warm, starry night and a girl he thought he knew.

'Atreu, are you listening to me?' Micah's voice cut through the memory.

'Sorry, Micah.'

Praether said, 'I would counsel against even trying to convince Lythos.'

'Why is he so important? I thought he was just one of the Cir-cle?' asked Atreu.

'Yes,' said Praether, 'but because he has responsibility for the Ascenders before Equinox, he can limit your movement as he wishes.'

Micah said, 'It is with his permission that I was allowed to bring you here – and to the librum. He could have chosen to con-fine you to your room until Equinox.'

'That's a lot of power,' said Atreu.

'He has it only because the Circle has elected to give him that power,' said Praether. 'And, under normal circumstances, all the

Ascenders would still be down at the Hold anyway, where there are not as many choices open to them.'

'But Lythos has to be told that Teyth changed because of his Zenith,' said Atreu. 'His Ascent was successful. He must be up here with the rest of us.'

'We have no proof of anything,' said Micah.

'Are you going to argue with me again, Uncle?'

'No, no. I believe you, Atreu. I can feel the truth that you speak. But I doubt if Lythos will feel it.'

Atreu sipped his wine once more. 'Surely he would not want to see the death of an Ascender, whether he has failed or not.'

'I have some idea how Lythos' mind works,' said Praether. 'Even if he believes what you have read in the Book of Maelur, he will consider it impossible to rescue Teyth.'

'But we must do something,' said Atreu. 'The impression I had was that Teyth may be very strong now, but Valkyra can still destroy him if she chooses to. She has already begun to do it.'

'What would you expect Lythos and the Circle to do?' asked Praether. 'The Faemir have taken the Hold and we need to wait for winter to set in to loosen their grip.'

Atreu's gaze flashed from Micah to Praether and back again. 'A small number could sneak – '

'Don't even think about it,' said Micah. 'There are probably thousands of Faemir at the Hold by now, with countless more on their way.'

'So,' said Atreu, 'no all-out assault is possible and no surreptitious path is open to us.' He sat in silence, looking into the goblet.

'You're certain Teyth won't be able to survive till winter?' asked Micah.

'How could he remain alive while all the Faemir are dying around him? He seems to have gained great physical strength and stamina, but I doubt if that would be enough.'

Praether said, 'I also think it's far from certain that everything will go the way the Holy Orders have planned. Perhaps the Faemir will make progress before winter. The battle is far from over if they are aware of the strategy being used against them.'

'The Circle should at least be made aware of that,' said Atreu.

'I will ensure that happens,' said Praether, 'but I'm afraid that won't help Teyth.'

'We have to do something.' Atreu ran his fingers through his hair.

'Don't open your eyes. You promised you wouldn't look.' Teyth's voice echoed through his head. *'Ready, little brother.'* He felt everything spinning. Around and around. *'You promised you wouldn't look.'* He fought the urge to fall down.

'Atreu – what is the matter with you?' Micah's voice jolted him.

'I ... I ... don't ...'

'I was just saying,' continued Micah, 'that there may be another way. It's never been tried before – we could bargain for prisoners with the Faemir. We have one here and there are others downslope in the Mid-Reaches.'

'Wait a moment.' Atreu jumped up and grabbed Micah by the arm. 'Who is the prisoner you have here?'

Micah glanced nervously at Praether. 'I shouldn't be telling you this either.'

The old librer shook his head slowly. 'You'll have no argument from me. You do what you think is right. I still trust your judgement in your moments of clarity.'

'It is who you think it is,' said Micah.

Atreu released his grip and slowly sat down. 'Verlinden. Here? And I thought she was with the Faemir ...'

Micah said, 'The windriders found her three days ago not far from the Hold. She was unarmed but apparently she still put up quite a fight. In the end they had to drug her to get her up here.'

'So she is up here in the Keep?'

'Well, not exactly ... look, all of us know what you did with her. It took a great deal of arguing by both Praether and me even to get you up into the Keep.'

'Lythos wanted to leave me there?'

'He, and others in the Circle. But look, you were not meant to know about her, and you certainly can't see her.'

Atreu thumped the table with his fist. 'Micah, damn it, tell me where she is.'

Micah turned away. 'I can't.'

'Look,' said Atreu. 'She can help us solve our problems. She can help us save Teyth. We don't need any other prisoners to bargain with.' He leaned forward so that Micah couldn't avoid looking him in the eyes. 'She's Valkyra's twin.' He moved even closer. 'Did you hear me? She's the twin sister of the leader of the Faemir.'

Atreu saw recognition register in his uncle's eyes. 'Yes,' he said, 'I'm betting they'll do anything to get her back.'

*

Darkness had well and truly claimed the day by the time Atreu and Micah entered the Felsen monasts. Gone were the towering spires, gone were the feather-light bridges, gone the soaring arches and buttresses. The monasts were a jumble of narrow arches and solid, squat buildings that clung to the ground with the same determination that the Liche towers strived for the heavens.

At first their path was lit faintly by the reflected light of the Liche heart, but with every corner turned and every twisting alleyway they negotiated, the light faded further and further into memory.

Praether had wanted to come, but Micah had argued that the arch-librer's age would put him at a disadvantage in such clandestine activities, and that being a member of the Circle, he had far more to lose if they were discovered.

Atreu and Micah moved quickly and spoke in hushed tones.

'I can't believe we haven't seen any Felsen,' said Atreu. 'Where are they all?'

'This is a good time to make our way through here. Most of them will be doing their evening meditations. We'll probably run into some, but as long as we appear as if we have business here, it shouldn't be a problem.'

'Perhaps it would have been better if we had travelled later tonight.'

'No, Atreu. There may be little reason for a Liche to be in this part of the monasts after sunset, and almost no reason for an Ascender to be accompanying him, but the later it was, the more suspicion it would generate.'

A dark shadow suddenly appeared from around the corner in front of them. Atreu felt a wave of panic but quickly composed himself and matched Micah's purposeful stride. As they walked past the cowled Felsen, Atreu watched him out of the corner of his eye. There appeared to be a slight turning of the head, but he couldn't be sure.

'Will that one be a problem?' asked Atreu after they had rounded two more corners.

'I don't think so,' said Micah, 'but ... well these Felsen are sometimes hard to judge. They take in a lot of information without appearing to do so.'

'What have they been doing with Verlinden?'

'Did I say the Felsen had her?'

'No, you haven't told me exactly where she is – you know that.'

'Atreu, please don't start again. I'm taking you to her, isn't that enough?'

'There are so many secrets in this place.'

'Secrets are power. The Holy Orders learnt that lesson long ago.'

'That's funny,' said Atreu. 'I thought knowledge was power.'

'Ah yes, Atreu, but what use is the knowledge if it is available to everyone?'

'Well – everyone would benefit from it. It seems the Holy Orders want to keep knowledge for themselves the way a wealthy merchant wants to keep his jewellery and works of art.'

They turned another corner. 'That is not being entirely fair to the Holy Orders,' said Micah. 'Knowledge must be kept by those who understand it. It would be destructive in the wrong hands.'

'But, Micah, who decides who can understand it? Who decides who can use it properly?'

'That is what we Holy Men spend our lives doing. The Circle makes the final decision as to who can enter the Holy Orders at Equinox.'

'I'm not convinced of the rightness of keeping all the knowledge.' Atreu realised he had been speaking loudly, and he lowered his voice. 'How different are you to the merchant who says he has the right to keep his jewellery and works of art because he appreciates them? So, he keeps them away from others because they would never understand them. Of course they can't understand them if they haven't seen them – and who is he to decide anyway?'

'Atreu, I have wrestled with some of these thoughts myself, long ago. But there are some things you shouldn't question. I seem to remember saying that to you long ago.'

Another Felsen appeared suddenly from the darkness in front of them. It was impossible to make out any of his features because of the cowl pulled over his head, but a chill shot through Atreu as the monk stopped to watch them walk past. Atreu followed Micah's lead and just kept walking, but it was only after turning several corners that he realised he had been holding his breath.

Exhaling, he said, 'Surely it's too dark for him to recognise us.'

'These Felsen have remarkable night vision – they have to. So, who knows? Anyway, we're nearly there.'

'Where? Sometimes I still get the feeling, Micah, that you're playing games with me. You still have secrets that I have to coax out of you.'

'I don't have too many left, Atreu. You may be right – it is a deeply ingrained way of doing things. But I deliberately don't want to tell you exactly where the Faemir is being kept. She has a hold over you that I can't understand, and my concern is for Teyth.'

'So is mine – you know that.'

'I'm not so sure that he is your prime concern.'

'How can you say that?'

'Atreu, you abandoned your brother once for her. How do I know you won't do it again?'

Atreu fell silent. He could hear the soft thudding of their footfalls on the cobbled alleyway.

'I didn't abandon him,' he said finally.

Micah's voice seemed to deepen and sink down the back of his throat. 'I'm sorry for what you did, Atreu. I can't understand it, and I can only hope that the Faemir's hold over you has weakened. And I am glad you have a chance now to make amends. But, my dear Atreu, if you had completed the final Zenith with your brother as you were supposed to, he would be safe and alive now.'

Atreu took a deep breath. 'So you're saying that if Teyth is killed, it is my fault?'

Micah didn't answer.

'Uncle, did you hear me?'

'Yes,' he said finally. 'I'm leaving you to wrestle with your own conscience.'

*

A gust of cold air brushed Atreu's face as he peered over the cliff. The swirling darkness seemed to extend down forever.

'So she's not being kept in the Keep – am I right?'

'Did I say that?'

'You didn't have to.' Atreu looked back in the direction from which they had come. First the expanse of brooding blackness, and behind it, the dancing lights of the Liche. 'This is the edge of the Keep. There's only one way and that's down.'

'Well, if you're so sure, then you won't mind if I blindfold you.'

Atreu stared at him through the dark. 'You're not serious.'

'Think of it as a game.'

'You're mad, Micah. I'm not going to let you blindfold me.'

Micah pulled out a dark cloth from his pocket.

'Get rid of that,' said Atreu, between gritted teeth. 'I'm not putting it on. Take me to Verlinden right now.'

'Don't make demands of me, Atreu.'

'I'm not playing your games anymore.'

'Atreu,' said Micah, raising his voice. 'I have done so much to save Teyth. I've put my whole position in the Holy Orders at risk by arguing the case to bring him up to the Keep. I had given him up for lost, but now I believe there is a chance we can still save him – and I'm not going to let that chance go very easily.'

'Micah, we want the same thing.'

'Look, that's what I'm not really certain of. I think the Faemir had you as firmly as they now have Teyth. I just want to make sure they don't get you again. I don't want to lose one nephew while trying to rescue the other.'

Atreu sighed. 'So you don't trust me,' he said softly.

'I don't trust the Faemir – and I no longer make the fatal mistake of underestimating them.'

Atreu almost laughed. 'Are you sure I can't just promise not to look?'

'What?'

'Never mind. I just remember a time, before the games became so serious, when people used to trust each other.'

He turned around slowly and let Micah secure the blindfold.

Chapter Six

Where were the threads? Where were all the colours he used to see when he closed his eyes? This was not his darkness. Atreu squeezed his eyes tightly under the blindfold, but nothing happened. Only black. Like the part of the night sky between the stars.

He could feel Micah leading him by the hand. Occasionally, he felt the gusts of cold air that told him they must have been walking close to the Keep's edge. He strained to hear something that may help him to find the place again, but the only sound was their footfalls.

So much had changed, yet so little. He was still blind, being kept in the dark by others. He was still letting others lead him. He felt the knot pressing into the back of his head and his hands went up instinctively.

He stopped himself. *I still have no choice*, he thought. *I am not master of my own destiny – I'm not choosing my own Path.* He squeezed his eyes still tighter and a single pale thread appeared across the dark canvas he had made.

He was vaguely aware that Micah had turned several corners and was now doubling back, but he concentrated all his attention on the thread. *I can make you into anything I wish.* It started twisting in front of him, growing, taking on colour. First pale blue, then emerald, then the deepest of crimsons. Atreu steadied his breathing and felt the night air enter his lungs and fill his body. Small threads began to appear, but he willed them away. He wanted only the one now, and he wanted it to grow.

He felt the cold air blow on his cheeks and ears. Were they back at the edge?

'Step over this.' The thread started to falter and fade at the sound of Micah's voice, but Atreu held it firm.

Atreu reached down and felt what he thought was a thin, slightly curved wooden wall. It moved slightly as he touched it. What was happening? There was supposed to be no instability within the Keep. With Micah's help he stepped over it and onto the other side.

Suddenly the ground seemed to give way underneath him, and Atreu grasped at Micah to steady himself.

When he gained his balance, he said, 'What's happening here? I thought you said the Keep was the most stable part of the Mountain – or is this just another one of the secrets?'

'How do you know we're still in the Keep?'

'You can't help yourself, can you?'

'In what way?'

'You have to answer a question with another question.'

'Here, give me your hands.' Atreu could feel Micah guiding his hands back to the wooden wall. 'Hang onto this, I think you'll find we're going to be in for some more instability.'

Atreu heard a creaking noise and again the ground gave way. He gripped the wall tightly and only just managed to remain upright. Everything around him shook, but the tremors gradually eased, and he could feel a cold wind eddying around him.

'Micah, are you all right?'

'Yes, yes, just hang on and don't try to move so much.'

'How can I –?'

There was another jolt and the ground again gave way. He was thrown against the wall and only just kept on his feet.

The ground still seemed to be swinging underneath him, but he began to sense a certain rhythm to the movements and adjusted his stance accordingly.

'It may be easier for you, Atreu, if you sat down.'

'No, Micah, I want to stand.'

Atreu soon found the pattern in the instability. A sharp jolt, followed by a rhythmic swinging from side to side. He found he could predict each motion and shift the weight of his body so that he rode with the movements. If only he could always read instability as well as he was doing it now.

Where was he? He listened intently for clues. The wind blew around him in cold gusts, but apart from that, all he could hear was a creaking sound that seemed to be growing increasingly faint.

And the thread was still there. To his amazement he became aware that, despite the shocks and jolts, the thread still hung on the dark canvas in front of him, unchanged. How had he been able to do that when his concentration had been elsewhere?

Now that his body had adjusted to the impermanence, he focused again on the thread. He held it with his mind and willed it to grow. You are mine. It expanded, taking the form of a plant – the leaves, the stalk, and at the very top a bud.

And the bud opened up into a brilliant flower. And each petal formed into a new bud, which opened up into a new flower. Again and again, each new ring of petals opened up. Flower upon flower, each one brighter and more vivid than the one before. And with each explosion, more of the darkness was eaten away. The border of black thinned until it appeared merely as a dark thread around a canvas of light.

And then, finally, the thread of darkness rolled itself into a small ball in the top right-hand corner of his vision. This time I will make you disappear. His breathing deepened and he felt a warmth envelop him. *Now.* The dot shook, in what seemed like a final act of defiance, and then vanished.

Atreu could still feel the tightness of the knot at the back of his head and the folds of material across his eyes, but the light flooded in.

He could see.

It was as if dawn had just broken. He looked around and saw he and Micah were standing in what appeared to be a large basket. To one side was the cliff face of the huge pillar which formed the Keep; to the other, empty sky. Above him he could see a thick rope stretching up parallel to the cliff; below him was nothing but clouds.

They were swinging in mid-air.

Micah, he observed, was operating a handle connected to a series of pulleys. Each turn of the handle resulted in a jolt, which meant they had descended further.

'There's no instability, is there?' Atreu said.

'What do you mean?' Micah had stopped to stare at Atreu and was wiping the sweat from his brow.

'Hard work, isn't it, Uncle?'

'Am I breathing heavily?'

'Not particularly, but you are sweating.'

'As a matter of fact, I am.' Micah started to stroke his beard as he eyed Atreu curiously. 'Can you smell it?'

'Not that I'm aware of.'

'You're guessing quite well.'

'Perhaps I am. Let me guess some more. You're probably looking at me and stroking your beard at the moment.'

'What?' Micah pulled his hand away. 'How –'

'Come on, Uncle. Put your hands back on that handle and get back to work. I'm sure we still have a way to go.'

Micah stepped over to Atreu and the basket started swinging again.

'Careful,' said Atreu, 'we don't want to fall, do we? It's a long way down.'

Micah ran his hand along the blindfold and tested the knot at the back. 'Stop playing games with me. How are you doing that?'

'Would I play games with you?'

'All right, tell me how many fingers I'm holding up.' Micah put his hands behind his back.

Atreu smiled. 'Well if you'd turn around, Uncle, I might be able to see.'

Micah's legs gave way slightly and he had to grab hold of the side. The basket pitched and heaved.

'Careful,' cried Atreu.

'How can you see? How is it possible?'

'Do you remember the first Rituals at Teuron?'

'Yes, of course.'

'Do you remember the meditation, the way I folded the scene?'

'Yes, yes. It is a common Liche technique. What point are you making?'

Atreu laughed. 'That's exactly it. The point. You remember how I got it down to one small point?'

'Yes, Atreu, and very easily too. I knew you had a great deal of ability when you did that.'

'Well, this time, Micah, I've managed to get the point to disappear.'

Micah gasped. He slowly released his grip on the side of the basket. 'So, you really can see *through* the blindfold?'

'As easily as I can see through water in a cupped hand.'

Micah reached for the knot on Atreu's blindfold and started to untie it. Neither of them spoke.

Atreu felt the material slip from his eyes.

'You've got your eyes closed,' said Micah incredulously.

Slowly, Atreu opened them and the daylight that had bathed his vision disappeared. His eyes strained through the moonlit darkness. 'I can only just see you now.'

Micah ran his fingers through his beard. 'Atreu ... I'm ... sorry. That is the last time I try to conceal anything from you. The time for secrets between the two of us is over. If anything, you are the teacher.'

'Come, Micah, don't show so much humility. It doesn't befit you. There are still many things I can learn from you.'

'Perhaps, Atreu, perhaps.'

*

Atreu watched the rocky cliff face jerk past them. Occasionally his view would be obstructed as they descended through a dark billow of clouds. The rope line now disappeared in a grey haze above them, and below there was still no sight of the ground. Atreu had grown so accustomed to the motion of the basket, the rapid jolts followed by the rhythmic swings, that he barely noticed them. Only the gusts of wind which hit them from time to time tested his balance. Unlike the downward motion of the basket, they couldn't be predicted. He was also being constantly surprised by Micah's sudden willingness to give him so much of the information that he had previously withheld.

'So Verlinden has been with the windriders since she was captured?' he asked.

'Yes,' said Micah, 'she's been in the Eyries the whole time. She hasn't seen the Keep and doesn't know of its existence.'

'Didn't you just say a moment ago that the Eyries were in the walls of the Keep pillar?'

'In the cliff face, yes.'

'And that's not part of the Keep?'

'You know we Liche place a lot of store on the meaning of words, Atreu. No, the Keep is the name of the city we built on top of the cliff.'

'I seem to remember Riell putting it differently.'

'Here, you have a turn with this thing. I'm getting a bit tired.' Micah let go of the handle and indicated that the two of them should swap positions. 'Careful.' The basket dipped as they crossed over.

Atreu grabbed the handle and pushed it away from him so that it moved in a semicircular arc. The basket immediately jerked down. 'Riell, the windrider who brought me up, said the pillar itself was called the Keep.' Atreu strained to pull the handle up to complete the full circle.

'It's important to keep up a rhythm, Atreu, or else that second half is always difficult.'

Atreu nodded.

'Look,' said Micah, 'these windriders often overvalue their position. Some of them have even been known to argue that they should be considered a Holy Order.'

'They are not Holy Men, yet they see the Keep. But you've told me that only Holy Men can see the Keep – am I right?'

'Yes, but the windriders don't live there. They fly above it, they touch down briefly and then they go. They are very important to us: they protect us, bring us food, drink, everything. The Keep couldn't function without them – but they are not Holy Men. Their position is a unique one. They are somewhere between the Holy Orders and the rest of the Maelir. Which is why it is appropriate that they live halfway up the cliff wall in the caverns and tunnels of the Eyries.'

'And they're all failed Ascenders, are they?'

'Well, yes and no.'

Atreu laughed. 'I knew you wouldn't be able to help yourself. I was growing bored with all your direct answers anyway.'

Micah smiled. 'Some questions don't have simple answers – I can't help that.'

'Spoken like a true Liche.'

'Look, Atreu, I said I would tell you all that I know. I'm no longer playing any games with you. The games had a purpose and I think they achieved that purpose, but they have no value for you now. But I can't give you a simple answer if there isn't one. It isn't correct to simply say the windriders are failed Ascenders. As I said, their position is a unique one.'

A sharp gust of wind hit the basket and swung them towards the pillar face. Atreu was almost knocked from his feet.

'Micah, how likely are we to hit the cliff?'

'This is not the safest way to visit the Eyries. The basket is not used often. It's much better to be carried down by one of the windriders.'

Atreu continued rotating the handle. 'The last answer you gave me was yes and no.'

Micah smiled again. 'You're obsessed with the windriders, aren't you? I'm not supposed to tell you this under any circumstance.'

'But you will.'

'Yes, Atreu, I said no more secrets between us.' He paused, looking up at the darkness above as he stroked his beard. 'As you know from the Valesend festivals, there are two Equinoxes: autumn and spring. Not only is each Equinox a time of balance when day and night are the same length, the two Equinoxes also provide a balance in the year. Balance within balance – the perfect equilibrium –'

Another wild gust of wind hit them, and this time they both lost their footing and ended up sprawled on the floor of the basket.

Atreu laughed. 'So much for perfect equilibrium.'

They got up and Atreu resumed his position at the winches.

'As I was about to say,' said Micah, 'the first Equinox is the time when the Circle judges the success or failure of the Ascents. Those who fail must leave the Upper Reaches and return to their homes.'

'Like Father.'

'Yes, like Tyr, they still have an important function. As returned Ascenders they have an automatic place on their town's council. It is through them, as much as anything else, that we have been able to impose order on the Maelir. Most often they become leaders, and very rarely are they without great influence.'

'But what has all this got to do with the windriders?'

'That's exactly what I'm saying. The first Equinox decides who has failed, who must return home. But that is not the only time the Ascenders are judged. Now, you are not to know this, Atreu, and I am breaking a convention by telling you. No Ascender should know because it is crucial to our Rituals: all who have not already been judged as having failed are judged again.'

'A *second* judgement?' Atreu drew a sharp breath.

'Yes.'

'And this happens during the second Equinox?'

'Yes, and those who are considered unworthy at this time become windriders.'

'Why can't you let them return home if they want to?'

'Atreu, try to fit it all together. Think about it from the point of view of the Holy Orders. The most important thing is to keep the secrets of the Orders, and the most important secret of all is the existence of the Keep itself. Those who fail at first Equinox have only seen the Hold – they return with knowledge of nothing else. Those who succeed are taken to the Keep, and they believe they are about to enter one of the Orders. Once they learn of their failure at the second Equinox, they know of the Keep – we cannot send them back down the Mountain to live with the rest of the Maelir.'

'What if they *want* to return?'

'They can't, no more than they can enter a Holy Order simply because they *want* to. Their Path was determined by their Ascent.'

'Is that fair?'

'It's got nothing to do with fairness or unfairness, Atreu. Besides, can you imagine anyone who has seen the Keep yearning to be anywhere else on the Mountain?'

'That's not the point. I think it would be marvellous to learn to ride the winds. But they are barred from really being part of the Keep – you said that yourself. Perhaps most are happy with what they have, but to take that freedom to choose to return home, it ... it ...'

'Don't talk about fairness again. There is no choice – for anyone. You were born a twin, you had no choice. Because you were born a twin, you made an Ascent. You had no choice. I have no choice. Tyr had no choice but to return to Valesend, just as I had no choice but to enter the Liche. This is how we function.'

Atreu shook his head. 'It's how we *choose* to function.'

'Look who's playing games with words now.'

'I'm not –'

The wind whipped at them, and this time the basket went crashing into the cliff wall. The impact was a dull thud followed by the sound of splintering wood.

Atreu struggled to his feet as the basket swung back from the face. He blinked, Micah was gone.

'Micah?' He noticed two sets of fingers over the lip of the other side of the basket. Micah had been flipped out and was hanging on.

Atreu raced over and the basket tipped wildly.

'Careful,' cried Micah. His fingers slipped slightly.

Atreu reached down and grabbed his uncle by his robes. He strained to pull him in, but the movement of the basket made it difficult.

'Hang on,' cried Micah.

Atreu was suddenly aware that the basket was swinging back into the cliff wall like a giant pendulum. He braced himself for the impact. The crunch came and Atreu almost lost his grip of Micah who slid back down again.

Atreu looked down past his uncle's legs and saw nothing but swirling blackness. He knew he had to get him in before the basket swung back into the cliff wall again.

He pulled back on the robes as hard as he could. Come on. The basket was on its way back again. He grunted with exertion, his arms straining as lines of pain raced through them. Almost there.

Then he heard the sick sound of splitting wood and the basket flipped, pouring them both out into the night air like wine from a flask.

His feet found nothing. He kicked wildly in mid-air, but somehow was still hanging onto Micah who still had a precarious grip on what was left of the rim.

Atreu managed to get one hand on the basket so that Micah was no longer taking his full weight.

'Atreu, are you all right?'

'Yes – and you?'

'Couldn't be better.'

'It's a nice night for it, isn't it?' Atreu could see Micah's fear tinged smile mirrored his own, and felt the wind whistling past his ears as the basket headed back towards the cliff.

When the crunch came he hung on instinctively, and neither he nor Micah lost their hold.

As the basket swung away from the wall, Atreu shifted his right arm so he was now holding onto the wood with both hands.

'That last one wasn't as bad as the others,' he said.

'The arcs are getting smaller.'

'That's comforting.'

Another crunch came and more wood splintered under the impact, but they both kept their grip.

The basket hit the wall four more times, but on the fifth occasion it barely touched before moving away. Atreu and Micah clambered back onto what remained. Almost half of the basket had been destroyed, and Atreu saw that the handle he had been turning now dangled uselessly below.

'What are we going to do now, Uncle?'

Micah sat down on what was left of the wooden floor. 'Wait until dawn, I suppose, and hope the windriders find us.'

'Will we be missed up at the Keep?'

'In the morning, yes – unless Praether can somehow cover up the fact that we're not there.'

Atreu carefully sat down next to Micah. 'And I thought ascending was the hard part.' He laughed.

'Your Ascent was only the beginning, Atreu.'

'I suppose we should be grateful.'

'For what?'

'The wind has dropped. At least it won't happen again.'

'I have news for you. It has been quite still all the way down.

The gusts of wind that have been hitting us are completely unpredictable.'

'You're being so comforting.'

Atreu peered out into the darkness as the two of them sat on the broken floor of the basket. He fought the urge to sleep brought on by the gentle rocking motion.

Two black shapes seemed to be circling below them. 'Hey,' Atreu cried, 'we're up here.'

'What is it?' asked Micah.

'Can't you see them?' Atreu pointed to the ill-defined shapes.

'Yes ... I think you're right.'

'Hey,' Atreu shouted again. 'Come up and help us.' He started waving, but the basket shook so violently that he had to stop.

The figures flew closer.

'They've seen us, Micah.'

'I'm not so sure.'

'Hey – ' The words stuck in the back of Atreu's throat.

As the figures drew closer, he could see they weren't windriders at all, but simply two geyers. The two large birds swerved to avoid the dangling basket, looked perhaps slightly bemused at its two occupants, and flew past.

*

Atreu's eyes eventually grew weary of staring into nothingness and they began to lose focus.

'You're not going to fall asleep, are you?' said Micah.

'Never. There's a war going on down there such as the Mountain has never seen. Teyth and Verlinden are both prisoners. You and I are dangling halfway down the world's largest pillar in a basket which could fall apart at any moment. How could I possibly sleep?' Atreu felt his eyes close. The next thing he was aware of was Micah shaking him.

'Atreu ... Atreu ... I believe we have a visitor.'

'How could I possibly sleep?' Atreu opened his eyes.

'You two are a sight.' The voice belonged to a figure hovering just in front of them in pale pre-dawn light.

'We were on our way to the Eyries,' said Micah.

Atreu could see that the windrider had a slightly amused look on his face. He was hovering almost motionless in the air as wisps of cloud brushed past him.

The windrider said, 'Micah, as always we are honoured by a member of the Liche who chooses to visit the Eyries, but could I perhaps respectfully inform you that there are easier ways to reach our home.'

'The matter is quite extraordinary, believe me,' said Micah.

'Oh?' The windrider's wings tipped back slightly.

'Could you please take us to the Eyries and we'll explain every-thing?'

'I can only take one of you at a time, I'm afraid.'

'I'll wait,' said Atreu. 'I'm starting to enjoy it here.'

*

It surprised Atreu how close they had been to the Eyries. The sun had already risen by the time he and the windrider approached the myriad of openings in the cliff wall. He could see dozens of dark figures emerging and gliding out into the morning sun.

'Are all these natural caves?' he asked.

'Some are,' said the windrider, 'but most of them have been built by the guild over the generations. You can only see a small part of our work. The tunnels and caverns extend far back into the Keep.'

'Where are you taking me?'

'Wherever you wish to go. We are as always at the service of the Holy Orders.'

'But I'm only an Ascender.'

'At the very least you will be a windrider.'

'How can you say that? I am told nothing has been decided. I could still fail.'

'That's normally true, but as you are no doubt aware, things are different this year. All of you Ascenders are now in the Keep. Success or failure, none of you will be allowed to return home.'

Atreu felt the wind eddying around him as the openings on the cliff grew larger. Of course, he thought. Now that he had seen the Keep, he would never live in Valesend again.

'I assume you want to be taken to where Micah is,' said the rider.

'Yes, that will be fine.'

Then something occurred to him. 'Tell me – do you know Riell?'

A gust of wind seemed to buffet the windrider. 'Of course. We all know him. Why?'

'I'm just very grateful to him. He saved my life – twice. Perhaps you could just mention to him how much I owe him ...' He felt suddenly slightly embarrassed. 'And I owe you, of course.'

'The phrase has no meaning for us. The Holy Orders can't function without us. We know it, but we don't ask for any thanks or payment or gratitude. We have a covenant, and we do what we are asked to do.'

'I've met few Maelir with such a selfless philosophy.'

'Perhaps – but anyway, here we are.'

The windrider landed gently on a ledge in front of a large opening in the rock face. Atreu unclasped his harness and stepped away from under the wings.

Micah stood just inside the entrance to the cavern. Next to him was a tall man who, judging by his grey-green tunic, was clearly a windrider. It was the first one Atreu had seen without wings. As they walked towards him, he could see the tall man had an awkwardness to his gait, as if his feet no longer functioned effectively on the ground.

'Good morning,' said the windrider, 'my name is Theander. Micah is somewhat secretive about why you have visited us in such an unusual way.'

Atreu smiled. 'I suppose that's the prerogative of the Holy Orders.'

'I have told Theander who we wish to see,' said Micah. 'I think he understands the delicacy of our mission.'

'Although I am curious, I know it is not my position to ask,' said Theander. 'As always, I assume the Holy Orders are choosing the right course of action.'

'Do I detect a hint of sarcasm in your voice, Theander?'

'Never, Micah, never. This way, gentlemen. I'm sure the Faemir will be pleased to see at least one of you.'

Atreu turned to thank the windrider who had rescued them, but he had already gone.

Chapter Seven

Praether felt a strange tingling down his back as he unlocked the last chamber of the librum. It was as if he was suddenly given a vague awareness that something had just changed, or was about to change.

He opened the door and walked in.

'I thought you would be here,' he said.

An old man stood ankle-deep in dust by the bookshelf. He looked up from his reading and half smiled. It appeared as if a grey mist had started to snake its way up the Reader's body.

'Wait,' cried Praether. 'Don't go.'

The mist continued no further.

Praether gasped. 'Something *has* changed,' he said, more to himself. And then to the Reader: 'Why have I been able to stop you disappearing this time?'

The Reader raised his eyebrows as if to say, I think you know.

Praether shivered. 'No ... no I don't.'

The Reader motioned the arch-librer to come closer.

Praether walked slowly towards him, kicking up small swarms of dust with each step, until he stood so close he could have reached out and touched him. The mist started to twist its way up the Reader's legs as he slowly handed Praether the Book of Maelur.

'Tell me – please,' said Praether. 'Tell me what has changed.'

The mist continued up his torso, and his body began wavering in front of Praether's eyes.

'Please, wait,' cried Praether.

The Reader opened his mouth. 'Read,' he said, and Praether drew a sharp breath – it was the first word he had ever heard the old man speak.

The arch-librer watched the mist claim the remainder of the Reader's body. As his face faded, Praether could still make out the strange half smile. For a brief moment it was as if a human-sized cloud floated just above the floor, and then it dissipated into nothingness.

The tingling sensation Praether had felt on entering the room now shot through every nerve. As he looked down to read the words on the page, he knew what had changed.

Somehow, in some strange way, he had become part of the story.

*

Valkyra ran the palm of her hand along the smooth hardness of the cliff face. Each breath escaped her lips as cold, white vapour. It was considerably colder today than it had been since they had entered the Upper Reaches, and she knew there was a good chance snow would soon fall.

She and Rhea peered up into the white haze above them.

'The Watchers' reports are not conclusive,' said Rhea, 'but it appears that the windriders are up there.'

Valkyra nodded slowly. 'I have no doubt. I can sense that's where they are. I'm certain the Holy Orders and all the surviving Ascenders are with them.'

Rhea asked, 'How can we find out?'

'We have to get up there of course,' said Valkyra.

'What are we going to do – fly?'

'Perhaps. We *do* have a number of their wings, don't we?'

'Yes, about twenty. Most of them were taken at Crosanct. The problem is we've never been able to capture a live windrider, so no-one has been able to find out how they work.'

'It must be a skill that can be learnt.'

'That may be, Valkyra, but without a teacher, our progress is going to be painfully slow.'

Valkyra slammed the wall with her fist. 'That's because we've been wasting all our time endlessly searching for secret tunnels. We should have had more sisters trying to fly those things.'

'But what real use would it be if twenty of us learnt how to use them? Even if we somehow developed a skill equal to the windriders, which I doubt is possible in such a short time anyway, how can twenty of us mount an invasion force? We would be hopelessly outnumbered – '

'Quiet!' Valkyra slammed the fist against the pillar face again. 'I don't want to hear this sort of talk. We have been outnumbered from the very beginning. If I had allowed this sort of argument to affect our plans, we Faemir would still be where we were for generations – simply making small raids on insignificant towns and villages, and fooling ourselves that we were making progress.'

'But – '

'Enough, Rhea. This is what we do. I want you to call off the search of the Summit. I want all our attention focused on getting up this pillar. I want our efforts to use the wings we have in our possession increased one hundred fold ... We still have full control of the pass at Crosanct, don't we?'

'Yes, the Maelir forces are massing, but we can still move backwards and forwards at will.'

'Right. I want our best artisans working on making more wings based on the ones we have. Make sure enough material and tools are sent up to us to make a thousand more. Get – '

'Valkyra, have you gone mad? Our artisans can't make more

wings. They don't have the skill or the materials. The only things we've ever made are weapons –'

Valkyra motioned Rhea to be quiet. She began to pace backwards and forwards furiously. 'Don't tell me what we can't do. You, above anyone else, should know that, Rhea. Was it impossible for me to lead a coveyn before I was even ten years old? No. Was it impossible for me to unite all the coveyns across the whole Mountain in a single army? No. Was it impossible for me to capture the Summit? No.'

'Then give me a plan, Valkyra.'

'That's what I'm doing.' Valkyra stopped pacing and glared at Rhea. 'Look, if our builders can't copy the wings, if there is some secret we can't divine, capture some Maelir artisans and force them to do it. It *can* be done. We only have to get up there. The windriders must live on solid ground. That's where we will have the advantage. They will be completely unprepared for our attack.'

'You know, though, that we won't have our usual advantage – even if we can do all you are asking us to do. We have no idea what's at the top of this pillar and that sort of information is vital.'

'Yes, Rhea, there you are right. We need a Watcher as always to tell us what we need to know about our enemy.' Valkyra shivered as a chill wind sprang up. Again, she ran her hand along the surface of the cliff face. She looked at Rhea and smiled.

'Don't even think about it, Valkyra. No-one can climb that cliff. We can't even see the top of it, and there are no handholds or footholds.'

'It could be possible to hammer stone wedges into the cliff face to create holds. We've done it before on cliff faces.'

'Perhaps, but it would be very slow. And any Watcher could be seen easily.'

'Not if it's snowing.'

'Valkyra, you might as well order one of our Watchers to be put to death. It would have the same effect. You know the wedges need to be constantly re-used with that sort of climbing technique. How many of them do you think you can carry? This pillar is so high, they would eventually break under the repeated hammering and removal.' Rhea shook her head. 'And the wind currents must be treacherous up there. No-one would be able to keep their balance. And that's still assuming the windrider patrols don't see the Watcher.'

'Why is it, Rhea, that you seem to spend so much time lately telling me what is impossible?'

'So you are really going to order a Watcher to try to climb up the cliff?'

'No.'

'I thought you said – '

'No, I didn't say I was going to order anyone up there. I'm going up myself.'

Rhea fell silent and stared at Valkyra open-mouthed. 'You are mad. It's that Ascender we captured, isn't it? He has some sort of hold over you.'

'Don't you worry about the Ascender, Rhea. I have the control over him that I want now.'

'You are serious? You are going to try to climb this cliff?'

'A Faemir leader is always in front of any attack – I don't have to tell you that.'

'But right now we aren't yet fighting – we need a Watcher.'

Valkyra laughed. 'You know I was the best Watcher you ever had.' Then she stopped suddenly. 'And you know how my instincts work, don't you?'

Rhea nodded as the temperature dropped around them.

Valkyra continued. 'I've never been wrong, have I?'

'No,' said Rhea, 'no, you haven't.'

'Well, Rhea, I *know* I have to climb up there. Do you understand me?'

Rhea nodded.

'Come on then,' said Valkyra, 'I need to get ready. I think it's going to snow soon.'

*

Teyth sat crouched in the corner of the cell as usual when Valkyra entered. She smiled at the look in his eyes when he noticed she was carrying his battle-axe. She walked to the middle of the cell and stood with her legs wide apart, leaning on the axe.

'Well, my Ascender,' she said, 'I thought you might be interested in getting this back.'

Teyth eyed her curiously.

'You *do* want it back, don't you?' She fingered the handle as she continued. 'You know, you haven't even told me your name. Not very civilised of you, is it? I though you Maelir were very big on civilisation.'

She looked down at the handle. 'There's a T here. Now let me guess – that's the first letter of your name, isn't it? That's the way these Talismans work. Am I right?'

Teyth sprang to his feet.

'Ah, I was right.' Valkyra didn't move. 'I know quite a lot about Ascents. It's amazing what Ascenders will tell you if you put them in the right mood.'

'Try to kill me. I won't be telling you anything.'

Valkyra smiled. 'Oh, it speaks again. You do it so rarely, I always feel so honoured when words come out of that mouth of yours.'

'Try to kill me.'

'I heard you the first time: you won't be telling me anything. But that's because you have nothing to tell me, isn't it? Not only don't you have any idea where the others are, you have no idea where Verlinden is, or even if she's alive. Nothing. You know nothing.'

Teyth's body jerked involuntarily.

Valkyra continued. 'They left you behind, didn't they? That's what happened. You've failed, haven't you?'

'I ...' Teyth leant back on the wall to steady himself.

'They left you for dead. You failed at Zenith; you're of no further use to them. That's what happened, isn't it?'

Teyth started to tremble.

'They've shut you out. You're just like us now. Do you know that? We're shut out from Zenith too. You and I, we're the same now. They decide we can't have any power. No matter what we say, no matter what we think, no matter what we do – they decide we can't have any power. They decided your Ascent was worthless; they decided that your life is useless.'

'Stop ... please.'

Valkyra laughed. 'You must know that about me now. I never stop. Never.'

She lowered her voice suddenly. 'How many Faemir have you killed?'

Teyth tried to steady himself. 'Count the notches on the handle.'

'You know, T – that's what I'm going to have to call you, is it? You know, T, we are very similar. You and I, we've both done a great deal of killing. We've both been shut out by the Holy Orders.'

'I can live with the decision.'

'But I don't think you can, T. Not if you're like me – and I'm certain you arc. You won't let them do it.'

'What are you trying to do to me?' Teyth's voice was strained.

'All I've ever done, T, is to try to give you pleasure.'

Valkyra let the axe fall onto the stone floor and the clang reverberated around the cell. 'You see, I'm even going to give you a chance to get your axe back.'

She walked towards the corner of the cell diagonally opposite the one that Teyth was standing in, then turned to face him again. The battle-axe now lay in the middle of the cell, the same distance from each of them.

'You see how fair I am to you, T. I'm giving you another chance. That's more than the Holy Orders have given you. And

I'm going to play fair. To show you I've got nothing to hide, I'm going to take off my armour.'

Valkyra unclasped her breastplate and proceeded to remove her battle garb until she stood naked.

'See, T, how vulnerable I am?' She could see his chest heaving under his broadcloth. 'Now, are you going to play fair as well?'

Teyth struggled for air. He could see Valkyra's lithe yet well-muscled body tensing in front of him. Her thick dark red ringlets cascading around her shoulders looked like they were on fire. He felt the blood course through his veins as he pulled his broadcloth over his head. He stared at her, always keeping the battle-axe in the corner of his vision. Her taut breasts jutted out at him, and he traced the long, firm line of her muscle down her legs. He drew a deep breath. He could feel the effect she was having on him again.

Without warning, he raced towards the axe. Valkyra had somehow sensed his timing and had started running virtually as he had. They both lunged for the battle-axe at the same time and grabbed the handle simultaneously.

Teyth pulled it towards him but Valkyra's strength was such that it didn't move. They both got to their feet, each straining but gaining no advantage as they faced each other. Teyth could see Valkyra's stance mirrored in his own. Sweat beaded her face just as he felt it come out of his own pores. They stared into each other's eyes, the battle-axe trembling slightly, but otherwise immobile between them.

Teyth gritted his teeth, then pushed back towards Valkyra. She was thrown off-balance and fell backwards but didn't let go of the axe, so Teyth fell down on top of her. He pushed down so that the handle pressed against her throat.

Valkyra's face was flushed and the veins stood out on the side of her neck. Teyth knew he had the advantage now because he was pushing down.

All he had to do was push harder ...

He felt a subtle shift of Valkyra's legs and pelvis and suddenly he was enveloped in a yielding softness. He felt a wave of pleasure wash through him.

Then everything spun in front of him, and he realised that he was now on his back and Valkyra was sitting astride him. And she was pressing the axe handle into his throat.

'Well, my T,' she said, 'you had your chance.'

'It's Teyth,' he said, his voice struggling to escape his constricted throat. 'My name is Teyth.'

As he spoke he pushed up into Valkyra, and her body responded with its own urgent rhythm. Almost as one they rolled over onto their sides, still locked in their embrace. They let go of the axe handle and let it fall to the ground.

The last thing Teyth was certain he saw were the two blades gleaming with the reflection of candlelight.

*

Snow flurries eddied around Valkyra's body and shot up along the pillar's face. Her battle armour offered little protection against the cold, but she barely noticed. She was confident that it was almost impossible for her to be seen. She was also confident that, despite the unpredictable gusts of wind, she was in no danger of losing her balance. What she was unsure of was how long the wedges would last under the stress of constant re-hammering.

She sat on one of the wedges and braced herself as she pulled hard on the one just below her. She jiggled it slightly, knowing removal of the wedges was more a matter of finesse than force. The hammering in, on the other hand, required brute strength.

She lifted out the wedge and examined the fault lines in the stone. It was hard to tell how long it would last before it shattered. She had more in her pack, as many as she could safely carry, so she wasn't overly worried. Then again, she had no idea how high she would have to climb.

She looked up. Through the falling snow she could see a grey mist which suggested another cloud line. If it was, it would be the third one she had encountered. She removed the hammer from her belt and tapped the blunt side of the wedge as she held it against the cliff face, on a spot several spans above her head.

Confident that the wedge was now embedded, she returned the hammer to her belt and stood up. A current swept through her as she reached back for Teyth's axe. Every time she touched it, she felt as if she was embracing the Ascender again. She swung back in a wide arc and then came forward and hit the wedge with the flat of the double-sided blade. This was always the hardest part, because she had to make sure she didn't lose her footing on impact. As usual, though, she kept her balance and the wedge sunk deeper in the rock.

She swung the axe back and struck the wedge three more times to secure it in the cliff wall. Testing to see if the newly embedded wedge would take her weight, she smiled. The rock was much harder than any cliffs she had ever climbed, this pillar was much higher, and the conditions far from ideal, yet she knew she was going to make it.

She slid the axe into place behind her back and tried not to think about Teyth, but his image invaded her brain again. She shivered as she automatically went through the motions of climbing up onto the next wedge. What was happening to her? He had been asleep after their last encounter. She could have killed him with his own axe. How fitting that would have been. It was the sort of irony she had always been fond of. She knew from her own experience that baresarks were partly vulnerable when they were asleep. She would have had to move quickly, but it would have been possible to kill him. And now, although he was imprisoned, he was potentially dangerous – especially since she had left the others. Yet, instead of killing him, she had simply taken his axe and left.

Valkyra could see now that she had been partly deceiving herself since Teyth had been found. Her visits to his cell had never really been to extract information from him. But neither had they been to dominate and humiliate him – not entirely. She had to admit she had a strange fascination for the Ascender, something she had never experienced with any of the others. He matched her in so many ways. There was an explosive power there, yet he also had a control she had never seen in anyone else. And he was relentless, absolutely relentless – like her.

The snow flurries thinned as she entered a cloudbank. She knew she would regret not killing him when she had the chance. She was certain he had no information that would help her find the Holy Orders. She should have rammed his own axe into his heart. The Faemir never kept prisoners alive for very long – and Teyth had already lasted longer than anyone else. She should have killed him. She should have.

And yet ... and yet, the thought of him being in the cell, ready for her when she came back, gave her pleasure. Despite the chill of the night air, a pulse of warmth ran through the length of her body.

*

Praether became aware of someone looking over his shoulder. He turned his head to see the old face of the Reader steeped in the pages of the open book.

'Are you still here?' asked the arch-librer. 'I thought you had gone.'

'I'm always here, my young friend, when you read. You are simply not always aware of me.'

'*Young* friend?' Praether raised his eyebrows and felt the parched skin stretch across his ancient face. 'I haven't been called that in a long time.'

'That's strange,' said the Reader. 'I thought I always called you my young friend.'

'How can you say that? You've never spoken to me before today.'

'How peculiar, how very peculiar that you say that. I've been under the impression that I speak to you all the time.'

'Your impressions and my impressions must be quite different then.'

'I'm sure they are.'

'I have wanted to speak with you for such a long time.'

'But I have spoken to you every time you've opened my Book.'

'When I read it?'

'Yes, of course.'

'And you call it *your* Book?'

'Yes.'

'So you are ... you are Maelur?'

The Reader looked slightly puzzled. 'The name does sound familiar to me.'

'Of course, it should. This book I'm holding here – this is the Book of Maelur.'

The Reader hesitated for a moment and then said, 'Ah yes, I knew I had heard that name before. Yes, I understand a little more clearly now. You can call me Maelur if you wish, but only while you're holding that book.'

'I'm sorry, I don't understand what you're saying. Who are you? What is your real name?'

'I am what you call me in your own mind – the Reader.'

Praether gasped. 'How do you know what's in my mind?'

The Reader seemed genuinely perplexed. 'Why, it's written on the page in front of us.'

Praether turned back to the book and started to read: *Praether gasped. 'How do you know what's in my mind?'*

The Reader seemed genuinely perplexed. 'Why, it's written on the page in front of us.'

A wave of vertigo hit the arch-librer and his legs began to buckle under him. How could this be happening? It had to be a dream. His legs gave way and he fell to the ground, still clutching the book.

Fighting to retain consciousness, he looked back up at the Reader. He strained to form the words. 'Am ... am I dreaming?'

'No, I don't think so – although I am unsure that you and I would agree about what a dream is, my young friend.'

Praether's thoughts swum round and round, desperately trying to escape the whirlpool that had entered his head. 'What is happening here? Please tell me.'

'Read.'

'But you must tell me. I'll ... I'll go insane.'

'Read.' The voice was soft, yet insistent.

Praether nodded. 'I understand. You're going to tell me, aren't you? The answers are in the Book.'

Without getting up, Praether scanned the words on the page in front of him. When he found the name Valkyra, he started reading again.

*

As Valkyra emerged from the third cloudbank, the sky was clear. Although she was certain snow was still falling below her, above her was nothing but cluster after cluster of the brightest stars, and a moon which bathed the cliff face in a clear light.

Damn, she thought. She hadn't planned for this. She was now exposed. She looked up. The pillar still stretched up into the distance, and there was no end in sight.

Valkyra set about her climbing with increased urgency.

With every movement, she scanned the skies for any sign of windriders. There would be little she could do if they attacked her now.

Should she go back? The thought hit her like the clash of sword on sword. How could she even contemplate descending so soon? What was the matter with her? Never once in her life had she ever stepped back from what she considered to be her path. It had always been forward, ever forward. How could the thought of returning even enter her head? That would mean defeat. Had she been weakened somehow?

It was Teyth. He had wakened the mercy in her that she had

sought to ruthlessly expunge from her being since she was nine years old. She had to kill him. Of that she was now certain. She knew the seed of weakness that had shown itself within her could only be destroyed by his death.

She looked up. She would complete what she had to do and then return to visit Teyth one last time.

She continued her climb with a manic determination. The wedges were embedded deep into the rock wall after a single swing of the battle-axe. Two of the wedges she had been using finally shattered along their fault lines, but all she did was throw them through the layer of clouds below and pull out two new ones from her pack.

Sweat bathed her body. Her arms ached yet she shut out the pain. The more her lungs struggled for air, the faster she went. Climbing up with ever increasing speed, she almost willed the windriders to find her. Please come, she said softly to herself. See how exposed I am here? She smiled. Let them come. She knew she was most dangerous when her back was to the wall, and just now she had her back to the biggest wall anyone had ever seen.

Then, with a start, she realised there was a ledge above her. She pulled herself up and saw that it was actually the entrance to a small cave. She could see lights shining somewhere inside.

The smile on her face broadened. With her back to the rock, slowly she inched her way in.

*

Praether looked up from the Book. 'Someone has to warn them.'

The Reader had crouched down next to where the arch-librer was lying and had been reading with him. 'Why don't you keep going, my young friend?' he asked.

Praether got up. 'I can't stay here reading – I have to do something. The entire Keep is under threat.'

The Reader again looked genuinely puzzled. 'I think the words must have an urgent meaning for you that I can't divine ... but ... yes, perhaps I see.'

'Please, I need to take your Book. I need to show people. I need to learn from it. Can I take it with me?'

'Of course,' said the Reader. 'You are the arch-librer – you have always been free to take the Book. To tell you the truth, I have grown a little tired of this dusty room. Just a word of warning, though, my young friend. Be a little wary of the meaning you extract from the Book. Trust it only as far as you trust your own judgement.'

As Praether stared at the old man, he wavered and then disappeared.

The arch-librer shook his head. 'And I thought I was old enough to be the one spouting enigmatic dictums.'

He was laughing to himself as he left the room.

Chapter Eight

'Are you sure you don't want any of us to come in with you?' asked Theander. 'She's extremely strong.'

Atreu, Micah and Theander stood outside a locked door which was flanked by two windrider guards. The three had been walking for some time through labyrinthine tunnels and corridors. Atreu had tried to memorise the path that they were taking, but he was unsure if he had been successful. What he was certain of was that they were now deep inside the pillar.

'I know how strong she is,' said Atreu. 'Just leave me alone with her and I will call out if I need any help.'

Theander glanced curiously at Micah, and said, 'I'm sure you two understand far more about such things than I.'

Micah nodded and Theander indicated to the guards to let Atreu in. Atreu stepped into the dimly lit room with the uncanny sense that he had experienced this before. Multi-hued glimmerstones lined the walls and bathed the room in a pale light. There was a chair and a small table pushed up against the wall on one side. On top of the table was an unlit butter-lamp, a goblet and a bowl of half-eaten broth. On the other side was a bed, and under the blankets he could see a figure curled up with its back to him.

Atreu walked over to Verlinden and could see her rhythmic

breathing as the blanket rose and fell. A mane of dark red ringlets lay sprawled across the pillow. He leant over her so that he could see the soft snow-whiteness of the part of her face which was exposed.

He bent down and kissed her cheek gently. She stirred briefly, a soft glow emanated from her face, and then she curled up still more and the rhythm of her breathing returned.

Atreu ran his fingers through her hair. 'Oh, Verlinden, how could I have been so foolish.' The words emerged with the softness of silk.

Verlinden's breathing remained steady as he spoke. 'Knowing the way isn't enough. We both know that now. It's not enough to know the truth. Others have to be persuaded, they have to be shown or else nothing happens.'

Atreu sighed. 'Perhaps we were both blinded by Zenith. Perhaps we were wrong to stare into the sun. It was all so clear to me, so crystal clear, that I couldn't accept that the world wouldn't suddenly change because of my new understanding.'

He lifted her crimson locks to his mouth and brushed them against his lips. 'And you know, Verlinden, I'm not even certain of what we can do now. I've told Micah that we can exchange you for Teyth. I have no idea how, or what it would achieve. Or even if I want to do it. I don't know, Verlinden, I don't have a path anymore. I've gone as high as I can go and I don't see which direction I should take.'

Atreu felt a warmth not unlike that of the R'angkur burgeoning from inside his chest. He carefully lifted up the blankets and got into the bed beside her. He wrapped his arms around her as she slept and curved his body softly into her back.

As he lay there, his thoughts started to clear. 'I'm unsure of the way, Verlinden,' he whispered into her ear, 'but I'm certain from now on we have to be together.'

He held her until his breathing perfectly matched her own and then he fell asleep ...

The light of the tunnel was blue and cold, and he knew he had been there before. He heard the crunch of gravel under his feet as he walked along the rocky floor, and he was vaguely aware of a dim figure walking with him. Suddenly he came to a fork and he stopped.

Motionless, he stared at the three openings in front of him. He examined each one closely, straining for a clue as to which one to take, but he could see nothing in any of them but darkness.

Then he became aware of an old man beside him.

'Where did you come from?' he asked.

'I have always been here, with you.'

'But I haven't always been here.'

'Yes, you have – look at your feet.'

Atreu looked down and saw that his feet now formed part of the rock. He tried to move but nothing happened.

'You don't know which way to go, do you?' asked the old man.

'No,' said Atreu giving up the struggle to move his feet.

'Why?' asked the old man. 'You've had no problem with any of the others.'

'There are three forks this time.'

The old man shook his head. 'You'll have to learn to count more than two, Atreu ...'

'Atreu' the voice came slightly muffled through the door. 'Atreu, are you all right?'

'Yes ... Micah. Give me just a little more time.'

Atreu looked down at Verlinden who was now stirring. She opened her eyes and smiled. 'Atreu,' she cried and they embraced.

For a brief moment Atreu forgot everything, but then Verlinden pulled away. She looked around and frowned.

'I had such a beautiful dream,' she said. 'We were floating above the clouds, you and I, and three snow-white birds were flying with us and watching over us. But it's not true, is it? I'm still here and the door is still locked.'

Atreu pulled her closer. 'There is a way out, but I'm not sure how to find it.'

*

Valkyra made her way through into the Eyries. There were surprisingly few Maelir around, and she found she could easily avoid the ones that she came across by hiding in a crevice of the rock wall or quickly rounding a corner. Fortunately, her time as a Watcher had trained her in moving silently and furtively while observing others.

She found it strange that the Maelir that she saw all wore the grey-green garb of the windriders – there were no Holy Men and no Ascenders. Clearly the windriders felt safe from attack up here. They carried no weapons apart from small knives, and there appeared to be no guards as such. They think they're safe, thought Valkyra. Again they underestimate us.

She heard the sound of crunching feet behind her so she quickly dashed through an entrance to her left. To her surprise, it was filled with dozens of wings and harnesses. She crouched down low as she made her way through the room, checking to see that there was no-one there. Once that she was confident the room was empty, she examined the large wooden doors on the far side. She pulled at them tentatively. They're not even locked, she thought. And she peered outside.

A gust of cold air hit her face as she saw that it opened out onto a large ledge and past the ledge was nothing but the star-filled night sky.

Valkyra's lips thinned into a cold smile. Opportunities always come when you make them.

She grabbed the frame of the set of wings nearest her and lifted it above her head. It was surprisingly light. Once she worked out how to balance the wings, she carried them through the doors and onto the ledge. She walked as close to the edge as she could.

'Here, use these,' she said, heaving the wings off the cliff face. She watched in fascination as the wings careered like some massive dead bird through the night sky below her.

She then sprang into furious action, dashing back into the

cavern, grabbing another set of wings and tossing them over the edge as well. One after other, she lifted and discarded the wings – until the sweat glistened on her skin, despite the cold, and her arms ached. Nothing swayed her from her purpose.

How she loved to turn what the Maelir thought of as their strengths against them. Another set of wings was launched riderless into the night sky. Not only was she immobilising a whole squadron of windriders, but her own people would be able to make use of the wings to launch their final onslaught.

She had almost emptied the room when she heard a shout behind her. She turned to see a windrider running at her, brandishing his knife. She kicked him in the stomach and he crumpled to the floor. She had just drawn her sword when she saw five more charging through the door. The second one to reach her was also only carrying a knife so she thrust at his stomach. She had withdrawn the blade even before the bleeding started, and he quickly collapsed. On seeing this, the third Maelir stopped in his tracks and threw his knife at her. She quickly deflected it in mid-air with a flick of her sword.

Then everyone froze.

Valkyra watched their eyes, trying to read their next move.

The sole windrider with a sword stepped towards her. 'Get more help,' he cried, and one of the others ran back out.

Valkyra didn't wait for him to make the first move. She feinted and then lunged for the heart. He parried and threw back a counter thrust. It was a weak manoeuvre and Valkyra knew immediately that she had his measure. These windriders were dangerous in the air, but on the ground they were only ordinary soldiers.

She wasted no time with complicated feints. She skipped forward and in two swift movements the windrider lay at her feet.

The remaining riders backed nervously towards the entrance.

'So you are the greatest warriors the Maelir can produce?' She threw the taunt at them. 'You make me sick.' She picked up another set of wings, and ignoring the windriders behind her, she carried it to the edge and threw it over.

On her return she saw they still hadn't moved. She reached out to pick up one of the remaining sets of wings when she felt a sharp, searing pain in her calf. She looked down.

Damn. The first windrider had recovered. He lunged at her leg again with his knife. She jumped out of the way and calmly ran her sword through his throat.

Valkyra looked up at the others and saw the fear in their eyes. 'That's the last time I make the mistake of not killing one of you when I have the chance.'

The bleeding had started on the cut on her leg. She reached down and pulled the two sides of the skin apart to see the depth of her injury.

'It's going to take a lot more than that,' she said as she picked up another set of wings and threw it over the side.

Valkyra returned to see dozens of heavily armed windriders pouring through the door. As they attacked, she could tell by their haphazard formation that they had no idea how to fight under these sorts of circumstances. With several flourishes of her sword, half a dozen lay bleeding in front of her.

The others stopped dead and backed away. At least the windriders weren't stupid, she thought. They knew when they were outmatched. Valkyra sensed they weren't going to charge again as they backed up all the way to the door. There they stood still, their swords pointing in her direction.

Valkyra shrugged. 'So you think you've got me trapped, do you?' She returned to the work of throwing the wings over the side.

She was about to release the last one when six windriders suddenly attacked her from above. She dropped the wings onto the lip of the ledge and drew her sword almost in one motion.

Still it wasn't fast enough because one of the rider's swords had found its mark through the padding on her left shoulder and had drawn blood. She fought back, swinging her sword with all the skill she possessed, but the windriders always managed to fly up just out of reach. They were in their element in this sort of fighting. One moment they were hovering almost motionless in mid-air, and the next, they lunged like birds of prey, all in a tight coordinated formation.

Their blades grazed past her skin several times and she still hadn't been able to lay her blade on one of them. This was not the sort of battle she was used to. She was expending all her energy simply defending herself. She needed to counter-attack – that's what she was good at.

She pulled out Teyth's battle-axe and started to swing it with one hand while continuing to thrust with her sword in the other. This new approach gave her the element of surprise she needed. The tight formation they had been using was suddenly thrown off-balance. She felt the blade of the axe slice through soft flesh, and she watched with pleasure as one of the windriders tilted in mid-air and then plummeted down the cliff face.

The formation quickly realigned itself, but she sensed the balance had swung her way slightly. It was only when another windrider flew in to join the remaining five that she realised what was happening. Six was obviously the most effective fighting number under these conditions. They were simply going to keep replacing riders if any fell.

The windriders had now adapted to her surprise two-weapon attack, and the axe was starting to feel heavy. She knew that the battle-axe would soon be a disadvantage because it was designed to be used double-handed. So they think they're going to wear me down, do they?

Valkyra allowed one of the thrusts to graze her skin and she fell to the ground, letting the axe fall from her grasp. Just as the windriders moved in, she lashed out ferociously, mortally wounding three of them. The remaining ones flew back up out of reach, obviously in shock.

Valkyra stood straight and raised her sword above her head.

'Come to me,' she cried, her voice filling the night air. 'Every last one of you, come to me.'

Almost as if in reply three new windriders flew in to re-form the six, and they moved in again.

The new grouping was more wary of her. They didn't lunge as quickly or as often. They no longer came close to laying a blade on her, but Valkyra soon realised this was not an advantage to her. They were going to try to tire her now, and they wouldn't be fooled by another one of her tricks.

It was a stalemate. How she hated stalemates.

Just then she heard a whistling noise and a sharp pain in her thigh. She looked down and saw to her horror that an arrow had embedded itself deeply in the muscle.

Another whistling noise and she jumped to avoid another arrow hitting her. Staring up into the night sky, she saw about twenty windriders hovering within firing range and loading their bows.

She dived to one side as several arrows just missed their mark. She was an open target on the ledge. As more arrows whistled through the air, she ran back inside. The windriders still lined the far door, standing shoulder to shoulder with their swords pointed at her.

Trapped, she thought. A wave of raw fury gripped her as she felt the baresark rage grow. She reached down to where the arrow still protruded from her thigh, grabbed it firmly, and with a single swift action, pulled it through her flesh.

She held the bloodied shaft up for the windriders lined at the door to see. The terror in their eyes only fed her power. A single chilling cry filled the cavern as she charged towards the door. Those who stood their ground were hacked mercilessly. Behind them stood others in the corridor who fell under her fury, her sword appearing to flash in all directions at once.

Panic reigned around her as windriders dived from her path. She slashed, whirled, thrust, lunged as she ran through the tunnels, turning corner after corner as the battle heat coursed through her veins. She ran through anyone who stood in her way. She ran until the shouts started to fade behind her. She ran until even the echo of screams had died. She ran until she was completely alone and there was no-one left to kill.

Only then did the baresark leave her.

*

'Praether, for your sake I hope you haven't had anything to do with these reports I've had about Atreu's unsanctioned visit to the monasts.' Lythos had the sneer on his face that Praether detested. 'The Ascender is lucky to be here, and you know it. I wouldn't tie my reputation too closely to his actions if I were you.'

'We have an urgent problem,' said Praether, ignoring his implied threat. 'Look at this.' He held up the Book of Maelur for him to read.

'You have an irritating obsession with books, Praether, and I grew sick of it a long time ago. Look, I'm very preoccupied at the moment. The Circle is about to meet – you know that. News of the war is coming in all the time. And now I have an Ascender without leave sighted in the monasts – and with his sage no less.'

Praether walked back and forth in agitation. 'Just read a small part of it. This is crucial. The Eyries and possibly the Keep itself are in grave danger.'

'I think you've finally taken leave of your senses. You've spent too long in that dust-filled librum.'

'Here, look at it, you fool.' Praether shoved the Book into Lythos' chest.

'Have you gone totally mad?' He grabbed the Book. 'This is the original Book of Maelur. What is it doing out of the librum?'

'I've told you. I want you to read it. Here, I'll even find the page for you.'

'Praether, I've read this many times. We all have. What could there possibly be in a centuries-old book that has been studied by thousands of scholars – '

'Copies. Everyone has been working from the copies we've made, Lythos.'

'The scribes would have been the best in the Holy Order. There is no difference between the original and the copies.'

'Just read it.'

'Praether, do you think you're the only one to read the original Book of Maelur? Is that the delusion you're suffering from? Come on, think a little more clearly. Many of us have read the original. I've looked at it myself when I first entered the Liche.'

'I've read it myself, Lythos, countless times, but it's changed now. We always knew it was our most important book. Now I know it's true. Just read it.'

Lythos sighed loudly. 'All right, if it will quieten you down and we can talk about Atreu. Let's see ... ah ...: *I learn with the breaking of each new dawn of the power of this Mountain. The sunlight seems to feed it at the same time as it feeds my inner strength –* '

'What?' Praether grabbed the Book back. He was trembling as he scanned the page. 'How can you not see the words. Listen ...: *she held the bloodied shaft for the windriders lined at the door to see. The terror in their eyes only fed the power. A single chilling –* '

'Enough, Praether, you have taken leave of your senses.'

'Listen, listen to me. How can you think I'm making this up? *A single chilling cry filled the cavern as she charged towards the door.*'

'Enough.'

'*Those who stood their ground were hacked mercilessly.*'

'I said enough!' He took the Book from Praether and slammed it shut.

Praether was shaking uncontrollably. 'Lythos, the woman in the part I just read is Valkyra. You know she's the Faemir leader, the one who's united them in the attack on the Summit.'

'Which has been unsuccessful.'

'But you're not listening to me. That's just it. She's in the Eyries wreaking havoc as we speak. She's a baresark, the most lethal one we've ever seen.'

'The windriders will keep the Keep safe, as they've always done.'

'They can't. She can't be controlled.' He grabbed Lythos by the shoulders. 'And Micah and Atreu are down there!'

'What? What business do they have in the Eyries?'

'Excuse me.' The voice came from the door.

Praether and Lythos turned to see the purple-robed Liche standing in the doorway.

The Holy Man said, 'The meeting of the Circle has been brought forward. Your attendances are required now.'

Lythos turned to Praether. 'I'm going to recommend that you be dispelled from the Circle, Praether. Your brother took leave of his senses a long time ago, and now the madness has gripped you.' He clutched the Book of Maelur to his chest. 'And the evidence is right here.'

*

Praether was still trembling as he took his place in the Circle. He looked around. There were still a few seats empty so he knew there would be a short wait before the meeting started.

His gaze followed the curve of the circular wall of the Areol ... the ornate frieze, and then up to the stars which decorated the domed ceiling. He stared at the highest point and then looked down to focus on the figure that stood directly below it in the centre of the Circle. It was his friend, the windrider Riell. He looked exhausted, as if he hadn't slept for a long time.

When the last seat was filled and all sixty Holy Men were present, Leyvin started to speak. Praether flicked a glance from Leyvin to Lythos and back again. He had always felt a little uneasy about twins being in the Circle at the same time. But what really troubled him was when one of the twins had the role of First Speaker. It had never happened before Leyvin took the position a number of years ago. Praether had argued at the time that it meant a subtle shift away from the perfect balance of power the Circle was supposed the achieve, but, as had occurred so often in the past, his views had been discarded by the majority.

Praether barely listened to Leyvin's introductory words. He only started to take in what was being said when Riell began to speak.

'As you've just heard,' said Riell, 'things are not going as well as we had hoped. Maelir battalions are massing near Crosanct, but the Faemir have obviously worked out our plan and many are now holding back and fighting for control of the pass itself, rather than simply pouring through and up to the Summit as they have been doing until now.'

'So who controls the pass?' asked one of the Holy Men.

'I would have to say neither of us does at the moment. No-one has a clear advantage. There are reports of Faemir troop movements further downslope. Many of their battalions which had been blocking exits from the Rimforest and access across the Maelstrom have now started moving up through the Mid-Reaches. They will eventually add weight to the Faemir numbers at Crosanct, but the balance will swing our way again once the Lower Reaches start emerging from the Rimforest in larger numbers.'

'But all this isn't of immediate importance to us,' Lythos interrupted and Praether shuddered at the sound of his voice. 'I can't really see why this meeting was brought forward. However, as we have assembled now, I would like to discuss another matter.'

Praether stood up and said, 'And I would like to bring to the attention of the Circle something which is of the utmost urgency, First Speaker.'

'Please, Liche Praether, sit down. You know the rules. Liche Lythos, I will have to ask you to wait as well.' Leyvin motioned in the direction of Riell. 'The windrider hasn't given us all the news as yet. Please continue.'

'My name is *Riell*,' he said, with a look on his face which was hard to decipher. 'The urgent news that I have is that the Faemir are a lot closer than we think. One of them has been discovered the Eyries – '

A murmur went around the Circle.

'Did she do much damage before she was captured?' asked Leyvin.

'That's the real problem,' said Riell. 'We haven't been able to capture her.'

'What?' Leyvin's voice rose above the general outcry.

'We couldn't,' said Riell, raising his voice until the noise died down. 'She is the most fearsome warrior I've ever seen. And she had us at a real disadvantage. We never expected any Faemir could reach us. We simply weren't prepared for an attack on the Eyries.'

Praether caught Lythos' eye and held him in a stare as Riell continued, 'We don't know where she is now – we believe she is somewhere deep in our tunnel system. We haven't worked out how she got to the Eyries or how many others are to follow or if an attack on the Keep is imminent.'

'Riell, the warrior you are speaking of is Valkyra, the Faemir leader.' All eyes turned to Praether as he spoke, but he kept his stare locked on Lythos. 'She is a baresark.'

'How do you know this?' asked Leyvin.

'Just let me finish before I tell you how. She is alone. She climbed up the face using wedges hammered into the rock. The other Faemir are busy trying to work out the secrets of windriding. They plan to attack the Keep in numbers once they have perfected the technique.'

'That can't be done,' said Riell. 'It's taken us generations – '

'Wait.' Leyvin interrupted the windrider. 'How can you possibly know this, Liche Praether?'

'Before I tell you, I want no-one to doubt the truth of what I say. Riell, tell me if this is not true. The Faemir was first seen throwing wings over the edge.' The windrider's mouth opened in amazement. 'She survived your six-formation attack partly through use of a battle-axe. She ended up escaping by breaking through a wall of dozens of armed windriders.'

Riell's legs seemed to give way slightly. 'That is impossible. You weren't there ... I flew here as fast as I could ... you ...'

'Liche Praether, how do you know?' asked Leyvin.

'I'll answer you, First Speaker Leyvin.' He pointed to Lythos who still clutched the Book. 'I read it in the Book of Maelur, which your brother has in his hands over there.'

'You can't be serious. Liche Lythos, what's written in the Book you are holding?'

'The story of Maelur, the first Ascent,' said Lythos. 'We all know it well.'

Leyvin shook his head in confusion. 'So, Liche Praether, you said you read about the attack on the Eyries in this Book?'

'Yes, and the Faemir battle plans.'

'Well this will be easily resolved,' said Leyvin. 'The Book please, Liche Lythos.'

'Here.' Lythos gave the Book to the monk sitting next to him and it was passed along the Circle towards the First Speaker.

'There's little point in you looking at it,' said Praether as Leyvin took possession of the Book. 'You won't see the words I see.'

'What nonsense are you babbling, Liche Praether?' Leyvin flicked through the pages of the Book, reading a passage here and a passage there. 'I don't see anything about Valkyra here.'

'Listen to me,' said Praether. 'We all know this is our most precious book – the account of the first Ascent as written by Maelur's own hand. Countless scholars have studied it since it was written. Thousands of the most meticulous copies have been made.'

'I fear we are about to hear another in the line of endless ravings about the importance of books,' said Lythos.

'No, Liche Lythos, this time I'm talking specifically about the Book of Maelur. It is the work that gives everything we do direction. And all of you know how the interpretations have changed over the years. We understand it more clearly with every Zenith. The meanings are always changing.'

'The meanings, yes,' said Leyvin, 'but not the words themselves. You're saying the words you are reading in here are different to the ones I am reading.'

'Yes, don't ask me how. The Book is special in ways we have not yet discovered. The changes in interpretation over the years have hinted towards this, but nothing has been as clear cut. This is a new power that has been given to us since the last Zenith.'

'A change that only you can read, Liche Praether,' said the First Speaker, 'doesn't strike me as particularly *clear cut*.'

'So you claim only you can read these new words?' asked one of the monks.

Praether hesitated for a moment. 'No, there is one other who I believe is even more skilled than I in reading the words. He has seen things in those pages that I couldn't see.'

'Who is it, Liche Praether?' asked Leyvin.

'The Ascender Atreu.'

Chapter Nine

'Micah, you said you would trust me and my judgements from now on.' Atreu was sitting on the bed next to Verlinden while his uncle sat on the chair by the table.

'That's not quite what I said. I think my words were there shouldn't be any secrets between us anymore.'

'And that's not the same thing? You can't leave the word games behind, can you?'

'No, I don't think it's quite the same thing, Atreu. I didn't say I was going to blindly follow your judgement even if I thought it was wrong.' He smiled. 'You didn't follow mine when I was your sage.'

Atreu looked at Verlinden for a moment and smiled. 'That's true.'

Micah tapped the table with the side of his hand and grimaced. 'You know, I cannot bear to see you like this ... with her. It goes against everything I've always believed in.'

'Her name is Verlinden.'

'And I can speak for myself.' Verlinden removed Atreu's arm and stood up. 'I'm sick of the two of you discussing me as if I'm not here.'

Micah said, 'Can I remind you that you *are* a prisoner here at the moment? Can I also remind you that you are extremely lucky that we Maelir treat their prisoners in a far better manner than the Faemir do?'

'It's a weakness.'

Micah stopped tapping on the table. 'What?'

'We consider it a weakness that you don't kill your prisoners.'

'You are barbarians.'

Verlinden took a step towards Micah. 'Only because you have forced us to become barbarians. You've shut us out from everything.'

'Come on you two – this is not resolving anything.' Atreu tried to grab hold of Verlinden's hand, but she evaded him.

'No, let her speak, Atreu. I've never had a chance to hear a Faemir try to justify the actions of her people.' Micah stared directly at Verlinden. 'So we shut you out from everything, do we? You know that's not true. Our cities and towns and villages are filled with women. We live in peace, or would if it weren't for your people. And how many men do you allow to live with you? And I mean *live*. You Faemir make me sick – you kill Maelir prisoners, and I've seen you even kill your own kind.'

Atreu could see the blood had risen in Verlinden's face.

'Faelen,' she spat.

'What are you talking about?' asked Micah.

'We don't kill our own kind,' she said slowly. 'We kill Faelen – the women you've already destroyed. It's like killing a crippled dog to put it out of its misery.' She started pacing up and down. 'So you *allow* women to live with you in your cities and villages? How noble of you. And what do they have to do for the privilege? Clean your homes, work in your fields, have your children.'

'There are many places on the Mountain which have a tradition of marriage,' said Micah.

'Is that the tradition where the woman has to obey one man above all the others for the rest of her life? How generous of you to ensure they have only one master.'

'The women are usually treated very well.'

'Perhaps they are. Perhaps most of the dogs kept by you Maelir are also treated very well. But that's my point. The dogs have no choice. Faelen have no choice. Whether their lives are happy or not is completely dependent on the Maelir.'

'Power belongs to those who can exercise it wisely.'

Verlinden glared at Micah. 'My sister would say power belongs to those who can take it.'

Micah slammed his fist on the table. 'Enough. Atreu, I don't trust this Faemir. I believe she still wants her people to destroy all we've built since we came to the Mountain.'

'No, she doesn't, Micah. The two of us want to resolve the conflict. We know it can be done. There doesn't always have to be a winner and a loser. There must be a place for Faemir in the Inner Sanctum.'

Verlinden looked back at Atreu. 'Perhaps we don't agree,' she said. 'What I want to build is something new. I don't want to simply fit in with what's already there.'

'Listen carefully, Atreu – you're hearing it from her own lips. She wants to destroy what we have, just like the rest of the Faemir. She will abandon you once you've served her purpose, just as she did at the Summit.'

'Micah, I've told you what our plan after final Zenith was. It was a child's plan. It was stupid. I've done a lot of stupid things on my Ascent. Verlinden and I were both just caught up in the euphoria of it all. I thought all Verlinden had to do was to tell her people that it was possible to share Zenith with a Maelir. I thought that would be enough. It was all so clear to me.'

Micah stroked his beard. 'Do you know how many days after the last Zenith the windriders found you?'

Atreu shook his head. 'I ... I don't really know. I fell asleep after looking at my Book.'

'It was five days.'

'Five? How can that be?'

'And Atreu – I know I shouldn't be asking you this because

any discussion of Talismans after Zenith should be confined to the Circle … where is your Book?'

Atreu's head was spinning. 'I … I don't know. When I woke up, I was confused. I didn't know where I was. I … I sensed somehow that Teyth was in danger, but that was all.'

'Was your Book next to you when you woke up?'

'I don't … think – no it wasn't.'

'Even if you were disorientated, you would have taken it instinctively, wouldn't you?'

'I'm not … I suppose I would have. Five days? How could I have been there five days?'

'As I told you, Atreu, the Circle had virtually decided to leave you for dead. It was my arguments and with Praether's help that you were allowed to come up. But the Book, Atreu, your Book. Where is it? You didn't have anything with you when you arrived at the Keep.' Micah suddenly pointed at Verlinden. 'I believe she knows where it is.'

'What?' Atreu felt his voice straining. He looked at Verlinden and she had gone pale.

'Where do you think we found her, Atreu? It was two days after the last Zenith, and she was walking around the cliffs of the Keep.'

'Is it true, Verlinden? Why didn't you do what we'd planned? You were supposed to go back to your people and I was going to join you.'

Verlinden's lips thinned and grew white. 'It *was* a stupid plan, Atreu. I realised that very soon after I started walking downslope. There was no way I was going to convince Valkyra or divert her from her plans. You blind my judgement when I'm with you, Atreu. You always have.'

Micah said, 'I told you, Atreu. She can't be trusted. She will always have the Faemir cause in her heart.'

'He's right,' said Verlinden.

Atreu felt a wave of nausea hitting him. Despite it, he struggled to his feet. 'What are you saying?' He took two shaky steps towards her and grabbed her hand. 'How can you say *that* is in your heart?'

Verlinden started taking deep breaths. 'He is right, the Faemir cause is in my heart … but so are you.' She appeared to be struggling for air. 'Atreu, I didn't return to my people. I realised nothing I could say would sway their course of action. I have no privileges being Valkyra's twin. Perhaps my life is worse for it. I am just a Watcher – I am not trusted in pitched battle. I am half Faelen so my judgement is worth very little. I … I didn't know what to do. It was clear the Holy Orders had all but abandoned the Summit, and it wasn't going to be long before Valkyra and the others arrived and took control of it. I … I only knew I wanted to be with you.'

Atreu's grip on Verlinden's arm softened as she continued. 'I returned to the Summit and tried to find you.' She sighed. 'And when I finally did, you were in a strange sleep from which I couldn't wake you. I tried everything, but nothing worked.'

Atreu encircled her with his arms and pressed her close while she spoke. 'I didn't know what to do. I … knew Valkyra would soon be there, and it wouldn't be long before she found you.' Atreu could feel her trembling.

'And the Book,' said Micah. 'What about the Book?'

'Your brother and I argued about it.'

'Teyth?' Atreu pulled away slightly.

'Yes, I found him as well. He was in a bad way. At least your sleep appeared to be peaceful. He seemed to always be half-awake and half-asleep, beset by the worst nightmares. Sometimes he was lucid, and that was when we argued. He said that your Book needed to be kept safe from the Faemir. One moment he was telling me about the time when the two of you first found your Talismans, and the next he was threatening to kill me.'

'So who has my Book now?' asked Atreu.

'No-one,' said Verlinden. 'It's buried in the snow.'

'Where?' said Micah.

'I would have to take you there.'

Micah stroked his beard. 'I see, something to bargain with.

Atreu, I hope you are getting some idea of how the Faemir mind works. She's the only one who knows where the Talisman is. We need her now.'

Verlinden glared at the Holy Man. 'Teyth knows as well.'

'How can that be?' asked Atreu quickly.

'It was his idea to bury it, during one of the times when he was thinking more clearly. He was starting to half trust me. He agreed it was a good idea that we both knew where it was.'

'And what happened?' asked Atreu.

'He turned on me just after we had finished burying it. There was a madness in him – I don't know. He was tortured somehow. One moment he had unbelievable strength and the next all his power was gone. Anyway, after we fought he just collapsed in the snow. Every time I went near him, the rage would grow again. I didn't know what to do. In the end I simply left him. There was a demon in him neither he nor I could control.'

'You just left my brother there, in the snow?'

'Yes ... I would have gone back, Atreu, but it wasn't long afterwards that the windriders attacked me and brought me here.'

'Teyth is still alive,' said Atreu simply.

'How do you know?'

'I read it – I know that doesn't make sense, but I read that Valkyra had imprisoned him.'

Verlinden stared at him open-mouthed. 'How can you possibly read about something like that?'

'I can't explain it, but I *did* read it – and what's more I'm absolutely convinced it's true.' Atreu shook his head. 'Valkyra has a technique for killing Maelir where she presses into their throats – right?'

'Well, yes, but – '

'And the Faemir second-in-command is called Rhea, right?'

Verlinden's eyes widened. 'How could you possibly know that, Atreu?'

'I told you, Verlinden, I read it all. I read about Valkyra's actions, her thoughts.'

'Can we get to why we're here?' interrupted Micah. 'To put it as directly as we can, our plan was to somehow arrange an exchange of prisoners – you for Teyth, although it sounds to me like Atreu is no longer particularly warm to the idea.'

Verlinden sat back down on the bed. 'There's another plan doomed to failure. Even if Teyth is still alive, there's no strong reason why Valkyra would want me back. I'm a reminder of failure to her. I'm – '

The door burst open suddenly and Theander rushed in.

'Sorry for the intrusion,' he said, 'but an evacuation has been ordered.'

'What are you talking about?' demanded Micah.

'Sorry, Micah, but there is a Faemir loose in the Eyries.'

'One Faemir? Can't she be captured?'

'No, from all reports we've tried everything. Look, I'm just passing on the orders. They come from the Circle, so hurry up. Everyone has to abandon the Eyries.'

'For one Faemir?'

'Yes, there are rumours she's a baresark.'

Atreu and Verlinden looked at each other.

'So the plan is to just leave her here alone?' asked Atreu.

'Yes,' said Theander. 'We can't risk trying to kill her.'

'And everyone is going to abandon the Eyries and imprison her there?' asked Atreu.

'Right – let's go.'

'And her?' asked Micah, indicating Verlinden.

'The orders were to take her with us. She can be trouble too, but she's manageable.'

'To the Keep?' asked Micah incredulously.

'Yes, yes. Now quickly – here's her blindfold.'

*

Valkyra strained to hear the sounds of any activity. She had found a dark corner and was examining her wounds. The lacerations on her upper body where the blades had sliced through her armour had begun to ache, and the cut to her calf would need to be looked at. What most worried her, though, was the wound where she had removed the arrow from her thigh.

It was at these times, when there were no enemy present, that she felt most vulnerable. She hated silence at any time, but the silence that followed a battle was always the worst. It was always the same when the fury left her – the pain and exhaustion that her body had held at bay would overwhelm her. An all-consuming ache crept through every nerve ending, and she shut her eyes to try to fight it back. She knew the battle with her own body was always the hardest battle of all.

'No!' she cried, as the blackness came for her.

She tried to scream again as it reached her throat.

Before another thought could enter her head it had consumed her ...

She blinked her eyes open to a cold, blue light. An old man stood in front of her. She instinctively reached for her sword, but to her dismay it was gone.

The old man appeared to be laughing at her confusion.

'I can kill you with my bare hands,' she said.

'Perhaps,' he said, 'but it won't get you out of here.'

Valkyra shook her head to clear her vision because the old man had seemed to waver for a moment.

'Look,' said the old man, pointing behind him. She saw the openings of three tunnels. 'Which one do you take?'

Valkyra stared at them in confusion. She didn't remember seeing them before. 'None,' she said. 'After I kill you, I'm going back the way I came.'

'There is no way back,' said the old man.

She looked around and saw that he was right. She was surrounded by rocky walls on all sides and the only openings were the three tunnels in front of her.

Valkyra felt dizzy. 'So I'll strangle you until you tell me which is the way out.'

'Wrong again,' said the old man, shaking his head sadly. 'You will have to learn.'

Valkyra went to get up but found her legs were paralysed. She looked down and screamed and screamed and ...

... and the blackness came for her again.

... and then it faded to grey.

What was going on? The dull, throbbing ache had returned. The rocky walls swam around her. Strange, dark birds seemed to circle above her. She tried to fend them off but found there was no strength in her arms.

Somehow, she got to her feet, instinctively aware that she had to get moving. She looked down and remembered the blood. The bile rose in her throat but she managed to swallow it back down.

Valkyra staggered along the rocky path, sharp pain shooting up her leg with every step. And always the silence followed her, like a shadow.

Where were they all?

Come on, her mind screamed. Attack me. Give me strength.

Still there was no sign of anyone. The corridors were all empty. Most of the rooms had recently had occupants but now there was no-one in sight.

A wave of nausea hit her. As she vomited, her legs buckled and she fell to the floor, fighting the blackness that invaded her once more.

She wouldn't let it defeat her.

Valkyra started crawling on the gravelly floor, and then finally she stood up again. Her gait was still unsteady and she could see the trail of bright red blood she was leaving behind, but still she kept walking.

Finally, she felt a gust of fresh air. She saw the light of day coming through the entrance in front of her.

To her surprise, she had somehow instinctively returned to the first cave she had entered. She walked to the edge and saw that the last two wedges she had embedded were still there. She felt around to her backpack and remembered she still had the other wedges there. The battle-axe was gone but her hammer could perform the same function with a little more effort, particularly since the holes had already been hammered into the cliff face.

With her arms and legs quivering, Valkyra lowered herself onto the first wedge. She stopped to draw several deep breaths before she started to climb down to the second wedge.

It was then that the windriders attacked her.

One of them had already sliced into her arm before she could draw her sword. She cried out and stared down in disbelief at the new wound.

The windriders moved in again, but this time she was ready for them. The bloodlust of the baresark had gripped her once more.

'You had your chance,' she cried, swinging her sword and wounding two of the riders.

All six of them quickly backed away from the cliff face, the formation broken. The two injured riders tilted their wings and allowed the updraughts to take them away. Almost immediately, two replacements flew in from above.

Valkyra looked up and saw a group of archers hovering not far away, their arrows pointing in her direction. She was an open target.

Without warning, she flipped herself up past the first wedge and back onto the ledge. A volley of arrows hit the spot where she had just been.

The formation of six windriders now came at her again. She counter-thrusted but could see from the corner of her eye that the archers were loading their bows again.

She dived, rolled out of the way, and ran back inside.

She stood and looked back out the entrance and saw the windriders were making no attempt to come after her. She strained to hear any sounds back in the tunnels but only silence called to her, and she realised what they had done.

Trapped, she thought, they couldn't kill her, but they had just locked her up in a prison with no key.

*

Atreu knew Lythos was trying to use his tall frame to intimidate him. There was little he could do except try to keep his distance so that the Holy Man didn't tower over him.

'Why am I confined to my room?' asked Atreu, glaring at Lythos and trying to match the Liche's dark gaze.

'I think you must realise that you've broken almost every rule we have. I'm convinced you can't be trusted, so you have to be controlled.'

'Perhaps it's about time some of the rules were broken.'

'Keep that sort of talk up,' said Lythos, 'and the Circle will really be impressed.'

'The Circle? When do I get to speak to them?'

'Tonight. Because of your recent actions, I've arranged for your audience to be earlier than it would normally be.'

'Good – I want to take Verlinden with me.'

'The Faemir?' Lythos spat the word at him. 'You have gone truly mad.'

'I'm serious.'

'I'm sure you are serious – that Faemir has so much power over you.'

'It's got nothing to do with power.'

'*Everything* has to do with power. Hasn't your Ascent taught you that yet? That's one of the first lessons Zenith should have taught you.'

'What about balance?'

'What are you talking about?' Lythos eyed him curiously.

'Balance. Equinox – you know what I'm talking about.'

Lythos took a step towards Atreu. 'What do you know about Equinox? Who's been talking to you about it?'

Atreu swallowed, and he knew straightaway Lythos saw the sign of weakness.

Lythos bared his teeth in a smile-like grimace. 'It was Micah, wasn't it?' He took another step closer. 'I can see it in your face. It was Micah. Well, well. Thank you very much. I think this will just about finish his aspirations in the Inner Sanctum.'

How was he going to protect Micah? 'One of the windriders spoke of it,' said Atreu quickly.

'What was his name?'

'I ... I don't know.'

'You're lying – no member of the guild would ever speak to an Ascender about Equinox.'

Atreu looked him straight in the eyes and struggled to steady his voice. 'A windrider spoke to me about it.'

'Did he, Atreu? Well, we'll see. The Circle will find out the truth. It always does. Just remember, you won't be able to lie to the Circle. Start preparing yourself. You're going to have to do a lot better than this.'

He was still smiling when he turned to walk out.

*

Micah stroked his beard. 'I find this very hard to believe, Praether.'

The arch-librer flicked through the pages of the Book which lay open on his table. 'But I can prove it to you. Just wait – I will be able to tell you exactly what you said to Verlinden. Here, listen to this and try to tell me they're not your words ... *No, let her speak, Atreu. I've never had a chance to hear a Faemir try to justify the actions of her people ...*'

Micah went white. 'I *did* say that – show me.' He swung the Book around slightly and scanned the page in vain.

'It's no use, Micah. You won't be able to read it. Just like I couldn't at first read what Atreu saw in there.'

Micah shook his head. 'What is going on here?'

'You know what we have spoken of before.'

'Praether, you have always placed too much value in books.'

'It was the truth of my Zenith. Have I taught you nothing?'

'Of course you have. I knew Atreu's Talisman was the right one for him.'

'No, Micah, you were only ever half convinced of the power of books. That's why you confirmed the battle-axe as a balance.'

'You know me too well, Praether.'

'I've always been convinced I was right. I know my truth has often been disparaged among the Inner Sanctum.'

'That's not true – '

'Don't humour me, Micah, I'm far too old for it. You know my views have often been considered dubious – particularly within the Circle. The power of my truth led to my acceptance into the Liche, but the details, the clarity of it, never have been fully accepted.'

'Praether, you know you were denied your turn at First Speaker for other reasons.'

Praether shook his head. 'It all ties together, Micah. It always has for me. I just have never been able to convince anyone else – the best I've ever done is to half convince you.'

'So, you believe you've been right all along?'

'Yes, and now I have evidence.'

'And the Circle will accept it?'

'Probably not everything, but they will have no choice but to change their views about what I've been saying all these years. The immediate advantage to them now is unsurpassed, and I won't have to argue too hard for them to see that. To know the movements of your enemy in times of war is a supreme advantage, but to have access to their plans and even thoughts gives undreamt of power.'

Micah continued to run his fingers through his beard. 'And you have access to that power. You can now control every decision we make.' He looked up into the lined face of his old sage.

'Perhaps, Micah, perhaps, but I must remain true to my Zenith. I know that my role lies with the knowledge of the Books, not with any battle plans.'

'But, Praether – '

'No, Micah,' Praether put his hand on Micah's shoulder. 'I have lost count how many years I've been arch-librer. I cannot even begin to remember the number of times I've opened the Book of Maelur. I've devoted my life to finding the meaning in the words, but despite my small triumphs, my life so far has been a failure.'

'Don't say –'

'No, we both know it. And what has changed since the last Zenith? Why can I suddenly read what I couldn't read before? It wasn't anything I did. I've been dragged into the story through Atreu's presence here in the Keep. No, I may have knowledge, but the true power, as I have always known, lies somewhere else.'

Micah shifted a little uneasily, aware of the consequences of what the arch-librer was saying. 'So you're saying Atreu is possibly the most powerful Maelir on the Mountain?'

*

Atreu looked up in surprise when Micah and Praether walked through the door of his room. 'I thought Lythos told those guards out there that I wasn't allowed to have any visitors.'

Praether sniffed. 'Lythos thinks he has more authority than he really has.'

'You mean he can't keep me in here?'

Micah said, 'Yes, he can do that, but there's no way he can prevent anyone from seeing you.'

'Yes,' said Praether, 'although it took us some time to convince those two guards out there of that.'

Atreu looked at his uncle and drew a deep breath. 'I'm afraid, Micah, that I may have given Lythos some fire with which to burn you.'

'How so?' asked Micah.

'I'm afraid I mentioned Equinox, and he guessed that I could have only heard it from you.'

The Holy Man waved his hand as if it didn't matter.

'Micah, didn't you hear what I said?'

'Yes, yes, Atreu.' He reached back and closed the door behind him. 'So I've revealed some of our secrets to you. Lythos gets obsessive about minor transgressions in conventions – Praether should be able to deal with them. Those secrets are nothing compared to what we are about to tell you.'

*

Lythos carried the two goblets and the bottle of wine to the table. He put one of the goblets in front of his brother and started to pour.

'I still don't think we have that much to worry about.' Lythos finished pouring.

Leyvin fingered the stem of his goblet. 'I think you're wrong, Lythos. Praether may have often been seen as an old fool with some strange ideas, but many of the Circle have found him a likeable old fool – and he can present some convincing arguments at times. The problem is if he convinces them that his ideas are not as strange as we have tended to believe, then our control is going to disappear.'

'Once an old fool, always an old fool – that's what I say.'

'Lythos, I think you're the one being foolish here. He's convinced me that he's able to read something in the Book of Maelur that the rest of us can't.'

'I still don't see the real problem. We use what he has to tell us. If he's wrong, then he's in disgrace and no-one will listen to him again. We will even be able to expel him from the Circle. If he's right then he can give us valuable information on the Faemir. The decision on how to act on that information still belongs to the Circle, and you know the influence the two of us have there.'

'Let me tell you about influence, brother.' Leyvin sipped from the goblet of wine. 'Our influence on the Circle is a subtle one. You are too prone to making demands and orders, the dramatic gesture. It doesn't work in the long run, and you don't have to look for any more proof than the fact that I was the one nominated for First Speaker. You know my philosophy – never use a sword when a knife will do the job for you and never use a knife when a bare hand will do. There are ways of getting the Circle to come to a decision without even stating which side you are arguing for. A word here, a question there, let certain people speak longer than others – that's all it takes and the Circle thinks it has come to a certain conclusion without me exerting any sort of influence.'

Lythos drank deeply from his goblet. 'We've had this argument before, Leyvin, and I still say without me pushing our cause so loudly, your way would lead nowhere.'

'I never said I did it on my own. What I'm trying to say is that it would be of no value to us if I also started charging in with sweeping statements and bold assertions.' He took another sip. 'The problem I see here is twofold. Firstly, even if Praether does little more than supply the Circle with information, there will be a subtle increase in the esteem in which his comments in matters of judgement are concerned. The others will listen to him much more carefully and, rather than dismissing much of what he says, they will now credit his comments with extra weight.'

'He has years of ineffectiveness to overcome.'

'True, but I could see it starting to happen at the last meeting. See how his pronouncement about Atreu was taken.'

Lythos nodded.

'And that brings us to our second, and as far as I can see, far greater problem: the Ascender Atreu.'

'The obsession he has for this Faemir has all but destroyed him in the eyes of the Circle already. His Ascent has been filled with failure, his final Zenith a disgrace, and now I have enough to bury his sage, Micah.'

'I suspect your approach won't be enough, brother.'

Lythos drank the last draught of wine and reached for the bottle again. 'The Circle won't stand for the contamination of Zenith.'

'Perhaps you're right. But the potential danger with Atreu is far greater.'

'How so?'

'If he can read the Book the way Praether can, then he won't be dismissed easily. He also has an advantage over Praether in that he is totally unknown. There are no known limits to the understanding he gained at Zenith. As with any Ascender before Equinox, he is only potential, and only after Equinox will his limits be decided upon.'

'I still believe I can totally discredit him.'

'I think you'll have to, brother, because I'm starting to feel more than a little uneasy about our Ascender Atreu.'

They both raised their goblets to their lips, paused, and then drank.

Chapter Ten

Atreu leant out his window to watch the play of light as the sun set over the Keep. The weather had grown unstable as the afternoon progressed, brief snow showers and fast-moving clouds had been punctuated by the most brilliant bursts of sunlight. But now the sky was a cold, clear shade of purple. He had occasionally wondered why the Liche, the Order of the Light, usually wore purple robes, but he could see now why that was the most appropriate colour.

As the sun sank below the lip of the Keep, the horizon glowed with a most exquisite shadow of light which kept night's fingers at bay. The balance was held for less time than it took Atreu to blink, and then the Maelir lights of the Keep started to dominate. Atreu gasped when he realised the transition had occurred. The deep purple had darkened to black, and the brightly lit spires and towers now danced in the night sky.

Atreu had given up trying to rehearse in his mind what he was going to say to the Circle. He was convinced the words would come when needed because it was all clear to him now. He had been right in what he'd said to Teyth after the last Zenith. The answers had always been in his dreams – the past, the present and the future had always been there for him. Yet even now, as the clarity grew with every moment, there were some nagging doubts.

He shuddered as he remembered the last dream he had while lying with Verlinden in the Eyries. He had some idea of what it was trying to tell him, but doubt lingered. The three forks in the tunnel were something new. There had only ever been a choice of two ways for him, the path had only ever had two forks. This third way added a complication he wasn't used to. Perhaps the windriders' talk of the third way between the Rock and the Light was where the answer lay. He knew it was part of what he was looking for, but he also knew there was more significance to the number three than that.

Atreu pondered over what Praether and Micah had revealed to him. He shook his head. So many secrets had tumbled out – how very different from the confusion of his Ascent. Praether had told him about his own Zenith, about his truth that books were of vital importance to the direction of the Holy Orders and the Maelir. It was the arch-librer who had always argued for the use of books as Talismans. None of the attempts had succeeded and his ideas gradually lost favour within the Circle. When Micah had been appointed sage to Teyth and himself, Praether had what would be probably his last chance to encourage the confirmation of a book as a Talisman. Now, with the arrival of Atreu at the Keep, Praether believed his faith in books had been vindicated.

Although he didn't say so at the time, Atreu sensed that Praether had only a limited idea of what he saw as the power of the Book of Maelur. Either that, or he was still keeping something to himself. Praether certainly still didn't trust Verlinden, and Micah was only partly convinced of her trustworthiness. Atreu had promised himself that whatever happened in the Circle, he had to somehow ensure that Verlinden was freed so that they could be together.

There was a knock at the door and Atreu looked over his shoulder at the Felsen messenger who opened the door.

'Ascender Atreu,' he said, 'your presence is requested in the Circle.'

'Requested? So I have some choice?'

The Felsen monk looked a little confused. 'Please come with me to the Areol.'

'Praether was right,' muttered Atreu. 'You Felsen have no sense of humour.'

*

Atreu stood in front of the huge double-arched doors of the Areol. He had never seen such workmanship as that of the intricate bas-relief wood carvings. Holy Men in flowing robes were rendered in the most exquisite detail. Throughout the carving was the motif of the circle within circle, so brilliantly executed that the design had no edges or corners. His eye turned from one circle to the other without being aware of what was happening, an endless spiral leading out, then in, then out again.

'Ascender Atreu.' The Felsen's voice broke the hypnotic effect.

'Yes, I'm sorry, but the carvings in this door ...' Atreu tried to look away but the pattern had taken him again, and he was lost in the endless circles.

'Ascender Atreu – you must enter now. Your presence is – '

'I know, I know, *requested.*' He deliberately forced his eyes to go out of focus.

'Please, walk straight to the middle of the Circle. You must remain there until you are dismissed.'

'Is that another request?' He could see the Felsen was about to open his mouth. 'Don't worry – I'm not expecting an answer to that.'

Atreu pushed the doors open. They were surprisingly light. He stepped in and couldn't help but draw a breath. The room wasn't particularly large, but it was unlike any he had seen. There were no corners anywhere. The wall was one perfect circle, decorated by a series of interlocking stucco arches all the way around. The ceiling above was a large dome which was painted, with the most gorgeous clusters of stars, to look like the night sky.

He took another step forward and, to his surprise, almost fell. The floor was also slightly curved and he tried to make adjustments for it with his next step. He felt slightly giddy. There was no sharp edge for his gaze to lock onto – even the wall gently curved into the floor.

Atreu glanced at the sixty seated figures in front of him to see if they had seen him stumble, but they were all silently staring at a marked dot in the middle of their circular formation.

Slowly he walked between two seated monks and up to the dot. He looked around at the Holy Men who now surrounded him. The purples, crimsons and earth-browns of their robes seemed to merge into a continuous line for a moment.

'Welcome, Ascender Atreu.'

Atreu turned his head to see who was speaking. His eyes came to rest on Lythos – no, it was Leyvin. Praether had told him the First Speaker would have to be watched closely, far more closely than his twin, Lythos.

'I'm a little confused about my status, Leyvin.' Atreu decided it wouldn't hurt to go on the attack from the very start. He knew it would probably surprise Leyvin that he knew his name.

'Please address me as First Speaker Leyvin.' If Leyvin had back-footed, it didn't register on his face. 'Why are you confused about your status?'

'Am I still an Ascender? Your brother has told me that now that my Ascent is over, I no longer have that status. Which one of you is right?'

'As you may have had the good fortune or skill to learn on your Ascent, Atreu, truth comes in many guises. Of course, in this matter we are both correct. The term Ascender in a strict sense does not apply to you or to any of the others. Your Ascent is over, its judgement is not. Yet all of us still find it convenient to continue to use the term even if it is, strictly speaking, no longer accurate. And I am glad you asked me about your status because, as you are aware, that is exactly what we are here to ascertain. Your future will be determined by the judgement of your address here tonight. Circumstances have made it desirable for us to hear you before your normally allotted time, however you will find that the functioning of the Circle depends on a number of important conventions which I will, no doubt, have to make you aware of as we proceed.'

Atreu bit his bottom lip. This Leyvin was extremely skilful. He had already turned Atreu's question around to suit his purpose.

'Now, Ascender Atreu,' continued Leyvin, 'we heard your sage's report of your Ascent some time ago, and we have a number of questions we believe you would like the chance to answer.'

'I will answer what I can.'

'I'm sure you will. I'm sure you will. We can ask no more of anyone. Liche Lythos, could you please begin?'

Lythos cleared his throat and Atreu swung around to face him. He was sitting in the Circle, directly opposite his brother.

'Ascender Atreu,' began Lythos, 'a number of irregularities in your Ascent have been brought to the attention of the Circle. Firstly, you chose to deviate from your Path on occasion.'

The room was silent. Atreu's eyes followed the interlocking arches along the wall. 'Are you expecting me to answer that?' he asked finally.

'Whether you choose to speak at any stage or not is up to you,' said Leyvin, and Atreu swung around to look at him again. 'We simply give you the chance to respond, if you so wish. Just remember, however, that you are here to argue your case, and silence rarely wins arguments.'

'I cannot believe I am seriously being charged with deviating from my Path.'

'Please address your comments to Liche Lythos.'

Atreu swung back to face the other side of the Circle. 'Aren't there more serious matters to discuss here?'

'Please note,' said Lythos to a Liche scribe who was busily writing a few seats away from him, 'that the Ascender Atreu does not consider his path to be of serious concern.'

'That's not quite what I said. You want an answer: yes, I did deviate from my Path – several times in fact. There was a war going on, in case no-one here is aware of that. If you're going to charge me with that, then you may as well charge all the other Ascenders. I can't see how any of them could have stayed on their exact Path as it was outlined in their scrolls.'

'No-one is charging you with anything.' Atreu again turned to look at Leyvin who was now speaking. 'This is not a trial. We are assessing the worth of your Ascent.'

'That's not quite how it seems to me.'

'Ascender Atreu,' continued Lythos, 'how did the war with the Faemir affect your deviation through the Plains of Vygird when your Path was to walk around the edge?'

'I ... er ...'

'Please register that as a non-answer,' said Lythos to the scribe.

'No wait – I couldn't see the point of spending weeks walking around it. I chose the most direct route.'

'The most direct route?' The question came from one of the other Holy Men, but Atreu didn't catch who it was.

'Yes, and as it turns out, I was correct to do it. There was no way I would have made it to Zenith in time if I had followed my set Path.'

'But you didn't know that at the time,' said a small balding Felsen.

'No ... but sometimes things just feel right to me.'

'An interesting reason for disregarding a Path,' said Lythos. 'Now, tell us how you escaped Crosanct when all of the other Ascenders who were there for their final Rituals were killed.'

'I was rescued by Riell, one of the windriders.'

'We are familiar with Riell,' said Lythos. 'He has also revealed to us that he carried you through the Pass. Is that right?'

'Yes, it is.'

'Were you aware that such assistance was forbidden to Ascenders?'

'Yes – ' He looked at the faces around him. 'I can't believe any of this can possibly be relevant to the judgement of my Zenith.'

'The accumulation of small concerns can affect the judgement,' said Leyvin. 'You would have to agree that while a single pebble weighs almost nothing, a thousand of them are not an insignificant weight.'

'But a thousand pebbles don't make a rock. Why waste time looking for pebbles if you are really after a rock.'

'Thank you for the philosophy lesson.'

'No, thank *you*.' Atreu felt himself getting angry.

'Please note,' said Lythos to the scribe, 'that Ascender Atreu has resorted to sarcasm during the initial stages of the judgement.'

'Is it fair to interpret my reactions in this way?'

'It is the usual procedure,' said Leyvin. 'It is part of Lythos' duties to maintain written records of the addresses of all Ascenders. However, each member of the Circle will judge you through his own eyes. The interpretations are for Lythos' reference only. Can we continue?'

Atreu nodded.

'Is it true,' said Lythos, 'that you carried a sword with you for part of your Ascent?'

'Yes.'

'You know of the ban on Ascenders carrying weapons?'

'Yes,' said Atreu. 'A silly ban in time of war. Perhaps you could look at that in the future.'

'But you fully understand the rule?' asked a Holy Man to Lythos' right.

'Yes, although I find it more than a little vague and confusing. Why is it that a knife is not considered a weapon, when it can be easily used to kill someone? How is it possible that a weapon as destructive as a battle-axe can be a Talisman?'

'Please note,' said Lythos, 'that Ascender Atreu does not have sufficient understanding of our rites and Rituals at this stage.'

Atreu felt the blood rush to his head. Addressing the scribe, he said, 'Please note that Ascender Atreu expresses his displeasure at the commentary on his answers, and he questions the interpretation.'

'You understand,' said an old Felsen monk, 'that the members of the Holy Orders are all men of peace.'

'Only because you have others doing the fighting for you. I can see that none of you want to get your hands bloodied, but I don't know if you can call yourselves men of peace when there is a terrible war raging on the Mountain which you are responsible for.'

'How is a victim responsible for being attacked?' asked Lythos.

'It depends what the victim has done to justify that attack.'

Leyvin asked, 'Are you seriously suggesting that there is some justification for the Faemir attack on us?'

Atreu stared straight into his eyes, 'Yes.'

A murmur travelled around the Circle.

Lythos began, 'Please note – ' and Atreu swung around towards him.

'Please note,' Atreu said loudly, 'that the Holy Orders have been responsible for the deaths of tens of thousands of Maelir and that although they have the power to prevent further bloodshed, they have not considered the alternatives.'

There were several outbursts from members of the Circle.

One of the Liche asked, 'What sort of alternatives are you suggesting we consider?'

Lythos interrupted before Atreu could answer. 'I have a number of other matters to bring up before we pursue this line of questioning. Now, on his failure to complete the Ritual of R'angkur at Crosanct – '

'This is a new matter,' said the Liche Holy Man, 'that must be reserved for discussion at a later time. It is appropriate at the moment for us all to hear the Ascender's answer to my question.'

Other Holy Men voiced their support.

'Ascender Atreu,' said Leyvin, 'perhaps you can answer the question for us. What are the alternatives we haven't considered?'

Atreu hesitated for a moment. He found Leyvin impossible to read. Praether had warned him that the First Speaker was a deft manipulator, and Atreu was concerned that he had been given a chance to say what he wanted to say so early. He knew that the more skilful the manipulator, the less aware the victim would be that he was being manipulated.

'I believe no-one has ever tried talking to the Faemir,' he said finally.

The Circle fell into uproar.

Lythos' voice was audible above the others. 'Do you propose we talk to murderers?'

'Yes,' said Atreu, 'and I propose that they should talk to murderers as well.'

'What are you implying?' asked the balding monk sitting next to Lythos.

'Well, we have murdered many of their people, haven't we?' said Atreu.

'Are you equating killing in self-defence,' said the monk, 'with unprovoked butchery?'

'I find it difficult to believe that no-one here has ever felt that perhaps the Faemir may have some justification for their cause.'

'Cause?' said Lythos. 'You're suggesting that they have right on their side?'

'The Faemir have never been allowed to take part in Zenith. We have never even allowed them into the Upper Reaches. In fact, if it were possible, we would banish them from the Mountain. Yet, all our records show that they have always been here with us. If we see it from their point of view, we are keeping for ourselves what we should be sharing with them.'

'Sharing?' asked Lythos. 'I've never heard any suggestion of sharing from them. The Faemir don't want to share anything with us, they want to destroy everything we've built.'

'That's only because we've given them no option. But I am not here to argue the case for the Faemir. What I am suggesting is that you allow them to argue their own case.'

Leyvin asked, 'Are you seriously suggesting that we have a Faemir appear within the Circle?'

'Ridiculous,' said one of the Liche, and this was followed by similar outbursts.

'I believe,' said Atreu, 'that the Circle should consider all its options and that while it has no blood on its own hands, it should do everything it can to ensure others no longer continue to have blood on their hands.'

'Is this the truth of your Zenith?' asked Leyvin.

'My truth goes far deeper than that. I know the Maelir have always sought to bring the opposites of life together: the rock and the light, the Felsen and the Liche, the Mountain and the sun. We have always known that the answer lies in how we bring them together. After my final Zenith, I realised that the next step towards truth is to bring the Maelir and the Faemir together.'

'And which part of the final Zenith made you realise that?' asked Lythos, with a sneer on his face.

'As you've informed me, you already know.'

Leyvin broke in. 'We have discussed the matter before, and I would have to say that you can consider yourself quite fortunate simply to be here.'

'I shared the last Zenith with a Faemir. I am not ashamed of it.'

'Please note,' said Lythos, 'that Ascender Atreu shows no remorse.'

Atreu bit his bottom lip. 'It was the right thing to do.'

'You are aware,' asked Leyvin, 'that the Holy Orders require you to shun the ways of the flesh?'

'I am, although the practice makes little sense to me.'

'It is to stop the sort of insane conclusions you have come to from occurring,' said Lythos suddenly. 'I'm getting sick of this time-wasting dressed up as a profound discussion. Ascender Atreu has clearly been unduly influenced by the ways of the flesh. We have seen it before and have quite quickly recognised it and dismissed the Ascender. That in this case a Faemir is involved only makes the crime more serious and the Ascender more foolish.'

'He has made some interesting points,' said Leyvin, without conviction.

Lythos said, 'They are, at best, rationalisations to cover up his guilt.'

'Please,' said Leyvin, 'can we leave our detailed assessments for afterwards? This is not the time.'

'I'm growing a little tired of waiting.' The ancient voice belonged to Praether. Atreu turned to watch the arch-librer as he spoke. 'We haven't discussed the most important matter here, and that is the Talisman.'

'Perhaps that is because not everyone shares your obsession for books,' said Lythos.

'I think we can move onto the Talisman,' said Leyvin. 'Please tell us, Ascender Atreu, what truth you believe your Talisman gave you.'

Atreu shuffled nervously.

'Can you tell us what you read in the Book of Maelur?' asked Praether.

Leyvin interrupted. 'We will come to that in good time. I realise all these matters are related, but I don't think anyone would deny that we need to find out about the Talisman first.' He gestured for Atreu to speak.

Atreu swallowed, then spoke. 'My Book contained the story of my Ascent, beginning on the day when I was first told about it as a nine-year-old.'

'When did you write it?' asked the Felsen monk next to Leyvin.

'I ... I didn't exactly write it.'

'What do you mean?' asked the Felsen. 'If you didn't write it, then who did?'

'I ...'

Praether broke in excitedly. 'So you are saying the Book somehow predicted your journey?'

'No, no. I only found I could read it after the final Zenith.'

'You are going to have to explain yourself more clearly,' said Leyvin.

'The ... the pages were all blank at first. They gradually filled as I proceeded with my Ascent.'

Praether asked, 'What do you mean? Did the pages write themselves before your eyes?'

'No,' said Atreu. 'It was just that every time I looked, some of the pages had been filled.'

'So you could read one day about the events that happened to you the day before.' Praether spoke quickly and his face was flushed.

'No – that didn't happen either. For all of my Ascent up until the last Zenith ... it was ... it was as if my Book was written in a strange language. I tried to understand it – it seemed to me as if I could almost make sense of it. But no matter how hard I tried, I couldn't.'

There was a brief moment when no-one spoke.

Leyvin finally asked, 'When you finally were able to read the words, how close were the descriptions in the Book to your actual experiences?'

'I ... er ...'

Lythos began, 'Please note – '

'Please note nothing. I didn't read much of the Book.'

'How much did you read?' asked Praether.

'Well ... two ...'

'Chapters?'

'No.'

'Pages?'

'Er ... no.'

Leyvin said, 'I'm not certain if playing guessing games here is appropriate. Could you please tell us how much of your Talisman you read?'

'Two lines.'

'Two lines!' Lythos voice boomed through the room. 'This has become a farce. It is obvious Ascender Atreu has no idea of the meaning of his Talisman.'

Praether asked, 'Why did you only read two lines?'

'I felt I knew the story. I had already lived through it, so what was the point in experiencing it again?'

'How could you be so certain after only two lines that the Talisman contained your story?'

'I ... I just knew. Everything was so clear to me at that moment.'

'An apotheosis,' muttered Praether.

'Don't be such an old fool,' cried Lythos.

'What are you talking about?' asked Atreu, suddenly feeling quite strange.

'There is a moment of extreme clarity that all successful Ascenders feel after the final Zenith,' said Leyvin.

'Yes,' said Atreu. 'Yes, everything made sense to me then. It was all so clear. Is that the apotheosis you are speaking about, Praether?'

'No,' Leyvin cut in, 'the moment of supreme clarity is only brief for all of us, as sharp and precise as a shaft of sunlight hitting a rock, but just as elusive. The apotheosis is the much higher state which all of us aspire to, but which none except Maelur have achieved. It is permanent clarity, the ultimate wisdom, the ultimate truth.'

Praether asked, 'Do you still feel the clarity?'

Atreu drew a deep breath. 'Sometimes I – '

'Sometimes is not good enough,' interjected Lythos. 'There is no evidence of apotheosis here. Can I remind the Circle that the success of the Ascent is still very much in doubt.'

'I still say there could be an apotheosis here,' said Praether.

'I'm afraid I can't let that claim go unchallenged,' said Leyvin. 'It is far too serious. We have no evidence here of anything other than a moment of clarity after Zenith – and even that moment is under challenge.'

'Yes,' said Lythos. 'I don't have to remind all of you that the Circle has been deceived before.'

'Are you suggesting that I'm lying to you?' demanded Atreu.

'Don't jump to conclusions,' said Leyvin. 'It is possible for an Ascender to fool himself regarding the outcomes of his own Zenith. That is exactly what we are assessing here.'

Lythos said, 'Can we please look at the Talisman a little more clearly? Here we have a book of which Ascender Atreu only read two lines. Even if we accept everything he says and the Book related the account of his Ascent – so what? What has he learned from it, what could the Holy Orders possibly gain from it?'

'But can't you all see how the Book has functioned during his Ascent?' began Praether. 'First, he knew nothing about our ways or what was in store for him – the pages were blank. Then he came to know the Rituals, but he failed to understand them – the words appeared to him as an incomprehensible language. Then it all became clear to him after Zenith – now the Book made sense to him. The experience of his Ascent gave him clarity.'

Leyvin said, 'You present a fine interpretation, Praether, but forgive me if I say it sounded more like an interpretation of a book, than of a real life Ascent.'

'I have always argued that the two are inseparable.'

'Can we deal with Praether's book obsession later?' asked Lythos.

'Yes – ' began Leyvin before Praether interrupted.

'You want to silence me now, Leyvin, because you know what my interpretation will lead to.'

'Praether, please, over the years you have been given more than enough time to speak about your books. The Circle has given you and your beliefs due respect. We have even elevated books on occasion to the status of Talismans in response to your arguments. And need I remind you that we wouldn't be having this discussion at all if it wasn't for my support as First Speaker for the very book which we are now speaking about.'

'Nevertheless,' said Praether, 'I wish to continue my interpretation now.'

Leyvin continued to train his eyes on Praether. 'Please don't force me to name you, Liche Praether,' he said, slowly.

Atreu looked around in confusion, unable to follow exactly what was going on.

Praether said, 'My request to speak is not unreasonable. I will challenge your naming.'

Atreu looked from one pair of eyes to the other. Neither Leyvin nor Praether flinched, and it was almost as if a cold wind had sprung up in the room.

Leyvin broke the silence. 'Praether of the Liche, arch-librer of the Keep, I name you.'

The Circle drew a collective breath.

'I challenge the naming, First Speaker Leyvin.'

Both Leyvin and Praether stood up.

Leyvin's voice was measured. 'Second Speaker Holthim. You are now first.'

'Ascender Atreu,' said the Felsen monk who was sitting near Leyvin. 'You must leave the room with them. This is a matter entirely for the Circle.'

Atreu tried to catch Praether's eye, but the old man was looking straight ahead. He was suddenly acutely aware of the crimson, purple and brown robes around him. He hesitated. Was there any point in standing firm? Or was this not the time? In the end, Atreu glanced at the clusters of painted stars on the dome, and then simply followed the arch-librer and Leyvin out the door.

Once outside, Leyvin sat on one of the chairs lining the walls, while Praether continued to walk a considerable distance down the long corridor. Atreu hesitated for a moment and then rushed to catch up with him. The arch-librer stopped when Atreu reached him.

'Praether, can you tell me what's happening here?'

'I'm sorry to interrupt your assessment in this way, Atreu, but I have a number of important things to say and I know that now is the best time to say them.'

'Why have we been asked to leave?'

'I've been named – it is the First Speaker's prerogative to name a member of the Circle if they are unruly or insulting or insist on speaking out of turn.'

'And only he can do it?'

'Yes.'

'That's a great deal of power. I thought everyone in the Circle was equal. How can he have the power to decide who is being insulting or is speaking out of turn?'

'He doesn't really.'

'But you just said – '

'Look, I have faith in the way the Circle works. The system has functioned well for generations. Anyone can challenge a naming and the result is what you see now.'

'So what happens next?'

'The remaining fifty-eight members of the Circle decide who is right and whether I should be allowed to speak.'

Atreu thought about this for a moment. 'It's not as serious as I thought. At best you'll be allowed to say what you wanted to say, at worst Leyvin will continue the judgement in his direction and you'll have to speak later.'

'It's not quite so simple, Atreu. If it was so easy then we would have namings and challenges all the time. No, I'm afraid this is far more serious for me.'

'How do you mean?'

'Well, a member of the Circle can only fail in a challenge nine times. After the last one he is expelled from his seat in the Circle and another Holy Man is voted in to take his place.'

'And this is – '

'Yes, Atreu, I've already lost eight times. I've been in the Circle for many, many years. Perhaps I've been a little lucky not to have been expelled before.'

'So Leyvin had little to lose in naming you?'

'That's not entirely true. A First Speaker can only have three successful challenges against him before he must relinquish his position as First Speaker. Even then, though, he can continue to sit in the Circle under the normal conditions.'

'How many successful challenges has Leyvin had against him?'

'None.'

'None?'

'He is extremely clever, Atreu. I've told you that already. He influences the Circle in such subtle ways that they don't know they are being influenced. He never seems to say a word in the wrong place. Even before he was elected First Speaker he was never named successfully – in fact that's one of the reasons he has the position.'

'Your situation is a bit grim then, isn't it?'

'Well ... I really think I should have been given the right to speak. Leyvin had anticipated me – he's good at that – he knew what I was about to say. I think he may have made a mistake here because he was keen to silence me.'

Atreu moved a step closer. 'What were you about to say?'

Praether shook his head. 'This is not the time. If I win the challenge then you will hear it when the others hear it. If I lose, I promise I will still tell you, but in that case it won't make any difference.'

'You think you'll win?'

'I know I'm right, Atreu, but as you've probably already seen, that is not enough. The problem is Leyvin knows he can rely on his own reputation for infallibility. Many of the members of the Circle are simply going to assume he was right in naming me – without question.'

Their attention was taken by the opening of the huge arched doors.

'Wish me luck, Atreu,' said Praether. 'Leyvin and I are required to go back in now to hear the pronouncement. If you see me come back out of those doors not long afterwards, that means I've sat in the Circle for the last time.'

'Good luck, Praether.' Atreu watched as the arch-librer

walked back down the corridor and followed Leyvin back into the room.

After the doors were closed, Atreu stared at the carved circular designs for what seemed like an eternity. He knew that somehow Praether's fate was linked to his, that what the arch-librer wanted to say was of vital importance to him.

With a start, he realised the doors were opening again. He watched as an old Holy Man slowly emerged through the gap. His stomach turned cartwheels.

It took him a moment to realise it wasn't Praether, and that it was in fact a Felsen and not a Liche.

'Ascender Atreu,' called the monk, 'your attendance is required. Your audience is to continue.'

Atreu allowed himself a small smile and started to walk towards the door.

Chapter Eleven

'Thank you, Felsen Fystaff,' said Leyvin, nodding in the direction of the old monk who had called Atreu back in.

If the successful challenge against his naming had had any effect on Leyvin, then it didn't register on his face. Atreu still found it impossible to guess what was going on in the First Speaker's mind as he spoke.

'As always,' said Leyvin, looking at a spot just past Atreu's shoulder as Atreu resumed his place at the centre of the Circle, 'I accept the decision of the Circle. I have no doubt that the decision is the correct one. Liche Praether, you may now continue with your interpretation of Ascender Atreu's Talisman.'

'Thank you, First Speaker,' said Praether, 'and I thank all of you for giving me this chance.' He started coughing but quickly swallowed to get himself under control. 'As I was trying to point out earlier, Atreu's Book mirrors perfectly his Ascent. The ignorance which gave way to confusion which finally gave way to total clarity.'

'But you spoke of apotheosis,' said a dark-haired Felsen seated not far from Praether.

'Yes, I did and I believe we already have some evidence of it. Atreu could read in the Book of Maelur what no-one else could read. It is the sort of sign we have always been looking for – a miraculous event, an event whose origin lies beyond our reason and our understanding. Something greater than the sum total of what we have created.'

'I'm sorry,' said Leyvin, 'but I'm a little confused. We have had no evidence as yet that Atreu can read anything other than the literal words of the Book of Maelur. The only evidence of any kind that you have presented to us is that you are the one connected with this miraculous event.'

Praether coughed again before he spoke. Atreu shifted his weight from one foot to the other. He was rapidly growing impatient with the proceedings. 'All of you have at some stage referred to what you call my obsession with books. I have never denied that I have been totally preoccupied with them since my Zenith. That was my truth and it was accepted, although I have never been able to impress on the Circle the extent of my truth.'

'Are you claiming that we haven't given you a fair hearing in the past?' asked Leyvin.

Praether shook his head. 'No. The fault has been with me – I have been unconvincing.'

Lythos broke in. 'Could you make your point now, so that we can move forward with the audience.'

'Yes,' said Praether, 'of course. I am in the middle of saying exactly what I want to say. I have been totally involved with books since my Zenith. I must have read the original Book of Maelur we have stored in the librum a thousand times. And it was not until after I had met and spoken to Atreu that I could read the hidden words.'

'It proves nothing,' said Lythos. 'You can't claim anything for Ascender Atreu on that basis.'

'Can I speak?' asked Atreu. 'Why is this proceeding as if I'm not here? Why not ask me what I read in the Book of Maelur?'

'Of course you may speak,' said Leyvin, 'but you must realise that an audience with the Circle involves as much discussion about you as it does discussion with you.'

Atreu cleared his throat. 'I read that my brother Teyth had been found lying in the snow by the Faemir. I read that he was still alive and was being held prisoner, and that the Faemir leader, Valkyra, was trying to destroy him, but that it was going to prove almost impossible because somehow he had been transformed into a baresark.'

There was a commotion around the Circle at the mention of the word.

'That's ridiculous,' cried a young dark-haired Felsen.

'The last confirmed Maelir baresark was over a thousand years ago,' said another.

'But there have been reports of Faemir baresarks,' said Atreu, 'and we have one currently trapped in the Eyries, have we not?'

Leyvin spoke above the commotion. 'Please, we are not focused on the task here. All of this needs to be discussed, but it is not directly related to the matter at hand.'

'Ah, yes,' said Praether, 'but it is. If Teyth has transformed into a baresark then it could only have been as a result of Zenith. Another change we can't explain, another miraculous event.'

'So you're claiming we may have another apotheosis?' asked the dark-haired Felsen.

'I'm claiming that it certainly needs to be assessed,' said Praether. 'And that we have made a grave mistake in not allowing Teyth's Ascent to be judged.'

'We made a decision on that some time ago after a full discussion,' said Leyvin.

'Perhaps we need to reassess it. It's not too late if he is still alive,' said a tall Liche near Leyvin.

'This is all of great interest,' said Leyvin, glaring at the Holy Man, 'but I must insist on bringing the discussion back into line with our original aim. Please address only the matter at hand with your comments. We are discussing Ascender Atreu, not Ascender Teyth. And more importantly, we are discussing his Book. Praether, please return to the matter at hand.'

'It is all related,' said Praether.

'Yes,' said Leyvin, 'we all know the Ascents of twins are related, but will you please return to the topic for which you won your challenge.'

'I believe we need to discuss ways of rescuing Teyth as quickly as possible.' Praether was overcome by a coughing fit which seemed to take an eternity to finish.

The tone of Leyvin's voice changed slightly. 'We have considered the Ascender Teyth's case at length, and I personally believe there is no point in reconsidering our decision. Despite this, I am willing to have the Circle hear you out again – but I think we would all agree that now is not the time. You have strayed too far from the consent which was granted you after the last challenge.'

'But Teyth is – '

'I'm sorry, arch-librer Praether, but I am naming you again.'

There was a stunned silence around the room.

In between coughs, Praether stuttered, 'I challenge the naming again.'

The Second Speaker, Holthim, took charge of proceedings again, and, as before, Atreu followed the two Liche out. Leyvin seemed to move more abruptly this time.

Again Atreu and Praether walked far enough down the corridor to be out of Leyvin's earshot.

'What are you doing?' asked Atreu. 'Leyvin is right this time. You haven't really told the Circle what you said you would tell them.'

'I know.'

'What's going on? Do you want to lose your place in the Circle?'

'No, Atreu, of course not. I'm playing a rather dangerous game here. Leyvin was right to name me there. He had no choice.'

'Have you gone mad?'

'No, I think I'm going to win this challenge as well. Think about it. All of them in there discussing my fate know that I am deliberately putting my place in the Circle at risk. They may think I'm obsessive, but they know I'm not stupid. Why would I do it?

The only conclusion they could come to is that what I am going to say is of the most vital importance.'

'I don't want to dampen the logic of your thinking, Praether, but from their point of view, they could assume that your revelations are only of vital importance to *you*.'

'That's the gamble, Atreu, but we've both given them so much to think about now. They know that technically they should uphold the naming, but they also know that they will never find out what I was about to say if they do that. I'm gambling that curiosity will get the better of the majority of the Circle.'

'But what will you have gained – ah I see, Leyvin will then have two successful challenges against him.'

'Yes, one more and he's out of the First Speaker's chair. Now, I may not be able to trap him again like this, but for the first time since he has been in the Circle, he will feel the pressure. He may start to hesitate, be not quite as confident of his judgement – his control may start to falter.'

Just then the doors opened, and Praether and Leyvin were recalled.

This time Atreu walked back and stood right in front of the closed doors of the Areol after the two Liche had re-entered. He strained to hear what was being said inside, but it was impossible. He ran his fingers along the curves of the relief carvings, quickly pulling his hand away on several occasions when he thought he heard someone walking towards the door on the other side.

Like a true Liche, Praether was playing a game – one which had a high risk factor. Up until now, Atreu's desire to rescue Teyth was unfocused. He had a vague idea of how it could be done, but the problem had always been convincing the Circle to accept his brother in the Keep. Praether was clearly working towards that.

The door had opened almost before Atreu had realised it. The words of Fystaff were an anticlimax. 'You may return again. The judgement is to continue.'

When Atreu resumed his position in the centre of the room, he could see this time that Leyvin was visibly affected by the results of the challenge. His lips were tighter, his expression more stern, and when he spoke the tone of his voice had changed slightly. As a man who had never known defeat, he was struggling to come to terms with it now.

'Arch-librer Praether, the Circle admonishes you for your convoluted approach and asks that you strive for greater clarity, however you may proceed with whatever it is you want to say.'

'Thank you, First Speaker. As I was saying, Ascender Teyth is crucial to our discussion here. We must somehow retrieve him from the Faemir and bring him to the Keep. Partly because his transformation needs to be judged in light of Zenith, but also because he is the only Maelir to know the whereabouts of Atreu's Book.'

'What?' cried Lythos. 'You mean Ascender Atreu no longer is in possession of his Talisman?'

'How is that possible?' asked a Liche Holy Man addressing Atreu.

'I ... I fell into a strange sleep after reading my Book – '

'All two lines of it,' snorted Lythos.

Atreu continued, '... and when I woke up it was gone.'

'The explanation,' said Praether, 'as I have discovered, is that Ascender Teyth, unable to wake his brother and expecting the imminent Faemir invasion of the Hold, decided to bury the Talisman deep in the snow. And might I say we should all be grateful to him for that.'

Leyvin said, 'Can I point out to the Circle that we have not yet attributed any importance or value to Ascender Atreu's Book, which is what Praether originally claimed he would do.'

'And,' said Praether, 'which I am about to do.'

'Can I further point out a fact which may have escaped the attention of many of you: if Praether fails to establish the importance of Ascender Atreu's Talisman, then his whole argument collapses.'

'I am aware of that, First Speaker.' Praether broke into a coughing fit before he composed himself enough to continue.

'Atreu's Book is clearly a true reflection of Atreu's Ascent. I think I have established that.'

'And it's lost at the moment,' said Lythos, smiling. 'I think we can agree on that. Where does that leave his Ascent?'

'A faulty piece of logic,' said Praether. 'We have the power here to find the Book and to give direction to Ascender Atreu's truth.'

Lythos interrupted, 'I move that we cease this judgement because Atreu has failed in the most fundamental duty of an Ascender and has allowed himself to be separated from his Talisman.'

'You can't do that,' cried Atreu. For a split second, he lost all points of reference as the Areol seemed to start spinning.

'And further,' continued Lythos, 'I would like the Circle to note that this is not the first time Ascender Atreu has lost his Talisman. He arrived at the Summit without it, and only thanks to the windrider Riell was it returned.'

After the noise died down, Praether began to speak. 'First Speaker, I demand you uphold my right to speak on the importance of Ascender Atreu's Book.'

Leyvin gritted his teeth and glared at Praether. 'No motions can be made until Liche Praether has made his point.'

'Thank you,' said Praether. 'As I have already said, since we have established that Ascender Atreu's Talisman literally mirrors his Ascent, and his understanding of it mirrors his understanding of his Ascent, it must follow that if he can now, nine days after the final Zenith, still read the Book, then his clarity must have extended into permanency.'

'Hence your claim for the apotheosis of Ascender Atreu,' said a Liche.

'Yes.'

The Circle sat in stunned silence.

Atreu scanned the faces that surrounded him. Despite his frequent contact with the Holy Orders since he set out on his Ascent, he still found them strange at times. He had never seen a group of people so affected by the force of a logical argument.

How is it possible to remove yourself to such a degree from the physical world that ideas had such impact? Only Leyvin didn't appear stunned – his demeanour was one of resignation. Obviously Praether had been right and the First Speaker had anticipated the line of argument all along and had been trying to circumvent it.

When Atreu spoke, the Circle appeared to look at him with different eyes. 'Are you saying,' he asked, 'that if I could still read my Book then you would all accept it as proof that my clarity is permanent, that my ideas and beliefs would be accepted as ultimate truth?'

'That appears to be the general thrust of his argument,' said Leyvin, somewhat wearily.

'And you would accept that as *proof*?' asked Atreu again, sensing the mood of the Circle had shifted in his favour.

'The argument is yet to be scrutinised in detail,' said Leyvin.

'And,' said Lythos, 'there are the possible insurmountable problems of getting the Book back and of Ascender Atreu being able to prove to the Circle that he can, in fact, still read it.'

Praether said, 'I believe that I have argued sufficiently well to justify making the retrieval of the Talisman our major priority.'

'Yes, we will have to review our options in that regard,' said Leyvin.

'But, please,' said Praether, 'before we proceed, I would like to point out a number of other consequences which result from my argument. Firstly, the value of Ascender Atreu's Ascent cannot be judged without the Talisman, so I would suggest that we need to suspend his address until the Book is retrieved. Secondly, as the Ascents of twins are always linked, I believe it is now essential that Ascender Teyth be judged by the Circle. Thirdly, if my arguments are all accepted as correct, then I believe some of the other claims that I have made in the past and, which were dismissed, need to be examined again.'

Leyvin said, 'You can't seriously expect us to re-examine every decision where you were outvoted during your time in the Circle.'

'No,' said Praether, 'but I believe that the original pronouncements I made relating to the importance of the three Books should be looked at again.'

'Why am I surprised,' said Leyvin, 'that you have returned to the three Books? Is there really anything you haven't said on the subject?'

'As a matter of fact, there is.'

'Your requests have been noted, Liche Praether. I agree the address of Ascender Atreu must be suspended and an attempt made to retrieve the Book. Unless I hear a voice of protest, I hereby suspend Ascender Atreu's address.'

There was silence until Atreu spoke.

'And what about Teyth?'

'I will open the rescue of Ascender Teyth up for discussion as well, although I can't see how it can be done.'

'I have a suggestion,' said Atreu.

Leyvin frowned. 'Ascender Atreu should now leave the Circle, as his audience has been suspended.'

'But there may be a way – '

'You no longer have a place here.'

'What?' Atreu felt a wave of anger well within him.

'You have no status. Your audience is under suspension.'

Atreu spread his legs wider and folded his arms across his chest. 'I am going to offer my suggestion anyway. You will have to name me to stop me.'

Leyvin smiled a sardonic smile. 'Only members of the Circle can be named. Others are forcibly removed if necessary.'

Atreu looked across at Praether for support, but the archlibrer shook his head softly. Atreu frowned. Despite all the discussions about his Ascent and apotheosis, Atreu could see that he still had absolutely no influence.

'You function by shutting people out, don't you?' said Atreu.

Leyvin was still smiling. 'Please leave, Ascender Atreu.'

Atreu unfolded his arms and started walking towards the arched doors.

*

Once back in his room, Atreu stared out of his window at the dazzling dance of the Keep's night-lights. For some reason he thought of his time in the village of Heimfell in the very early days of his Ascent. There, the lights had also danced a wild and alluring dance in the night sky. He remembered the music spinning him round and round in the warm summer air, the laughter, the giddiness, the warmth of Danae and the soft tender rhythms. He could also remember the anger and frustration he had felt the next day when the Vows of Silence were again in place.

How little things had changed. The Holy Men of the Circle had made little effort to speak to him or even to listen to him.

A chill wind suddenly blew through the open window and he closed the shutters before getting into bed. There was too much in his head and he sought respite from the constantly whirling thoughts. Finally, he was rewarded with a dreamless sleep.

He awoke to find Praether sitting on the chair opposite him, looking exhausted.

'Sorry,' said Praether, 'did my coughing waken you? We were quite happy to wait.'

Atreu then became aware that Micah was sitting on the end of his bed. The Holy Man also had large dark rings under his eyes.

'Am I the only one who has slept tonight?' asked Atreu.

'I managed to get a little,' said Micah, 'but Praether had to wait for the Circle to cease meeting.'

Praether rested his head in his hand. 'And it was almost dawn when Leyvin finally ended proceedings.'

Atreu propped his pillow up against the wall and sat up. 'Praether, I want to thank you for everything you said and did last night.'

Praether gestured the comment away. 'There's no need to be too grateful, Atreu. Like most Liche members I love a stunning, well-thought-out argument. And, besides, I would have to say I argued with such persistence because my interests coincided with yours. And now, Leyvin's position as First Speaker is vulnerable for the first time – and that is to my advantage.'

'Do you believe what you said? About my apotheosis?'

Praether cleared his throat. 'I believe my reasoning is sound. As with any argument though, it is with the assumptions that its weakness lies. I think the Circle was too overcome with the audacity of what I was saying last night to question the assumptions too closely. And the major problem will be retrieving your Book.'

'The obvious solution is to rescue Teyth,' Micah said. 'That would solve all our problems. Teyth knows where the Book is and Praether has convinced the Circle that a judgement of his Ascent is required after all.'

'Have they agreed to that?' asked Atreu.

'Yes, it was decided after you left, but again we have the almost insurmountable practical problem of rescuing him from a Summit overrun by thousands of Faemir.'

'And how was it decided it was going to be done?' asked Atreu.

'That's one of the things that took so long, Atreu. We discussed all the options from full-scale attack to surreptitious infiltration by a single Maelir.'

'And?' Atreu stared at the arch-librer.

'I'm afraid we couldn't really come up with anything.'

Atreu punched his blankets with frustration. 'I told them I had a suggestion. Why wouldn't they hear me out?'

'It's not your place,' said Praether. 'You have to earn the right to be heard.'

'Look,' said Micah, 'let me explain how our system here at the Keep functions. I know it appears as if only the sixty members of the Circle have any say in how things are done. That's not quite true. If you want your voice to be heard, you must be able to convince one of the members to argue your case as if it was his own. I've done it many times, haven't I, Praether?'

The arch-librer smiled and the many creases in his face turned upwards. 'If someone can't convince any of the sixty members of the Circle to argue a case or express a view, then the argument probably is of little worth in the first place. It's a good system, Atreu, and it has worked very well for a long time.'

'Then will you argue my case, Praether?'

'If I believe in it – tell me what your suggestion is.'

'All right,' Atreu sat up straight. 'I believe you should allow Verlinden to find the Book.'

Praether shook his head. 'I suspected that's what you were going to say. We discussed the option but it was quickly dismissed, and I would have to say I agreed. We would simply be releasing her. We can never trust a Faemir, no matter how obsessed you are with her.'

Atreu shifted uncomfortably. 'You of all people shouldn't be dismissing obsessions.'

'I've spoken to Verlinden,' said Micah. 'I believe she can be half-trusted, particularly if Atreu is there to persuade her.'

Praether stared at Micah for a moment and then said. 'Half-trust is worse than no trust. You never know where you stand.'

'No, wait,' said Atreu. 'Listen to my full suggestion before you dismiss it. I believe Verlinden can help us get Teyth back as well.'

'Yes,' said Praether, 'the exchange of prisoners. We've discussed that already. That involves negotiation, something which neither we nor the Faemir have done before. I don't think it will work. The Faemir will simply torture and kill anyone we send down there.'

Atreu sighed. 'You're doing to me what the Circle did to you last night. Just let me finish.' He drew a deep breath. 'As you know, Verlinden is Valkyra's twin sister. They are identical. According to what I read in the Book of Maelur, Teyth couldn't tell them apart. I think she could pass for her sister if she wanted to.'

'How can you ensure that she would want to?' asked Praether, straightening up a little.

'I think I can persuade her. She would then be able to find my Book and negotiate with us for the release of Teyth.'

Micah said, 'So you're saying that we send down a negotiator with her?'

'A brilliant plan, Atreu, may I commend you,' said Praether. 'As always though, the weaknesses are in the assumptions. I don't believe you can persuade her – and even if she says she is prepared to do it, how do we know she is not simply lying to us so she will be released?'

'She won't – I can ensure that.'

'How can you?' asked Micah. 'You heard yourself that the Faemir cause still beats in her heart.'

'Yes,' said Atreu, 'but not their methods. And besides, even you would have to agree that she would never harm me. She has had dozens of opportunities to kill me. When I was lying asleep after the final Zenith, she stayed with me instead of returning to her people.'

'You're right,' said Micah, 'but she also hates being kept prisoner and she could lie to gain her freedom, re-join her people, and kill or imprison our negotiator without harming you.'

'Not if I was the negotiator.'

'What?' Praether and Micah spoke almost simultaneously.

'If I went down with Verlinden, then it would work.'

'But, Atreu –'

'Look, Micah, you yourself said she would never harm me. I can talk to her. I know it can work.'

Micah ran his fingers through his beard.

'What do you think?' asked Praether. 'You know more about Atreu's relationship with this Faemir. Can the plan work?'

'I think there is a chance. As I said, she can be only half-trusted but with Atreu by her side and in potential danger I see the balance of trust swinging further in our direction. One problem I see is: who do we use as a swap in the negotiations for Teyth's release?'

'I thought that part was easy,' said Praether. 'As far as the Faemir are concerned, Verlinden will still be a prisoner up here.'

'From what she said, though,' said Micah, 'she isn't much of a bargaining tool. The Faemir don't hold her in high esteem for some reason.'

'She was lying when she said that to you,' said Atreu quickly. 'She obviously didn't want you to overvalue her status. I know she is crucial to the Faemir.'

'Is she?' asked Micah, raising his eyebrows. 'So she is capable of lying?'

'Aren't we all?' said Atreu.

Micah eyed him curiously before he spoke again. 'I believe Atreu's suggestion is worth a try. No-one's come up with an alternative to save Teyth, and that's always been my number one concern.'

'You could end up losing both your nephews,' said Praether.

Micah nodded. 'I know – if Atreu is willing to take the risk then I'll support him. The problem, as you know, however, is not my support, but how the Circle can be persuaded to allow the plan to be put into action.'

'Don't worry about that,' said Praether. 'That is my task.'

'Do you think you can do it?'

'Frankly, yes. Perhaps I'm overconfident after my successes last night, but I feel the Circle is receptive to direction from me at the moment. I have to pretend, of course, that the idea was mine, or else it will carry little weight. I actually think both Leyvin and Lythos will support the plan – for their own reasons.'

'Why is that?' asked Atreu.

'Because they consider you a real threat to the power structure. They may not be happy about losing our only Faemir prisoner but neither of them wanted you up in the Keep anyway. I think they'll be quite pleased to leave you at the mercy of the Faemir down there.'

Atreu smiled and pushed his blankets back. 'So you really think it will work?'

'I don't know if you should be smiling so broadly about it, Atreu. I think I can get you and Verlinden down there. Whether you'll be successful or not is another matter.'

'I'm suddenly very hungry,' said Atreu, standing up. 'Let's break the fast.'

Micah put his hand on his nephew's shoulder. 'I don't have to tell you how happy I would be if you and Verlinden could get Teyth to the Keep.'

Atreu smiled. 'You know, Uncle, that's the first time I've heard you say Verlinden's name.'

Chapter Twelve

Valkyra examined her wounds as she had done every day since she had been trapped in the Eyries. She was pleased with the way they had healed. She rarely suffered from wounds very long – the bleeding always stopped quickly and the pain usually disappeared after a day or two.

As the windriders had left the Eyries in a hurry, Valkyra had found food, water and blankets everywhere. At first she had spent much of her time sleeping, but as her strength returned and her head cleared, she spent most days exploring the hundreds of caverns, tunnels, corridors and caves.

She understood the Maelir strategy only too well now. They would keep abandoning places so as to trap her. It was the second time they had done it to her now – first the place she had thought was the Summit, and now this place which was clearly nothing more than the home of the windriders. From the very beginning she was determined that the third time was to be the last. She knew they must be running out of places to escape to – they could only retreat so far before they had nowhere to go.

The Eyries was far more comfortable than the caves at the Summit. There were fireplaces everywhere, comfortable chairs, soft rugs and even decorations on the walls. This was obviously a place of permanent residence. She could see now that no-one actually lived down at the Summit – the Faemir had taken control of a place of only temporary importance.

At first Valkyra had felt the rage boil inside her. How could they do this to her? She was completely trapped – the sole prisoner in the Mountain's largest gaol. All the doors were open, but there was no way to escape.

In the early days of her imprisonment when the rage took her, she would charge out onto one of the hundreds of ledges and call her captors to her. The windriders would always be waiting and would move in. But never to try to kill her, only to hold her back from the ledge so she couldn't try to climb down. Despite their caution, she would usually manage to wound at least one of them – but, frustratingly, a new one always flew in to replace him.

And it was never long before the archers took aim and started firing from such a close range that any arrow that hit its mark would pierce her armour, so she was again forced to retreat into the caves.

Valkyra had soon realised that a less direct method was going to be needed. She had tried the more furtive approach of sneaking out onto a new ledge and commencing a descent using the remaining wedges. Somehow, though, the windriders who patrolled the cliff always spotted her before long and moved in. She had no choice but to return.

There was no escape.

She grappled with the thought for a long time. Her natural impulse when she was trapped was to fight, but she could see that simply wasn't going to work this time. She had to control the rage. Focus it. Use it. She had always prided herself in both outfighting and out-thinking her opponents. There had to be a way.

She had continued searching the caves of the Eyries, desperately looking for something that could help her. Nothing had ever held her back before. She had come so much further than any Faemir could have dreamed of.

One day she had entered a room filled with the windriders'

wings. Her first impulse was to start taking them outside and throwing them over the edge as she had done with the others. But she had stopped herself. There had to be a way to escape – she just had to find it. She had no idea how to use the wings. She couldn't simply fly back down – even if she could somehow teach herself the basics, she would be even more vulnerable than trying to climb down using the wedges. And yet, there had to be a way.

She remembered running her palm along the material between the wooden frames. She knew that whatever she was going to do would have to be totally unexpected.

At that very moment a smile had crept onto her lips as a plan began to take form – and it had rarely left her face since.

*

Snow was falling softly, like the autumn leaves of a giant white tree, as Atreu and Verlinden touched down on the Mountain. The Upper Reaches' summer had now fled, chased from the slopes by pale phantoms. Theander and the windrider carrying Verlinden had decided to drop them some distance downslope to avoid attack by the Faemir, although no place in the Upper Reaches was totally free of that danger.

Atreu felt good to be finally putting his plan into action after the weeks of frustrating waiting. From what Praether had told him, the Circle never rushed a decision. Everything had to be looked at from all angles. Conventions needed to be followed strictly, and the lead-up to Equinox was always a busy time when the Ascenders' addresses had to be heard. Praether had been confident that Atreu's plan would be accepted, but he had pointed out that Leyvin was probably employing a deliberate tactic of delaying the decision to make the task more difficult.

Atreu felt his feet sink deep into the snow and he quickly reached back and undid the harness. He looked across as the second windrider untied Verlinden's hands and removed her blindfold. The Keep's leatherworkers had done an impressive job in attempting to recreate Valkyra's battle armour. He just hoped that the descriptions from the windriders, together with Verlinden's help, would be enough for the armour to withstand all but the closest scrutiny. And Teyth's battle-axe slung across her back was more than a nice touch. According to Praether, actually persuading the Circle of the importance of letting her have the axe was one of the most difficult things to do. The Holy Men were reluctant to give a Talisman, even one that belonged to an Ascender who had been pronounced a failure, to a Faemir. But Praether's reasoning that the axe was crucial had prevailed in the end – and Atreu was grateful.

'Good luck, Atreu,' said Theander as he prepared to take off again.

'We will return here at the times agreed on,' said the other windrider, also addressing Atreu. He shot a cautious glance at Verlinden, and both riders tilted their wings to allow the updraughts to make them airborne again. Atreu watched them quickly disappear behind the curtain of gently falling snow.

'When are they going to return?' asked Verlinden, rubbing her wrists to improve the circulation.

'I'm not supposed to tell you.'

Verlinden turned away. 'Why is trust so hard for us?'

'You don't know what it's like, Verlinden. I still don't know who to trust completely up there. It seems to me that everyone is simply striving to do what's best in their own interests. I'm sure Praether only agreed to my plan because he knows it will be the only way my Book can be retrieved. He's only interested in his beliefs about books. Even Micah really only wants to get Teyth back.'

'And what do you want, Atreu?' Verlinden turned and looked at him through the gossamer veil of falling snow.

'I want ...' Atreu felt the words somehow trapped in his throat. 'I want to be with you. I don't want us to be separated again. I want us to trust each other the way no man and woman on the Mountain have ever trusted each other.'

'When are the windriders going to return?'

'Every evening, just after dusk.' He stepped towards Verlinden. 'And they are not going to return here. That was supposed to mislead you in case you planned to ambush them when they returned. The place they will fly to is an outcrop surrounded by three hills just west of here.'

'You didn't have to tell me that, Atreu.'

'I know, but you don't know whether I'm lying to you, do you?'

'I believe you.'

The two embraced as the snow continued to fall. Atreu pressed his lips against hers and felt her soft warmth pass through to him. Everything was still. Nothing seemed to exist beyond the pure white curtain of snow.

Atreu pulled away slowly, unaware of how long the two of them had been embracing. 'You asked me what I wanted, Verlinden.'

She nodded.

'I want us to be together – but more than that, I want us both to be free together.'

Verlinden laughed. 'Do you think I'm going to throw you in a cell?'

'No,' said Atreu, 'but I still believe we can persuade our two people to make peace. We have to – that was the way of truth of my Zenith. The problem was that we were both too naive to know how it could be done. I want more than simply to retrieve my Talisman and rescue Teyth. I'm supposed to be a negotiator here – I want the two of us to negotiate a peace between the Maelir and the Faemir.'

Verlinden's gaze dropped.

'What's wrong?' asked Atreu.

'You still aren't very different from the rest of the Maelir.'

Atreu was puzzled. 'What do you mean? How can you say that? I want us to – '

'See, you're doing it again.'

'What?'

'You're saying what you want, what you want to do, what the truth of your Zenith was. Have you ever thought to ask me what I want, what the truth of my Zenith was?'

'I'm sorry, Verlinden. I just thought your truth was the same as mine. I thought I sensed that.'

'I do want peace, Atreu. You were right about that, but I want an equal peace, not something the Maelir allow us to have. I don't want your people to simply allow the Faemir to take part in Zenith. It has to be more than that. Everything the Holy Orders have built up has to be examined and much of it may have to be broken down and built anew.'

'What exactly is it that you want broken down?' Atreu stared at her intently.

'Don't look at me like that. You can't keep everything as it is now and simply add the Faemir. It's impossible. Look at what the Holy Orders have achieved with the way they go about things: a Mountain devastated by war. That can't be the right way.'

'But they have achieved so many good things.'

'Well, let's keep those and throw out what hasn't worked. That's the only sensible way to go about things. But if we are going to do that, then we are going to have to really negotiate as equals. The ultimate truth of my Zenith may have been the same as yours, but that doesn't mean we are going to agree at first how to achieve it.'

Atreu ran his fingers through Verlinden's dark red ringlets. 'You're right.' He pulled her head gently to his chest. 'Since Zenith, I've had this overwhelming sense that I am right about things.'

'That's funny,' said Verlinden, 'so have I.'

They both laughed.

'Come on,' said Atreu, 'let's get up there and negotiate.'

*

'You want to speak with me, Rhea?'

'Yes. Close the door – I don't want anyone to hear our conversation.'

The dark-haired Faemir eyed Rhea curiously. 'Do you have news of Valkyra?'

'No. Still nothing. Just sit down will you.'

The Faemir sat down at the table opposite Rhea. 'We are making some progress with the wings,' she said, 'if that's what you are worrying about. The ones we believe Valkyra sent down to us were easily repaired. We have been able to make a few copies as well, but because – '

Rhea motioned her into silence. 'We've been together from the very start, haven't we?'

The Faemir nodded. She ran her finger around the deep scar in the palm of her hand.

Rhea continued. 'We were the first two she defeated, weren't we, Ahrai?'

'I think I know where this is leading,' said Ahrai. 'Look, I have no love for Valkyra. None of us do. But she wins – all the time. And she's given us a direction no-one else had been able to give us.' She went to get up.

'No, wait,' said Rhea. 'You have no idea what I'm going to say to you. Just hear me out.'

Ahrai sat down again.

'You know Valkyra better than almost anyone,' said Rhea. 'You are one of the few people who engaged her in hand-to-hand combat and lived to tell the tale.'

'That was ten years ago, Rhea.' She held her palm up for Rhea to see. 'I haven't forgotten the scar. How can I? But I blame you more than her. She was the one who spared me in the end, not you. So don't try to get me to switch my allegiance.'

'Do you think I'm mad? I stood aside for her when she was a mere girl of nine years. Do you think I'm going to challenge her now?'

'As you said, Rhea, we've been together from the very start.

I'm not sure how well I know Valkyra, but I'm fairly certain I understand you.'

Rhea raised her eyebrows. 'You think so? Now listen to me, will you? Valkyra has been gone a long time. The only evidence we had of what she's doing up there was the wings that came down to us on the first day. Since then, nothing.'

'There have been slight changes in the flight patterns of the windriders.'

'Yes, I know, but nothing too drastic, and the supply lines appear to be functioning as normal.'

'I don't really see what you're getting at,' said Ahrai. 'She went up as a Watcher. No-one could have seriously expected her to single-handedly disturb their supply lines.'

'I wouldn't rule that possibility out entirely, Ahrai, but my point is that she could have done one of two things up there. Either she has fulfilled a Watcher's function and remained hidden, or she has been unable to help herself and has engaged those up there in battle. The disturbance in the windriders' flight patterns, and what I know of Valkyra, suggests that she would involve herself in fighting in some way.'

'Are you suggesting she has been killed? I doubt if you would be able to get too many of us to accept that.'

'No, we both have seen enough to know how difficult it would be to kill her. I believe she can be imprisoned, though. We have to look at the possibility.'

'What do you want from me, Rhea?'

'I want your support.'

'I'll never support you against Valkyra. I may not like her, but she has always given support to those who she considered worthy of it among the Faemir, regardless of whether they had once opposed her. Look at me – I'm a battalion leader because of her. And you yourself are second-in-command of the entire Faemir army. We'd both still be in the coveyn doing raids on small villages if it wasn't for her.'

'I don't want your support against Valkyra. I would be mad to ask anyone for that. But if she has, as I now suspect, been captured, I have to begin making decisions and giving some orders.'

'You want me to back those orders?'

'Yes, and build up as much support as you can among the other battalion leaders.'

'Most of them will say we should stick to Valkyra's original strategy – and I'm inclined to agree with them.'

'But look, Ahrai, we both know one of Valkyra's strengths is her adaptability. She has always changed strategies midstream if that was what was needed. I think it could be disastrous not to make any new decisions.'

'Perhaps you're right, Rhea, but how do we know the new decisions are going to be the correct ones?'

'We know it because they'll be our decisions.'

Ahrai stared at Rhea. 'Are you saying what I think you're saying?'

'Yes, Ahrai. If I'm going to command the Faemir army I want you to be my second.'

'The other battalion leaders won't like the idea – you know that. They'll probably challenge your right to appoint me.'

'I realise that, which is why I don't want to make an official pronouncement yet. What I'm proposing is that I appear to consult with the other senior battalion leaders, but that you and I be the ones to make the final decision. I want you to support me in private discussions with the other leaders and in public conclaves, and when my authority is assured, I will officially make you my second.'

'And if Valkyra returns – or when we rescue her?'

'In that case, are you any worse off than you are now?'

'No, perhaps not – but I think one of those two things will happen eventually.'

'*Eventually* is the right word, Ahrai. I'm beginning to realise we are going to be here for quite some time ... Look, at least think about what I've said.'

Ahrai nodded. 'All right, Rhea, I'll think about the offer.'

There was a knock at the door and they both looked up as a tall Faemir warrior entered.

'Rhea, your attendance is required immediately,' she said. Rhea looked at the warrior with momentary bemusement. 'What do you mean, my attendance is *required*?' Who can require my attendance?'

'Valkyra,' said the Faemir. 'She has returned.'

Rhea and Ahrai exchanged a glance.

*

As Rhea entered the room, she saw the figure of Valkyra silhouetted against the roaring fire on the far side.

'Ah, Rhea, it's so good to see you again. Why do you look so surprised to see me – don't tell me you'd given up hope?'

'No, Valkyra, I knew you would return. It's just ... well ... it has been some time. And I'm surprised at the fire. We have so little to burn up here.'

It was then that Rhea realised with a shock that a figure standing to Valkyra's right was Maelir. Instinctively, she drew her sword.

Verlinden gestured for her to re-sheath the sword. 'No, this one remains alive,' she said.

Rhea eyed them both curiously. She stepped towards the fire to get a closer look at the Maelir.

'When did you release him?' she asked.

Verlinden hesitated for a moment. 'No, Rhea, this is not Teyth.'

'What are you saying, Valkyra? Did you take leave of your senses up there? Of course, this is the baresark.'

'How dare you doubt my word, Rhea. This is the twin of the one we have imprisoned.'

'I am Atreu.'

Rhea ignored him. 'Valkyra, can you explain to me what is

happening here? We all like our sport with Ascenders, but this one is untied and standing there as if … as if he were your consort.'

'And he will remain untied – as I've already explained to the others here.'

Rhea's eyes narrowed. 'What happened to you up there?'

'Many things which I will explain to you in good time.'

'I think you had better start now.'

'Perhaps you've grown too used to giving orders in my absence, Rhea. I'll reveal to you what has happened when I think it is appropriate. Meanwhile, I want to be briefed on how the war is faring.'

'With him here?' she asked incredulously.

'You won't be telling me anything I don't know or haven't already guessed,' said Atreu.

'Someone cut his tongue out,' said Rhea.

Atreu swallowed, hoping that the Faemir would think the sweat on his brow was a result of the heat of the fire behind him.

'You are no closer to victory in the battle for Crosanct, am I right?' said Atreu. Rhea brandished her sword, but he kept speaking. 'All the new forces arriving from downslope are being more than matched by increased Maelir battalions.'

'One Faemir warrior is worth a hundred Maelir soldiers,' said Rhea.

'That may be,' said Atreu, 'but even at that rate, you will eventually be outnumbered.'

'Put the sword away, Rhea. I have granted Atreu asylum while he is with us.'

'What?' A look of utter disgust crossed Rhea's face. 'How can you grant a Maelir asylum?'

'The war is not going well, Rhea. You know that.'

'We are a long way from defeat.'

'Yes, but we are also a long way from victory.'

Rhea slowly sheathed her sword. 'So you are finally coming to the conclusion that we've failed. You know I've been arguing that for some time.'

'No, I don't think we've failed,' said Verlinden.

'What we have is a stalemate,' said Atreu, 'an impasse.'

'Do I have to listen to him?' asked Rhea.

Verlinden said, 'What harm is there in listening?'

Rhea looked straight into Verlinden's face. 'There's something strange about you, Valkyra. I've known you a long time and I've never heard you say anything like that.'

Verlinden felt the heat of the flames on her back. 'I've always listened to you, haven't I?'

'A little,' said Rhea, 'but you have always followed your own counsel. And we are talking about a Maelir here.'

'I'm going to speak anyway,' said Atreu, 'and whether or not you choose to listen is up to you. You may not have succeeded in your aims, but there is a real chance that you may still have possession of the Summit at the time of the next Zenith. The Holy Orders realise this is a possibility and that the future of their grip on the Mountain is not assured. The situation we are in now could continue indefinitely, and in the meantime, both our people are dying in numbers so great we can no longer count them.'

'There are many more Maelir than Faemir dying,' said Rhea.

'That may be,' said Atreu, 'but there are so many more of us. I think the time has come for peace between our two peoples. I am here to discuss this with Valkyra and the Faemir.'

'Peace? Discussion? Are these the things you want, Valkyra?'

'I'm going to listen to Atreu, and I want you to do so as well.'

Rhea spat on the ground. 'I agree that we have to change our strategy – but peace, that is insane. What sort of peace are you Maelir going to give us? To live in your towns and villages like Faelen. That peace has always been on offer to us and we have always refused it.'

'I want peace on our terms,' said Verlinden.

'The peace must be acceptable to both Maelir and Faemir,' said Atreu, 'or else it is no peace at all.'

Verlinden said, 'Now, Rhea, tell me about the progress we have been making in my absence. Then I want you to organise a conclave of all the available battalion leaders. Send the order out to those in other parts of the Upper Reaches. And try to get as many as you can through Crosanct and up here to the Summit.'

'A conclave? Why do you feel it is necessary to call a conclave now?'

'We need to discuss some important matters.'

'More discussions? Why not make your decision and tell the others as you've always done?'

'I want to hear what the others have to say, Rhea.'

Rhea stared first into Verlinden's eyes and then into Atreu's. 'There is something very strange about this. I will do what you ask, but I think you've been with the Maelir too long, and there is something happening here that I don't yet understand.'

As Rhea's gaze bored into him, Atreu felt as if the flames of the fire were licking his skin.

*

Teyth was half asleep when the door to his cell opened. He sat up and watched the Faemir step in and close the door behind her. The familiar mixture of thrill and raw terror pulsed through him as his eyes followed the lithe, well-muscled frame of Valkyra. His heart missed a beat, as it always did, when he saw the glint of his double-bladed axe.

'Where have you been?' he asked. 'I've missed your visits.'

'Teyth, it's me – Verlinden.'

'What sort of games – '

'No, Teyth, it is me. Valkyra is imprisoned. I've returned to find Atreu's Book and to try to get you out.'

'Atreu's Book? What book are you talking about?'

'You remember, Teyth, we buried it in the snow.'

'I ... I don't know what you're talking about.'

'I'm glad I'm so convincing, but I know one person who may be able to persuade you.'

Verlinden pushed the door open again and called out, 'You can let him in now.'

A man walked through the door which then clanged shut again.

Teyth felt as if the Mountain had suddenly shaken. A wave of euphoria washed through him. 'Atreu, little brother, is it really you?'

They rushed towards each other and embraced, clasping their hands and raising them in the air.

Teyth pulled away suddenly. 'So they have you now too?' His smile dropped.

'No,' said Atreu. 'This really is Verlinden. The Orders are holding Valkyra prisoner.'

Teyth's head spun. He sat down on his bed again. 'I don't know what's going on anymore. Everything has been a haze since the last Zenith. Valkyra, Verlinden – I don't know the difference anymore.'

'You sound better than you were just after the Faemir captured you,' said Atreu.

'What? How do you know what I was like?' He ran his fingers through his hair. 'Nothing makes sense to me anymore. I don't know. I thought Zenith was supposed to clarify everything. For me it's been as if my mind is no longer my own.'

'I'll explain all I can to you,' said Atreu.

'They left us both, didn't they?' said Teyth, dropping his head. 'We both failed our Ascents.'

'No,' said Atreu. 'The Holy Orders have already deemed my Ascent worthy of judgement. They want to judge yours as well.'

'What do you mean?'

'Don't worry, Teyth. There is hope for all of us. We are going to try to negotiate your release.'

'Since when do the Faemir negotiate anything?'

'Since they think I'm Valkyra.' Verlinden stepped towards the two brothers.

Teyth stared at her open-mouthed. 'You won't be able to get away with it.'

'I fooled you, didn't I?'

'And from what I've read, you were getting to know Valkyra very well,' said Atreu.

'What do you mean – from what you've read?'

'That, I would have to say, is a long story.' Atreu laughed.

Teyth looked at his brother in bewilderment.

'Listen,' said Verlinden, 'this is what we plan to do.'

*

'It was just as I expected,' said Praether, taking another sip of butter-tea as he and Micah sat in the arch-librer's chambers.

'So the words have now faded, have they?' asked Micah.

'It's not quite that simple, Micah. The ability seems to come and go, but I know it's been waning for some time. It was gradually becoming an effort for me to read, as if my eyes were getting tired, although it was more like the words were getting tired – if that makes any sense. But last night I was getting towards the end of a chapter, and words and even whole sentences started becoming incomprehensible. It got to the stage where there was no point in me continuing.'

'That means you were right when you said Atreu was the key.'

'Yes – he is the one with the real power. I'm sure I could only read the Book of Maelur because he was here in the Keep.'

'And now that he is back down at the Summit, your ability has gone.'

'Yes, Micah, I'm afraid so.'

'That means you've lost your advantage in the Circle.' Micah stroked his beard thoughtfully.

'Not necessarily,' said Praether. 'Only the two of us know that I've lost the ability to read the Book. I think I can bluff my way effectively. Besides there was enough information in the chapter last night for me to use for the time being.'

'You haven't told me what it is Atreu and Verlinden actually plan to do.'

'I don't know exactly – except that they are seriously trying to negotiate peace between the Maelir and the Faemir, as preposterous as that may sound.'

'Could they get the Faemir to retreat from the Upper Reaches?'

'Not without the Maelir giving ground.'

'What sort of ground?'

'I'm not sure, but I suspect they will want to take part in Zenith, perhaps even join the Holy Orders – who knows?'

'Atreu and Verlinden are both mad,' said Micah. 'No-one here will agree to that. Their problem won't be convincing the Faemir, it will be convincing us.'

Praether took another sip of the butter-tea. 'You're right, Micah, but let's just wait and see. If they get Atreu's Book and Teyth safely up here, then that's all that matters, isn't it?'

'Yes – and you still think we have to fear Valkyra?'

'I do. If she somehow escapes and returns to the Hold, the plan will fall apart completely, and we will have lost Atreu as well as Teyth.'

'And there was no clue in the Book about how she thinks she can escape?'

'No, none – except that it's got something to do with the wings she found.'

'She can't possibly plan to fly back down. Even if she could somehow gain a rudimentary mastery of the techniques, the windriders would cut her down very quickly.'

'I know, Micah. It seems impossible. But all of us thought it would be impossible for the Faemir even to reach the Hold – and they have. No-one ever thought that a single Faemir could force the windriders to abandon the Eyries – but that is exactly what's happened. This woman is the most dangerous thing on the Mountain. That's one thing we should all be convinced of.'

Micah ran his fingers through his beard as the room suddenly seemed very quiet.

Chapter Thirteen

Valkyra carried the wings to where the cavern opened out onto the ledge and peered out. She had found night-time to be the best. The small snow flurries of early autumn also helped her. Anything that could mask what she was doing for even a short while.

She thought she could see dark shapes hovering in the distance, but as usual it was impossible to tell exactly how many windriders were out there waiting for her to emerge. What she was certain of was that, no matter how dark it was or how much snow was falling, she had very little time before they would attack her.

She strapped on the harness, careful not to tie it too tight because she knew she would have to be able to remove it quickly.

Drawing a sharp breath, Valkyra grabbed hold of the overhead bar on the frame and charged out into the night air. She was aware from experience that any time spent out on the ledge was wasted, so as usual she ran towards the edge and stepped out into nothingness.

The first time had been the worst, but she had now grown accustomed to the sensation. The updraught, the sudden lift which had surprised her initially, was now expected. She no longer feared she was going to fall.

What she did fear was the windriders. Hovering, forever waiting for their chance to mortally wound her.

But every time they failed, every time she had a few minutes to improve her skills, she was that one step closer to escaping the prison.

On this particular night she had longer than usual. She pointed the wings up so that she quickly gained altitude, revelling in the control she was starting to achieve. She always looked around in all directions for any sign of approaching windriders. Perhaps it was because the snow flurries were slightly heavier than usual, but she still couldn't see any of the swooping formations of six which she had grown to hate. As usual, though, she remained alert and kept close to the cliff face and to entrances in the rock that could provide an escape route once the inevitable attack began.

She leant to the left and then to the right, weaving her way through a band of mist. Although she knew her attempts at turning were still clumsy, she was learning all the time. Finding and using the updraughts was important, but she had learned that shifting her body and tilting the wings at just the right angle was where all the skill was.

She knew it would take her years to gain the sort of control needed to engage the windriders in airborne battle. But if everything went according to plan, she would never have to do that.

She was flying through another band of mist when she realised the windriders were almost upon her. Damn. She almost preferred the clear nights. Although she was more exposed at those times, at least she could see them coming from a further distance.

With a rapid tilt she headed towards the nearest entrance, but this time the riders had a great deal of momentum on their side and swooped dangerously close on an updraught she had missed.

There was a crack and Valkyra felt a sudden drop. The lead rider had snapped one of her major struts with his sword. The riders knew exactly which points on the wings were the most vulnerable.

Fortunately her sudden drop also meant the formation was now some distance above her. She tilted the wings again and found that although it took longer for her to head in the desired direction, she wasn't entirely without control.

The riders dipped towards her again, just as she touched ground on a ledge. She drew her sword immediately and fended them off while she undid the straps.

The windriders went through the motions of an attack but they soon backed off. They always did. They knew from experience that once she touched ground, there was little point in continuing the battle. They couldn't win, and besides, she was still imprisoned so that was all that mattered.

Valkyra watched the riders fly off again. The mist was thickening and they soon disappeared. She sheathed her sword and examined the damage on the wing. The main strut was in two pieces and part of the material stretched across the top frame had torn. She knew she had neither the expertise nor tools to attempt a repair.

Well, never mind, she thought. There are plenty more wings inside. She lifted the damaged set and threw it over the edge. She would never know whether it reached the ground and the Faemir retrieved it, or whether the windriders caught it first. Ultimately, it didn't matter to her.

She watched as further plumes of mist ascended the cliff face. It was only a matter of time, she thought.

*

Verlinden realised it was going to be difficult when Saretha, the first of the battalion leaders, entered the chamber.

Saretha's jaw dropped when she saw Atreu, already sitting at the table.

'Give me your sword,' said Rhea.

'What?'

'You know the rules of a conclave,' said Rhea. 'All weapons are to be removed.'

'I'm not going to unarm myself with a Maelir in the room,' said Saretha. 'If I unsheathe my sword, the next home it will find for itself will be in his chest.'

'Remove the sword – and your knife,' said Verlinden, 'and give them both to Rhea.'

Verlinden knew the origins of the removal of weapons at conclaves. Leaders of different coveyns had always done so because of the Faemir tendency to resolve arguments through combat. The convention ensured that discussions continued longer than they otherwise would. It was particularly important that it was going to be adhered to in this conclave.

Saretha glared at Verlinden and refused to move. When she spoke, her words were slow, deliberate and filled with venom. 'I will not remove my sword while there is a Maelir alive in the room.'

Verlinden could feel herself trembling slightly, but she fought for control. She reached back for Teyth's battle-axe and held it in front of her. 'If you think you need your weapon in here,' she said, 'then let us see how you use it.'

She wasn't sure how convincing she sounded, but she didn't take her eyes off Saretha as she took a step towards the other Faemir. She prayed Saretha would back down because she had no familiarity with battle-axe technique.

Saretha suddenly went pale. 'All right, Valkyra, there's no need to bloody the floor here.' She threw her sword and knife into the corner and sat down on a chair as far away as possible from Atreu.

Verlinden lowered the battle-axe and then leant it up against the wall behind her.

Ahrai was next to arrive, and Verlinden noted that she gave Rhea a sideways glance as she surrendered her sword. The battalion leader then eyed Atreu curiously before she sat down, although she didn't appear to be surprised to see him there.

The ten other battalion leaders to enter the room were all reluctant to remove their weapons, but it became easier to persuade them to do so with so many others already sitting weaponless at the table.

When the last one was seated, Verlinden began. 'I'm not going to waste words on what I'm about to say. We've come a long way – all of us. I've known some of you my whole life, so you know that I always mean what I say, and I always do what I say I'll do.' She paused, knowing the impact the words were about to have. 'We are not going to win this war.'

A stunned silence fell onto the room like a leaden weight. The battalion leaders looked at each other.

'What happened to you up there?' demanded Saretha finally.

'You've led us all the way to the Summit,' said Rhea, 'and now you expect us to accept defeat?'

'I've never spoken about defeat,' said Verlinden. 'I said we can't win this war. That's not the same thing.'

'It sounds like the same thing to me,' snorted Saretha.

'So what do you expect us all do to?' asked Kaithen, one of the other battalion leaders. 'Go home and just re-form the coveyns?'

Verlinden put up her hand to demand silence. She hoped it was the right gesture and was a little surprised when it worked.

'Now listen to me, all of you. I said we are not going to win this war, but I also know that the Maelir won't win this war either. We have the Summit, but the Holy Orders are still running their affairs as they always have done – way above our reach.'

'You managed to get to them, Valkyra,' said Ahrai. 'The rest of us can follow.'

'I came as a total surprise,' said Verlinden. 'They weren't expecting me. It is going to be almost impossible for anyone to get up the pillar without being attacked.'

'We'll go up in numbers,' said Saretha. 'Just like we originally planned. We won't need the element of surprise. Hundreds on wings and thousands scaling the cliff itself just as you did.' She glared at Atreu as she spoke. 'And don't think you will return safely to report what you're hearing here tonight.'

'I'll decide what happens to him,' said Verlinden. She continued. 'I believe the defences are too strong and the windriders have a huge advantage over us under those fighting conditions. We know we can defeat the Maelir on the open plain, in towns and cities, and in forests – but in mid-air or pinned to a cliff face I'm not so certain.'

'What exactly are you proposing?' asked Rhea.

'I believe neither Faemir nor Maelir can win. Perhaps we can hold the Summit through winter until next Zenith, but even if we do, we will be weakened – and the Holy Orders will still be powerful and capable of controlling things. Perhaps we can stop any Ascenders from reaching the Summit next time, perhaps the next Zenith will be ours. What then? The Holy Orders will still be controlling the Maelir. Will we be able to survive another winter in order to gain another Zenith? Will we be truly able to say Zenith is ours?'

'You sound strange,' said Ahrai. 'You would have drawn your sword if any of us spoke these words before you left us.'

'I have learnt some things,' said Verlinden. 'I do feel that I have changed.'

'Grown weaker?' asked Saretha.

'I'll show you how weak I've grown when we've finished here,' said Verlinden, 'if that's what you want.'

The two glared at each other, unflinching.

'All right, Valkyra,' said Rhea. 'You are actually agreeing now with what I've been saying for some time. We haven't achieved what we set out to achieve.'

'Not yet,' said Verlinden, breaking eye contact with Saretha.

'How can you say not yet,' said one of the others, 'when you've just taken away our hope?'

'The Orders know that if they are ever going to wrench the Summit back from us, then it will take a long time and many more

Maelir will be killed.' Verlinden paused. 'The battle of Crosanct has no clear winner – no-one controls the Pass and from reports we have, there doesn't appear to be much chance of that changing. We each hold a prisoner – everything is in balance. Neither side can win.'

'What Faemir prisoner do they have?' asked Rhea.

'Verlinden. She is still alive. I saw her.'

'Most interesting,' said Rhea.

'You still haven't told us what you think we should do,' said Ahrai.

'This is why Atreu is here,' said Verlinden. 'He speaks for the Orders.'

Atreu got up and started to speak. 'We find ourselves in exactly the same position you find yourselves in. We have started to realise we might not be able to win this war, but we also know defeat is totally unacceptable.'

The stunned silence rapidly turned into howls of outrage.

'I'm not listening to this.' Saretha stood up and started to walk out. Several others also rose to their feet to follow her.

'What harm does it do to listen to him?' asked Verlinden, her mouth tight.

'Listening?' Saretha spat. 'That's what Faelen do. They always listen and obey their men. I've had enough of this Faelen talk.'

Verlinden felt the blood drain from her face. She knew she had to do something. Would the bluff work a second time? 'Don't go for your sword,' she said. 'I want to feel my hands on your bare throat.' She pushed her chair to the ground and took a step towards her opponent.

Perhaps Saretha had noted a lack of conviction, a slight hesitation – this time she didn't back down.

The others drew their breath. The Faelen slur was unforgivable.

To Verlinden's surprise, Rhea tried to dampen the conflict. 'This should be something we no longer do,' she said, standing up quickly. 'Remember that it was only when we united and stopped fighting among ourselves that we achieved anything.'

'You don't have to tell me about unity,' said Verlinden, desperately hoping her voice sounded steady. She knew that while she was a strong fighter, she was not a match for the aggressive Saretha. 'The only unity we've ever achieved is under my leadership.'

Saretha went into a battle crouch. 'Perhaps the time of your leadership has passed if all you ask us to do is listen like Faelen.'

Verlinden knew she had to do something or else all was lost. She let out a bloodcurdling cry and up-ended the table so that it crashed into the Faemir sitting opposite her. Then she too assumed a hand-to-hand battle crouch. She could see the fear in Saretha's eyes. No Faemir had even attempted to best Valkyra in combat for a long time, and her reputation was terrifying.

They circled each other. Verlinden prayed for her to back down, but she knew there was almost no chance. The humiliation would mean she was finished as battalion leader.

Then Rhea stepped in between the two. 'This is not getting us anywhere. Saretha, if you don't want to listen to the Maelir, get out. Anyone else can join her. I, for one, agree with Valkyra. There's no harm in listening. Are we afraid of words?'

Saretha straightened slightly. 'I have no fear of his words, I just have no time for them.'

'So what are you going to do with the time you save by not listening?' asked Rhea.

Saretha didn't answer.

Rhea addressed the others in the room. 'How many times have the Maelir bothered to send anyone to speak to us? Never. Don't you see, we have them on their knees. They are contemplating defeat. The fact that this Ascender is here is a sign of their weakness. Listening to him is not a weakness – what we do afterwards will determine our strength.'

Verlinden sensed the subtle power play behind Rhea's words.

The second-in-command was clearly trying to position herself as first, and her actions were aimed at getting her closer to that goal.

Well, it didn't matter what Rhea's aims were. To Verlinden's relief, Saretha backed down and watched in silence as the other Faemir righted the table. The battalion leader continued to stand while the others resumed their seats. She was refusing to take her place, but she remained in the room.

Verlinden motioned for Atreu to continue.

Atreu struggled for control. The threat to Verlinden had affected him. 'I thank all of you for your time. As I said, we believe both our peoples have come to an impasse. There must be a way out for Maelir and Faemir. We are willing to listen to any demands you have, and perhaps we can come to a solution which is acceptable to both peoples.'

'You want one of us to speak directly to the Orders?' asked Ahrai.

'Yes,' said Atreu.

'And what if our demand is Zenith?' asked one of the other battalion leaders.

'Then we will consider it.'

Loud shouting suddenly filled the room. 'You will actually consider giving us control of Zenith?' asked Ahrai, when the noise died down.

'You will concede defeat?' asked Kaithen.

'No,' said Atreu, 'but we will consider sharing Zenith with you.'

'Impossible,' said Saretha, who was still standing with her arms folded.

'No,' said Atreu, 'it is not impossible. I shared my Zenith with the sister of your leader here.'

'What?'

Verlinden waved the room into silence. 'It's true,' she said. 'I spoke to her while I was at the top of the pillar.'

'And they let Verlinden live?' asked Rhea, her eyes narrowing.

'Yes,' said Verlinden, suddenly feeling very uncomfortable. 'She's imprisoned, but she's alive.'

'So, sharing Zenith is possible,' said Atreu. 'Not every Holy Man is convinced it is desirable, but I know they can be persuaded if all of you decide it is what you want.'

'Sharing Zenith?' said Ahrai.

'Yes.'

Saretha said, 'I think we would be mad to even consider it.' The others turned towards her.

Verlinden glared at her. 'Are you at this conclave or not, Saretha? If you are, please sit down at the table like the rest of us.'

'I'll remain standing, and I'll choose to comment how I please.'

'Valkyra – what do you think we should do?' Verlinden again felt uncomfortable under Rhea's gaze. She knew this was the crucial part. If she appeared too enthusiastic about the plan then it would arouse suspicion, on the other hand hesitation was not one of Valkyra's character traits.

'I think we should be very careful in dealing with the Maelir,' she said. 'I have never trusted them and I still don't trust them.'

'That's the best thing I've heard you say since I walked into this room,' said Saretha.

'But,' continued Verlinden, trying desperately to find just the right words, 'if they give us a chance to speak to them, we should take it. I'm not entirely convinced that sharing Zenith is possible, or even if I want it, but we can only learn more about the possibilities if we are speaking to them.'

'We know our enemy already,' said Saretha. 'We know that he bleeds to death when his heart is pierced with a sword. We know he dies a slow, choking death when his lungs are punctured. We know his carcass stinks in the hot sun if it is left lying on the open plain after battle. What else do we need to know?'

'I can't see what we can hope to achieve,' said another Faemir. 'We would learn nothing if they killed whoever we send up to speak to them.'

'The Orders haven't killed Verlinden,' said Atreu. 'They obviously see her as a link with the Faemir that they don't wish to sever. If you allow me to return safely, they will honour any agreement.'

'Honour.' Saretha spat the word. 'There is only honour in battle.'

Rhea ignored her and said, 'So, Valkyra, you agree with him that Verlinden is capable of speaking to the Orders on our behalf?'

'She's the one who has taken part in Zenith. The only Faemir who's ever done so. Yes, she could speak.'

'But what does she know of our cause?' asked Ahrai. 'She is half Faelen. She's always been a Watcher, and she knows little of real battles.'

'Yes,' said another battalion leader, 'and we haven't even seen her since Crosanct.'

'I agree,' said Verlinden, 'that she cannot speak for us on her own. I am going to return and join her.'

'Why wouldn't the Orders have you killed?'

'Why didn't they have me killed the first time I went up there?'

'I'd be interested to hear the reason for that as well, Valkyra,' said Rhea. 'That's something you've told us very little about.'

Atreu jumped in before Verlinden could answer. 'She created havoc in the Keep,' he said quickly.

'The Keep?' said Rhea.

'Yes, that's what we call the place up there. She destroyed many of our buildings and killed dozens of windriders. We kept attacking her but no matter how exhausted she was, she continued to fight back. We had her backed into a corner but we couldn't defeat her. She couldn't break out but she also couldn't kill us all. In the end we decided to talk to each other.' He paused. 'That's what we have here on the Mountain – two sides who can't defeat each other, and the only way to resolve it is to start talking to each other to see if we can come to an agreement.'

'This is making me sick,' said Saretha.

'So, Valkyra, you're just going to go back up to the Keep with him, are you?' asked Rhea.

'They won't harm me,' said Verlinden.

Saretha spat. 'They won't harm you because they know you're now on their side.'

Atreu took a deep breath and steadied his voice. 'Look,' he said, 'we can start quite simply. We can't expect to begin trusting each other from the outset. The trust has to be earned a step at a time. First of all the Orders want a gesture of goodwill from you.'

'A gesture of what?' shouted Kaithen.

'Goodwill. To show both sides are serious about negotiation, we should have an exchange of prisoners. We have Verlinden imprisoned in the Keep while you have my brother Teyth here in the Hold. We could release our respective prisoners, and that would free Verlinden to return to negotiate with the Orders.'

'I'm totally confused,' said Kaithen. 'What would such an exchange achieve?'

'It would show we are prepared at least to begin to talk about cooperating,' said Verlinden.

'You agree with this?' asked Kaithen.

'Yes, Kaithen, I do. What do we have to lose? If we reach a point where we can't agree, then the battle continues.'

'We have everything to lose,' said Saretha. 'Time is on the Orders' side. We are the ones who could freeze or starve to death here during winter.'

'We could allow food and wood for fire through the Pass while our two peoples are negotiating,' replied Atreu.

'Why would you do that?' asked Kaithen.

'To show you we were serious about talking peace.'

'I see it now,' said Saretha suddenly. 'This is all a plan to rescue his brother.'

All eyes turned to her.

'Where is the fair exchange?' she continued. 'We've all heard the rumours about this Teyth. He's a baresark. Just think how much damage he could do once he's free.'

There was a murmur of assent.

'And what is Verlinden to us, anyway?' said Kaithen. 'She is one of our best Watchers, but we have little need of Watchers now. We need warriors.'

'I should know about baresarks,' said Verlinden quickly, knowing she was in danger of losing the ground she and Atreu had gained. 'He is a strong fighter, but he's no baresark.'

'Why are you so keen to release him?' asked Kaithen.

'I don't want to release him in particular. What I want is my sister returned to us.'

'Do you?' asked Saretha, sarcasm dripping from her tongue. 'So let me see if I have this right. You are going back up to this place they call the Keep with both Maelir, and we are expected to believe Verlinden will be released and will be allowed to speak for all Faemir?'

'This is an insane plan,' said Kaithen. 'I've heard enough.'

'The baresark has done something to you, Valkyra.' Saretha's face was flushed. 'We've all heard the rumours. He's weakened your mind and I think he's weakened your body as well. I'm not listening to your ridiculous arguments anymore.' She walked over to the corner to retrieve her sword.

Kaithen and several other battalion leaders stood up as well.

'Wait,' said Rhea. 'Valkyra has always been right in the past.'

Again Verlinden was slightly taken aback at Rhea's open support.

Saretha stopped as Rhea continued. 'Do I have to remind all of you that you have all opposed Valkyra at some point – and you've all been wrong.'

'But those were all battle plans,' said Kaithen.

'This is surrender,' said one of the other Faemir who had stood up.

'Why not just consider what has been said tonight?' said Rhea. 'I don't know if I agree with Valkyra but I'm going to think about it. Let us form another conclave in three days without the Maelir and make a decision.'

Verlinden knew Rhea was deliberately taking charge and the second-in-command's authority was growing as a consequence, but the course of action was the best she could hope for at the moment.

'So your decision isn't final, Valkyra?' asked Ahrai.

'I wanted to hear all your views,' said Verlinden.

'Talk, talk,' said Saretha. 'Since when do we spend so much time talking? I won't be back for the next conclave – you all know my views.' She shot a venomous glance at Verlinden. 'And don't rely on the support of my battalion for any of your plans.' She sheathed her sword and stormed out.

'This doesn't sound like war to me anymore,' said Kaithen. She collected her sword and also walked out, followed by three other battalion leaders.

Verlinden scanned the faces of those Faemir who remained. Apart from Rhea, she had no idea who would support her.

'We meet again in three days,' she said.

Chapter Fourteen

Valkyra smiled as she watched the thick, grey mist billowing past the cliff face. This was what she waiting for. The light snow reduced visibility even further, and she sensed now was the time. Though she was still clumsy with the wings, she felt her mastery was sufficient for what she had planned. If she was attacked in mid-air, she knew she was dead – but if everything went well, the windriders would have no idea what was happening until it was too late.

Moving through the cave, she quickly made one last check of all the straps to ensure that the blankets and weights were all securely tied. Valkyra drew several deep breaths. So much relied on speed and timing, and she knew she would have to draw on all her strength and stamina. She ran a finger along the scar on her leg which had fully healed – she was ready for battle.

Tensing every muscle in her body, she let out the cry which always energised her during combat. She grabbed the frame of the first set of wings and rushed outside onto the ledge. She tilted the frame, and allowed the wind to lift the wings. With an almighty force, she threw them out into the chill night air. The wings arced upwards for a brief moment and then the nose dipped and they soared down into the grey mist.

Without catching her breath, Valkyra raced back in and grabbed another and returned to the edge to launch a second set of wings. She had no time to watch its progress because she ran back into the cavern for a third.

Again and again, Valkyra launched wings into the billowing mist, confident that each one would draw more windriders in pursuit. Because of the poor visibility, the riders would never be sure which one she was strapped into until they flew close – and that would buy her the time she needed.

Valkyra's shoulders ached, but she redoubled her efforts. Time after time, she returned to the edge and threw yet another set over. And with each one her strength grew – she ran faster and the wings soared further away from the pillar before the nose dipped towards the ground.

And when the last one disappeared into the mist and Valkyra was bathed in sweat, she ran back into the cavern, out into the tunnels, up several flights of stone stairs and into the room which contained the set of wings she was going to use.

She strapped herself in and raced out onto the ledge which was well above the one where she had launched the others.

Without hesitating, she tilted the nose upwards and ran off the edge. She felt the rush of wind under her wings and a surge of power coursed through her body.

Always the unexpected, she thought, that had been why she was so successful in battle. She swung the nose so that she could use the full force of the updraught. Let those stupid windriders attack one set of blankets after the other. Who would be expecting her to go *up*?

She smiled as the grey mist raced silently past her ears.

*

'You know, little brother, one day they're simply not going to let you out. Then you'll be trapped in here like me.'

Atreu paced up and down in the cell. 'I'd have to say, Teyth, that it's not going as well as I thought it would. I don't think the Faemir are ready for peace.'

'And you think we are?'

'But it all makes so much sense to me. Maelir and Faemir sharing Zenith. The twins of life brought together.'

'I'm just glad we are together now, Atreu. With every visit, I can feel my mind clearing. I've been a mess since the last Zenith. It was like a fever had taken hold of me.'

'You were a mess during most of Zenith as well. Can you remember?'

'When I look back, it's like I was looking through the thickest of snowstorms, Atreu. All the details are gone, and all I can remember is endlessly fighting Faemir after Faemir.'

'Do you remember your last Zenith?'

Teyth frowned. 'No, not really. Why? Did I tell you about it?'

'No ... I ... I don't really know. You must have. You finally found out who it was you were protecting while you were fighting the Faemir.'

'I ... can't remember – yes, I can. It was Verlinden, wasn't it?'

'Does that tell you anything?'

Before Teyth could answer, a low rumbling sound echoed through the walls of the room and the ground started shaking.

Atreu steadied himself until it stopped. 'I don't remember ever feeling any instability in the Hold,' he said.

'That's the first time I've felt anything in here,' said Teyth.

'I don't like the look of this.' Atreu knelt down and examined the stone floor.

'What is it?'

'Cracks – they're very fine. You have to get really close ... but here, have a look.'

Teyth crouched down next to his brother. 'Do you remember the first day of our Ascent, when you tried to walk the pattern and fell into that chasm?'

'Yes, of course I do.'

'Well, little brother, I hope your technique has improved since then, because you may need it.'

*

Saretha looked up as Ahrai walked through the door. 'What do you want?' she snarled.

'What sort of greeting is that for a fellow battalion leader?'

'I'm not listening to any more talk of peace and negotiating. If Valkyra no longer has the stomach for war, then I want nothing more to do with her. I'm going to take those who support me and we'll continue the battle. Anyone else is my enemy. That's the way it's always been with me, and that's the way it always should be with the Faemir.'

'How do you know what I think?' asked Ahrai.

'You didn't walk out with me during the conclave, and you're going to the next one tonight.'

'I like to know what the enemy is thinking.'

'A dead enemy doesn't think much.'

'Listen, Saretha, I agree that Valkyra has gone mad.'

'I didn't hear you argue very strongly against her madness.'

'No, but I'll tell you why. How do you think it has been possible that, after hundreds of generations, we have been able to take control of the Summit in one year? I agree it's been Valkyra who has brought us together. But it's our unity which has given us power. When the different coveyns simply organised their own separate raids, we were nothing.'

'What are you telling me?'

'I'm telling you we need to stay unified,' said Ahrai. 'Nothing will happen if you take your supporters away and go your own direction.'

'I'm not going to support Valkyra.'

'Neither am I.'

'What?'

'I'm going to support Rhea.'

Saretha spat on the ground. 'Rhea's always backed Valkyra. Weren't you listening to what she said at the conclave? They're both mad.'

'Don't be too hasty in your judgements, Saretha. The two things we need for success are unity and strong leadership. Right?'

'Of course, but if the leader has gone insane and is consorting with Maelir and talking peace, then I can't follow that leader.'

'Rhea wants war.'

'How do you know?'

'She's told me. She would have told you, but you've refused to see her or Valkyra.'

'What was all that talk about listening and thinking?'

'She knows unity is important. Listen, Saretha.' Ahrai stepped closer and lowered her voice. 'Rhea is going to challenge Valkyra at the meeting tonight.'

'What?'

'She will only do it if she knows that as leader she will have the full support of all the battalion leaders. There would be no point otherwise.'

'You can't be serious, Ahrai. If Rhea could best Valkyra in combat, she would have done it a long time ago. We've all seen Valkyra in action – she would destroy any of us.'

'Yet, you were set to fight her.'

'I was angry. I wasn't thinking. It was stupid of me and I couldn't back down. There would be no way I would ever plan to challenge her. If Rhea is seriously thinking of challenging Valkyra, it sounds to me as if Rhea must be going mad as well.'

'Rhea knows Valkyra better than any of us. She was the only one of us to ever lead her.'

'Yes, when she was a young girl.'

'Nevertheless, she has knowledge of certain weaknesses which Valkyra keeps hidden.'

'What weaknesses?'

Ahrai rubbed the scarred hole in her right palm. 'I have some idea, but Rhea wants to keep it to herself for the moment.'

'So why hasn't Rhea used these weaknesses before?'

'The time hasn't been right. She realises how important unity is to the Faemir. She needs the support of all the battalion leaders.'

'So you want me at the meeting?'

'Yes.'

'And Rhea promises she will forget all this talk about peace, and the war will continue if she is successful?'

'Yes.'

Saretha thought for a moment. 'Then I'll be there,' she said finally.

The two Faemir reached for support as the ground started trembling underneath them.

*

Verlinden made slow progress through the deep snow. A thin, grey mist had descended and she knew it would make her task more difficult, but she was thankful that she was protected from the prying eyes of too many of the Faemir warriors. She knew no-one would question the fact that she was walking outside alone at night, but she also knew many of them were looking at her curiously. She had relied totally on Valkyra's fearsome reputation and bluff since returning to the Hold, and she suspected it might soon wear thin.

When she and Teyth had agreed on the hiding place for Atreu's Book, they had anticipated that it might have to be retrieved under less than ideal circumstances. The snowfall since then would also increase the difficulties of her task. She only hoped that not enough snow had yet fallen to completely cover the rocks which they used as their orientation.

She heard a deep rumble somewhere behind her, followed by the crashing sound of an avalanche of snow. She shuddered as she remembered what it was like to be buried alive. The instability seemed to have increased drastically as the day progressed.

What was that? As a Watcher, Verlinden was used to moving

silently while listening for signs of others around her, but the conditions tested her skills. The mist seemed to muffle and distort all the sounds, so she couldn't be sure if what she heard was footsteps or simply a sheet of falling snow.

She scrambled over a large mound which was only barely recognisable from the last time she had been there. The light fall of snow made it hard to see as she searched for the outcrops of exposed rock.

Verlinden was beginning to think that she was in the wrong place when she saw a small dark outcrop to her right.

She trudged over and removed some snow from around its base. This was one of the outcrops all right. She was thankful she hadn't waited any longer to retrieve the Book. It was obvious it was only a matter of a few more snow showers and the outcrop would have been totally buried.

She strained to see the others, and finally she focused on the two dark rocks barely jutting out past the snowline.

Using her outstretched arms, she judged the midpoint between the two rocks in the distance. She began walking, taking slow, measured steps and counting silently to herself. When she had reached thirty, she stopped and looked around. Was there anyone there? Perhaps she had been imprisoned so long that her senses could no longer be trusted. There was no sign of anyone, but the mist was thickening and the visibility deteriorating.

She got down onto her knees and started digging. This was going to be much harder than when she and Teyth buried the Book – she had to do it alone this time and the snowline was considerably higher. She scooped out large armfuls of soft snow and piled it up around the hole she was digging.

It was easy at first but gradually the snow became more icy. Her hands turned numb but she continued to dig her fingers in. When the ice became too hard and she found she could no longer penetrate it with her bare hands, she took out her knife and continued.

There still was no sign of the Book. Could she have made a

mistake somehow? Impossible – the markers were a clear guide. The ice was now so hard that the knife was ineffective.

Verlinden reached back for the battle-axe, when the earth suddenly shook. A wave of panic swept through her as some of the snow she had piled up above her fell down. She shook her head, surprised she could still breathe, and the snow which had been trapped in her hair fell to the ground.

Although the amount of snow which had fallen on her was small, her fear of being buried alive hit her with full impact. She looked up past the lip of the hole she was digging and felt a sudden urge to climb out.

What was she doing here? She didn't have to find Atreu's Book. It made no difference to her.

Verlinden closed her eyes and fought the urge to climb out. She remembered a river of white washing over her. She remembered the thick, pale sludge blotting her face and entering her lungs. She remembered the whiteness turning black.

Then she remembered Atreu's soft lips on hers and his breaths filling her body – and a calm washing over her.

She cleared away the snow that had just fallen and reached for the axe to continue digging.

Chunks of ice broke away easily under the impact of the battle-axe. As each block was separated, she flung it out of the hole.

She must be getting close. Another swing of the axe and ... there was a dull thud. She knelt down and pushed away the ice.

There was the Book.

She reached down and touched the capital A on the cover. To her dismay, she then noticed the axe had sliced off a corner.

She ran her fingers along the cut edge. Thank goodness it was only small. Hopefully none of the writing inside had been cut off.

She opened the Book and scanned some of the pages. It didn't appear as if she had removed any of the words.

Her attention was caught by the name *Valkyra*.

She stared at the word for a moment, unable to believe it was there. She tried to read what followed the name, but the mist seemed to make the letters swim together.

Verlinden blinked and suddenly the mist started to clear. She felt a tingling sensation behind her eyes. What was happening here? The letters stopped swimming and started to form words. She became aware of someone at the lip of the hole. She glanced up and thought for a moment that she could see the face of an old Maelir, but then was certain it was only the mist playing tricks.

She looked down at the Book once more, and it was as if all the mist between her eyes and the page had disappeared.

She found the name Valkyra again and started to read.

*

Valkyra stayed as close as she could to the cliff face. It became increasingly obvious to her as she continued her flight that her prison had been nowhere near the top of the pillar. She scanned the vertical face for ledges and openings, but there were none. No matter – there were no signs of any windriders, and as long as the updraughts continued, she would make it to the top.

She knew that from the very beginning all the Maelir had ever done was run away from her. They had never been able to stop her – and now they would have nowhere to run to.

*

Verlinden's eyes drifted off the page for a moment. How could she be reading what she was reading? So this was what Atreu had experienced. She felt suddenly dizzy. Was this true? Had Valkyra escaped? The implications of the answers made her feel ill. No wonder the Orders were so keen for her to retrieve this book.

She looked down at the page again: *Valkyra stayed as close as she could to the cliff face ...*

When was this happening? Was it happening now? Did it happen yesterday? She shuddered – was it going to happen tomorrow? Was Atreu's Book able to tell the future? Verlinden flicked through the next few pages trying to read what else it said, but none of the words made sense. She looked further towards the back of the Book but the pages were all blank.

She turned back to where she had been reading: *They had never been able to stop her – and now they would have nowhere to run to.*

She looked at the next line. It was blank, and the one after that read: *Verlinden's eyes drifted off the page for a moment. How could she be reading what she was reading?*

Verlinden steadied herself on the wall of ice she had created. She was part of the story. She struggled for air as the words imprinted themselves on her mind. She was part of the story. Right now. What she was doing, perhaps even what she was thinking, right now, could be read.

A voice cut through the turmoil of her thoughts. She looked up to see a face staring at her from over the edge of the hole. The sharp sting of recognition hit her like an arrow piercing flesh.

It was Rhea.

'Can I help you up?' she asked again.

Verlinden instinctively closed the Book.

'Come on,' said Rhea, 'it's not going to be easy to get out of there yourself.'

Verlinden looked at Rhea's hand as she reached down for her. Something told her she couldn't be trusted. And yet ... and yet her face was open, the palm of her hand was up. From what she knew of her, she had been a loyal second-in-command ever since Valkyra had assumed leadership of the coveyn.

She tucked the Book under her coat, reached out to grasp Rhea's hand, and allowed herself to be pulled out of the hole.

'What are you doing here, Rhea?' Verlinden brushed snow from her legs.

'I might ask you the same question,' said Rhea.

'Why did you follow me?'

'You haven't been entirely honest with me since you returned, have you?'

Verlinden stared at her. 'What do you mean?'

'We've known each other a long time,' said Rhea. She pointed to the bulge in Verlinden's coat. 'What's in the book?'

'Don't question what I'm doing, Rhea. I'll explain it to you in good time.' Verlinden tried desperately to assert her authority but she knew her words rang hollow.

'It must be an important book,' said Rhea, 'for it to have been buried so deeply.'

'It's important to me, yes. But can we continue this conversation inside. The snowfall seems to be getting heavier.'

'All right – we'll continue our discussion inside if you want. You seem to want to do a lot of talking since you came back, Valkyra. Or would you prefer me to call you Verlinden?'

'What?' Verlinden felt suddenly cold.

'I just asked you what you preferred to be called.'

Verlinden tried to compose herself. 'You've gone mad, Rhea.'

Rhea smiled. 'As I said, we've known each other a long time. What has it been? Nine, ten years since we found you in that village? A lot of things changed for all of us on that day, didn't they?'

Verlinden stood tight-lipped as Rhea continued. 'That was the day Valkyra effectively took control of the coveyn from me. It was the day her twin Faelen sister was admitted into the coveyn despite her age. It was the day that led to the two of us standing here.'

'You must have some sort of fever, Rhea. Let's go back and you can lie down.'

'I could expose you so easily, Verlinden. I could have from the very first day. It didn't take me long to work it out.'

Verlinden's heart raced as the tone in Rhea's voice acquired an increasing edge. 'Tell me about our battle strategy at Ariathe. How did we manage to overrun the city so quickly? And Rathsheed – what was our strategy there? You must remember. It was your strategy ... wasn't it?'

Verlinden's shoulders slumped. 'You knew from the first day that I wasn't Valkyra?'

'Yes – I know Valkyra and the way her mind works better than anyone. The two of you may be impossible to tell apart physically, but the things you were doing and saying, they were nothing like Valkyra. And there's something that Valkyra gives off that you just don't have.'

'Does anyone else know?'

'Ahrai does, but we are the only two leaders to have known both of you so well. The others sense you're not the same person you were, but they simply think you've gone mad.'

'What are you going to do?'

'I'm not going to expose you. If I had wanted to expose you, Verlinden, I would have already done it. I've supported you, haven't I? In the conclave. You were in a great deal of trouble there, weren't you?'

Verlinden eyed her curiously. 'Why did you support me?'

'I want peace, Verlinden. Just like you. We've brought the Maelir to the point where they have to bargain with us. Why have any more killing if they are going to give us what we want?'

'You've never argued that before.'

'We've never been in this position before. And Valkyra has always preached war and more war. With her gone, we now have the freedom to direct the Faemir in our own way. The others will follow you if you have my support.' She hesitated for a moment. 'By the way, where is Valkyra?'

Verlinden pressed her hand against the bulge of the Book. 'The windriders imprisoned her. They couldn't kill her, but she's now trapped in a place she'll never get out of.'

'Are you absolutely certain of that?'

'Yes,' said Verlinden. 'She won't be back to interfere with our plans for peace.'

'Good,' said Rhea. 'I've persuaded Saretha and the others who walked out of our last conclave to attend the one tonight.'

'How did you manage that?'

'I can be very persuasive – which is why I think with your

authority and my persuasiveness we can achieve what we both want to achieve.'

Verlinden nodded. 'So we are fortunate we have the same aims.'

'Now, let's get to this meeting.'

Rhea gestured palm up for Verlinden to start heading back to the Hold.

*

Another shock ran through the floor.

'Are the cracks any larger?' asked Teyth.

'Yes – a little,' said Atreu. 'I think we're a long way from having a chasm right here in the Hold, but who knows what will happen if the impermanence continues.'

'Tell me some more about the Keep.'

'Teyth, do you remember that game we used to always play when we were children?'

'When we used to blindfold each other and – '

'No, not that one. The one where each of us pretended we could see the Summit, and we tried to convince each other that we actually could.'

'It was a silly game, wasn't it?'

'You only decided it was silly when you realised you couldn't win, remember?'

'No-one could win – I couldn't see the point after a while.' He laughed. 'Isn't it funny how things work out? You've seen the true Summit and I haven't. You, who were never interested in winning or losing, succeeded on your Ascent, and I failed.'

'That's not true, Teyth. You haven't failed until you've been judged by the Circle – and they're going to judge you now.'

'If I ever get out of here.'

'Verlinden and I will get you out.'

'I'll wait until I see it.'

'Don't feel too sorry for yourself, Teyth. I haven't succeeded in my Ascent either. Neither have any of the others, as far as I know.'

'How is that possible?'

'The final decisions are made at Equinox.'

'At Equinox?' Teyth sat down on his bed. 'It looks like you've got a lot to tell me. The Keep, Equinox – all of these things I know nothing about.'

'The Keep is easy to describe,' said Atreu. 'Remember how I used to describe the Summit as a glorious city with spires of silver?'

'Yes, I do.'

'Well, that's exactly what it's like. It's almost as if I had made it exist by pretending it was real.'

'You also said some funny things about dreams just after the last Zenith, from what I can remember.'

'Yes,' said Atreu. 'It's the same thing. Since I started my Ascent, my dreams ... well they've been real, if that makes any sense.'

'It doesn't, little brother, but I still like you around even if you talk nonsense. I've been feeling so much better since you arrived.' He put his hand on Atreu's shoulder.

Another tremor shook the room, and they both watched as the cracks in the floor widened.

Atreu headed towards the door. 'I'm going to find out how widespread this instability is. They can't keep you in a room which could collapse into a chasm at any moment.'

He knocked on the door. 'This is Atreu. I wish to be let out now.'

There was no reply.

Atreu knocked again, louder this time. 'Is anyone there? I said, this is Atreu – I wish to be let out.'

The voice of a Faemir finally answered. 'My instructions are that you remain there.'

Atreu stared at Teyth, open-mouthed.

'Well, little brother,' said Teyth. 'It looks like you've got a lot of time to tell me everything you know.'

Chapter Fifteen

Valkyra's wings caught another updraught, and suddenly she found herself under a crystal clear night sky. The stars shone like the brightest of torchlights, and her lungs breathed in the crisp, acid air. She looked down and saw the lake of motionless grey mist below her. And all around her was silence, the delicious silence of a conquered foe. The all-encompassing mist had been slowly deadening her senses, but now every nerve suddenly sprang to life. Her eyes followed the cliff face as she continued to ascend, until finally they came to rest.

She could see the top of the cliff.

And still the updraughts pushed her higher. This was it, she thought, this was the Summit. This was the pinnacle, and now she was going to be the first Faemir to see it.

One more sudden rush and she raced past the pillar's lip. And her senses swarmed. She stared in awe at the magnificence of the city below. So many lights – even more than there were in the heavens above her. Shining, glowing, flickering, reaching out to join their sisters in the sky.

Valkyra flew over the dark buildings on the periphery towards the glowing heart of the city. Rathsheed, R'in, Spa, even the mighty city of Ariathe had been nothing compared to this. She had viewed them simply as an impediment to her path, something to be destroyed because it was in the way. But this city, this was different. The others had been mere shadows of what she saw before her. This was the final prize. She knew now that she didn't want to destroy it, she knew she had to own it, to take possession for the Faemir.

She tensed as she spied three windriders soaring past a spire to her right. Her hand went down towards her sword as she watched and waited for their attack. But nothing happened. They simply continued on their flight path.

Valkyra laughed. They think I'm a windrider. No-one expects me to be here. There must be a whole army of windriders searching for me below, and here I am. This place will barely be guarded. I'll be able to claim it on my own.

She tilted her wings so she could get a closer look at one of the towers, a shining pillar of silver and glass. Below, she saw a lacework of bridges which seemed to flash in and out of view like fragile ghosts. To her right, a series of arches, one piled upon the other, all encrusted with glimmerstones and precious gems of every imaginable colour. To her left, a long row of giant, slender obelisks, tapering to the sharpest of points.

It took her a moment to realise she had been struck by a volley of arrows.

She looked at the two arrows now embedded in her arm in disbelief. The first pain to register was in her shoulders. She glanced back and saw with horror that five more arrows had pierced her armour.

A wild rage unlike any other she had ever experienced suddenly consumed her. She shifted her body weight so that she would move quickly to the right. Her timing was fortunate as she heard another volley of arrows whistle past her.

She looked down in the direction they had come and saw a formation of nine windriders hovering just above the flat roofs of a line of buildings. Their bows were again aimed in her direction.

She tilted the wings, but they were sluggish to respond. One of the next volley of arrows hit her side, again piercing the leather work of her armour. *Damn.* She looked up at the frame and saw the material had now been slashed a dozen times and shreds trailed in the wind. No wonder the wings weren't responding too well. There was no way she was going to be able to manoeuvre quickly enough to avoid the arrows.

She was bleeding now, but as each drop of blood escaped her veins, she grew stronger. Always the unexpected. She drew her sword and dipped the nose of the wings so that she was plummeting directly towards the windriders.

When the next volley of arrows came at her, she flashed her sword with lightning speed, blocking most of them in mid-air. One pierced the wing material, but it didn't matter now – her course was set.

The riders took aim and shot again. Valkyra again managed to block all but one, which took a small piece of her thigh with it as it shot past.

The windriders were loading their bows again when she was close enough to see they were now fumbling with their arrows. By the time they had taken aim, she could see the raw fear on their faces. None of the arrows were fired. They scattered like a flock of frightened birds just before she arrived at the spot where they had been hovering above the building.

Valkyra didn't look back. She no longer had enough control of her wings to do anything but continue her descent. She was vaguely aware of more arrows coming at her from all directions, but if any of them hit her, she didn't feel it.

It was only just as she touched down on one of the flat roofs that she felt any pain at all. Her legs screamed as she demanded them to bear her weight.

She quickly unstrapped the harness and tried to run to the roof's edge, but her legs wouldn't move with the speed she was used to. She felt another arrow tear the flesh of her calf muscle, and she turned to face the riders who now hovered dangerously close.

She flashed her sword at the next volley of arrows and somehow managed to block those which would have hit their mark.

'Cowards!' she cried, waving her fist at them as they reloaded their bows 'Come down here and fight me.'

Valkyra dived and rolled out of the way of the next volley of arrows, but barely managed to get to her feet again. By rolling, she had accidentally forced some of the arrows sticking out of her legs even deeper into her flesh.

Leaving a trail of blood behind her, she staggered to the edge of the roof. She looked at the ground below and was about to jump, when a sharp pain hit her at the base of her spine and the lights of the Keep went out.

*

The twelve battalion leaders were already seated when Verlinden and Rhea entered the room. Rhea put her sword in the corner with the other weapons, and then held out her hand to indicate Verlinden should give her the battle-axe.

Verlinden hesitated. She knew the convention applied to Valkyra as well, and the battle-axe wasn't much use to her as a weapon anyway, but Rhea's gesture indicated a subtle shift in the power balance between the two.

Ultimately, though, she had no choice. She couldn't realistically talk peace while she was the only one in the room to keep possession of her weapon. She gave the axe to Rhea and the second-in-command sat it blade down in the corner.

Verlinden took her place. 'I hope all of you have given good thought to what I said during the last meeting.' She scanned the faces of the battalion leaders. Her eyes locked on Saretha's for a moment, but it was impossible to tell what she was thinking.

A shock wave hit them before anyone could speak and the chamber quaked beneath their feet.

After it had subsided, Rhea looked around anxiously. 'This damned instability has followed us up the Mountain.'

'Has anyone seen how much damage has been done in the eastern caverns?' asked one of the other leaders.

'Can we discuss the instability later?' said Verlinden. 'We have more important matters to talk about here.'

'Valkyra's right,' said Ahrai. 'We've been coping with impermanence all the time. Our battle plans have often worked around it – you all know we've even used it for our purposes on occasion. Let's not worry about it now.'

'Oh yes, I remember now why we're here,' said Saretha, her voice laden with sarcasm. 'Valkyra wants us to talk about surrendering.'

'I want us to talk about peace. I believe Atreu means what he says about the Maelir,' said Verlinden.

Saretha nodded slowly. 'I'm sure you do, Valkyra, I'm sure you do. You must know him well by now.' She slapped her palm on the table and glared at her. 'Perhaps as well as you know his brother.'

'What are you implying?' demanded Verlinden.

Saretha sneered. 'It's no secret that you spent a great deal of time with the other one before you left.' She drew closer to Verlinden. 'Are they truly *identical* twins?'

'Right,' said Rhea, 'that's enough. We need to make some decisions here.'

'Surrender or war,' said Saretha. 'The decision is simple.'

'All I'm suggesting,' said Verlinden, 'is that we try to negotiate with the Maelir. If they give no ground, then we continue the war – as long as there is no other option.'

'I believe we should negotiate,' said Rhea.

'What?' Saretha stared at her and then across at Ahrai.

'Let me finish,' said Rhea. 'We should negotiate, find out what we can from them, and then use what we've found out to destroy them.'

'That's not what I'm – ' Verlinden was shocked when Rhea interrupted her and motioned her to be silent.

'Think about this,' said Rhea. 'We know nothing of what they have up there. They know our situation down here. We gain an advantage if speak to them because we have everything to learn. We're fighting and planning blind at the moment. That's the problem. We need to know the physical layout of this place they call the Keep. We need to know the Orders' strengths and their weaknesses. And we need to put them off guard. When that happens, we pounce and finish them.'

'Yes,' said Ahrai, 'let them allow food and wood through Crosanct for us, if they're stupid enough to do it.'

There was a murmur of agreement and even Saretha was starting to smile.

'Wait,' said Verlinden. 'There is no fairness or honour in such a plan. We need to at least assume there is a chance we can negotiate peace.'

Rhea looked at her with her eyebrows raised. 'Do you mean, Valkyra, that this has not been your plan all along?'

'No, of course not.'

Rhea frowned. 'I had assumed that it was what you had in mind from the very beginning.'

'How could you assume that?'

'You wouldn't have revealed your strategy in front of the Maelir – and you always seemed to be with him.'

Verlinden looked around at the faces in front of her. 'I meant what I said. I believe we can share Zenith with the Maelir.'

Rhea said, 'I didn't think you could be so stupid.'

A low rumble echoed through the room as Verlinden and Rhea glared at each other.

Verlinden suddenly felt as if her lungs couldn't take in enough air. So this was her game. Rhea was seizing her chance to take leadership of the Faemir. No risk, maximum benefit.

'Let's talk about this,' said Verlinden, but her voice sounded thin and faint.

'You really believe we should end our war?' asked Rhea.

'I think –'

'You're not thinking at all, Valkyra. What happened to you up there? They've turned you into a Faelen.'

The battalion leaders all tensed at the sound of the word. There was no turning back from such an insult. This was a real challenge to their leader's authority.

Verlinden slowly stood up, desperately trying to control the trembling in her legs. Rhea had her – there was no way she could bluff the second-in-command. She was trapped.

Rhea got up and moved to the open space away from the table. 'You're no longer fit to lead us, Valkyra.'

Verlinden's jaw tightened. 'Who supports me here?'

As she looked at the faces around her, she saw no response. The Faemir were still a long way from talking peace.

Verlinden tried desperately to put some authority in her voice. 'Anyone who fails to support me now will be dealt with later.'

Saretha was smiling. 'The challenge is there,' she said. 'I for one will only think about supporting you once you are again our unchallenged leader.'

Verlinden knew she had no choice but to fight. She moved away from the table and assumed a battle crouch. Sucking in a deep breath, she readied herself. Although Rhea had relied considerably on Valkyra's influence to reach where she was in the chain of command, she was a fearsome fighter. And Verlinden knew she had only the slimmest of chances of defeating her in hand-to-hand combat.

Then another shock wave hit and they were both knocked from their feet.

The two Faemir jumped to their feet quickly and resumed the crouch, but Verlinden saw a slight hesitation on her opponent's part. Rhea hated instability – everyone knew that. One advantage Valkyra had always had over her was that she could use the Mountain's instability for her own ends. Perhaps Verlinden could now do the same.

Rhea lunged at her, but Verlinden skipped away. As a Watcher, she was quick and light on her feet. She could probably avoid serious contact for some time – but that would not win the challenge for her.

Rhea charged straight at her and Verlinden only just managed to step away.

'You're fighting like a Watcher,' cried Saretha.

Verlinden ignored her as Rhea came at her again. As she stepped aside, the ground shook violently underneath her. She managed to regain her footing quickly but Rhea now lay sprawled on the floor.

Without hesitating, Verlinden seized her chance and jumped on the still-startled Rhea. She pressed her forearm into the back of Rhea's neck, pinning her face down to the ground.

Verlinden was about to speak when another shock wave reverberated through the chamber – but this time it wouldn't stop. Instead of dying, it increased in intensity, growing ever more violent.

There was a crashing sound in the distance, and Verlinden tensed as it came closer. Even though she had braced herself for the final impact, the force of the tremor was unlike any she had experienced. It was as if a gale-force wind of solid rock struck her, and she was thrown clear.

Then everything came crashing down around her. Chairs and bodies flew through the air as the room convulsed like an animal in its death throes. She heard screams and shouts in a welter of panic. The image of Atreu's face flashed in front of her eyes, his expression one of utter terror.

Then there was nothing.

*

'So the baresark is alive?' Leyvin addressed Riell, who was standing in the middle of the Circle.

'Yes,' said Riell, 'but only just. We have taken her to the Halls of Healing.'

'Have you taken leave of your senses?' asked Lythos. 'How much more damage do you want her to do?'

'If she's not conscious then she can't be too much of a threat,' said one of the Felsen.

'She's lost a good deal of blood,' said Riell. 'The last arrow was from such a close range that it pierced her armour and hit deep into her lower back. I don't know what sort of damage that will do, but baresark or not, she's not going anywhere right now.'

'We have to kill her while we can,' said Lythos.

'Need I remind all of you of the covenant between the guild of windriders and the Holy Orders?' said Riell.

'This is an exception,' said Lythos. 'This is one prisoner we must kill.'

Several others voiced their approval.

'There are no exceptions to the covenant,' said Riell. 'The guild doesn't kill prisoners. If we start breaking that tenet then the entire covenant falls apart.'

'Why didn't you kill her in battle?' asked a Liche.

'We tried – she must have taken a dozen arrows.'

'Is she invincible?' asked a thin, stooped Felsen.

'No,' said Riell. 'We could finish her off now. She's not in a fit state to fight.'

'And we're healing her?' asked the Felsen.

'Yes,' said Riell, 'but she may still die from the wounds we inflicted.'

'And that would save your sense of honour?'

'Without our sense of honour, we have nothing,' said Riell. 'And may I say, without our covenant with the Orders all of you would have nothing. If it wasn't for the windriders, the Faemir would now have Zenith as well as the Summit.'

'Riell is right,' said Leyvin. 'To make only one exception to the covenant is to destroy it completely.' He addressed Riell. 'How securely is she guarded – one thing we have learnt is that she has remarkable powers of recuperation.'

'Even if she recovers, there is no way she will ever be at full strength again,' said Riell. 'Nonetheless, the door to the room we have her in is double barred and heavily guarded. Any healers who see her will also be guarded.'

'I can't believe this,' said Lythos. 'The only Faemir to ever see the Keep and the most dangerous woman we've ever experienced, and we're healing her. If the windriders won't do it, I'll put the knife in myself to finish her off.'

'We couldn't allow that,' said Riell.

'Couldn't allow it?' spluttered Lythos. 'Who gives the orders here?'

'The Holy Orders do,' said Riell calmly, 'except in matters directly related to our covenant. We cannot kill prisoners or allow them to be killed. It is quite simple.'

There was a silence. 'Thank you, Riell,' said Leyvin. 'You may leave the Circle now.'

After Riell left the room, Leyvin addressed Praether. 'You've been strangely silent through that report.'

Praether suspected what was about to come. 'I agree with your position on this matter, First Speaker,' he said. 'As, I assume, do all the others – judging by the lack of protest.'

'That's not what I meant, Liche Praether. I want to know why you didn't warn us of Valkyra's escape.'

'The Book is no longer as clear to me as it once was,' said Praether, feeling the subtle menace in Leyvin's voice.

'How clear is it?'

Praether knew he was in trouble. The Circle had always been a place of truth. You always spoke what you believed and the Circle as a whole sat in judgement. He had occasionally seen an attempt at deception during his long years in the Circle, but none of them had ever been successful.

'I can no longer read the Book,' said Praether. 'Since Atreu left for the Hold, the words have grown unclear for me, and now I see only the words of Maelur again.'

'We have met many times since Ascender Atreu left us. When exactly did you lose the ability to read the Book, Liche Praether?'

Praether swallowed and immediately started to cough. When he finished, he said, 'The day after he left.'

'Do you realise you placed the entire Keep at risk by your deception?'

'I don't think that is entirely fair.'

'Fair? We had no idea of the baresark's plans.'

'I told you she believed she had found a way to escape.'

'But I, for one, was relying on your knowledge to tell us when her escape was imminent. Because you pretended to have knowledge you didn't possess, you have placed us all in the gravest danger.'

Praether was overcome by another coughing fit. 'I ... I never claimed to have read anything that I didn't actually read.'

'Misleading the Circle by deliberate omission is the same as misleading by a direct lie.'

Praether knew his fortunes had just sunk. How could he have been so stupid? All that power after so many years of impotence had gone to his head. And now the Book had led him to the brink of his downfall. How was this possible? He closed his eyes and waited for the words.

'I name you, Liche Praether.'

'I challenge the naming, First Speaker,' said Praether, without looking Leyvin in the eye. He was going through the motions – he knew there was no hope.

They both got up and walked out of the room. Once outside, Praether followed Leyvin to the chairs pushed up against the wall.

Leyvin waved the arch-librer away. 'Don't talk to me, Praether. You're finished this time.'

'I'll be able to read the Book again when Atreu returns. You'll need my advice then.'

'Atreu won't be returning.'

'What?'

'You really are too old for all of this, Praether. Go back to your dust-covered librum.'

'How can you say Atreu won't be returning?'

'You understand nothing about our enemy, Praether. They are not like our windriders – they have no conscience, no humane covenant. You've been blinded by your desire to get hold of Atreu's Book. Atreu has almost no chance of returning from the Hold alive.'

'And you let him go.'

'No, Praether,' said Leyvin, 'you argued the case so well that the Circle agreed to let him go. You've sacrificed him for a book.'

Praether buried his head into his hands. 'What have I done? Could I have been so wrong?'

'It no longer matters whether you are right or wrong, Praether. Once you have been expelled from the Circle, your opinion will no longer matter.'

Praether looked up to see Leyvin's cold, dark stare boring into him. 'You're wrong,' he said. 'You have to be wrong.'

They sat there in silence until the doors opened and they were beckoned back in.

Both went to their chairs and stood behind them, unable to take a seat until the judgement was passed.

The Second Speaker, Holthim, shuffled uncomfortably in his chair. 'We realise,' the Felsen began, 'that the outcome of judgements of namings should not play a part in the judgement process. However, it was difficult to ignore the fact that one decision will end Leyvin's tenure as First Speaker, while the other will mean the expulsion of Liche Praether from the Circle. In the end, I hope we have, as always, been as dispassionate as possible and have ensured our judgement is based on clarity of thought.' He paused for a breath and Praether knew from the way Holthim avoided looking at him that he was finished.

As Holthim was about to continue, a faint tremor shook the Circle. Praether had little trouble keeping his balance, but after the shock wave passed, he looked around in amazement.

Everyone was stunned – not by the physical impact, but by the fact that the tremor had happened at all in the Keep, where no instability had ever been felt.

'We are no longer safe,' cried one of the Felsen monks, and suddenly the room was filled with a cacophony of panic-stricken voices.

Leyvin was quick to compose himself. 'The judgement, the judgement first,' he cried. 'Deal with that so we can deal with the implications of the impermanence.'

His voice had the desired effect of calming the Circle. Holthim cleared his throat but Praether interrupted before he could begin to speak, deliberately not using the First Speaker title. 'Leyvin has broken the prejudgement convention of silence, so I want to assert my reciprocal right to speak.'

Leyvin glared at the arch-librer but made no attempt to argue against him.

Holthim was still a little shaken, but he said, 'You're right, Liche Praether. You have the right to speak.'

'Praether doesn't have the right to speak,' cried Lythos. 'First Speaker Leyvin was merely calling us to the task at hand. We all lost sight of what we were supposed to be doing. Second Speaker Holthim, please pass the judgement now.'

'I have ruled,' said Holthim.

Lythos' face was flushed. 'This is insane. I demand you pass the judgement right now.'

Holthim drew a deep breath. 'Then I will have to name you, Liche Lythos.'

Lythos snarled. 'This is ludicrous. I challenge your ridiculous naming.'

'Third Speaker Baelren,' said Holthim. 'You are now first.'

The small balding Felsen monk who was Third Speaker Baelren indicated the door. 'Please,' he said, 'if all four of you leave now, we will make our judgement.'

As Praether, Leyvin, Lythos and Holthim walked out the door, the earth started shaking again.

*

Atreu and Teyth tried to ride out the tremors. They were growing in intensity with each wave, and the cracks in the floor were now clearly forming a chasm.

'We are moving further away from peace,' cried Atreu, once the instability had subsided.

'You don't have to tell me that, little brother. They've locked you up in here with me, haven't they?'

'No, I mean more than that, Teyth. The Mountain itself is moving further away from peace.'

'Atreu, this is not the time to be talking in riddles.'

The ground began shaking again.

'I've sensed it since my Zenith.'

'What?' cried Teyth, as the cracking sounds drowned out their voices.

When the rumbling died down again, Atreu repeated. 'I've sensed it since my Zenith. The instability and our war with the Faemir are tied together.'

'I don't know what you're talking about.'

'Yes, you do,' said Atreu. 'Think about it – as the war with the Faemir has escalated over the last year, so has the instability. We are tearing the Mountain apart with our conflict.'

'You're saying the Mountain *feels* what is happening between us?'

'Yes – we're killing it. There will be nothing left to fight over if we don't end the conflict.'

'Atreu, I can't believe – '

Another tremor hit and the chasm opened up to the body width of two Maelir. Atreu and Teyth took a step towards the wall.

'It won't matter soon whether you are right or wrong, little brother. The ground is about to swallow us.'

Atreu looked at the growing chasm in the middle of the room which separated him and his brother from the door. He drew a breath and jumped across, taking care to land on a solid juncture of cracks on the other side. Then he banged on the door with his fist. 'Let us out,' he cried. 'There's a chasm forming in here.'

There was no answer.

He tried again, slamming at the door with both fists but again no-one replied.

'Perhaps they would let you out if you were in here on your own,' said Teyth, 'but there's no way they'll let me out as well.'

There was a crashing sound and the roof started to crumble. Small pieces of rock rained to the ground.

Another tremor hit with such force that both Atreu and Teyth were up-ended.

Atreu lay prone, blinking to clear his vision. The chasm had now opened so wide that it gaped just in front of his eyes. He was drawn by the riotous array of colour before him. Crimson, gold and vermilion danced across his vision as warm air hit his face.

'This is it, little brother,' said Teyth. 'No death in battle for Tyr's sons.'

Atreu shook his head. He looked up to see Teyth pinned against the wall on the other side of the room, the chasm now so wide that he had almost no floor space on which to stand.

'Wait,' said Atreu, lowering his gaze. 'There's a way out.'

'You're not suggesting what I think you're suggesting, are you?'

Atreu nodded and pointed into the cavern. 'Do we have any choice?'

Teyth watched as the cracks continued to multiply and spread under his feet. The remaining floor of the room was now collapsing. He looked across at Atreu and grinned wryly.

'After you, little brother,' he said. 'After you.'

Chapter Sixteen

Praether knew this would be the last chance he would have to address the Circle. He had won the right to speak on a technicality, but there was little doubt in his mind that they would judge against him and he would be expelled. The best he could do with his last chance at directly influencing the Holy Orders' decision making was to sow some seeds which might come to fruition at a later date. If only there was some way he could bring Leyvin down with him.

'I thank you all for the right to speak before my judgement,' said Praether, 'and I particularly thank Second Speaker Holthim and Third Speaker Baelren for their adherence to our conventions.'

Lythos sighed loudly. 'Could Second Speaker Holthim please ensure that Liche Praether is aware of the urgency of other matters.'

Praether continued loudly and clearly. 'Second Speaker Holthim, please be informed that it is the urgency of the matters on our agenda of which I intend to speak. I respectfully request that owing to my advanced years, I be allowed against convention to be seated during my address.'

Praether stared at Lythos, almost daring him to protest. It was obvious to the arch-librer that he thought about it for a moment but then changed his mind.

'I will allow it,' said Holthim.

Praether sat down, knowing his words would have much more authority from the position of acceptance within the Circle. He glanced at the still standing Leyvin before he began.

'I have deceived the Circle by omission,' he said. 'That is something which I cannot deny. However, I believe my truths about the three Books have never been given sufficient consideration.'

'Not again,' moaned Lythos.

'I ask you not to comment until Liche Praether has finished,' said Holthim.

Praether continued. 'The recent evidence – and I believe this evidence has been accepted by the Circle – suggests that my truth about the power of the Books should carry more weight than it has. The only understanding I have ever claimed is of the importance of the Books – I have never claimed the mastery of detail therein as my truth. In fact I have always said that the power of the Books will work through someone else. That's why none of you should have assumed I would be able to continue to read the Book of Maelur after Atreu left the Keep.'

Praether was almost thankful for the coughing fit which overcame him. It gave him time for his point to sink in before he continued.

'I may perhaps appear to be a little over-focused when it comes to the Books, but I have spent my adult life arguing for my truth. My Zenith is now so many years ago that many of you were not even born, yet I remember the truth as clearly as if it were the last Zenith.'

'Yes,' said Lythos. 'We all know. The ultimate truth lies in the three Books. Do we have to listen to this again?'

'Please, Liche Lythos,' began Holthim.

'But this is wasting time,' said Lythos. 'Liche Praether is claiming he has had no influence on the Circle during his time. Can

I suggest he has had more than his share? He has persuaded the Circle on two occasions to have a Book as a Talisman. If we count Ascender Atreu, both of them failed disastrously. He has exerted far too much influence than his performance has warranted – and he is still doing so.'

'Perhaps he is,' said Holthim, 'but I will let him finish unless you wish to challenge my decision. I would also remind you not to prejudge Ascender Atreu.'

Lythos snorted but remained silent.

'As I was saying,' said Praether, 'the truth about the Books has started to be borne out, and Atreu has been the catalyst. I am convinced his is the second Book.'

'The Circle will judge that,' said Holthim.

'Of course,' said Praether. 'But I can only express my personal beliefs and truths.' He drew a breath. 'Just remember this: if you judge me as having misled you regarding my understanding of Maelur's Book, then you are accepting that it has certain qualities which match my predictions over the years, and further, you are accepting that Atreu's proximity is crucial in the activation of those qualities. Your expulsion of me, therefore, actually adds weight to the arguments I have been presenting to the Circle.'

A wry grin tugged at the corner of Praether's mouth. It was his masterstroke. The very act of his expulsion would ensure his truth would dominate the Circle's future decisions. By expelling him because they judged he had misled them, they were affirming that the Book of Maelur had certain power. In a way, there was little point in him remaining in the Circle and endlessly repeating his ideas. Through the act of his expulsion, the Circle would commit itself to his truth.

Praether looked at Lythos who was scowling, and then his eyes met Leyvin's. There was an exchange of pure venom before Leyvin's face hardened to a blank mask.

'Liche Praether,' said Holthim, 'could you please stand behind your chair for your pronouncement.'

When Praether had taken his place, Holthim continued,

'Unless there are any protests, I will now inform First Speaker Leyvin and Liche Praether of the Circle's decision.' He waited a moment but no-one spoke. 'Since the words you have heard have not led any of you to reconsider your position, I pronounce judgement in favour of First Speaker Leyvin.'

'Thank you,' said Leyvin and resumed his seat. 'Now I must inform the Circle that Liche Praether has failed in his ninth challenge and as required has now forfeited his place in the Circle. I would like to thank him for his many years of service.'

Praether listened to the steady monotone of Leyvin's voice. He knew the words even before they escaped the First Speaker's lips. The euphoria of his final masterstroke was gone and in its place was a dull, empty ache.

It was finished. Over sixty years in the Circle. He had seen more Zeniths than any of the other members. And now, finally, he could argue no more. A tear began to form in his eye but he blinked it away.

He knew they would probably indulge him in a few final words, despite the conventions prohibiting them, yet he felt he had, over the years, said all he could possibly say.

He straightened his old back as far as he could and scanned the faces of the Circle for the last time. He smiled a wry half smile and walked towards the door.

*

The chasm was filled with a strange fusion of brightly coloured rock-light, and the air was surprisingly warm. Atreu and Teyth exchanged incredulous looks as they climbed down the rocky surface. The deeper they went, the more bizarre everything appeared. Crystal clusters of the most delicate hues grew around them like semitransparent plants. Bright jagged-edged ferns jutted out from the stone. Thin grass-like tubes crackled like hay as they brushed past, bending and then swinging back into position. Points of light which Atreu had first thought were glimmerstones shone from the surface of the rock. He tried to touch them but each time he did they winked out as if frightened by him and only came back on again after he had walked past.

'This is beautiful,' said Atreu. The sound of his voice was thick and sluggish as if most of the volume was being drawn in by the rock around him.

'Who would have thought?' said Teyth, looking around open-mouthed as they clambered down further.

The slope was not as steep as it appeared from the surface, but with the chasm still expanding, they had to take care with their footing. Each new quake seemed to be accompanied by a sensation of the air around them being sucked into the depths of the chasm.

It was almost to Atreu as if the Mountain was inhaling with every tremor.

'Do you get the feeling we are being drawn in?' asked Atreu.

'Yes,' said Teyth, 'I know what you mean. There's something about the way the air moves in here.'

'I think I've felt this before.'

Teyth looked at his brother curiously. 'You mean in that chasm on the first day of our Ascent?'

'And since then.'

Teyth looked up at the chasm opening which was now well above them. 'We're going to lose sight of the surface soon.'

Atreu nodded. 'I know – it's possible for the chasm to close again at any moment, but we don't have any choice, do we?'

'We could go back,' said Teyth doubtfully.

'To what? Either the chasm's opened up to fill the whole room, or there's some remaining floor space up there but we're still prisoners – not much reason to go back, is there?'

'You're right, Atreu. It's funny how I've faced so many Faemir in battle and felt little fear, but this is making me nervous.'

The ground under their feet shook again and there was a rumbling sound from above them. Atreu looked up and saw a flurry of small stones raining down. He and Teyth pressed themselves against the sloping surface and tried to protect their heads with their arms.

The stones stung for one short, sharp moment and then they were gone, disappearing into the multi-hued depths below them.

Atreu looked up tentatively to see if anymore were on their way. 'I think the entire Hold is falling to pieces up there.'

'Come on, little brother, let's see where we end up.'

As they continued and the chasm opening receded still further into the distance, the colours of the crystals changed subtly. They seemed to Atreu to be more delicate and the crystals themselves longer and finer. He ran his fingers along the length of some of the slender tubes, and they trembled under his touch like the strings of a lute. Immediately the air was filled with the most exquisite sound. Atreu and Teyth looked around in fascination as the walls sprang to life. One after the other, the crystals started to vibrate in a melodic chain reaction and the chasm sang to them in subtle tones. Atreu felt the music vibrate through him as he watched the waves wash across the crystal fields and gradually fade into the distance.

After the sound died, he felt a hollow emptiness inside where the sounds had been. He reached down and strummed the flute-thin crystals again but this time they didn't tremble and no music issued from their delicate stalks. He looked up to meet Teyth's gaze, a gaze filled with sadness and loss. Perhaps this was their one song, and now it was gone forever. Atreu drew back his hand and they continued their descent.

The slope flattened out the deeper they went so that it was now possible to walk rather than climb. The sensation of being drawn in by the movement of the air was still there, but either it had weakened or Atreu had grown used to it.

Atreu looked up. Apart from the tiny light, which he knew to be the opening, there was an illusion of a sky filled with a glorious array of twinkling stars stretched out above them.

A feeling of utter strangeness enveloped Atreu as they walked in silence. It was as if a million tiny pinpricks were being gently pressed against his skin so that they didn't pierce the flesh but somehow made him aware of every part of his body. The air around him seemed thick with life, and he found a single breath sustained his body much longer than it ever had before. Atreu sensed the colours around him were nourishing his body and he was drawing them in directly through his pores. The sensation grew with each step, and as he continued, the colours also appeared to be melting into each other, almost merging with the air itself.

Then the surface on which they were walking flattened out completely.

They had reached the bottom of the chasm.

'Funny,' said Atreu, 'I half expected these to continue on for-ever.'

Teyth pointed to their right. 'I think there's an opening of some kind over there.'

They found what looked like a man-made tunnel.

'What do you think is going on here?' asked Atreu.

'I don't know.' said Teyth. 'Perhaps these are parts of the Hold which were never revealed to us.'

'We're a long way under the Hold,' said Atreu.

'Could be catacombs.'

'Do you mean we could find skeletons of dead Holy Men in there?'

'Who knows?'

'Well, Teyth, I went into the chasm first. I think it's about your turn to take the lead.'

*

Micah's eyes were red-rimmed and bloodshot when he entered Praether's antechamber at the librum. The arch-librer was sitting at his table with the Book of Maelur in front of him.

'I know,' said Praether, 'you are going to chastise me for not speaking to you since my expulsion from the Circle.'

'Of course, Praether, if you really don't wish to see me, I understand. It must be difficult for you. If you really don't want to talk to me, I'll go.'

Praether looked down at the Book again. 'This Book has finished me,' he said. 'Who would have thought? I have done what I can – and now, I fear, my time may be coming to an end.'

'Don't say that, Praether. You still have a role to play.' Micah spoke quickly as if the words were racing each other to escape his lips. 'You know it's possible to influence the Circle without being a part of it.'

'Whose ear do I have, Micah? I have made too many opponents over the years. You know that as well as I do. And I have never stooped to cultivating friendships to gain influence as some of the others choose to do.'

'When Atreu returns – '

'I think you mean *if*, Micah. I fear he is even further away than the last time I looked at the Book.'

'What do you mean? I thought ... I thought you couldn't read the Book anymore.'

'Oh, the words are now crystal clear to me, Micah. No haziness, no vagueness. The trouble is the words are again exactly what they appear to everyone else. They are again simply the words of Maelur to me, the same words that have been here for me for the past sixty years in the Keep.'

Praether cocked his head as he heard a faint rumbling in the distance. 'I fear for the Keep,' he said, 'and I fear for the Holy Orders.'

'You can't be serious,' said Micah, gesturing rapidly. 'How can you be serious? Apart from one Faemir near death, none have breached the Keep. The windriders continue to bring us everything we need.'

'And this year's Ascent?'

'You've heard the reports – some Ascenders are on their way. Who knows what will happen by next Zenith?'

'Who knows indeed, Micah? This instability concerns me

more than anything now. The Keep has always been immune from it – you know that. It was the most stable place on the Mountain. It was our sanctum: the place protected from the ravages and chance elements of life where we can contemplate and reason and judge in peace. And now that's gone. Yes, we're only talking about one Faemir on the brink of death, and yes, the tremors are minor and cause no damage, but I'm afraid the war has come to the Keep and it is no longer the place it once was.'

'You should be speaking these words to the Circle, not to me,' said Micah.

Praether looked at him suddenly. 'Nominate for the Circle. We still have a chance if ...' He stared into Micah's bloodshot eyes and his hopeful tone changed. 'You've taken some r'lung again, haven't you?'

'I ... I ...'

'Don't try to deny it, Micah. I've told you it is damaging you. There is no need to take it here in the Keep.'

'I was worried.' Micah's words tumbled out one after the other. 'About Atreu, about Teyth, about you. Everyone who is dear to me. I don't know, I – '

'Micah, I'm sick of your excuses. You know the r'lung has been taking hold of you for some time. I thought you had broken its grip.'

'I only took a small amount.'

'You know a small amount for you is much more than anyone else needs to take.' Praether slammed the Book shut. 'Micah, you are a fool. You have so much potential but you are still wasting it. You also know the r'lung was probably responsible for your fail-ure at the last Circle nomination.'

'But, Praether, it was my Talisman,' said Micah. 'How can I deny the truth of it?'

Praether buried his head in his hands. 'It is my fault. You're right – how I regret that decision.'

'But r'lung has been a boon to the Liche since then. The two of us brought a plant with great benefits to the Holy Orders. You can't deny those benefits, Praether. The Liche have been able to move so much more quickly and cover much greater distances than ever before. Our influence has spread greatly. We can monitor Ascents more effectively. We – '

'But at what cost, Micah, at what cost? I think now it was my biggest mistake. I regret choosing it as your Talisman. For you and for others it has been too dangerous. I doubt if it has been worth it.'

'Praether, listen to me. Listen.' He grabbed the arch-librer by his robes. 'Atreu would not have made it to Crosanct, let alone the Summit, without the r'lung.'

'Perhaps, Micah, perhaps not.' He pulled Micah's hands away. 'Perhaps it would have been better for all of us if he had never reached Crosanct in time. Who knows?'

Micah slumped. 'I'm sorry, Praether. I'm sorry.'

'I may not have any more influence on the Circle, but hopefully I can still influence you a little, Micah. Go and burn all the r'lung you have. Go now. Burn it, denounce it, get rid of every last shred – and then nominate for the Circle. It's our only chance.'

Although the ground was still, Micah started trembling. He ran his fingers through his beard and began nodding slowly. 'You're right, Praether, you're right.'

*

Atreu couldn't tell where the cold, blue light which filled the tunnel was coming from. It certainly wasn't daylight. Somehow it was emanating from the rock which encased the two of them as they hiked further into the Mountain. The ground was rough underfoot and occasionally he or Teyth would step on a loose rock, but the slope was gradual and the going relatively easy.

'Where have all the colours gone?' asked Atreu, fascinated by the strange light around them.

'I don't know,' said Teyth, 'but have a good look at these walls.

This tunnel is definitely man-made – you can see where the rocks have been chipped away by some instrument.'

'A lot of work has gone into this,' said Atreu, examining the surface of the rock. 'It's nowhere near as fine a workmanship as the Hold, and from what I can remember, the tunnels of the Eyries were much more skilfully carved. What I don't understand is what's the point of the Orders having a tunnel so far below the surface?'

'I have no idea,' said Teyth. 'I'm more concerned with getting out of here somehow. Instead we seem to be going further and further into the Mountain.'

'We can always go back.' Atreu laughed.

'Have a look at this,' said Teyth, and Atreu approached the wall where Teyth was standing. 'It's almost as if this was cut recently.'

'Impossible,' said Atreu, examining the surface. He drew back. 'It does look like it though.'

They continued walking, peering ahead to see if there was anything apart from the long featureless tunnel ahead of them.

'Have you noticed something funny about your breathing?' asked Atreu.

'You mean how we don't seem to be doing much of it?'

'Yes.'

'I thought it was my imagination at first, Atreu, but it does feel to me like I don't need to breathe as much as I usually do.'

'You know what that makes me think is happening?'

'We're dying.'

'You thought of that too?'

'Yes,' said Teyth, 'but I feel good. I'm actually glad to get my legs moving after being imprisoned for so long.'

'I feel fine too,' said Atreu, 'but how do we know that's not what everyone feels when they're dying?'

'We don't, little brother, but look at us, we're walking and carrying on a conversation. I don't think this is what dying is all about.'

Their attention was taken by what was ahead. A fork.

'Well, now this is getting interesting,' said Teyth.

They walked closer.

'We take the left,' said Atreu.

'What?'

'The left one – always take the left one.'

'What are you talking about, Atreu? How do you know which one to take?'

Atreu shook his head to try to clear his thoughts. 'I don't know ... somehow I just sense that the left one is the correct one to take.'

'They look identical to me – but if you're so sure, let's go.'

They entered the left fork. The cold, blue light still shone all around them.

'Do you realise we have no shadows here?' said Teyth, after a while.

'You're right – the light must be shining from all directions at once.'

'Little brother, do you think we're dead?'

'No – but it feels very strange.' Atreu tried to laugh but couldn't.

They stopped. The tunnel forked in front of them for a second time.

'We have to take the left,' said Atreu.

'I'm glad one of us is so sure – come on then.'

They entered the left fork and it wasn't long before the ground began to slope up.

'It looks like you made the right choice, little brother,' said Teyth. 'We may get out of here yet.'

Their legs soon felt the strain of the change in direction of the gradient, but the thought that they were heading back up to the surface buoyed their spirits.

Then they arrived at another fork.

Teyth looked at his brother. 'The left, always the left – am I right?'

'Yes – we should take the left.' Atreu frowned. 'You know, I've been here before.'

'Don't tell me we're going round in circles?'

'No – I've been here before. The first time was at the start of my Ascent.'

'Atreu – are you sure you're still breathing? You're not making any sense. How could you have been here at the start of your Ascent?'

'It ... it was in a dream.'

'A dream?'

'Yes – that's how I knew to take the left fork.'

'And that was how you got out in the dream?'

'Well no, the dream ended before I got out.'

Teyth shook his head. 'At least you seem to have made the right choices so far – so let's keep going.'

Once more they entered the left fork.

The new tunnel continued to slope up, and the gradient increased. The cold blueness of the light dimmed slightly and it was as if the air was beginning to thin again, making it necessary to breathe a little more often. Otherwise, the tunnel was identical to the previous ones.

They arrived at several more forks, each time taking the left one, and each time the slope of the new tunnel increased, taking them further up towards the surface. And with each tunnel, the air seemed to grow less thick and sluggish.

'Thank goodness for your dream,' said Teyth as he drew in a deep breath. 'If we were dead for a while there, we're certainly springing back to life.'

'I wish I knew how the dream ended,' said Atreu.

'Just get me to the surface,' said Teyth. 'That's all I want.'

'The dreams were real – do you remember I said that to you after Zenith? They cause things to happen.'

'I can't remember much of what you said, but I do recall you spoke about dreams. If you get us out of here, I'll – '

They both stopped. In front of them the tunnel forked again.

This time there were three choices.

'What happens now, little brother? The left one?'

'I ... I don't know.'

'Don't tell me this didn't happen in your dream.'

'Not in the first one, no. But I've had another one recently where I had three choices.'

'Well, that shouldn't be a problem. Which one did you choose in the dream?'

'That's just it, Teyth. I couldn't choose. Two were easy to deal with, but I had no idea what to do when presented with three.'

'You must have some feeling about which one is the correct one.'

Atreu frowned. 'No, Teyth, I don't. I have no idea. And what's more, I have this paralysing sense of dread about choosing.'

'All right, little brother, I'll make the decision. We'll take the left fork again.'

Teyth led the way and Atreu's legs felt to him as heavy as led-stones as he followed.

They walked in silence for a time. Atreu looked around anxiously.

'See,' said Teyth finally, 'the ground is sloping up even more. You have to learn to trust my judgement, little brother.'

'How could I have ever doubted you?' Atreu smiled weakly as he peered ahead.

They walked for some time, expecting more forks but nothing came. Atreu was unsure what that meant. Perhaps they were getting close to the surface.

They froze. The sound of approaching footsteps echoed towards them.

Atreu and Teyth looked at each other. Who could it be? Atreu scanned the tunnel for somewhere to hide, but they could see nothing but rocky walls in the cold, blue light. There was no way but forward towards the sound or back the way they came.

'What do we do?' whispered Atreu.

Teyth planted his feet firmly on the ground. 'I'm not running from whoever it is. It only sounds like one person. I say we wait.'

Atreu nodded and joined his brother in staring in the direction the sound was coming from.

The steps grew louder, but still they couldn't see anything. Was it a trick of sound in the tunnel? Atreu shuddered, suddenly very aware of his own breathing. Or was this some ghost?

Then the footsteps stopped.

They waited a moment but the tunnel was silent.

Teyth motioned to his brother to follow and they made their way slowly forward.

After a while, they could hear voices. Strange, harsh voices speaking in a language which they could make no sense of. Atreu hesitated but Teyth indicated that they should keep going. They continued for some time – clearly sounds travelled a long way downslope in the tunnels.

Finally they came to a sharp bend. The voices now seemed to be coming from just around the corner. They crept up to the bend and slowly looked around.

Atreu felt as if the cold blade of a sword had caressed his spine. In the blue light he could see a dozen dark-skinned people with thin, gangly limbs and angular faces, their eyes and teeth flashing a razor-sharp white. They were sitting and eating something that appeared to have blood dripping from it. Behind them was the beginning of a new tunnel, and strewn around them were digging tools. With a shock that hit him like the most violent of earth tremors, Atreu realised none of the people had eyelids.

Atreu and Teyth drew back slowly and silently. They stared at each other, each mirroring the other's raw fear. There was no need to utter anything, one brother knew what the other was thinking.

Dusk People.

Chapter Seventeen

'Riell, you don't know how much I appreciate this,' said Praether.

'You have been a friend to me and to the other windriders for a long time, Praether. We were all shocked to hear of your expulsion from the Circle.'

The Book of Maelur lay closed on the table in front of the arch-librer. The candle next to it was burning low and shed only the palest of lights into Praether's librum chamber.

Praether nodded slowly, in time with his own breathing. 'It seems that events have already moved past me. I am already starved of news. I didn't think I would miss it to this degree.'

'I will keep you informed of any windrider reports given to the Circle.'

'I thank you, Riell. Unfortunately, all I can do now is thank you.'

'Even that is not necessary, Praether.' Riell stopped and Praether sensed the windrider's eyes were trying to tell him something. 'I'm afraid none of the news is good.'

'Please, I need to know.'

'The Hold is all but destroyed.'

'What? How can that be? How can caves and chambers carved out of solid rock be destroyed?'

'The impermanence we have been feeling at the Keep is just an after-tremor of what's happening down at the Summit. It's total chaos below.'

'I thought you said none of the news was good. I know the Orders will have some rebuilding to do if we ever get control back, but surely the collapse of the Hold means the Faemir are totally exposed.'

'Yes, that's true – and the weather is starting to turn. However, many of the Faemir survived.'

Praether closed his eyes, fearing the answer to his next question. 'And Atreu and Teyth?'

'No sign of either of them, but we would be almost certain both of them would have been in the Hold when it collapsed.'

'And the Faemir, Verlinden?'

'We haven't sighted her.'

'The news is grim, but at least the Faemir will not last long once the snows start in earnest.'

'I'm afraid they may last longer than we think.'

'How so, Riell?'

'The Maelir grip on Crosanct has loosened. The same violent instability which racked the Hold has also hit at the Pass. We have reports of total chaos down there as well. Because of our position, the Maelir forces suffered far heavier losses, and the Faemir are again able to move through.'

'Let them,' said Praether. 'There's nothing but ice and snow waiting for them at the Summit.'

'We are more concerned that those battalions already in the Upper Reaches are now able to return to the Mid-Reaches to protect themselves from the ravages of winter.'

'So the war may not end before next Zenith?'

'No, I believe it will be a long time before we can again truly claim to control the Mountain.'

'And you have told the Circle this?'

'Yes.'

'Did they give you any clue as to what their response might be?'

'No – you know better than I how the Circle works. I suspect they may soon give up on Atreu and Teyth, and order that the windriders cease returning to the Upper Reaches for them.'

Riell cleared his throat and shifted the weight on his feet.

'Is there something else you wish to tell me, Riell?'

'Yes, Praether, there is – but it is something which has not yet reached the Circle.'

'You can tell me now. As I am no longer in the Circle, I am not required to divulge such matters.'

Riell cleared his throat again. 'As you know there have been many of us in the guild who have not been entirely happy with our relationship with the Liche and the Felsen.'

'I understand some of your concerns.'

'But do you appreciate them?' said Riell. 'We serve the Liche and the Felsen. We have always provided everything the Keep requires to function, and hence your control of the Mountain and of Zenith depends on us.'

'It depends on many things, but, yes Riell, I have always acknowledged the importance of the windriders.'

'We windriders are more than important, we are crucial.'

'I suppose we are playing a little with words here. Yes, most of us in the Holy Orders would probably concede you are crucial, but we would add that there were other factors which were also crucial.'

'Praether, I think you know the direction in which I am moving. There have always been those of us who have believed the guild of windriders should be a Holy Order.'

The arch-librer nodded. 'I have heard some of you refer to yourselves as the Order of the Wynde. The matter has been discussed in the Circle.'

Riell placed his hands on the table and leaned towards the arch-librer. 'Praether, the windriders have carried the burden of the protection of the Keep. There have been many deaths among us, many more in the weeks since Zenith than in my entire time in the guild. And not only have we lost many of our number, we have been forced to abandon our home in the Eyries.'

'You can go back now – you know that.'

'But that's just it, Praether, we're not going back.'

'What?'

'We want to stay in the Keep proper, to share the place with the Liche and the Felsen.'

'The third Order – the Wynde?'

'Yes,' said Riell. 'The time has come.'

'You believe this yourself, Riell?'

'Yes, and with every death and loss we have sustained in recent times, I have become more convinced. Praether, we report to the Circle, we give advice, but in the end we take no part in the decisions. And yet it is the windriders who are dying as a result of those decisions.'

Praether looked into the flame of the candle. 'You want windriders to sit in the Circle?'

'Yes, we want a full Holy Order. Our truth is the third way, between the light and the rock.'

Praether shook his head slowly. 'The truth of each and every windrider was judged to be a failure.'

'By a Circle which contained no windriders.'

'Your argument itself turns in circles, Riell.'

'Perhaps that's why we think it is right. Praether, the time has come for us.'

'Why now? When we have so many other problems? You yourself have said the next Zenith is now in real doubt. We have lost control of Crosanct, a Faemir baresark has breached the Keep itself – and you feel the time is right for this?'

'Yes, we are the ones carrying the burden.'

'As you are required to by your covenant.'

'The covenant can only be changed by mutual agreement. We

want the Circle to accept the change, to allow the Order of the Wynde to come into being.'

'And you feel now you are in the position to hold the Orders to ransom? At a time when we are dependent on you like never before?'

'Ransom is not a word we like to use, Praether, but we are talking about power here, and we now have the best chance to negotiate with the Liche and the Felsen.'

'And you're telling me all this before you reveal yourselves to the Circle – why?'

'As I said, you've been a friend to the windriders and to me personally for a long time. This was despite your disappointment in the failure of my Ascent.'

'As your sage, I judged you differently to the final consensus of the Circle.'

'Nevertheless, other sages have had little to do with their charges once their Ascents had been judged as failures at second Equinox. You have been an exception.'

'And you choose to tell me all this at a time when I have no influence.'

'We don't need your influence now, Praether. We believe the Circle will have no choice.'

'I wouldn't be so sure. They have many options open to them. Only one of them is giving you what you want. And even if they do grant you temporary status, they may strip you of it once the war is over.'

'We suspect that is a possibility, and we believe you can help us consolidate our position once we have gained it.'

Praether shook his head. 'I'm afraid I will never have another chance to make decisions again. My time is over.'

'Praether, we are going to force changes on the structure of the Circle itself.' The arch-librer looked up into Riell's eyes as he continued. 'I believe we will be able to make it possible for you to return.'

'You really think you can do this?'

'Praether, I'm telling you this against the wishes of some of the other riders, but we are prepared to do whatever it takes. We will request if that is enough, but if it isn't, we are going to be quite direct in our demands.' The windrider drew even closer. 'We are prepared to cut the lifeline we provide to the Keep if necessary.'

Praether started to cough – deep rasping coughs at the back of his throat. Once the fit passed, he struggled for the words. 'You cannot be serious. You may threaten to, but you would never actually do it ... would you?'

Riell stared back at him in silence.

*

Atreu and Teyth again stood in front of the three forks. They had returned along the tunnel as quickly and as quietly as possible. It was only now that they dared to speak.

'I was right,' said Atreu. 'I told you and Micah about this at Zenith. You didn't listen. Everything I experienced during Zenith has been proved correct. These tunnels – they are the work of the Nazir. They're here.'

'Now let's be careful, Atreu – we only saw a handful of them. We're assuming the tunnels were built by them.'

'Teyth, I'm sick of not being listened to. I know I'm right. My Zenith was crystal clear. The Dusk People are here, at the Summit. Who knows how many thousands of years it's taken them to burrow up from the Steppes to get here. And the instability – it all ties in. That's why the Mountain is collapsing. It's their work, don't you see? And now they're at the Summit.'

'Father was right.'

'Yes, Teyth – and he's been the only one who believed the Nazir were still a threat. You know how he's been laughed at and ridiculed for his beliefs. Even you never accepted his views.'

Teyth stared at the two forks to the right of the one they had just returned from. 'We still need to get out of here to sound the warning. Which one do we choose?'

Atreu expelled a deep breath. 'The middle way. We have to find a middle way.'

'Are you saying we should take the middle fork?'

'I'm ... not sure ... Yes, let's take the middle path.'

They entered the fork and walked along the tunnel, taking care to move as silently as possible.

They soon realised the ground was sloping down.

'Let's go back,' said Teyth in a low voice.

'No, wait,' said Atreu. 'Remember the surface of the Mountain is sloping at a much greater gradient than this tunnel. It's possible to reach the surface from a tunnel with a down slope.'

'I suppose you're right,' said Teyth, 'but this doesn't appear to be very encouraging.'

'I think we should see what happens.'

They walked on and, although the path kept sloping down, Atreu found his breathing rate was almost back to normal. The blue tinge to the light had also continued to fade. Now and then, he thought he heard a vague sound which could have been foot-steps or voices, but when he strained to listen, he could never be certain he could hear anything.

After rounding several bends, they stopped suddenly. Atreu's eye was caught by a flash of white on the ground ahead.

'It's snow,' he said and they walked towards it, glancing around all the while to ensure they were alone.

When they reached the patch of snow, Atreu scooped some up and held it in his palm. 'I can remember the first time I saw this. I didn't even know it was just water in another form.' He laughed. 'You know, that really wasn't so long ago.'

'I think we're getting close to the surface, little brother,' said Teyth. 'Look there's more.'

Atreu glanced further ahead and saw a trail of white starting in the middle of the tunnel.

After following the ever-increasing trail for some time, Teyth said, 'You know, I'm certain you're right. This is an exit tunnel.

Any tunnel leading to the surface has to slope down – if it didn't, snow would simply keep falling in and filling it up.'

'I think you're right,' said Atreu. 'The wind probably blew all this in ... look.'

In front of them, the tunnel ended in a wall of the purest white.

'This is the way out, little brother,' cried Teyth.

Immediately, there was a faint shuffling sound coming from somewhere behind them.

Atreu stared at his brother. 'I think you've just told them we're here.'

Teyth glanced back, but couldn't see anything. 'Let's hurry up and dig our way out of here.'

*

'Praether, will you stop staring at that Book.' The tone in Micah's voice made the arch-librer look up from his desk quickly. 'If you can't read it the way you want to, then staring at it for hours on end isn't going to help.'

'I was so close to my truth, Micah. So close, and now it's been taken away from me. Can you begin to understand what that feels like?'

'Don't tell me you've given up on Atreu and Teyth?'

'You must have heard the reports by now, Micah. The Hold is nothing but a pile of rubble now. I'm sure neither of them would have had the freedom to roam at will down there. What chance do you think they had?'

'And you think Atreu's Book will remain buried?'

'Micah, there is another explanation which I failed to give you before for my inability to read this Book. Perhaps I can no longer read it because Atreu is dead. Perhaps the power of all the Books is now lost forever.'

'Praether, at our last meeting you spoke to me of hope and of what I must do, and now you seem to have given up.'

'I don't know, Micah. I think I'm growing tired of it all. I feel that so much of what I have always known, and grown to love, is about to change.' He rubbed his rheumy eyes with his fingers. 'Sometimes I feel I have earned a right to rest now and let things take their course without me. Tell me, Micah, when will I be allowed to rest?'

'I don't think you want that sort of rest, Praether. That sounds to me more like the rest of death.'

Praether shook his head. 'Have you nominated?' he asked.

'Yes – my address is tonight. Eight others have nominated so it could be a long night. The judgement will be made tomorrow. Apparently the Circle has heard almost all the Ascenders' addresses now – which is good because Equinox is rapidly approaching. I only hope Atreu and Teyth can make it in time.'

Praether's eyes started watering. 'I don't know. The Summit has collapsed, we've lost control of Crosanct, the Mountain is in chaos, and we're up here going through the same procedures we've always gone through. Laboriously talking and sticking to our age-old conventions.'

'You need sleep, Praether. I haven't given up on Atreu and Teyth. The windriders are going down again tonight to see if they're there. Who knows, they may even have the Book with them.'

'You're right, Micah, I'm very tired. Perhaps it will all be different to me in the morning.' He looked up, but found it hard to focus on Micah's face because his eyes were still watering. 'Let me tell you something that may help your nomination. The guild of windriders are about to call for the consecration of the Holy Order of the Wynde.'

'What?'

'Riell told me. You know him – he was the windrider who returned Atreu's Book from Crosanct. He wants my support after the consecration has been completed.'

'You know such a consecration just won't happen.'

'Micah, I'm certain now it will. Riell has told me the guild will do whatever it takes to make it happen. If that means cutting off our food supplies and withdrawing their defences, they will do it.'

'You're not serious?'

'I am.'

'What should I do at my address – warn the Circle of the impending threat?'

'No – if I were you, I would argue for the cause of the Wynde.'

'How can you be seriously suggesting that?'

'I leave it to your conscience, Micah. You're on your own. I just ask you to seek out Riell, speak to him first, and then decide your course of action at the address. He is a reasonable man who has lived nobly with a great sense of shame since his Ascent was judged to have failed.' Praether's eyes were still watering. 'You share a bond with him, Micah. I was his sage the year before you and Tyr made your Ascents.'

'How is it you have never told me about him before?'

'It was his wish. Riell's shame was so great, he wanted to cut all his personal ties with the Holy Orders. It is not uncommon amongst the guild. I had to struggle at first to maintain any sort of friendship with him, and drawing him into any other interactions with Holy Men outside his official capacities was out of the question.'

Micah put his arm under the arch-librer to help him up. 'I'll speak to Riell,' he said, 'but please, Praether, get some sleep now.'

Praether nodded. He picked up the Book of Maelur and tucked it under his arm.

*

Atreu looked back into the tunnel as he and Teyth continued scooping out the snow. The noises were becoming more frequent now, although the tunnel was somehow distorting them so it was difficult to tell what they were.

'They don't sound like footsteps,' whispered Teyth, as he continued furiously shovelling snow.

'That's what worries me,' said Atreu.

The noise grew louder, but Atreu could still see nothing when he glanced over his shoulder.

'These tunnels do funny things to sounds,' said Teyth. 'It's almost as if whatever is making the noise is standing just over there and watching us.'

'Maybe it's still half a league away and we're only hearing an echo.'

'We can always hope.'

The sound grew louder still, and more distinct. Atreu froze. He had heard the noise before.

He turned slowly, as if he had lost full control of his muscles, and he saw what he hoped he wouldn't see.

Rounding the bend in the tunnel was a large beast with the unmistakable shuffling gait of a grale.

Atreu's eyes met the beast's and it growled a low, threatening growl. The all too familiar smell of scorched dung reached Atreu's nostrils.

'Keep digging,' said Teyth as he slowly straightened up. His voice was flat and firm.

'But – '

'I said, keep digging, little brother.' Teyth took several steps towards the grale. His back was perfectly straight, his gait steady.

'You've got no weapon, Teyth.'

'Keep digging.' His voice echoed through the tunnel.

Atreu started scooping snow again but kept glancing over his shoulder. The grale was now shuffling on the spot, its growls growing in volume, and Atreu sensed it was about to attack.

Teyth was walking towards it. 'Come on,' he said, gesturing at it to charge at him. *Was Teyth going mad?*

He picked up a rock and threw it at the beast, hitting it on the side of the face. The grale bellowed and threw its head back.

'Teyth, how can – '

'Keep digging!' His voice seemed to shake the tunnel like a tremor.

'I am,' cried Atreu.

Teyth picked up another rock and threw it at the grale, again making contact on the head.

'Come for me,' said Teyth, still walking towards it.

This time the grale charged.

Instead of waiting, Teyth started running towards the huge beast. There was a sickening crunch as the two connected and Teyth rolled off to the right and hit the side of the tunnel.

A scream of pain reverberated through the air, and it took a moment for Atreu to realise it came from the grale. Teyth had somehow managed to stab it in the eye with his finger at the point of contact.

The grale shook its head wildly from side to side, bellowing and screaming, blood pulsing from its damaged eye socket. Atreu saw Teyth lying on the floor of the tunnel and just starting to move.

Although the grale was now blind in one eye, it managed to locate Teyth and was now moving towards him.

'Teyth!' cried Atreu.

The grale's attention was momentarily taken and it jerked its head in Atreu's direction.

At the same time, Teyth lunged at the beast and rammed his finger into its other eye. The beast again screamed in agony, charging into the tunnel wall in a wild panic. Totally disorientated, it blundered into the wall on the other side, its twisted limbs appearing to be running in all directions at once.

Teyth raced back to Atreu at the snow wall. 'I told you to keep digging,' he said.

They worked furiously as the grale rammed the walls in a bellowing frenzy behind them. The snow was getting softer.

'I think we're getting close to the surface,' said Atreu, breathing heavily.

The screaming came to a crescendo and then it stopped.

'We'd better be close,' said Teyth.

Atreu glanced back into the tunnel and his stomach turned.

Two more grale had rounded the corner, and they were now feeding on the blinded one.

'I hope they're going to eat their fill,' said Atreu.

One of the grale looked up and saw the two brothers. Its face was streaked with blood and pieces of flesh hung from its mouth.

'Come on, Atreu, we must be almost there.'

Another handful of snow, and another.

The second grale had now also become aware of them.

More snow. Atreu's fingers had long since numbed, but he now redoubled his efforts.

The two grale had left the half-eaten carcass and were coming towards them, shuffling, getting ready to charge. Obviously, they much preferred Maelir flesh to that of their own kind.

'Can you handle two?' asked Atreu.

'Maybe,' said Teyth.

'Good.'

'But not three.'

Atreu glanced over his shoulder to see yet another grale had now rounded the corner.

He dug his fingers frantically into the snow again. 'Hey, I think we've reached the outside.'

Teyth had turned to face the oncoming grale, but Atreu sensed his brother was less sure of himself this time. With a shout, Atreu's fingers broke through the snow.

The grale started to charge.

'Quickly,' shouted Teyth.

Atreu scooped out an armful of snow creating a hole in the snow wall and a shaft of light from the outside pierced the pale blue inside the tunnel. He grabbed another armful and more light flooded in.

The three charging grale started bellowing.

'You've done it,' cried Teyth.

Atreu saw that the light from the outside was now shining into the eyes of the grale and they were in a wild panic. They crashed into each other in a frantic effort to escape back into the blue light of the tunnel.

With Teyth's help, Atreu dug a hole big enough to climb through.

They clambered out onto the snow-covered Mountain slope, and the cold sting of the morning air felt like caresses on their skin. The sun even shone briefly before being blanketed again by thick snow clouds.

The two brothers clasped hands and raised them above their heads.

'We made it, little brother,' cried Teyth.

'What if it had still been night?' said Atreu, looking back at the hole they had just climbed out of. 'What would have happened to us then?'

'Let's not worry about the what if, little brother.' He looked around. 'Do you know where we are?'

Atreu scanned the snowscape. A series of hills to his right, a ridge and some exposed rock in the other direction, and else-where, just a vast expanse of featureless white. Nothing looked particularly familiar, but then snowfall changed the appearance of the Upper Reaches constantly.

'It's easy, I suppose,' said Atreu. 'Upslope is the Summit, downslope are the Mid-Reaches.'

Teyth laughed. 'You know, little brother, I really don't know what to do. I've been a prisoner such a long time and before that I was simply following the path of my Ascent. I'm a little frightened about choosing which direction to go.'

'Stay with me, Teyth, and you'll be fine.' Atreu smiled as the sun came out again for a brief moment. 'The windriders arranged to be at a rocky outcrop between three hills just after dusk every day. I think we've got a bit of a walk, but we should be able to find it.'

'Judging by the position of the sun,' said Teyth, 'we have most of the day.'

Atreu frowned. 'I'm not going back without Verlinden though.'

'What are you saying, little brother?'

'Teyth, I'm not going back up to the Keep without her.'

Teyth fell silent, and it was a while before he spoke. 'You know, Atreu, there would have been a time when I'd have been furious with you if you'd said that.'

Atreu nodded slowly.

They pushed snow back into the hole they had just escaped from and then headed upslope.

Chapter Eighteen

Although it was just past midday, the sun was a long-distant memory. Dense, billowing clouds crowded the sky, fighting for space. Atreu and Teyth had spent the morning climbing uphill and avoiding the occasional Faemir they came across. It wasn't particularly difficult as the Faemir obviously were confident that they had control of the Upper Reaches and didn't feel it was necessary to be very vigilant.

The part of the Upper Reaches they found themselves in was unfamiliar to Atreu. They traversed, for the most part, a sea of hillocks and crests, with the odd rocky outcrop puncturing the white carpet. The snow underfoot was fresh and dry, and after the thick sluggishness of the atmosphere in the tunnels, the Mountain air seemed to bite into his lungs.

'Where did you learn to fight grale like that?' asked Atreu, scanning the horizon for signs of Faemir.

'I came across quite a few on my Ascent, but I always had my axe with me. That's the first time I've ever faced one unarmed.'

'What came over you?'

'What do you mean, little brother?'

'When the grale attacked. You changed somehow – it was almost as if you were possessed.'

Teyth sighed. 'I just did what I had to do.'

'Did you think about it?'

'Not really. I didn't have time.'

'Teyth, you've changed, you know.'

'So have you, Atreu. I suppose we both have. We've had to.'

'But I'm not sure if I like what's happened to you.'

Teyth's eyes narrowed as he looked at his brother. 'What don't you like? We'd both be dead now if I hadn't attacked the grale.'

'Don't get me wrong, Teyth. Of course I'm grateful. But I don't think any Maelir on the Mountain could have had the courage to fight a grale barehanded, let alone have the skill to defeat it. That frightens me a little – the Teyth I used to know would never have been able to do it.'

Teyth shrugged. 'I've done a lot of fighting during my Ascent. My responses have become automatic.'

'There's more to it than that.' Atreu fell silent for a moment and felt the rhythm of his footsteps. 'Do you know what a baresark is?' he said finally.

'I've heard the word – hasn't it got something to do with battle fury?'

'I don't fully understand it myself, but a baresark is a warrior who is somehow possessed by fury during a battle. They are the most fearsome opponents imaginable because they instinctively know the best course of action. The more threatened they are and the closer to death they are, the more dangerous they become.'

Teyth continued to walk in silence.

'That's not you, is it, Teyth?'

Teyth looked into the distance. 'I don't know. I was always good with my battle-axe during my Ascent, but since Zenith, I've felt different.'

Atreu hesitated, then he said, 'Valkyra's a baresark, you know.'

'She couldn't be. She couldn't defeat me – and, believe me, she tried.'

'I know.'

'What do you mean, you know? I haven't told you anything about that.'

'That proves it though, doesn't it?'

'Proves what?'

'That you're a baresark,' said Atreu. 'If she couldn't best you in battle, or in any other way, then the two of you must be the same.'

Teyth eyed his brother curiously. 'How do you know so much about what happened between the two of us?'

'I read it.'

'What does that mean?'

'Exactly what I said, I read it in a book up in the Keep. It was ... like a story ... and I read how you were found semiconscious in the snow and were brought before Valkyra. She threatened your life by pressing into your throat – that's when you gained consciousness. You thought she was Verlinden at first and – '

'Stop,' Teyth shouted. 'Stop. Am I going insane? How can you know all this?'

'I told you – I read it.'

'In a story? You were always making up stories when you were young that you were convinced were real.'

'Like the ones about the Dusk People?' asked Atreu. 'Did I make those up as well?'

'You ... I don't know what to think anymore. The Nazir are here at the Summit so those stories were true. Now you tell me you read a story about Valkyra and me and – '

'Teyth, strange things have happened to both of us since we started our Ascent. You told me notches mysteriously appeared on the handle of your axe, and you finally realised there was one for every Faemir you killed. Can you explain that?'

'No, unless I was somehow cutting the notches into the handle in my sleep.'

'And I didn't tell you this, but after the final Zenith, I could read my Book.'

Teyth shook his head in bewilderment. 'Is that when you read about me?'

'No,' said Atreu. 'I remember the first words I read clearly. They were *Don't open your eyes. You promised me you wouldn't look.*'

'So?'

'They don't sound familiar to you?'

'No ... not really.'

'The blindman game. You said those words.'

'That was a long time ago, Atreu. How do you expect me to recall the words?'

'I can remember them as if you spoke them this morning.'

'You always had a good memory for stories.'

'But listen, the story in my Book was about my Ascent. It started with the day we found out about our Talismans.'

'I'm sorry, Atreu, none of this is making any sense.'

'Look, Teyth, I can't explain what has happened, but we've both changed since Zenith and our Talismans have somehow determined that change. That's what is supposed to happen, isn't it?'

'So you think I'm a baresark now?'

'Possibly the most fearsome warrior on the Mountain.'

'I don't feel particularly fearsome right now.'

'That's because you're not threatened.'

'And you, little brother, you can read life as if it was a story?'

'That's right, and hopefully, when we find Verlinden she'll have both our Talismans.'

'Hey – watch out.'

Teyth held Atreu back as they both watched a large sheet of snow disappear silently into the ground in front of them.

'These snow-covered chasms are dangerous,' said Teyth. 'I nearly fell into one on my Ascent.'

They walked back a short distance and then skirted around the chasm, giving it a wide berth.

'Do you see the three hills yet?' asked Teyth.

'No, but I think we must be getting close.'

The clouds overhead darkened as they continued.

'So, little brother,' said Teyth after a while. 'Tell me what else you read about Valkyra and me.'

*

Praether was disorientated as he woke up to find Leyvin standing next to his bed and shaking him. 'What do you think you're doing?' asked the arch-librer.

'That's exactly what I want to know from you, Praether.'

The arch-librer rubbed away the sleep to see Leyvin's flushed and angry face glaring at him. 'What do you want?'

'The Circle has just met, and we heard what Micah and that windrider Riell had to say.'

'So why are you waking an old man out of a sound sleep?' He coughed and sat up.

'Don't try to hide behind your age with me. Micah, Riell – it doesn't take a flash of inspiration to see that you're the link.'

'The link for what?'

'Don't waste my time pretending you're innocent.'

Praether shook his head. 'My, my, such directness. Is this appropriate for a First Speaker?'

'Praether, do you realise what you've done? The windriders are demanding their Order of the Wynde, and you're helping them destroy everything we have here.'

'Leyvin, first of all I want you to get your hands off me.' Leyvin scowled and released his grip. 'And secondly, I can't see how you can blame me for what has happened. Yes, Riell spoke to me about the windriders' plans yesterday, but I gave him neither advice nor tacit approval. I told Micah to speak to Riell before he addressed the Circle. That was all.'

Leyvin leant back, 'I don't believe you.'

'I don't care whether you believe me or not. Don't blame me if you have a situation you can't deal with.'

'I can deal with it, Praether.'

'Oh, yes? What are you going to do?'

'There's no choice as far as I can see. We refuse the windriders' demands.'

'How long will the food we have at the Keep last?'

'The guild won't go through with it. Even if Riell has some supporters, the others will still fly in the supplies.'

'And the pass at Crosanct? How will we regain control of that?'

'We have enough forces there now to take it again.'

'And you've convinced the Circle of your course of action?'

'Don't you worry about the deliberations of the Circle.'

'Well, Leyvin, I'm sure you're in control of proceedings as always. So there's no problem is there? Not much point in working yourself into a frenzy and waking up an old man from his much-needed sleep.'

Leyvin's demeanour suddenly changed. 'You're right. If you're not supporting the windriders, then there's no point in me even talking to you.'

'Well, I'm awake now for nothing. Thank you for that, Leyvin.'

'Go back to sleep, Praether. In fact, sleep as much as you want. Your time is over.' Leyvin started to leave.

'I'd advise you to support them.'

Leyvin stopped dead. 'I didn't come here for any advice.'

'Then why are you standing there waiting to see what I'm going to say?'

Leyvin scowled and turned towards the door.

'Wait, Leyvin, I'll tell you why you stopped. Now that I no longer have any power, you actually want to hear what I have to say. See, I know you better than you know yourself. You actually have very few ideas of your own.'

'I'm not listening to this.'

'Yes, you are. You're still standing there. Your success in the Circle has nothing to do with the power of your ideas. All you ever do is react to other people's ideas. Your will may prevail in the end, but you actually create nothing.'

'Thank goodness there's been someone there to argue against your foolish ideas.'

'It's not just me, Leyvin. Although I can see you're now completely lost without me there.'

'You're deluding yourself, Praether.'

'Am I? Try to think of a single argument you put before the Circle that wasn't actually someone else's or wasn't a reaction to someone else's. Any positive argument you've ever put has originally been Lythos'.'

'You're ranting. You know there are many things I believe in.'

'Oh yes? Name one.'

'I'm not going to stay here and play games with an arch-librer who is past his prime.'

'Name one.'

'I believe in the Orders, in the Circle, in the way we control the Mountain.'

'The way we used to control the Mountain.'

'We'll regain control.'

'Without the windriders?'

'I've had enough of this. Go and wipe some dust from your books, Praether, and I'll go and regain control of the Mountain.'

'I hope I've given you enough ideas to work with,' said Praether, as Leyvin stormed out.

*

Light was starting to fade and the white blanket of snow took on a ghostly sheen. The air was still and cold, and thick clouds blotted the sky.

Atreu shivered as he and Teyth trudged towards the rocky outcrop which jutted out between the three hills just up ahead. 'I can't understand why I'm so cold all of a sudden,' he said. 'I thought I was used to it.'

'I can't stop shaking either,' said Teyth. 'Perhaps we're reacting to that little bit of sunshine we had this morning ... how's your R'angkur?'

'I usually can't concentrate enough while I'm walking.'

'But that's the place just over there, isn't it?'

'Yes.'

'And we won't have long to wait?'

'No, but I told you, Teyth, I won't be going back without Verlinden. I just want to tell them to pass on the message that we're all right. You go with them if you want to.'

Teyth shook his head. 'We've been separated too long. I'm staying with you.'

'Have you noticed something?' asked Atreu.

'Apart from the cold?'

'Yes.'

Teyth looked around. 'I can't see much. In fact, with this cloud cover, it's going to be pitch-black very soon and I won't be able to see anything.'

'And what can you hear?'

'Are we playing a game, little brother? I can't hear a thing except our own voices and footsteps.'

'That's just it – no instability, nothing.'

'Does that mean the Mountain is at peace?'

'It doesn't feel like it to me. The stillness is making me feel uncomfortable. It's as if the Mountain's waiting for something to happen.'

'Like what?'

'I'm not sure.' Atreu began shivering uncontrollably.

'Are you all right?'

Atreu pointed to the rocky outcrop which broke the line of ghostly white in front of them. 'We can wait there. I ... I need to perform the R'angkur.'

They reached the rocks and sat down facing the flat area between the three hills. Atreu struggled to control the cold which had invaded his body. He found it difficult to evoke the R'angkur – his shivering kept distracting him.

'It's not working,' said Atreu, after a while. 'I can't seem to focus enough.'

'I'm not having much success either, and I've never had any problem before.'

'It must be colder than I've ever experienced.'

'And it's still not fully dark yet.'

Atreu closed his eyes and tried to concentrate again. Each time a tiny pinprick of heat burgeoned inside him, it was like someone reached over and extinguished the flame of a candle with their thumb and forefinger. And with every failure, Atreu was left even colder than before.

'Having any success?' he asked Teyth.

'No.' Teyth's voice was uncertain. 'I'm going to have to get up and move around. I ... can barely feel my legs.'

'No amount of exercise is going to do us much good in these temperatures.'

'You're right ... we'll have to try a dual.'

'A what?'

'A dual R'angkur. It was one of the Felsen Rituals. You must remember it.'

Atreu shook his head. 'I didn't complete my R'angkur training.'

'All right,' said Teyth. 'Give me your hand.'

They clasped hands.

'Now, focus on the point in the middle where our palms are touching.'

The last vestiges of daylight now fled from the sky and the Mountain side was flooded with dark. The temperature dropped even further and Atreu felt the cold enter his bones.

'I ... I can't feel anything,' he said.

'Come on, little brother. We should be able to do this together.'

Atreu felt the moisture around his eyes freeze into tiny crystals.

'Teyth ... I ... I can't move.'

'Concentrate. Our palms. Come on.'

The pinprick of heat suddenly sprang up. Atreu focused on it. He felt the cold trying to extinguish it again, but this time another point of heat joined it before it was overwhelmed. The two points merged into one and immediately began to grow. There was an explosion of heat and it raced through every corner of his body.

Atreu slowly pulled away, but the warmth continued to pulse through him.

'How do you feel?' asked Teyth, his face obviously flushed with heat.

Atreu smiled. 'Much better.' He got up. 'Let's have a look around. There's a chance Verlinden may be here waiting for the windriders – perhaps she'll even have my Book with her.'

'You might be being a bit optimistic, little brother.'

Atreu smiled. 'Perhaps.'

They explored the area. Atreu's eyes soon adjusted to the deep darkness which blanketed the Mountain, a darkness not unlike the one Atreu had experienced at the Lhorong monastery. He noticed that although Teyth was coping, his brother's night vision skills obviously weren't as effective as his own.

'It doesn't look like she's here,' said Teyth.

Atreu sighed. 'You're right.'

'What do you want to do?'

'I need to find her.'

'I hope you're not going to suggest we walk straight into a nest of Faemir looking for her.'

'Teyth, I'm not going to leave without Verlinden. When the windriders come, you go up to the Keep. It makes no sense if we both stay.'

Teyth shook his head. 'I told you you're not getting rid of me that easily – besides she has my axe as well as your Book. I think it's about time I got it back.'

'All right,' said Atreu, 'we'll wait for the windriders to tell them to pass on the message that we're alive and well, and we can find out any news that they may have. Then it's back up to the Summit – right?'

'Right, little brother.'

'You're agreeing with me? I think I'm going to collapse.'

'Don't get too used to it. From what you've told me about the way things work up at the Keep, I don't think I'd be much use on my own. Persuading people was never one of my strong points.' He patted his brother on the shoulder. 'Besides, little brother, someone has to protect you from any more rampaging grale.'

'Don't laugh,' said Atreu. 'This darkness is going to suit them. I told you at Zenith that the grale were tied in with the Nazir. Remember, you didn't listen to me. I gave you the explanation why creatures obviously native to the Steppes were suddenly everywhere on the Mountain.'

'All right, Atreu, I'm listening now. At the time it just sounded like another one of your Dusk People stories. I thought the Faemir had been breeding them somewhere and had unleashed them on us to weaken the Maelir defences.'

'Verlinden told me that the Faemir thought they were our beasts. The grale have been causing havoc among their battalions as well.'

'So, it's been the Dusk People all along. There's been a three-way war for the past year and we didn't even know it.'

'Perhaps, although I'm not convinced yet that the grale have been a deliberate tactic of the Nazir. I think it's still possible that the grale and the Dusk-rats have simply escaped from the tunnel system the Nazir have been building. It made no sense to release grale onto the Plains of Vygird – who were they supposed to attack? And, believe me, there was a whole herd of them there.'

Teyth ran his fingers slowly through his hair. 'You're saying the Nazir have caused all that damage without trying? What would happen if they started using the Dusk creatures as a deliberate tactic?'

'I don't even want to think about it,' said Atreu. 'What do we know about the Nazir? Not much, except that if they are now almost at the Summit, they must have been tunnelling for thousands of years. They are very patient people, and they plan carefully.'

'So you think it's possible they haven't even begun their attack yet?'

'Yes, and I pray that we are prepared when they do. Atreu pointed up into the sky. 'Look the windriders are coming.'

Teyth stared in the direction Atreu was pointing. 'Your dark vision must be a great deal better than mine. It was never one of my favourite Felsen Rituals.'

'Looks like we have different strengths, Teyth. Here they come.'

Atreu started walking and Teyth followed. The two windriders circled slowly, obviously trying to scan the area for Faemir.

'We're here,' cried Atreu.

Teyth glared at his brother. 'Have you taken leave of your senses, Atreu? You'll have every Faemir within a league bearing down on us.'

'The riders were having problems seeing us. Besides, if Verlinden is hiding nearby, she'll know I'm here now.'

Teyth strained to stare through the darkness around him. 'I know why you're not worried – I'm the one who's going to do the fighting if there are any Faemir around.'

'Relax, Teyth. We haven't seen any all afternoon.'

The windriders hovered low and then landed in front of them.

'So you're both alive,' said Theander. 'There are those who thought there was no hope for either of you after the Hold collapsed.'

'What?' said Atreu.

'Are you deaf? I said the Hold's collapsed. Most of the Faemir in it were killed. How did you two escape?'

'It's a long story,' said Teyth.

'Well, tell us about it once we're back in the Keep.'

'I'm not going back until I find Verlinden,' said Atreu.

Teyth interrupted. 'Do you mean to tell us the war is over?'

'No,' said Theander. 'Far from it. There are still some Faemir at the Summit and we haven't made any attempt to reclaim it. Much of Crosanct has also collapsed because of the instability and the Faemir have gained the ascendancy there.'

'Let's go,' said the other rider. 'I want to get airborne.'

'Didn't you hear my brother?' said Teyth. 'We're not going till we find Verlinden – and our Talismans.'

'So, you're not coming?'

'Not yet,' said Atreu. 'Just tell the others that we're alive and well. And keep coming down each dusk as we arranged. We would also appreciate it if you could save us some time just now and take us closer to the Summit.'

'You're lucky we're here right now,' said Theander. 'It's only because some of your friends are offering us their support that we're down here at all.'

'Have you lost your mind?' said Atreu. 'What are you talking about? You're supposed to be serving the Orders, aren't you?'

'It's all changed now. We're sick of taking all the losses so the Felsen and the Liche can drink their wine and eat their fill.'

'The middle way,' said Atreu.

Theander seemed startled. 'Yes, what do you know about the Wynde?'

'Between the Rock and the Light is the wind.' Atreu peered through the darkness at the tall windrider. 'I owe my life to Riell and many other windriders. If you're looking for a third way, then I support you.'

The two windriders exchanged glances. 'We ... we thank you for your expression of support,' said Theander.

'I don't understand what's happening here,' said Teyth, 'but are you going to take us nearer to the Summit or not? If you aren't then we'll have to get going if we want to find Verlinden while we still have the cover of darkness.'

'Look,' said Theander, 'I suppose on a night like tonight and with the Faemir number decimated, we could take you closer without too much risk.'

'Let's go then,' said Atreu.

As the two windriders strapped them in, Atreu wondered how they were going to fly with the extra weight on a night as perfectly still as this one.

He glanced at Teyth who was looking at the wings anxiously. 'Don't tell me these things scare you?' said Atreu.

'I like to keep my feet firmly on the ground, little brother. Are you sure these things are safe?'

Atreu laughed. 'For a man who has faced and defeated a grale unarmed, you seem to be very nervous.'

'Now, both of you will have to help us take off,' said Theander, fastening Atreu's last strap. 'Just run downslope with us and lift your feet when we tell you.'

Atreu grabbed hold of the bar in front of him.

'Right, let's go,' said Theander.

The two of them started running as fast as they could down the Mountain. Atreu stumbled a little at first, struggling to match the windrider's stride. His lungs raked in air as they picked up speed. Faster and faster, as the slope pulled them to even greater velocity. Don't fall, he commanded his legs. Don't –

Atreu felt the harness pulling at his chest and shoulders.

'Now,' cried Theander, and Atreu raised his legs as the wings lifted the two of them into the air.

He looked down and saw the ground rapidly moving away from him. To his right he could see that his brother was also airborne. He laughed when he saw Teyth's face. 'Hey,' he cried, 'how about opening your eyes.'

Chapter Nineteen

Atreu found it hard to take in what he was seeing. The Summit below was ruptured and scarred like the worst battle wound. The hillside which had once been the Hold had collapsed in on itself and was now a giant jumble of white-streaked boulders. Chasms had opened up everywhere and steam was issuing out of many crevices. Here and there, giant black pillars had erupted from the ground and now stood like stark sentinels against the snow.

There appeared to be little sign of movement. Small fires had been lit next to various boulders and overhangs, and groups of Faemir clustered around them, huddling close in an obvious attempt to fight the gnawing cold of the still, frigid air.

The windriders continued to circle the scene from what they considered to be a safe height. Atreu felt gratitude for the Felsen at Lhorong for their training. He was clearly far more skilful in seeing through the oppressive darkness than the windriders.

'Any sign of your Faemir?' asked Theander.

'No – my night vision is not quite that good.'

'Are you ready to be taken down?'

'Not yet,' said Atreu. 'I just can't believe what's happened down there. They're finished. There used to be thousands of them at the Summit. Now look at them – the ones that are left look as if they'll barely survive the night.'

'Their losses were heavy, but our reports tell us that Maelir deaths at Crosanct were far greater. Don't be mistaken into believing the Faemir are a spent force. There are thousands more on their way through the Upper Reaches now that the pass is open again. They'll have food and supplies with them.'

Atreu closed his eyes for a moment, trying to grapple with the thoughts of devastation which twisted and roiled in his mind. *This has to end. Maelir and Faemir must take the knives away from each other's throats.*

'Your third way,' said Atreu, 'the way of the wind – is it the way of peace?'

'Peace?' asked the windrider. 'What do you mean by peace?'

'Between the Maelir and Faemir. Will your Order work for peace?'

'The Order of the Wynde will work towards what we think is the best course. What's important is that our voices be heard now.'

'Hey, little brother.'

Atreu looked at Teyth who was hovering next to him.

'Hey, little brother. I've had about enough of this. I can't see much down there anyway.'

'All right,' said Atreu, cocking his head in the direction of his windrider. 'Can you put us down somewhere?'

'I don't fancy having a volley of Faemir arrows in my back,' said Theander. 'We'll have to take you away from the Summit.'

Atreu felt a tilt and they glided downslope away from the rubble which was once the Hold. The windrider hovered closer to the ground as he looked for a dropping-off point.

'We're going to do this very quickly,' said Theander. 'This is a risk you want to take, and we've all grown sick of taking the risks for others.'

'That's fine with me,' said Atreu. 'I'll be happy as long as you keep returning for us as we agreed. Hopefully, we'll be ready tomorrow.'

The windrider grunted a reply. Atreu saw the ground coming towards him and readied himself for the landing. He had barely come into contact with the snow when he felt the harness being released. Before he knew it, he and Teyth were standing free and the riders were airborne again.

'Bring another windrider with you next time,' said Atreu, as they flew off. 'There will be a third person with us.'

*

The music had started and it seemed to merge with the warm eve-wind. She could smell the stalks of ripened grain. Zenith harvest was always her favourite time of year. The air itself was ripe and every breath nourished her. She stood awkwardly on the fringe, watching the dancers twirl in front of her, half afraid, yet half wishing that one of the boys of the village would ask her to join in.

She twirled her deep red ringlets of hair with her fingers in time to the music and sighed as she looked up at the clear star-strewn summer's sky. She knew at nine she was too tall for the boys her own age and far too young for those of her own height. The music and laughter floated upwards towards the stars and she felt she was being drawn up.

Then the sky exploded in a million slivers of colour. The fireworks had begun. She watched as shard after glistening shard was thrown into the night sky, only to fall back to earth and fade and die before it reached the ground. As in the past, she soon had to stop looking. The more vivid the burst of colour and the more breathless she felt, the greater her disappointment when the slivers died their death. Instead, she stared at the hillside just past the village.

She was the one who gave the first cry of warning.

'Valkyra – you must be able to hear me.'

The fires sprung up all around. The music faltered and was swallowed first by confused voices and then by cries of panic.

'Valkyra.'

She stirred and opened her eyes.

'Valkyra – we knew you were still alive.'

She looked past the face and into the small fire which burnt a short distance away. 'I'm freezing,' she said.

'I'm sorry, Valkyra, we have very few blankets and the night is bitterly cold.'

She looked around in confusion. 'They're attacking. We have to watch out.'

'We're not defeated, Valkyra, not by a long way. Now that you've come around we have some hope again.'

Verlinden's thoughts started to clear. 'The instability – what happened?'

'Everything fell apart, Valkyra. It all collapsed. Some of us got out in time. Some were lucky. I told the others not to give up hope when we found you. Rhea and several of the others are still breathing too – and I'm hopeful they will also regain consciousness.'

Verlinden tried to sit up but found her head was pounding.

'Valkyra, we have some broth for you. Don't try to move just yet.'

It was all coming back to her. The second conclave, the challenge by Rhea. 'So none of the battalion leaders are conscious?'

'No.'

'How many of us survived the collapse?'

'We're still counting, and we're still finding sisters half alive under the rubble. I would say two to three hundred altogether.'

'And the Maelir haven't tried to finish us off?'

'No, Valkyra. We still have enough able-bodied warriors to repulse them.'

Verlinden tried to sit up again but immediately felt dizzy. 'I think you're right. I need to rest a while longer.'

She closed her eyes, but try as she might, the music and laughter and warm summer air didn't return.

*

'I thought you would be back to see me, Leyvin,' said Praether, looking up from the Book of Maelur, his eyes red from constant reading. 'I see you brought your dear brother with you this time.'

Lythos scowled at the arch-librer. 'This wasn't my idea.'

'We have heard some news which may interest you,' said Leyvin.

'How nice of you to keep me informed.'

Lythos said, 'Both Atreu and Teyth have been reported as being alive.'

Praether straightened up. 'Indeed?'

'Yes,' said Leyvin. 'No sign of either Talisman, but apparently they intend to return with both the Book and the axe – and the Faemir – tomorrow.'

'That gives you some real problems, doesn't it, Leyvin. As if the windriders aren't giving you enough trouble already.'

'We can cope with it all,' said Lythos.

Praether snorted. 'Then why are you here, Lythos?'

'All right, Praether, enough of this,' said Leyvin. 'Yes, we are in trouble, but so is the Circle, so are the Holy Orders and so are you.'

'Me?'

'Yes,' said Lythos, 'your precious Riell has started something he now no longer has control of.'

'What do you mean?'

Leyvin started pacing up and down. 'There are members of the windriders who are, shall we say, more extreme in their views and demands than Riell. He assumed leadership but others have their own ideas.'

'What are they asking for?'

'That's just it,' said Leyvin. 'There's a large and growing group not asking for anything. They're just going to leave, abandon us here in the Keep, and go back to their towns and villages.'

'Are they mad?' said Praether, suddenly overcome by a coughing fit. Composing himself, he continued. 'Don't they realise that if the war continues, there may not be any towns or villages for them to return to?'

'There are others,' said Lythos, 'who now no longer simply want seats on the Circle, they want to control it.'

Praether covered his face with his hands. 'It's all falling apart, isn't it? Everything we've built.'

'And it's your fault, you old fool,' said Lythos.

Leyvin said, 'The Circle is paralysed. We can't make a decision. I'm constantly being challenged by some member.'

'You win, of course,' said Praether.

'Yes,' said Leyvin, 'because the challenges are stupid or ill thought, but we're spending so much time making judgements about challenges that we no longer make decisions.'

'Don't blame me for that, Leyvin.'

'Of course, I blame you. You were the one who gave Atreu such prominence. A large proportion of Circle members are now convinced that an apotheosis has occurred, and they are refusing to make any decisions until Atreu returns with the Book. Six days to Equinox and we haven't even completed the Ascenders' judgements, let alone decide what our new battle strategy will be now that the impermanence has become such a crucial factor.'

Lythos' face was flushed. 'How can we not make decisions during a war? You've effectively destroyed the Circle.'

'And now the windriders want a consecration of the Order of the Wynde,' said Leyvin, 'and you must be aware of the repercussions such a consecration would have for the Circle. And while we argue and bicker endlessly, unable to decide how to deal with it, the extreme elements among the riders become more and more vocal.'

'And you're the one,' said Lythos, 'who has given Riell the sort of encouragement he needed to make the stand. Of course you're to blame.'

'I've heard enough,' said Praether. 'The problem to me doesn't appear to be what I've said or done – it's the system we've built up here.'

Leyvin glared at Praether. 'You know as well as I do that what we have built in the Keep and on the Mountain has been the result of accumulation of one small truth on top of another for thousands of years. It has worked for countless generations and it's been improved upon for countless generations.'

'But it's not working anymore, is it, Leyvin?'

Leyvin's expression softened. 'Look, Praether, speak to Riell. Get him to change his demands or postpone them – or anything.'

'It would be of no use.'

Lythos snorted. 'I told you he would be no help. We're wasting our time here.'

'No, wait,' said Praether. 'I don't think anything I can say will make him change his mind, but let me give you some advice.'

'Come on,' said Lythos. 'We've had to listen to too much of his advice over the years.'

Leyvin held his brother back. 'Let's hear what Praether has to say.'

Praether shifted his gaze from one brother to the other and then back. 'There's not much point in me speaking to Riell. You two go to him yourselves.'

'He had his chance to address the Circle,' said Lythos. 'We spoke to him then.'

'You've never actually talked to him outside the Circle, have you?' asked Praether.

'Why would we?' asked Lythos.

'Other members of the Orders speak to the two of you all the time, hoping to have some influence through you on the decision making of the Circle. Just give Riell the same chance, outside the formality of the Circle procedures.'

'Do you mean treat him as if he is a member of an Order?' asked Leyvin.

'Yes,' said Praether. 'Hear what he has to say. Give him a chance to appear to the other windriders as if he is getting somewhere. Let all those with extreme views see that Riell is the one they should support. Perhaps even allow him to nominate for my vacant seat.'

'What?' cried Lythos. 'Now you've gone too far. You almost seemed to making a little sense for a while there.'

'No, wait,' said Leyvin. 'I think you may be right, Praether. We've steadfastly refused to negotiate at all, and we've given him no room to manoeuvre. No wonder the actions and demands have grown so quickly. Allowing him to nominate together with some vague promises could be enough to solve the crisis.'

'I'm not sure about that,' said Praether. 'I think you'll have a bigger headache when Atreu returns.'

'Perhaps,' said Leyvin. 'Perhaps. I want to thank you for your advice – you've given me some ideas which may be extremely helpful.'

Praether watched as the two brothers left the room, shook his head slowly, and then returned to the Book.

*

Verlinden took the Book from under her coat. She opened it and rifled through the pages, trying to make out the words in the flickering firelight. Her attention was caught by Atreu's name and she started to read.

*

Atreu and Teyth trekked upslope, protected from view by the icy overhang which reared above them. The strange stillness still pervaded the night air. Occasionally, they would come across a small pillar which was evidence of the recent instability, but otherwise it was almost as if the atmosphere itself had somehow frozen and was waiting to thaw. Although the R'angkur still warmed his body, Atreu shivered as an image from his Ascent through the Upper Reaches fought into his consciousness. Although the ice wall which they were walking along was opaque, he refused to look at it too closely for fear of seeing more figures eternally frozen in utter terror in an icy tomb.

Atreu also fought desperately against the thought that Verlinden was dead, but it constantly threatened to overwhelm him. She couldn't be. She must have been one of the survivors he had seen huddled together around a fire. What would he do if she perished? He simply couldn't conceive the rest of his life without her.

He felt tears starting to well in his eyes. He didn't have any idea how he would be able to find her. If he had looked at it rationally, he would have to admit there was a good chance that he and Teyth would be imprisoned again – or worse. Yet, here he was, returning to the Summit where the Faemir, though decimated, still ruled. It was blind faith in a way, and he knew he had experienced it before. Somehow, in Peleusar, one of the largest cities on the Mountain, he convinced himself he would be able to find Micah – and, with Belzalel's help, that's exactly what happened.

Teyth suddenly pushed him back up against the icy face of the cliff. Atreu was about to protest when he saw Teyth's finger held up to his lips, gesturing him into silence. Atreu leaned forward slowly and saw a low-burning fire just beyond the curve in the cliff. Around the fire were about a dozen Faemir, huddled together and trying to sleep. One Faemir was sitting with a straight back and obviously keeping watch.

It was impossible to tell whether any of the prone figures was Verlinden. Atreu could see Teyth looking at him and gesturing as if to ask, What should we do?

Atreu shrugged his shoulders, and Teyth grimaced.

Then Atreu stepped out from the protection of the cliff face, pulling Teyth by his broadcloth, and they both walked slowly towards the group of Faemir.

The Watcher drew her sword once she became aware of the approaching Maelir. She shouted a warning call and the others quickly roused and also drew their swords.

'We are unarmed,' said Atreu.

The Faemir were obviously finding it difficult to see through the darkness.

'There are two of us,' said Atreu. 'We are unarmed. We have returned to speak with Valkyra.' He felt his heart pounding inside his chest.

The Watcher pointed her sword in the brothers' direction as she approached them. 'Valkyra is not in a fit state to speak to anyone,' she said, 'least of all two Maelir.'

'You can put the sword away,' said Teyth. 'As my brother has told you, we are unarmed.'

'We have an important message for Valkyra,' said Atreu. 'She's expecting us.'

The Watcher hesitated for a moment. 'Tie them up,' she said.

*

Verlinden sat up and the blanket slipped past her chest. 'Hey, what's your name?' she called to the Faemir who had first spoken to her when she came to and who was now crouched in front of the fire warming her hands.

'Meirith – has your memory been affected, Valkyra?'

'Perhaps,' said Verlinden. 'Look, Meirith, the two Ascenders who were with us, they survived the collapse. Go downslope and bring them to me.'

'Valkyra, you haven't long been conscious. You must be slightly delirious. The cell they were in was in the worst affected area. They can't possibly be alive ... and how could you possibly know anyway?'

'I'm telling you, Meirith, they're alive, and it's crucial that I speak with them. Now either you go downslope to bring them to me, or I'll go myself.' Verlinden tried to get to her feet but felt light-headed.

'Just you stay here,' said Meirith. 'I'll see what I can do.'

Verlinden watched the Faemir head towards a group of warriors and then turned her attention back to Atreu's Book. She read the words she had just heard herself speak and everything started to dance and twirl before her eyes. She skimmed the next six paragraphs until she came to one which included Atreu's name.

*

'Valkyra won't be happy about this,' said Atreu, the cords around his wrists so tight they dug into his flesh.

'Valkyra's on her deathbed,' said the Faemir, 'so I'm not particularly worried about any of your threats.'

'Take us to her,' said Atreu.

'I'm not about to start taking orders from a Maelir, so hold your tongue or I may cut it out.'

'Look,' said Teyth. 'We're not threatening you. All we're asking is for you to take us to Valkyra. She will be the one who is demanding to see us.'

The Faemir pulled a blanket over herself and stood closer to the dying fire. She was clearly freezing and Atreu could see they had no wood left to burn. 'I don't know how someone who is unconscious can give orders,' she said. 'I'm not taking you anywhere until sunrise when I can see what I'm doing.'

'You're cold, aren't you?' asked Teyth.

'I will cut out both your tongues if you're not silent. The others want to try to get some sleep.' She pointed to the Faemir who had resumed their huddle on the ground.

'Come here and touch my face,' said Teyth.

'What?'

'I said, come and touch my face. I'm tied up and weaponless. What can I do to you?'

The Faemir looked at him strangely. 'I told you I don't take orders from Maelir, least of all from Ascenders.'

'All right then. Please, come here and touch my face. All I'm going to do is give you some warmth.'

'I felt the heat when I was tying you.' She was obviously curious despite herself. 'How is that?'

'It's a technique one of the Holy Orders teaches. How do you think we're not shivering the way you are?'

'Why would you give me some of the warmth?'

'Because you're cold.'

The Faemir gave him a look he couldn't decipher. It appeared for a moment as if she was going to come towards him, but then she changed her mind and turned back towards the fire. Apart from the occasional crackling sound, the Mountain side was still.

Atreu suddenly felt very tired. How long had it been since he had slept? He looked across at Teyth and saw that his brother was still watching the Faemir but that his eyelids were half-closed and he was fighting not to fall asleep.

'Was this a good idea, Teyth?' he whispered.

'What was that, little brother?'

'I said, do you think coming back here instead of going to the Keep was a good idea?'

'I want silence from you two.' The Faemir drew her sword.

Teyth looked at Atreu and shrugged.

A surge of fatigue overwhelmed Atreu and his vision began to blur slightly. Then he found his attention being taken by something that appeared to be moving in the distance. His eyes must have been playing tricks on him. It appeared to him as if a large flat rock which lay exposed just downslope of them had moved. He forced his eyes wide open to try to get a better look. It seemed to have moved again, this time rippling like the wave on a lake.

What was going on here? There were no sounds of any tremors, and the ground and air were as still as they had been all night. Besides, he had never seen a rock move like that.

Wait! He took a deep breath and let the air clear his head. He and Teyth had walked up from there, and they hadn't seen any exposed rock. How could there suddenly be a rock there anyway? He stared through the darkness, trying to focus on it more clearly.

It moved again. Unmistakably.

This time it gathered momentum, and as if sensing his awareness, it started heading upslope in his direction.

Atreu squirmed, trying to get to his feet. It came closer, moving, pulsing like a living being.

And then he realised that it was alive.

But it wasn't a single living being – it was hundreds of them. And finally, with a stab of fear that hit him in the back of the throat, he realised what they were. He tried to dredge up the words, but it was as if the words themselves were afraid to leave his lips. Finally, he cried:

'Dusk-rats!'

Again he cried as the horde drew closer, 'Dusk-rats!'

There was a brief moment of confusion as the Faemir got to their feet, but then they all quickly drew their swords as the Dusk-rats approached with increasing momentum.

'Untie us,' cried Atreu.

'Come on,' said Teyth, 'quickly. You can't leave us like this.'

The Faemir hesitated for a moment, but then cut their cords.

And the rats began to swarm over all of them.

Atreu screamed in agony as two bit into his leg.

'The eyes,' cried Teyth. 'The eyes.' He kicked at them furiously, trying to stun them before their razor-sharp teeth could hold.

Atreu rammed his finger into the eyes of one. It squealed, but it wasn't until he damaged the other eye that it let go. As he reached for the other one, another rat pierced the flesh of his arm and hung on. He staggered towards the embers of the fire and picked up a stick which was glowing at one end. Despite the heat searing his skin he pressed the glowing point into the eye of the rat on his right leg. It wriggled and squirmed ... and finally let go, running back downslope. He pierced the eye of the one embedded in his arm and the same thing happened.

He looked at the chaotic scene in front of him. The Faemirs' swords flashed in all directions, but it wasn't enough. Several of the warriors had been brought down and the horde swarmed over them in a feeding frenzy.

Teyth had somehow managed to get a sword from a fallen Faemir and was hacking and slicing at the beasts with unsurpassed fury.

Atreu kept near the glowing remains of the fire which seemed to keep them at bay. One Faemir staggered back towards him, covered from head to toe with feeding rats. Before he could do anything, she had fallen backwards into the fire. The rats screamed and tried to run off, some of them attempting to bury themselves into the embers in a wild panic.

Atreu reached down to lift the Faemir out of the flames but her arm came away from her shoulder. He looked at where her face should have been but all that remained was an open wound. Her body was still convulsing as blood poured out onto the fading embers of the fire.

Atreu felt a wave of nausea and reached down and took the sword from her other hand. He looked at the gaping wound which was once her body. Guessing where, in the sea of blood-soaked flesh, her heart must have still been beating, he ran her through with the sword.

Although he hadn't eaten for a long time, his stomach somehow found something to bring up.

He turned away from the fire to see Teyth surrounded by piles of dead Dusk-rats. And still his brother's sword flashed in a manic frenzy.

Atreu raced out to join him and added more bodies to the tally. Finally, the remaining rats gave up and followed each other in a mad race downslope.

Teyth continued to hack and thrust at invisible rats long after the last one had departed.

'Teyth,' cried Atreu, again and again. 'They're gone.'

His sword, however, flashed as if they were still attacking.

The remaining Faemir watched open-mouthed.

'Teyth,' cried Atreu again. 'Put the sword down. It's over. Put the sword down.'

Teyth only stopped as Atreu stepped dangerously close to his swinging weapon. The fury left him as quickly as it had arrived and his arm now hung limply by his side.

Atreu reached down and took his sword. 'It's over, Teyth, it's over.'

Teyth stood there, listlessly staring into space. Atreu could hear the Faemir whispering the word baresark to each other. He took the two swords he now had and handed them to the Faemir Watcher.

'Here,' he said. 'We don't want these. Just take us to see Valkyra.'

Atreu followed the Faemir as she viewed the carnage around them. A pale light suddenly leeched out from behind the Mountain as dawn broke.

'They're not your beasts, are they?' she said softly.

'No,' said Atreu. 'The Maelir have suffered from the attacks of the Dusk creatures as much as you have. I think we've both suffered enough.'

The Faemir exhaled a deep breath and a cloud of vapour dispersed in front of her face. 'All right,' she said. 'There's no point in staying here any longer. Let's see if Valkyra has regained consciousness. No doubt she will want to see you.'

'Are you going to tie us up again?'

They both looked at Teyth who had slumped onto the ground and was holding his head in his hands.

'No,' said the Faemir. 'I don't see the need.'

Chapter Twenty

The flames towered above her like bright, ravenous giants. Countless sparks escaped the fire and raced into the night sky. A tumult of sounds assaulted her – voices shouting, screaming, the clash of stone on stone, the whip-like cracks as the flames consumed whatever they could find. And above it all was the battle wail of the assailants, bringing everything together into one horrifying crescendo.

Each time Verlinden emptied another bucket onto the flames, the heat pounded her in waves, almost as if she was feeding the fire rather than trying to quench it. She looked across at the battleground which had once been the dance floor, and she saw the deadly new dance which was now taking place.

And underfoot the Mountain trembled, crying for the dance to end. It bucked and heaved as if trying to break the combatants' rhythms. And above the tumult rang another cry. She looked up and saw a giant angled pillar slicing through the Mountain side towards the village, and atop the pillar stood a figure, sword raised to the sky, wild flaming hair trailing in the wind.

The figure entered the melee and the villagers simply gave up and dispersed. Verlinden threw the bucket to the ground and started running, she had no idea where. Walls of flames blocked her path at every turn. Giants leered at her, laughing with open mouths and long, yellow tongues. And with every step, the ground tried to shake her off-balance and throw her into the giants' embrace.

And then she stopped. This was not going to be the way. Taking several deep breaths, she stared the flame giants in the eye and they shrunk and withered. The fires still burned and the ground still shook, but she could now see the way out of the inferno.

One of the attackers suddenly emerged from a side alley. Something awoke inside her, something which had lain dormant, and instinctively she pounced, bringing the Faemir to the ground. To her horror she felt herself being rolled over quickly – now she was at the Faemir's mercy.

Verlinden struggled, furiously shaking her head from side to side. Finally she looked into the face of her conqueror.

And she screamed.

And she screamed.

And the first thing she focused on was the open page of the Book.

What was happening? The fire had all but died out and daylight now touched the expanse of snow around her.

She shivered. Memories raced back into her mind. She had blocked out so much of that day – and her entire nine years as a Faelen. Had she really been that tall, awkward girl waiting for one of the village boys to ask her to dance? Could she really have been the panic-stricken girl running from laughing flame giants?

What had happened to that girl?

She looked at the words on the page in front of her, but somehow she could no longer decipher them. Had she read her story, or had she dreamt it?

Or had it been real?

She closed the Book at the sound of voices. Looking up, her eyes met Atreu's.

She smiled. 'We meet again, Atreu.'

'We do indeed,' said Atreu.

'Valkyra, it is good to see you have regained consciousness,' said the Faemir who had brought Atreu and Teyth upslope. 'I didn't feel it necessary to tie these two. Do you wish me to do it now?'

'No – these two are no threat to us.'

'Valkyra,' said the Faemir, 'some decisions need to be made. We have been leaderless since the collapse. I would like to speak with you.'

'Yes, but please, all of you, leave me alone with these two for now. I will discuss any plans that I have after I have spoken to them.'

The Faemir nodded and she and the others left, leaving Verlinden, Atreu and Teyth alone.

'Atreu, it is so good to see you again.' She embraced him.

Pulling away, she looked at Teyth. 'I'm sorry, I'm glad to see you again too. I was so happy when I read that you were alive.'

'Read?' asked Teyth.

Atreu spied his Book on the ground. 'So you found it.'

'Yes,' said Verlinden, smiling, 'and I read some very interesting things about you.'

Atreu raised his eyebrows. 'Show me.'

'I'm sure we'll have time for this later,' said Teyth. 'Can we talk about what we're going to do now?'

'You're right, Teyth,' said Verlinden. Her face suddenly dropped. 'I didn't fool Rhea, you know. She knew I wasn't Valkyra.'

'Is that why I was imprisoned?' asked Atreu.

'I suppose so. I didn't know she had ordered that.'

'Who else recognised you?' asked Teyth.

'One other member of my former coveyn knew, but neither of them told anyone. Rhea was using the knowledge to take control of the Faemir army. It was to her benefit that the others all thought I was Valkyra.'

'And where's Rhea?' asked Atreu.

'I've been told she's unconscious. I'm not sure exactly where she is.' Verlinden frowned. 'Look, it's all over anyway, isn't it?'

'What do you mean?' asked Teyth.

'Well look at us. We're finished. The few of us who are left are going to either freeze or starve to death very soon. Many of the survivors are either badly injured or unconscious. The Maelir have won. It would take only one concerted windrider attack and it's all over.'

'Is that what all the others think?' asked Atreu.

'I haven't spoken to them about it, but what other conclusion can they draw? They're hardened warriors, and they'll continue to fight if required, but they must be devastated. Before I came to, they had been totally leaderless since the Hold was destroyed.'

'But it's not all over,' said Teyth. 'Not by a long way.'

Verlinden stared at him. 'Of course, it is. We have nothing to bargain with anymore.'

'Yes, you do,' said Teyth.

'Verlinden, this may be our chance.' Atreu felt his heart starting to pound. 'Look, the Maelir are in a mess as well. The instability which hit here was even worse at Crosanct. There the Maelir forces suffered far more casualties than you did here. Your people are able to get through the pass again and, from all reports, thousands of them with food and wood are on their way to the Summit.'

Verlinden nodded. 'You're right. We will be able to get support from the surviving warriors here at the Summit to start talking peace. They believe all is lost anyway, and it will appear as a large concession by the Maelir to begin negotiations.'

'But we'll have to move quickly,' said Atreu. 'The new Faemir battalions will be arriving in a few days.'

'Of course, we still have the problem of getting the Holy Orders to consider peace,' said Verlinden. 'While they remain safe and protected up at the Keep, what does it matter how many Maelir are killed or how long they have to wait for us to freeze to death?'

'I think that's changed as well, Verlinden. Perhaps I can make some things happen when I return with my Book. Praether is convinced it will make a difference. Besides, the Holy Orders can no longer afford to be so smug. The windriders have cut their lifeline and are refusing to fight anymore until their Holy Order of the Wynde is consecrated. Why do you think the survivors here haven't been attacked?'

Verlinden's face was flushed. 'So we really do have a chance for peace?'

'Yes,' said Atreu, 'and I think coming to some sort of agreement is crucial now.'

'Why?'

Atreu expelled a long breath. 'The Dusk People are here too.'

'What? That old legend.'

'It's true,' said Teyth. 'Atreu and I both saw them. They have a network of tunnels under the Summit.'

'Here ... what ...?'

'It looks like the Faemir aren't the only ones who want to wrest control of the Summit from the Maelir. The Nazir have just been more secretive about it.'

'And you saw them?'

'Yes,' said Atreu. 'They're here. Who knows how many thousands of years it's taken them to tunnel up through the Mountain from the Steppes. I don't know exactly when they'll attack, but they've done untold damage already without even revealing themselves.'

'What damage?'

'Look around you,' said Atreu. 'I think their constant tunnelling has destabilised the Mountain and has resulted in this, and all the carnage at Crosanct – and much of the other damage we've been hearing reports about over the past year.'

'And the grale and the Dusk-rats,' added Teyth. 'Don't tell me they haven't inflicted a great deal of injury and death to your forces.'

'They played havoc with our battle plans at times,' said Verlinden.

'It's all obvious now,' said Atreu. 'The beasts were light-sensitive – they had to be creatures of the Steppes. The only way they could get to places on the Mountain away from the base would have been through a system of tunnels.'

'So the Nazir have been inflicting damage on both Maelir and Faemir without our knowledge and without suffering a single casualty.'

'And they and their Dusk-spawn are at the Summit now,' said Atreu. 'Who knows what will happen when they finally decide to launch a full-on attack.'

'All right,' said Verlinden. 'I'm going to speak to some of the others. Peace negotiations have to start immediately.'

Teyth looked around. 'What about my battle-axe? It may have killed its last Faemir, but I've got the funny feeling I'm going to need it again.'

'I'll find out if it was retrieved from the rubble,' said Verlinden. She looked down at Atreu's Book. 'I suppose you'll want that back now.'

'Speaking of feelings,' said Atreu. 'I suspect I still don't know how important my Talisman is.'

He picked up his Book and tucked it under his broadcloth next to his chest. And as he did so, he felt a surge of power, as if his heart started beating stronger.

*

Praether awoke into darkness with the sensation that someone was in his room. He froze, trying to steady his breathing so that he still appeared to be asleep. He scanned the room as best he could from his bed without turning his head. Who was there? A dark shadow seemed to be crouched in the corner.

The arch-librer fought the urge to cough. Why would anyone want to be in his room at this time of the night? What could they possibly hope to gain? With a start, he saw out of the corner of his eye that the Book of Maelur, which was lying on the table next to his bed, appeared to be glowing.

Someone was going to steal the Book.

The thought struck him with the swiftness of an arrow. He had to do something. The shadow which he had seen in the corner was now moving slowly towards him. The glow around the Book grew as the shadow approached.

Praether sat up. 'Who are you?' he cried.

The shadow stopped.

'I won't let you have it, you know,' said the arch-librer.

He leant over to pick up the Book but found it was suddenly too heavy. Have I grown suddenly frail, he thought.

The shadow started moving towards him again. Praether fumbled with the flint to light his butter-lamp, but his hands were trembling too much.

'No-one owns the Book,' said the voice from the darkness.

He knew that voice. Praether stared as the shadow stepped into the halo of light being shed by the Book.

It was the Reader.

'Have you come to take the Book back?' asked Praether.

A bemused look lined the old Reader's face. 'No, I have come to return it to you.'

'I ... I don't know what you mean,' said Praether. 'It has been with me ever since I took it from the librum.'

'Ah, yes,' said the Reader, nodding slowly. 'I forget how to see things from your point of view.'

'I'm sorry ... I don't – '

'From the point of view of the one being read.'

'The one being *read*?'

'Yes, I have told you before, have I not, that we are all a tale within a tale within a tale?'

'I've hardly spoken to you before.'

The Reader shook his head as if trying to rid his mind of an unwelcome thought. 'Of course, that may have been someone else. I'll have to re-read that part – then again, I don't suppose it matters. I've told you now, haven't I?'

'Yes, I suppose you have. So you've returned the Book to me? Does that mean I can read it again?'

'As always, you read what you can. Take your meaning – you have always been so close.'

'You're speaking in riddles. Tell me about the Book.'

The old man laughed. 'You must know you have to read it for yourself. You have always been so close.'

The Book's glow now filled almost half the room with a soft light. 'There are three, aren't there?' said Praether. 'Three Books?'

'Count them yourself.'

'I've been right all along about the search for the three Books, haven't I? With each Book the power will grow.'

'The power, yes – and the balance.'

Praether thought for a moment. 'Power and balance. Perhaps that is where I have been wrong. Power and balance. Strength and judgement. Zenith and Equinox.'

'You are closer,' said the Reader.

Praether suddenly became aware that the halo of light was shrinking again.

'Don't go,' cried the arch-librer. 'I don't want to be just close. I've spent my life being just close. I want to know.'

The Reader smiled. 'Don't we all.' The light continued to contract and he stepped back into the shadows.

'Please,' said Praether. 'Something's happened. I can feel it. Tell me what it is before you go.'

The dark shadow which had been the Reader pointed at the Book of Maelur and then held up his hand. Praether strained to see what the gesture was, and although he wasn't sure, it appeared to be three extended fingers.

As the remaining light was drawn into the Book, the shadow moved slowly back towards the corner from which it had come, until Praether could no longer be certain there was anything there at all.

The Book of Maelur now glowed like a glimmerstone, although almost no light shone past its covers. As Praether stared at it, the glow faded to a pale afterimage and then died. It took the arch-librer a moment to adjust to the darkness. He reached for the Book and felt a tingling in his fingers as he touched it.

And suddenly he knew.

Atreu had returned to the Keep.

*

'They have gone back on their word,' said Riell. 'How do I know you won't do the same?'

Micah placed a hand on the windrider's shoulder to try to calm him. Riell pushed him away. 'I can't trust any of you anymore. Perhaps all the others who have been urging more radical action have been right. The Circle will never give us what we want.'

'Now wait,' said Micah. 'Listen to me for a moment. Leyvin and Lythos didn't want me in the Circle. I supported your cause in my nomination speech.'

'More vague promises. We want the consecration of the Order of the Wynde now.'

'They didn't promise you that you would win the nomination, did they? They couldn't do that. It's the decision of the Circle. They only gave you the chance to nominate. Leyvin and Lythos didn't lie. That's not their way.'

Riell glared at Micah. 'What did they promise you?'

'Nothing,' said Micah. 'They know I'm going to support Praether's views in the Circle. Leyvin went through so much to dismiss him, the last person he would have wanted to succeed would be me.'

'You've done particularly well, considering.'

'Look, Riell, you can take my winning a seat in the Circle as some sort of victory. I was successful with my nomination because I convinced enough of the Circle that the status of the windriders has to change. They weren't prepared to take the giant step of appointing you, but they've come halfway by choosing me.'

'Sounds like the sort of crumbs you throw out to birds,' said Riell bitterly.

'I can only repeat the promise to argue your case. Both Praether and I had some reservations at first, but I'm convinced of your cause now.' He tried again to place his hand on Riell's shoulder but the windrider moved away. 'I want to change the Circle from within. We can't throw away centuries of truth and start again. You're right, the Orders have treated the windriders with scant regard. But, please, help me to help you get what you want. Give us all a little scope.'

Riell spoke through clenched teeth. 'The guild must bargain from a position of strength. Now is the time. We may not have such leverage ever again.'

'Do you want to destroy the Circle, the Keep, the Orders and the entire system we have carefully built over the years?'

'No, of course not, Micah. We want to be a part of it, to have our worth recognised. We no longer want to be servants to the system.'

'Please, Riell, just give me a chance. Look, from what I've heard, there have been so many disputes and challenges that there are bound to be a number of expulsions soon. I'll ensure that your nomination is again accepted when another seat becomes vacant. Who knows, now that I'm in the Circle, I may be able to persuade the others to vote you in next time.'

Riell expelled a breath and relaxed a little. 'You believe that's possible?'

'Yes,' said Micah. 'I still believe the Circle can work. I don't want to destroy everything we've built. I don't really believe you do either. Take a positive message to the other windriders. I think you could still make it into the Circle before Equinox.'

'And it's about time too.' The voice wasn't Riell's, but Micah recognised it immediately. He turned, open-mouthed, to see Atreu and Teyth standing in the doorway.

'You do talk, don't you?' said Atreu, after a moment.

'Well?' Teyth raised his eyebrows.

Micah felt tears fill his eyes.

*

'You don't know how dangerous she is.' The windrider stood firm and refused to move away from the door.

'I think I do,' said Teyth. 'Besides, she's hardly in a fit state to attack me, is she?'

'Don't believe that,' said the windrider. 'She nearly strangled one of the other riders to death the other day when he tried to bring her food.'

Teyth eyed him curiously. 'And you're still trying to keep her alive?'

The windrider nodded. 'We don't kill our prisoners, by starvation or anything else – it's part of our code. It's difficult with her because she doesn't always eat, but we keep trying.'

'Look, why not let me take her something to eat. She knows me. I was her prisoner down in the Hold.'

'I don't know – you'll have to leave that battle-axe of yours at the door.'

'My axe? Why?' He instinctively grabbed the handle. He had been so grateful when the Faemir had found it and returned it to him that he was now unwilling to part with it.

'Partly because there are many members of the Holy Orders who want her killed. We simply can't allow that to happen.' He hesitated.

'There's another reason?' asked Teyth.

'Yes – she would be even more dangerous if she got hold of the axe. I've seen her in action, and I don't ever want to see her with a weapon in her hands again.'

'Even if she's bedridden?'

The windrider nodded.

Teyth pointed to a plate of bread, dried meat and cheese which sat on a chair next to the door. 'Is that food for her?'

'Yes.'

'Let me take it in.'

The windrider stepped away from the door. 'All right,' he said. 'Just give me your axe first – and be careful.'

Teyth hesitated, and then handed him his battle-axe. The windrider unbolted the door and slowly pushed it open. Grabbing the plate, Teyth walked in. He heard the door being shut behind him as he looked around.

The room had a high ceiling and was flooded with natural light through a series of windows which had been carved high into the walls. The floor was of a highly polished wood and the cornices were filled with intricate carvings.

On the bed at the far end lay Valkyra, staring at him.

'A bit better than the cell you kept me in, isn't it?' said Teyth.

Valkyra didn't move.

'Look,' said Teyth, lifting the plate. 'I've brought some food for you.'

Again no response.

'Not hungry?'

Valkyra clenched her teeth as Teyth stepped towards her.

'Isn't that funny?' said Teyth. 'There was a time when I was the one who didn't feel like speaking. I don't know, it must be something to do with the baresark rage.'

She blinked quickly at the sound of the word.

'So you escaped?' she asked.

'Don't blame your guards, Valkyra. It was beyond their control.'

Valkyra blinked rapidly again. 'What do you want?'

'Nothing – I came to bring you your food.'

'What do you want?'

'I really don't know why I'm here. This place, the Keep, is so wondrous, yet so strange ... I'm not sure ... the thought that you were here, it somehow ...' He trailed off, unable to finish the sentence.

'You're repaying my visits – that's what you're doing. But don't think it's going to be easy to best me, even the way I am now.'

'I wouldn't dream of trying.' He raised the plate again. 'Do you want this food or not?'

Valkyra stared at him.

Teyth stood there in silence, and finally said, 'You asked me what I wanted – what about you, what do you want?'

Valkyra's words were slow and deliberate. 'I want to climb out of this bed and tear down every building and tower in this place, one wall at a time, until there's nothing left.'

Teyth drew a deep breath. 'You know there was a time when I wanted to kill every Faemir on the Mountain. During my Zenith that's all I was doing – killing Faemir after Faemir after Faemir. I was doing so much killing that I'd built a wall of bodies around me, but still more came at me. I finally realised they'd probably be coming at me forever. The thought almost killed me.'

'So you gave up?'

'In the end the wall of bodies around me was so high I couldn't climb out. I'd trapped myself.'

Valkyra looked away. 'You were a fool then.'

'I want the fighting between Maelir and Faemir to end,' said Teyth. 'What do you want?'

Valkyra turned towards him again, her eyes burning. The words this time were spoken with even more venom. 'I want to climb out of this bed and tear down every building and tower in the place, until there's nothing left.'

Teyth felt a flash of anger. 'Well go ahead and try to do it then. Go on, get out of that bed. Just remember, the first Maelir you'll have to get past is me.'

Valkyra didn't move.

'Well go on, Valkyra, get out of the bed. What's stopping you?'

'I can't move my legs,' she shouted. 'I can't feel anything from my waist down.'

Teyth saw for the first time how pale and gaunt she looked. Her face was hard but he could see that her anger, now that she was bedridden, was turning in on itself and eating away at her.

'I'm going to give you this food,' he said softly. 'You can try to strangle me, or tear out my eyes, or break my arms, but you know you won't succeed.'

He slowly walked towards her and put the plate on the table next to her bed. She just lay there, half propped up against the bed head and stared at him, her deep red ringlets spilling out over her shoulders and onto the pillow. He looked into her eyes and for a brief moment saw something he had never seen before.

'I'm going to leave you to eat now,' he said, 'but I'll be back.' He turned and walked back towards the door.

'You asked me what I want,' said the voice behind him. He looked over his shoulder. 'I want to die,' she said.

Chapter Twenty-one

Atreu was surrounded by darkness. There were no threads, no dreams. Not even thoughts of threads and dreams entered his mind, just blackness, stretching upwards and outwards, blanketing his vision like a shroud.

He opened his eyes slowly. A hooded figure tended a fire in front of him. His surroundings were bathed in a sombre pre-dawn light, and dark mounds lay scattered across the landscape.

'Where ... am I?' asked Atreu. He had to dredge the words up from the back of his throat.

The features of a vaguely familiar face flashed across his vision and the dizziness returned.

'Relax, it will come to you in time,' said the voice. 'Atreu, please let it rest for a while.'

'Atreu? Yes, that's who I am.'

The darkness began to clear and he found he was slumped face down on the open pages of his Book. He sat up and tried to vanquish the giddiness from his head. The bearded face slowly came into focus.

'Micah, it happened again, didn't it?'

'Yes, Atreu, I'm afraid it did,' said Micah, 'but you're letting it happen to you. You don't have to keep reading your Book.'

'I have to, Micah. There are clues there, I just know it. I made the mistake once of thinking I knew the story and look what happened. It was all too much for me after final Zenith, but I'm going to fight it this time.'

'But, you collapse every time, and it seems to be taking you longer to come round after each collapse.'

'I have to read it, Micah. It's my Zenith – I need to know everything I can before I address the Circle.'

Micah stroked his beard and frowned. 'Of course, you're right Atreu ... but, well, I'm the one who keeps watching you come round. I'm the one who's wondering whether this time you won't be able to remember who you are and where you are.'

'I'm all right.'

'Yes, Atreu, this time.' He absently tapped the table top with his fingers. 'Look, I suppose I'm particularly sensitive about it because of the way you look when you recover. It reminds me of when I was feeding you the r'lung as we travelled towards Crosanct.'

'Don't worry about me,' said Atreu. 'After all I've been through, I'm not going to let a book defeat me. See, I'm up to chapter twenty-one – I haven't got very far to go.'

'Atreu, you know there's no point in me looking at your Talisman. I can't see anything there except a jumble of strange half-words.' He glanced at the open page in another attempt to make sense of the writing. 'You have a gift, Atreu, that I don't have.'

'Some gift!' said Atreu. 'Since I've come back to the Keep, all I can read about is my Ascent. There has to be more. It would help if I could read about what the Faemir are doing, or better still, when the Nazir are planning their attack.'

'You're convinced about the Nazir?'

'Yes – you've spoken to Teyth, haven't you? I didn't imagine it.

We both saw them – we just have no idea how many of them there are or how and when they plan to attack.'

'And the Book of Maelur is no longer any help?'

'No, Praether and I have both been trying, but Maelur's original words are all that's coming through. I feel I have to finish my own Book before we can progress.'

'And you're exhausting yourself in the process. You always seem so pale when you wake up. It's almost as if your Talisman is drawing part of you out as you read.'

Atreu took a deep breath. 'For me it feels the complete opposite – it's as if I'm taking more of myself out of the Book as I finish each chapter. Isn't that funny?' His eyes turned to the open page.

Micah laughed. 'I believe we've had this discussion before haven't we?'

'What?' asked Atreu, looking up again.

Micah looked puzzled. 'I didn't say anything, Atreu. Look, I'll leave you to it. If you feel you need to finish reading your Book, then I'll trust your judgement. I have to go – the Circle is meeting again soon. I don't have to remind you how important the next time will be.'

Atreu nodded slowly and returned to the Book.

*

Verlinden saw the fire ignite from Valkyra's eyes when she entered the room.

'I thought you were long dead,' said Valkyra, after she had recovered from the shock.

'I'm resilient for someone who is half Faelen,' said Verlinden.

'So they have you as well, do they? At least you can still walk.' She looked her sister up and down. 'What are you doing in battle garb. Who promoted you from Watcher to warrior?'

'No-one.'

Valkyra's eyes narrowed. 'What have you been doing?'

'Whatever I think is right.'

'What would you know – you've never planned a battle in your life.'

'Just now I'm planning a peace.'

'Peace? Don't make me sick. There's no such thing.'

'I'm sorry that's what you believe. Have you ever stopped to think how many Faemir have been killed since the war started?'

'I know many more Maelir have been killed.'

'I'll give you another question, Valkyra. Do you know how many more Faemir are going to die in this war?'

Valkyra shrugged. 'What's more important is how many more are prepared to die in this war. And it looks to me like the answer to that question is all of them except one.'

'I'm going to organise a peace with the Maelir.'

Valkyra laughed. 'Under whose authority?'

'Yours,' said Verlinden.

Valkyra's eyes widened. 'So that explains the battle garb. You've been passing yourself off as me.'

'And it's worked.'

'I don't believe you.'

'You can believe me or not believe me – I don't care. I'm going to negotiate a peace, and the war between Faemir and Maelir is going to end.'

'What sort of peace is that? The one where we work in fields and sit in houses and bear children? You're a fool, Verlinden. I should have killed you all those years ago. I was mad for thinking I could turn a Faelen into a Faemir just because she was my sister.'

'Our people can share Zenith with the Maelir.'

'I don't want to listen to this talk about sharing. The Maelir think they are sharing their homes with the Faelen – is that the sort of sharing you want? That's not sharing. What you want is permission to live with them. You want permission to take part in Zenith.' She waved her arms at her sister. 'Go away. You're making me sick. There's only one way to get what you want and that is to take it.'

Valkyra reached out with her hand and grabbed at the air, pulling a clenched fist towards her.

'You've got nothing,' said Verlinden. 'Have a look. Open your fist and you'll see there's nothing there.'

Valkyra let her arm fall listlessly. She turned to stare at the wall. Verlinden could see her body was trembling.

'Tell me, Verlinden,' she said slowly, her voice unsteady. 'Where is the glory in this? Why couldn't I have died in battle? This ... this is nothing, not life, not death. Not victory, not defeat. Give me one or the other, but don't give me this. Anything but this.'

As Verlinden walked towards where Valkyra lay, she saw the shaking was growing in intensity. With tears in her eyes, she put her arms around her bedridden sister.

The room felt strangely silent as she held her till the trembling stopped.

*

'Don't open your eyes. You promised you wouldn't look.' Atreu nodded as his brother led him slowly by the hand.

Atreu closed the Book and laughed softly to himself. He already knew the story, and there were other tales he wanted to read.

A wave of utter exhaustion washed over him. His eyelids felt like ledstones and he felt his head being drawn down towards the last page of his Book.

Had this happened before?

He fought the sense of weariness which overwhelmed him, but in the end sleep won the battle ...

He was riding on the back of a snow-white bird and Verlinden was at his side. The air was warm and still, and tufts of delicate cloud drifted past as they flew. Atreu laughed as he reached out to grab hold of one of the tufts but it slipped through his fingers. He made another attempt and almost overbalanced, but Verlinden grabbed hold of him.

He looked into her eyes and saw the deep blue of the sky reflected in them. She leant towards him and pressed her lips lightly against his. He drew back for a moment and then returned the kiss. He shut his eyes and held her close, feeling the warmth of her body and the beating of her heart. When he opened them again, he saw there was no bird under them and they were floating on the wind.

Below was the Mountain side: golden fields, deep green pockets of forest, and towns and villages teeming with life. And through the middle flowed the vibrant blue waters of the Maelstrom, wild and alive as it raced downslope to the Base. And in the river he could see reflections of faces from his Ascent – Tyr, Micah, Danae, Audum, Cluric and Belzalel. Still with one arm around Verlinden, he pointed to the river and they laughed and kissed again.

They were buffeted by a wind and Atreu pulled away. He looked down and the scene had changed. The colours had darkened and the air appeared to be filled with smoke.

He coughed as the smoke reached him. To his horror, the Maelstrom had turned black. He searched desperately for the reflections that he had seen a moment ago, but the blackness only drew in the light and gave nothing in return.

Another gust of wind hit him and he felt Verlinden being ripped away. He searched the sky for her but the smoke obscured his vision.

The Maelstrom groaned and cried below. As he watched, it began opening like an unhealed scar being pulled apart. The blackness grew to the sound of ripping flesh – deeper and wider – until village after village, field after field, forest after forest, all disappeared into the void.

And out of the blackness they came: Dusk-spawn – screeching, hooting, bellowing, shrieking, clamouring, howling, pale-eyed and misshapen, wild-haired and twisted, gaunt and angular – like broken and charred bodies rising from the grave.

Atreu felt himself falling ...

... and willed himself to wake up.

As he opened his eyes, he felt the room shaking around him.

He sat up in confusion. Where was he? Who was laughing at him. He looked around. Ugly, angular faces leered at him from the walls, pale lidless eyes stared through the stonework.

'Go away,' he cried. 'Go away.'

They crowded in on him, laughing, squealing, louder and louder.

He raised his arms to push them away but still they came, calling his name, shrieking it, groaning it, hissing it, bellowing it so that it echoed into a grotesque crescendo.

He looked down and saw his Book on the table. Lifting it up, he brandished it like a shield.

'I know who you are,' he cried.

The cries stopped and the room fell silent.

*

Night had fallen, but the lights of the Keep seemed to Atreu to have been tarnished in some way. They still flashed and winked at him as he crossed one of the delicate suspension bridges, but it was as if a grey pall had descended to smother the brightness. The air that had always been so clear, somehow immune from the mists which ravaged the Upper Reaches, had acquired an opaque sheen.

The rumbling started again and the suspension bridge began swinging from side to side. Atreu grasped hold of the handrail and prayed that the structure would not fall apart. A crashing sound raged in the distance, and he looked across at the far side of the Keep to see a reed-thin spire snap and fall onto the buildings below, shattering like glass.

Atreu's grip on the rail tightened, his knuckles whitening under the pressure as the bridge continued to swing. The Keep fell strangely silent and Atreu became aware of the rushing of air past his ears. The lights around him lengthened to streaks which stained the night sky.

When the swinging had finally steadied to a gentle sway, Atreu released his grip and continued walking. He entered the building and turned right towards the librum.

He found Praether in the main chamber standing on a box and stacking books. Several of the desks were occupied with scribes busily dipping their quills in the inkwells.

'I thought I would find you here,' said Atreu.

Praether put the two large volumes he was carrying on the shelf.

'Couldn't some other librers do that?' asked Atreu.

Praether looked at him. 'I think you mean the younger librers, don't you?'

'I didn't say that.'

'To tell you the truth, Atreu, I enjoy stacking books. It helps me to think.'

'I've brought my Book with me, Praether. I thought you might want to see if you can read it.'

'I'm not sure if there will be any use in me trying. It's your Book, Atreu. It was never meant for me.' Praether looked away for a moment and started coughing.

'But I've finished reading it now – I felt that completing it was important somehow.'

'You've finished? Micah tells me it wasn't easy for you.'

'No. Please come down, Praether. There are many things I want to discuss with you.'

'Of course, Atreu, of course. These books can always wait.' The arch-librer's legs trembled a little as he stepped down. For the first time since their initial meeting, Atreu really saw his age. Once Praether was on the ground and he had straightened up, Atreu saw how deeply the lines were etched on his face.

'It's a wonder you didn't fall off when the tremor hit,' said Atreu.

'I think it was centred on the other side of the Keep. We barely felt it in here.'

'It certainly affected the bridge out there,' said Atreu. 'Tell me, I thought the Keep was supposed to be the most stable part of the Mountain.'

'It probably still is,' said Praether, 'judging by reports we've had – but, of course, only in relative terms.'

'That last one caused some real damage. The structures here aren't made to withstand much instability.'

'You're right, Atreu, we've never had any before.'

'When did it start?'

'While you were down in the Hold.'

Atreu chewed his bottom lip. 'That's what I was afraid of.'

Praether looked around at the faces of the scribes who were glancing at the two of them. 'Come, Atreu, into my chambers where we can talk more freely.'

They entered the adjoining room, and as Praether closed the door, Atreu saw the Book of Maelur sitting on the table in the middle of the room. He took out his own Book and placed it next to it. For a moment it appeared as if both started to glow, but the sensation vanished suddenly, and Atreu was unsure if the effect hadn't been a trick of the flickering of the butter-lamps.

Praether stood at the door and stared at the two Books on the table. It seemed to Atreu as if the arch-librer didn't want to get any closer.

'I've had the feeling since my return,' said Atreu, 'that you've been avoiding looking at my Book.'

Praether drew a deep breath. 'You're right, Atreu. Perhaps I've been trying not to admit it to myself, but I *have* been avoiding seeing your Book, and I've been putting off the time when the Book of Maelur and the Book of Atreu sat side by side as they do now.'

'Why?'

Praether's shoulders slumped and his body seemed stooped and tired. 'I don't know, Atreu. Lately I've been feeling my age. Perhaps I'm just a foolish old man after all.'

'You know that's not true. There are still many people relying on you. You may have lost your place in the Circle, but you know Micah is depending heavily on your advice.'

'It's not that, Atreu. In recent days I've had the time to doubt myself. Sometimes it's a problem if you have too much time to think.'

'But your truth is your truth. How can that change?'

'The conviction with which you hold it can change.'

'Are you doubting your own Zenith, Praether?'

'It was so long ago. Memory is a funny thing. It can be as elusive as a play of light.'

'And you are unsure about what you've said about the Books, about me?'

'The time for proof has come,' said Praether. 'Either I've been right all these years, or I've been wrong. Either the two Books together deepen our knowledge and understanding, or they don't. What I've been saying is no longer a belief – it's either true or it isn't. And the thought terrifies me.'

'You claimed in the Circle that if I could still read my Book, there has been an apotheosis.'

'It was a clever argument, Atreu. Sometimes I get caught up in my own reasoning.'

'I can read it.'

'I know – I believe you, and you will possibly be able to persuade the Circle, but it may not be enough. I'm not totally convinced myself now. Perhaps I never was.'

'So you think my judgement is far from assured?'

'I only know that ultimately what you say when your judgement is resumed will determine what the decision will be.'

'Can we try now, Praether?'

The arch-librer shrugged. 'I suppose the time has come for me to discover whether my entire life has been a delusion.' He smiled wryly as he walked towards the table.

Atreu and Praether stood side by side.

'You open yours,' said the arch-librer, 'and I'll open the Book of Maelur.'

They both turned to the first page. 'What does yours say, Atreu?'

Atreu looked at the page and read: '*Don't open your eyes. You promised you wouldn't look.* Atreu nodded as his brother led him slowly by the hand. It's my story – shouldn't it have changed now that I've finished reading it?'

'Perhaps you haven't learnt all the truths that are hidden in it.'

'Are you going to try to read yours now?'

'It's not mine. I can't claim Maelur's Book the way you can claim yours.'

'You're going to have to look at the page if you want to read it, aren't you?'

Praether looked down and read out loud: '*I write this for the gen-erations to come so that they may learn of the great Mountain which is the axis of the universe, its spirit the heart of the world. And as with any heart, when it is broken it cries in pain for what has been lost, and when it has been mended it cries in joy for what has been regained.*' Praether closed his eyes and began trembling. 'They are fine words,' he said softly, 'and I've read them many times ... but they are the words of Maelur which have always stood at the beginning of his Book.'

Atreu put his arm around the old librer. 'Praether, don't give up.' Praether continued to tremble. 'I'll advise you as you advised me: perhaps you haven't learnt all the truths of the Book of Maelur. Perhaps that is what you are being told.'

Praether shook his head and looked at Atreu. 'I thank you, Atreu, but I can't see how that can be. I have read this Book a thousand times. I have committed great sections of it to memory. It has been the focus of my life. I have learnt all I can from it. If appears, Atreu, that my wisdom has come to an end.'

'Praether, please, don't give up yet. Here, let's exchange Books. See what you can read in mine.'

The arch-librer sighed and took the Book of Atreu. He looked at the open page.

'Well?' asked Atreu.

'Nothing, Atreu,' he said softly. 'I can't read a word.'

'Try again – concentrate. Can't you see it? Look at the first sentence, the first word ...'

Praether put the Book down. 'I'm sorry, Atreu. It looks like your story is your own.' He turned towards the door.

'Let me read this, Praether. Wait. Don't go. Please, maybe the Book of Maelur will change for both of us again.'

'It's over, Atreu.' He started to go.

'No, listen: *I write this for the generations to come –* '

'Read that again,' said Praether suddenly.

'Why?'

'Just read those first few words again.'

'*I write this for the generations to come.*'

'That's what I thought you said.' Praether walked back to where Atreu stood. 'That's what I read as well, wasn't it?' He held out his hand. 'Here, let me have a look at it again.' He stared at the words. '*For the generations to come.* Of course. How could I have missed it? *For the generations to come.*'

'I don't understand. What is so important?'

Praether looked straight at him. 'Of course, you wouldn't be able to work it out. You are barely familiar with the Book of Maelur.' He straightened up and his eyes were shining.

'Please, Praether, tell me what is so important about those words.'

'They're different,' said Praether, breathlessly. 'They are not the exact words which have always been there. The change is a subtle one but it makes a world of difference. The truth is there. I was wrong in searching for some big sign of the power of the Books. Power doesn't have to hit you like an axe. Don't you see?'

'Praether – the words, tell me how they've changed.'

'Atreu, the opening words to the Book of Maelur have always been: *I write this for the generations of Maelir to come.* Can you see what a difference that makes, what an earth-shattering difference?'

The room seemed to Atreu to suddenly light up. 'Of course. That changes everything. I've been right. It confirms my Zenith. The Mountain belongs to Maelir *and* Faemir.'

'Yes,' cried Praether. 'Our truths have come together, Atreu. The heart that has been broken is that between our two peoples; the war is its cry of pain. Now we must mend it so that the Mountain can be regained.'

The arch-librer stared at the page again, almost afraid to see the words change back to what they had once been, but they remained resolutely on the page. 'Proof,' he shouted. 'We need proof.'

He rushed towards the door and opened it. 'Werther,' he shouted at one of the scribes sitting quill in hand at a desk. 'Don't look at me like that, you damn Felsen. Just grab that copy of the Book of Maelur behind you and come in here ... and what are the rest of you looking at. I'm the arch-librer here and I'll raise my voice if I want to. Just get on with your work.'

Praether returned to the table where the scribe entered the room with another book tucked under his arm. 'Come on, Werther, you Felsen are always so slow. No time for meditating now.'

'Praether, I – ' began the Felsen.

'Don't ask any questions,' said the arch-librer. 'Just open the book you've brought in and read the first paragraph.'

Werther looked confused, but he complied with Praether's wishes. He opened the book and looked at the page.

After a moment, Werther looked up.

'Well?' said Praether.

'Well what?'

'Aren't you going to read it?'

'I just did.'

'No, you Felsen fool. I mean out loud. Make some noise for a change.'

Werther returned to the book. '*I write this for the generations of Maelir to come –* '

'All right, stop there, and read the original Book here.'

'Praether, I have a lot of work I want to get through tonight.'

'Humour me – if that's possible – for a few moments. This won't take long.'

Werther took the Book of Maelur.

'Out loud again,' said Praether. 'From the start.'

Werther sighed. His voice flat and monotone. *'I write this for the generations to come –'*

'Yes!' Praether banged his fist down on the table.

Werther looked at him as if he was insane. 'Perhaps you may wish to speak to one of the healers,' he said.

'Where's your eye for detail? You're supposed to be a scribe. Use your skills. You've got both books in front of you.'

Werther glanced from one to the other and frowned. He held up the book he had brought in. 'This must be a bad copy,' he said. 'Two words have been added in which weren't in the original.'

'Have there?' asked Praether.

'Well ... no wait. As far as I can remember, the opening line should read *generations of Maelir*. In fact, now that I think about it, I'm positive that's what it should read.'

Praether smiled. 'Look at the original again. Just make sure you haven't made a mistake.'

'No,' said Werther. 'It's quite clear the words aren't there.' He turned the book around to look at the cover. 'Are you certain this is the original?'

'Yes, absolutely certain.'

'Then how can this be? A scribe would not make such an elementary transcription mistake.'

'How indeed. How indeed. Werther, go out there and check every copy of the Book of Maelur we have in the main chamber of the librum. See what the opening sentence is.'

'We must have dozens of them here, Praether.'

'Good, then you'd better get started.'

Werther nodded in a surly fashion and left the chamber.

'You have your proof, don't you?' said Atreu.

The lines on Praether's face seemed to have smoothed. 'Yes, Atreu, that is the sign I've been waiting for. Not just the elusive flash, but permanence.'

'But neither of us has been able to read about the events happening around us.'

'It doesn't matter, Atreu. That will come back. The revelation here is much more important, far more wide-reaching. And some permanence has been gained. I always felt that would happen as we found the Books. With each one our understanding would deepen and gain more permanence. It's started to happen exactly as I have always thought. Werther can read the changed sentence – so will all the members of the Circle. So will the entire Inner Sanctum. And it's only the start, I can feel it. We will discover more and more from both these Books and still more from the third Book when we find it. And it won't be just you or I who can read them. The knowledge will belong to all Holy Men. Permanent, there on the page forever, so that we can all share in it.'

'Praether, you've never really told me about how you know there must be three Books.'

'That was my Zenith, Atreu. I know my path has been to put the three Books together. There have always been three. The signs during my Ascent, the revelation I had at Zenith. Three. Always three.'

'What power will the third Book bring, Praether?'

The arch-librer suddenly became more subdued. 'I've only ever had a vague sense of what the third Book would bring, Atreu. I always imagined it to be like walking over the top of a rise. With each step more and more comes into view and the scope of your vision widens until finally you're at the top and everything lies before you.'

'Like an Ascent?'

'Yes. A single Book on its own gives a narrow vision – the story in your Book, from what you've told me, was a very personal one. Two Books together give us a wider view of what's happening – the thoughts and actions of those on whom the destiny of the

Mountain depends. Two can show us the directions we should be travelling in, but the third ... once we have found the third, who knows what knowledge will be in our possession. Perhaps we will come to know the thoughts of the Mountain itself.'

'Praether?' Werther's voice came from the door.

Atreu and Praether looked around.

'There is something strange happening,' said Werther. 'All the copies of the Book of Maelur I have looked at appear to be at odds with the original.'

'Good,' said Praether, smiling. 'I'm most pleased to hear that.'

He and Atreu looked at each other and then down at the two Books on the table.

Chapter Twenty-two

'Why do you keep doing this?' asked Valkyra.

'You're pleased to see me, aren't you?' said Teyth, placing the steaming broth on the table next to her bed. 'There's a goblet of wine for you here as well.'

'There's no point, you know. They won't want me back.'

'What are you talking about?'

'I'm talking about the food, the healers, the reason why you want to keep me alive.'

'Haven't the windriders told you? They never kill their prisoners.'

'Weakness,' she spat.

'They have their reasons.'

'Like I said, there's no point in keeping me alive. My people won't want me back. They don't want a crippled leader. Our strength has been that our leaders always led the way in battle – unlike you Ascenders and the damn Holy Orders: weaponless, hiding up here like timid rabbits.'

'The Orders need time to think and argue and discuss.'

Valkyra snorted. 'Cowards. Spineless weaklings. I always think most clearly in the middle of battle. Give me an immediate threat and I'll make the right decision every time.'

'I'm the same.'

'You're the only Ascender I've ever seen with a weapon. Why is that?'

'It's one of the rules: no weapons. My battle-axe was my Talisman.'

'Stupid rule.'

'In time of war perhaps, but not in time of peace.'

'There's always been a war on the Mountain. We've never accepted your rule.'

'Eat your broth.'

'So I can stay alive?'

'Yes.'

Valkyra looked at him strangely. 'Come here.'

Teyth hesitated. He wasn't sure about the look on her face. She appeared less gaunt every time he visited her, and her deathly pallor had begun to fade.

'What do you want?' he asked, the huskiness in his voice betraying his uncertainty.

'Just come here.' She motioned him to come closer.

Teyth took a step towards the bed, and the next thing he knew, Valkyra had him by the throat and was squeezing.

'Tell me why I shouldn't kill you,' she cried.

Teyth grabbed her arms and tried to pull them away, but she hung on. He felt giddy – instinctively he tried to suck in air, but nothing reached his lungs.

'Tell me why I'm not going to kill you now,' she said again, tightening her grip.

Teyth felt a power awakening as he strained at her arms with all his might, at the same time twisting his body to free himself from her vice-like hands. And with a final surge of strength, he pulled himself free.

'Because you can't,' he said, as he raked in breath after breath. He looked up and their eyes met. 'And you don't want to.'

When his breathing had steadied, he picked up the broth and pushed it towards her face. 'Now, eat this,' he said.

Valkyra swung back and knocked the bowl out of his hand, and the hot broth spilled over the bottom of her blanket. She shouted and pulled the blanket away.

Teyth's eyes narrowed. 'Don't tell me you're starting to get feeling back into your legs.'

*

Atreu felt the wind whistle past his ears as Riell carried him through the sky. The Keep stretched out below him in a carpet of light, yet somehow it was no longer the same. The sun struggled to fight its way through a blanket of cloud. Sparks of colour still flashed through the air, but it was as if the vivid spontaneity had been overtaken by a lethargy, and the colours themselves were older and more tired.

Atreu knew Equinox was approaching, and soon day and night would be equal. His final address and the judgement of his Ascent were imminent, and the weight of the Mountain was resting heavily on his shoulders. The freedom of soaring through the skies with Riell alleviated the burden he was feeling. So much had happened since the first time the windrider had lifted him from the ground at Crosanct. He had known nothing then; his obsession had been to get to the Summit in time for Zenith, and nothing else had mattered. He had given no thought to the time after. With understanding and clarity of vision, though, came responsibility – he knew that now. And there was no turning back.

'You know,' said Atreu, breaking the silence, 'the dream I think I have most often now is one where I'm on the back of a giant bird.'

'I'm not surprised, Atreu.'

'How do you know what I dream?'

Riell banked to the right, catching a thermal and soaring higher.

'It is a dream I've often had. Many riders have told me they've had it as well.'

'But I'm not a windrider, Riell.'

'No, that's true. Perhaps everyone has that dream.'

Riell dipped slightly as Atreu continued.

'And sometimes the bird disappears and I'm floating through the air like a wisp of cloud.'

Riell fell silent again and the two seemed to Atreu to be hovering motionless for a moment before the windrider's wings caught another updraught and the lights of the Keep shrank below them.

'Riell, you said you wanted to talk.'

'It's over, you know,' he said finally.

Atreu nodded although he knew Riell wasn't looking at him. 'The guild will no longer remain what it has been. The Circle, the Keep – it will all have to change.'

'I know you've expressed your support for us, Atreu, but ...' Riell trailed off, leaving the sentence unfinished.

'The Liche and the Felsen don't own the Mountain.'

'They have owned us for a long time. We have been in the service of the Orders for thousands of years, somehow believing we were hanging onto a place at the true Summit. And we've been grateful – did you know that, Atreu? – grateful that we've been allowed to serve them, to bring food and drink to them, to die for them.'

'Why have you never questioned it before?'

'Some have, of course, Atreu. Over the years, I myself have often thought about it. But we were all so grateful to be part of it, to be able to fly over the Keep like this, to see the play of its exquisite lights when millions of Maelir didn't even know of its existence.'

'But you've never been allowed to live here.'

'No, Atreu, you're right. We accepted that, we accepted everything because we had been judged as failures. Can you imagine what that's like: to have been given a taste of something as sweet as the lights of the Keep and then to have it wrenched from your grasp. We failed, all of us, and we wanted to hang onto a shadow of what we had been denied – at any price.'

'And all that's changed now.'

Riell swooped in a downward arc before he levelled off.

'Atreu, I believe I have started something I no longer have control of.'

'You don't think the Order of the Wynde will be consecrated?'

'Yes, I believe it will, but many of the riders believe it will be manipulated in some way, or it will only be short-lived. They do not believe the Liche and the Felsen will give up power permanently. When the crisis is over, all will return to how it has always been.'

'Do you share that belief?'

'It doesn't matter what I believe. Many of the windriders no longer listen to me. There are those who, as we speak, are preparing to leave the Keep forever.'

Atreu listened to the wind whistling past his ears and watched as the cloudbank above them seemed to be snaking grey tendrils in their direction.

'I support your cause, Riell. I owe my life to you and the other windriders many times over.'

'I was hoping you would say that, Atreu, but we need more than your support.'

'I will speak for you at my judgement, be assured of that, Riell.'

'We need even more than that, Atreu.'

'Please, tell me what you want.'

The grey, wispy tendrils reached still closer. It was a moment before Riell spoke again. 'Do you remember the first time we flew together?'

Atreu nodded to himself.

Riell continued. 'You wanted me to go high, so that we could see the whole Mountain.'

'I remember,' said Atreu, 'and you said the only way to see the whole Mountain is to get to the Summit. You were right, Riell. I saw it during my final Zenith.'

'I'm glad, Atreu, I'm glad.' His voice was tinged with sadness.

'What's wrong?' asked Atreu.

He hesitated. 'I've never seen it,' he said finally. 'No matter how high I've flown, I've never seen the whole Mountain. None of the windriders have.'

'What does it matter?'

'It matters, Atreu. It matters more than you can imagine. We believe that is our truth. We will be redeemed only if we can fly high enough to see the whole Mountain. And none of us have been able to achieve it. We need guidance, we need someone to show us how.'

'Riell ... I think I know what you're asking me ... I don't know ...'

'Please, Atreu, we need more than support in the Circle. We need more than clever arguments and carefully considered opinions. We need to know we are not failures. Please, Atreu, I'm asking you – join the Order of the Wynde. Of your own free will, succeed in your judgement and then join us.'

Atreu felt a gust of air brush past his face. 'And fly the winds like you do?'

'Yes, and show us how to see the whole Mountain.'

Atreu looked down at the sparkling lights below and then up at the grey cloud serpents writhing above. And in between, the air was suddenly still, and he and Riell hung motionless, waiting for the wind.

*

'Ah, Rhea, you're alive.'

Rhea struggled to find focus. Her mind was a void, empty of thoughts, of emotions.

'Rhea, there is hope for us yet. First Valkyra and now you. I was right not to give up. I believe Ahrai and even Saretha may eventually gain consciousness.'

The words were confused, jumbled. Rhea recognised the meaning of each one, but somehow the whole made no sense to her.

'Here, Rhea, drink this broth. It is still hot, although the fire is now quite low.'

A familiar smell wafted towards Rhea's nostrils. She brought the bowl to her lips and sipped the warm liquid. The steam misted her eyes but as she drew the bowl away, her vision miraculously started to clear. She struggled for the sounds deep in her throat. 'Thank you ...'

'Meirith.'

'Meirith – of course.' Rhea looked around. 'What has happened?'

'The instability – it has destroyed everything.'

Rhea drew a deep breath. Around her was white on white, punctuated only by the occasional small fire or dark rocky outcrop or the bent figures of huddled warriors.

'Faemir were never meant to live in caves in sides of hills,' she said, as the void began to fill itself with a pounding pain. 'That was our mistake.'

'You know yourself the cold made it necessary, Rhea.' Meirith handed her a piece of dry bread. 'We won't survive out here if we don't find shelter soon.'

'How long have I been here, Meirith?'

'Six days.'

Rhea shook her head. 'Six days? Have we been under siege?'

'No,' said Meirith. 'The collapse alone reduced us to this. There have been no Maelir attacks, although there have been swarms of Dusk-rats attacking those of us who have ventured downslope.'

'No Maelir attacks? Why?'

'Valkyra returned up the pillar with the two Ascenders. They are going to talk peace.'

'Valkyra?' Rhea shook her head.

'She survived the collapse as well. I was tending to her. I had faith with you and with her – both times I was right.'

'Valkyra.' Rhea turned the name over in her mind as the pain spread across her forehead towards her temples.

'Just rest,' said Meirith. 'She said she would return with food and fuel for our fires.'

'And where will she get those from.'

'She says the Orders will give them to us.'

'And you believed her?'

'Why would Valkyra lie to us?'

Rhea stared at her reflection in the bowl of broth. The steam had now thinned in the frigid air, and she could see the glint of her own eyes clearly. 'You heard the reports of her visits to the first Ascender, the one we all believed to be a baresark?'

'Yes, I heard what was being said.'

'She never killed him. We've all had our fun with Maelir prisoners, some of us with Ascenders, but we've never allowed them to live for very long, have we?'

'Valkyra must have known what she was doing. We didn't reach the Summit by questioning her actions or her judgement.'

'No – and look at us now.'

'She will find a way out for us.'

'You think so? I wonder what she's doing up there now with that Ascender.'

'Rhea, I think you need to rest more.'

'Look at all of you.' She waved her hand at the scene of pitiful figures huddled together against the cold. 'Is this the Faemir army that has struck fear in the hearts of the Maelir?'

'Rhea, it is so cold. You won't be feeling it right now. We allowed the fire in front of you to burn higher than any of the others to help you gain consciousness. Wait until night falls and the temperature really drops – once the cold is in your bones it never seems to leave.'

'Meirith, I am not going to have us sit here and wait until we freeze to death. That's been the Maelir plan all along. For all we know, the Maelir could have been somehow responsible for the collapse itself.'

She started to get up. Her legs trembled and her head ached, but she managed to get to her feet. She stood, slightly unsteady, but glaring steadfastly at Meirith.

'If I can stand up,' said Rhea, 'then the rest of you can still form an army. We're not going to stay here and die of cold. We need to go back downslope, fight our way through Crosanct if necessary and regroup. We're a long way from defeat and the Maelir are a long way from victory. Call all the others – I'm going to speak to them.'

'But, Rhea –'

'Don't question my authority, Meirith. Where is the food and the fuel promised to us? It's not going to come. We're just going to die here. No battle, no glory. Just death. The Maelir are even going to rob us of our honour.'

Meirith nodded. 'I'll get the others.'

Rhea looked at the cliff wall of the giant pillar in the distance. Grey mists crawled up its vertical face, obscuring it from view. *Verlinden, she thought, next time we are locked in combat, you will die.*

She smiled to herself as she had the sensation that Verlinden had heard her.

*

Verlinden looked up from Atreu's Book and repeated the last words, '*She had the sensation that Verlinden had heard her.*'

Atreu was propped up on his bed and staring at her as she sat by the table. 'Isn't that strange?' said Atreu. 'It's almost as if Rhea knows you're reading about her.'

'Are you sure you can't see what I've just read?' asked Verlinden.

'No,' said Atreu. 'The power of these Books is elusive. Even

Praether doesn't fully understand them. He says that there is no permanence – like the instability on the Mountain, we never quite know how and when it will manifest itself.'

'But it's your Talisman, Atreu. How is it possible that I can read things that you can't?'

'Perhaps because you shared the final Zenith with me, it's partly yours as well.'

'Perhaps, Atreu.' She looked down at the page again, but it was as if the words had died. She frowned.

'What's wrong?' asked Atreu.

'The words – they've disappeared for me again. Do you want to have a look?'

'No, Verlinden, I've grown tired of reading about my Ascent. That's all I see there. It's as if there's something in my story that I need to understand before I can progress, but I just can't see it.'

Verlinden nodded slowly. 'And while we sit here and wait for your judgement tonight, the war continues below.'

'Will Rhea convince the Faemir to return downslope?'

'Yes, I've no doubt.'

'And they'll meet the ascending forces and regroup.'

'Yes – it will be impossible to talk peace then. Right now is the moment of despair among the warriors when we must strike.'

Atreu laughed. 'It's almost as if you're still talking about war.'

'So much depends on you now, Atreu. We have run out of time. Everything depends on your address to the Circle.'

'And yours.'

'You think you can convince them to listen to me?'

'I have to. Too many voices haven't been heard. That's been the problem.'

Verlinden smiled, got up from the chair, and walked over to Atreu's bed. 'Do you remember our Zenith?' she said, sitting down and running her fingers through his long brown hair.

'As clearly as I can remember what happened this morning.'

Verlinden laughed as she grabbed hold of both his hands. 'We thought it was all going to be so easy, didn't we?'

Atreu relaxed his hands as he allowed her to guide them around her waist and then onto the small of her back. 'I understood it all just at that moment – do you know that? But I realise now that understanding isn't enough. We have to make the changes happen.'

'You're right, Atreu. Nothing happens if you don't make it happen. A sword is no use unless someone uses it.'

Atreu smiled and looked into Verlinden's eyes. 'And a book is no use unless someone reads it.'

He drew her towards him and they kissed. Verlinden ran her fingers through his hair and stroked the back of his neck. Still locked in their embrace, Atreu gently pulled her down so that they were now both lying on the bed.

Verlinden scattered kisses on his face and throat, and he pulled at her tunic so that it came away to expose her body to him. He returned the kisses, first here, then there, seeking to cover her naked flesh. She sighed and loosened the cord on his broadcloth, and then ran her hands slowly up his legs, taking the folds of his robes with her.

Then he pressed himself against her and felt the warm, gentle rhythms take their hold – first softly like the lapping of waves on a lake, and then stronger and more turbulent like the swirling waters of the Maelstrom. Again and again, the rushing churned through him. He had no control, he wanted no control because the rhythm had now consumed his very being, and he surrendered everything, losing himself to their union.

Verlinden cried and he felt the power that had consumed her. She cried again and the power overwhelmed him too so nothing existed but that moment, that time, that place where they lay locked in their embrace.

And she cried one last time, and it raged through his soul ... until he realised the cry was his own.

Still locked, sharing the warmth that grew between them and the cry which now floated like the echo of a memory, they drifted off into a deep sleep.

Atreu was unaware of the beam of light which flashed through the window, unaware that it danced and gyrated through the room until it finally came to rest in front of him, unaware that it remained there calling to him as the ground started to shake again. And as night claimed day, Atreu had no awareness that the beam finally gave up the wait and faded into the oncoming darkness.

*

The shadows from the two flickering candles intertwined on the walls behind Lythos and Leyvin like grotesque serpents. Leyvin sat staring into the flames while his brother paced up and down behind him.

'You should let me restrict Atreu's address, Leyvin. There are many urgent matters to discuss, and he doesn't deserve another full address since we've already heard him once. I could still cut him short – with your support.'

Leyvin had both hands palm down on the table and was almost motionless. 'You don't see changes in circumstances, Lythos. We may have been able to do something like that at one time, but I'm afraid that's no longer possible.'

'You've lost your nerve, haven't you? Praether did more damage with his two challenges than anyone else has in all your time as First Speaker.'

'You may be right, Lythos. I have no idea what the outcome of Atreu's address will be – and I don't think I've ever had that feeling with any other address.'

'You're still First Speaker. Control the debate – you've always been able to do it in the past.'

'Things have changed. I have no authority anymore. Only one successful challenge against me and I lose my position to Holthim.'

'Don't make me laugh, Leyvin. You never had authority anyway, you had control.'

'You don't have to tell me what I had. The Circle knows now that I make mistakes, that I can be successfully challenged. That's why it's a free-for-all every time we meet. I'm no longer invincible.'

'All the other challenges have failed – and there have been dozens of them since Praether was expelled.'

'But that's the difference, Lythos. As always, you fail to see the subtleties. They challenge me because they believe they can defeat me now. They know it's possible. That's the main difference – the frame of mind. I only ever controlled proceedings because they believed that I did.'

'Leyvin, for me it's very simple. Either you get what you want, or you don't.'

Leyvin looked up at his brother. 'Tell me what you want then.'

Lythos stopped pacing. 'I want Atreu's truth to be dismissed and his Ascent declared a failure. I want us to order the windriders to fly to what's left of the Hold and finish off the Faemir, and I want the Circle to return to the way it once was.'

The ground suddenly shook under their feet, and the shadows on the wall writhed and squirmed as if they were struggling to escape their stony prison.

Leyvin grimaced as the tremors started to ease. 'You have to adapt, Lythos. Nothing is the way it once was. We're not safe anymore, not even in the Keep. The war has come to us and the Mountain is reminding us of it.'

'I'll tell you something, Leyvin,' said Lythos, pointing his finger at his brother. 'The war has come to us because we've opened our gates and bid it welcome. That Faemir baresark, we should have had her killed or at least allowed her to die. That was weakness on your part.'

'I can't impose my will to get the windriders to break their covenant.'

'Look what they've done now. The covenant is in tatters anyway.' Lythos started pacing again, his steps more frantic and his arm movements more agitated. 'Besides, we could have done the killing ourselves.'

'Have you gone mad, Lythos? Since when do the Orders kill?'

'Since when do the windriders refuse our command? Since when is an Ascender, who by rights shouldn't even be before the Circle, suddenly so important to the future of the Maelir? Since when do we have Faemir in the Keep? And not just one, but two. One, the most dangerous woman on the Mountain, responsible for the deaths of goodness knows how many Maelir, and the other the only woman to ever usurp the place of an Ascender and experience Zenith. What do we do with the first one? We heal her, feed her, keep her warm. And the second one gets to roam through the Keep almost at will. It wasn't long ago that not a single Faemir even knew the Keep existed. Now we have two here, almost as our guests. How many more are we going to let in?'

'Lythos, you're ranting. This does neither of us any good.'

Lythos stopped again, and Leyvin could see the two candle flames reflected in each of his eyes. 'Tell me why I shouldn't go and kill the baresark now, in her sleep. Tell me why I shouldn't murder the other one as well.'

'Why stop there, Lythos?' Leyvin's voice grew louder. 'Why not kill Atreu as well. Why not butcher Riell while you're at it – he'll cease to be a problem for us then. Why not even put a knife through old Praether's heart?'

Lythos slumped. 'You mock me.'

'No, Lythos, you're right. Just kill those who stand in your path, obliterate them and the problem disappears.'

'And what is your way achieving?'

'We're still here, aren't we? I'm still First Speaker. The Circle is still functioning.' He glared at his brother. 'And you're still failing to see the intricacies of it all. The damage was done by Praether and his reasoning before he was dismissed. Can't you see that? Do you understand how that works?'

'You and your intricacies and subtleties.'

'So your answer is now a knife through a sleeping heart? Has it come to this? A member of the Order of the Liche killing?'

Lythos clenched his teeth. 'We've always killed, Leyvin.'

Leyvin looked away and watched the grotesque shadow dance on the wall.

*

Valkyra was aware that someone was in her room. The baresark sense which had served her so well in the past was still functioning, even if her ability to move had been impaired. The transition from deep sleep to alertness was almost instantaneous. In less time than it took to blink, she knew where she was and that someone had entered the room under the cover of darkness and was approaching her. Her breathing didn't miss a beat as she maintained her sleeping rhythm.

Lying there motionless, she watched a dark shadow draw nearer. She waited, tensing her muscles without moving any part of her body.

The figure now stood above her and was bending down ...

Valkyra lunged at it, raking at the hard Maelir face as she pulled the body towards her.

She wrapped her hands around the throat, squeezing hard against the Maelir's Adam's apple. To her surprise, the Maelir had the strength to wrench free and roll to the other side of the bed. She lunged at him again, but he managed to throw her back and pin her to the bed.

A moment of clarity hit her. 'Teyth, it's you,' she cried.

She let her arms relax, and he lowered himself so that his body was now in contact with the length of hers. She thrust her hips towards him and he responded. It was some time after the waves of pleasure started to wash through her that she realised she had regained control of her legs.

Chapter Twenty-three

'Ah, Ascender Atreu, we have been waiting for you.'

Atreu looked at the cowled Felsen, unable to make out the features of the monk in the shadows. 'How is it that you could be expecting me? I didn't know myself until earlier this evening.'

'The Ascenders, they all come to the Felsen before their time of judgement. The compulsion overwhelms them. We all know how it is, for we have felt it many times. The agitation, it rages within you, and you want to still it.'

The ground rumbled again and Atreu could hear a crashing sound in the distance. He went to turn his head in its direction, but the Felsen seemed to be willing him not to.

'Leave the light for now,' said the Felsen. 'It draws all of us in some ways, but we must all find the time to be true to the Rock.'

'The instability is growing,' said Atreu. 'I know what that means. It will destroy the Keep.

'The towers of glass and gold may fall, but the soul of the Keep is here forever alive in the monasts of the Felsen. Our structures are not so easily toppled. It would take the Mountain itself to fall for our buildings to collapse.'

'That's what I'm afraid will happen.'

'Your fear must flee.'

'I have the truth within me, but I also have the fear. Please, help me to not just know the truth at my judgement but to speak the truth.'

'Of course, Atreu, of course,' said the Felsen. 'Come inside. The others are waiting.'

'Others?'

'Please.' The Felsen gestured Atreu through the doorway.

Atreu drew a breath and stepped through. The darkness of night was immediately replaced with a deeper darkness. Despite his finely honed night vision, he struggled at first to see where he was being led.

He thought of Verlinden still lying curled in his bed. When he had been pulled out of his sound sleep, he had been surprised she had not also woken up. A sense of impending doom had drawn him from his slumber, like an arrow being extracted from living flesh, and it had taken him a moment to realise he alone had been affected.

He had lain there next to her for some time, looking at the ceiling and listening to his heart pound in his chest and his blood race through his ears like the rushing wind.

It was about to happen. He could feel it, all that he had feared. No dream had taken him this time, no dark opening wound, no black, leering faces. There had been no invasion of his sleep by screaming, groaning hordes. There had been no giant birds, no trees, no river, no villages, no rocks, no clouds, no snow, no sky, no sun, no Mountain. Nothing. Only a void, a deep, echoless void filled his sleeping mind until the nothingness was sucked out into reality and the aching premonition that some unspeakable horror was about to happen overwhelmed his every thought.

Again, Atreu felt the sweat break out on his brow as he followed the Felsen down a twisting corridor. The air was stale, as if it had clung to the stone walls for an eternity. The compulsion to come to the monasts of the Felsen had been a strong one. The longer he had lain wide-eyed and awake next to Verlinden, the greater his agitation became. It grew until his blood screamed in his ears and a heat more intense than the hottest fires racked his body, a R'angkur over which he had lost control.

In the end he had no choice. He had to find peace somehow, to still his mind, and he had followed his instinct to the place of the Felsen where he now found himself. How had he known the exact place? It was as if an unheard voice had called to him, leading him to this monast. Atreu had learnt from experience that although the ways of the Rock were often difficult to fathom, their results were very real.

As they rounded a corner, the bare stone corridor opened up into a low-ceilinged room. On the floor, cross-legged, sat dozens of figures. They all had their eyes closed and were sitting in con-centric squares, all facing inwards.

With a start he realised they were all wearing the broadcloth of Ascenders. He had not seen any Ascenders since his return to the Keep, and even when he had first arrived, he had never seen one outside the Great Dining Hall. Is this where they had all been? He noticed there was an empty space on the length of one of the squares, and the Felsen motioned that he should sit there.

'How long have the others been here?' asked Atreu, his voice echoing dully against the bare walls.

The Felsen motioned to him again in silence.

'Please, answer me,' said Atreu.

'This is the place all Ascenders come to before their final address to the Circle. They return here to await their judgement at Equinox.'

'What happens here?'

'Please, sit down. They need you so that the square can be complete.'

'You called me here, didn't you?'

The monk nodded. 'We called you when you were ready. As

always, we wait for the right time. But, please, no more questions. You know all your answers without me.' Again, he indicated the place on the floor between two other Ascenders.

As Atreu took his place, he glanced at the youth sitting, eyes closed, to his left. What could you tell me of your Ascent, he thought. What tale do you have to tell?

What about Teyth? The thought struck him like a flurry of arrows. He looked around for the Felsen monk, but he had already left the room and disappeared into the shadows.

Atreu scanned the figures all around him. He sensed Teyth wasn't there, and he knew now to trust his instincts. He could see, too, that there was no place for his brother here. Atreu himself had been the last required to complete the formation. The Felsen had been right – he knew the answers to his own questions now.

He carefully removed his Book from under his broadcloth and placed it in front of his crossed legs. The Ascender to his left had a gold bracelet in front of him. As he looked around, he could see the other Talismans: rings, bracelets, precious stones which shone in unusual colours, a goblet, wooden statues, shards of glass, a strange stone carving, and things he couldn't identify or were obscured from his view. He drew a breath and focused on his Book.

The chanting started – almost imperceptibly at first. A soft, rhythmic whisper like the rustling of leaves. Instinctively, he knew the words, the tones and cadences coming to him as if he had given voice to them every day of his life.

He found himself joining the chant before he was even aware of it, joining the subtle textures of its euphony, its rolling pitch, its suspension and prolongation, its repetition and variation. At first his mind jumped from one thought to another like a stream across rocks. He was underground with Teyth, walking the tunnels of Dusk. Then he was in the librum, pouring over books with Praether. Then he was in the air with Riell, flying through cloud after feather-light cloud. Then he was dancing under warm star-lit skies with a girl whose name he couldn't remember. And finally, he lay next to Verlinden, feeling the warmth of her body and the steady rhythm of her breathing.

And as Verlinden's breathing pulsed through his being, his mind too joined in the chant. He felt himself being drawn into his Book, or that his Book was drawn into him – he was unsure which. He was vaguely aware that his body was swaying in harmony with the words, matching the rolls and dips of the chant, but soon even his awareness of this evaporated. He was at one with the other Ascenders. The strength of their Talismans merged with his, and a single voice made up of a multitude of tones rose like a living being.

And above the rolling cadences was Atreu, and below them was Atreu, and within them, and through them was Atreu. And with Atreu, they all rode the waves of the great river called Ocean, plummeting the troughs only to be raised again to still greater heights. And with him, they trekked across a vast desert, their steps an endless unvarying rhythm until, finally, they stood before the great Mountain.

And with Atreu they heard the soft lapping waters of the lake, the voice entreating him not to look, the music of a warm summer's night, the howling winds of the sirocco, the soft whispers of the Rimforest, the rushing of the Maelstrom, the clangour of Peleusar, the racing of ice-cold wind, and finally, finally, the breathless cries of a Faemir.

When Atreu opened his eyes, he saw a room bathed in the clearest of lights, although no window opened to the outside, no candle or butter-lamp burned its flame, no glimmerstone shone from the ceiling or walls. The chanting had ceased to be anything but a memory and the other Ascenders sat in silence, heads bowed and barely breathing.

Atreu looked down at his Book and it was as if an unseen hand was flicking rapidly through the pages. Afterimages flashed through his mind as the pages raced past. A lake. A river. A star-filled night. A Faemir. An old man. And as the last page was turned, Atreu felt an overwhelming sense of completion. The unseen hand slowly turned the back cover, so that now the Book lay closed in front of him.

Atreu stood up. He knew what he had to do.

Clutching his Book to his chest, he turned to go.

*

'Night beasts!'

The cry rang across the Summit as the Faemir drew their swords and rushed into battle formation. Grale, dozens of the giant, red-eyed, misshapen beasts, circled them with slavering tongues and deep-throated growls.

'Peace!' Rhea spat on the ground. 'This is the sort of peace the Maelir offer us. The cowards won't even come down to finish us off themselves.'

The grale continued to circle, wary of the glowing embers of the Faemir fires. The Faemir stood tensed, battle-ready, waiting for the onslaught. Yet it didn't come. Rhea knew from bitter experience that arrows had little effect on the tough grale hide. Face-to-face confrontation was the best way to deal with them.

'What are they waiting for?' cried one warrior.

'They're looking for a weakness in our formation,' said Rhea, 'and they haven't found one yet.'

'We only have to wait till morning,' said Meirith.

'No,' cried Rhea. 'As always, we attack.'

She gave the cry and the formation fanned out at the grale, swords flashing. The Faemir battlewail pierced the frigid night sky, and soon the bellows of wounded grale joined the cacophony.

Rhea felt the soft resistance of flesh as her sword pierced beast after beast. Warm blood spilled onto her arms and legs, and the sickening grale smell which pervaded the air made her want to retch.

And almost as quickly as the beasts had emerged from the night, they had disappeared again into the darkness. Rhea took quick stock of her losses. Two Faemir lay dead and another five were seriously wounded. Ten grale had been so severely injured they had been unable to run away with the others and now lay in the snow, surrounded by growing circles of blood. Several of them weren't moving, but Rhea went to each one and pierced their throats anyway, to ensure their deaths were swift.

'At least we now have some food,' said Rhea, after she had pierced the last one and watched the light in its eyes die. 'Prepare the meat and we'll make ready to leave.'

It was then that the grale attacked again. They came from a completely different direction, almost as if they weren't the same group of beasts that had just run off. The Faemir re-formed, but not before three others had been mortally savaged. Like the first time, the warriors fanned out from their tight formation and repulsed the grale, but once again they sustained losses and injury.

After the third attack, they decided to remain in battle formation and wait for dawn.

*

Atreu stood outside the Areol with Teyth and Verlinden; the huge arched doors remained closed in front of him.

'How long are they going to make you wait?' asked Teyth.

Atreu shook his head. 'You haven't seen the Circle in action. There's no such thing as a quick decision.' He looked around. 'Somehow I thought Praether would be here, despite what he said about not wanting to be near the Circle.'

'You know you're not on your own,' said Verlinden.

Atreu squeezed her hand. 'I'm going to get them to listen to you, remember? Micah will help me – we'll be able to do it.' As he held on, he felt the weight of his Book in his other hand.

There was a creaking noise and the doors opened. A Felsen monk emerged. 'Ascender Atreu, your presence is now requested.'

Atreu looked into his brother's eyes, and Teyth simply nodded once. He then shifted his gaze to Verlinden and her eyes shone softly. He opened his mouth to speak, but then changed his mind. The understanding they now had was wordless.

He walked through the door and heard it close behind him. The Felsen indicated the centre of the Circle and Atreu walked straight towards it, his eyes scanning the faces around him for Micah. He found his uncle among the sixty Holy Men, sitting in the chair Praether had once occupied. Their eyes met briefly and Atreu turned his head when he heard Leyvin speak.

'Ascender Atreu, you know your purpose for being here, and from your previous experience, you have some understanding of our conventions.' Leyvin's tone was cool and measured.

'First Speaker,' said Lythos. 'May I read the charges I initially presented against the Ascender Atreu together with the reactions noted by my scribe?'

'I don't think that's necessary,' interrupted Atreu. 'It would only be a waste of time. All of you – apart from Micah – heard them the last time, and he, being my sage, is perhaps more familiar than the rest of you with my Ascent.'

'Convention suggests – ' began Leyvin.

'I demand we waive the convention,' said Micah, looking steadfastly at Leyvin, challenging the First Speaker to name him.

Leyvin hesitated for a moment then said, 'I waive the convention.'

Lythos glared at his brother.

'I think you must all be sick of the way the Circle has been operating,' began Atreu. 'I want to state my truth as clearly as I can, and I trust all of you will come to the right conclusion.'

'That is what you are here for, Ascender Atreu,' said Leyvin. 'Proceed.'

Atreu took several deep breaths. 'Let me start with some facts that are not a matter of judgement. Yes, I shared my final Zenith with a Faemir. I did so with my brother's blessing, which you can easily verify. I also want to continue to share my life with her.'

There was a collective gasp in the Circle.

'You know,' said one of the older Felsen monks, 'that there are rules prohibiting such a lifetime liaison between a member of the Holy Orders and any woman, let alone a Faemir.'

'Yes,' said Atreu, 'I realise a liaison, as you call it, with a Faemir is unthinkable, but I'm going to speak of many unthinkable things before I'm done.' He paused and looked around, almost waiting for some sort of protest but nothing came. Praether had done his work well – they were all eager, at least, to hear what he had to say.

'You don't need me to tell you of the other facts,' he continued. 'You are aware that over the last year almost everything that the Holy Orders have created on the Mountain has started to fall apart. The war with the Faemir has caused massive destruction – whole cities have been burnt and destroyed. You seem to concentrate your efforts on Crosanct and the Upper Reaches, but believe me, I've seen the damage this war has inflicted on the Mid-Reaches, and who knows what has been done since the time I travelled through.'

'You speak of the war causing the damage,' said a tall Liche, whom Atreu remembered from the last time, 'yet it would be more accurate to speak of the Faemir as the cause.'

'I maintain that the blame doesn't lie entirely with the Faemir.'

There were shouts of protest which Atreu allowed to subside before he continued.

'We don't need to be scholars of the history of our people to know that the Faemir have always been troublesome. Their raids have caused death and destruction for as long as we have been on the Mountain. The difference in recent times is that they have been united and more organised. The war has always been with us, and we have chosen to treat it as a mere nuisance and have never made any attempt to resolve the conflict.'

'We are all giving you some latitude here, Ascender Atreu,' said Leyvin, 'but we are here to judge your Ascent and the truth of your Zenith. This is not the time to give lessons in Maelir history to the Circle, many of whom have far greater knowledge of it than you.'

'Knowledge perhaps,' said Atreu, 'but not understanding, it

seems to me. You have only succeeded in ruling the Mountain for so long because of the weakness of your enemies, not because you have right on your side.'

'All of us are noting your use of the word *you*,' said Lythos.

Atreu turned to him. 'By the word *you*, I mean the Holy Orders, of which, I have already been told, I am not as yet a member. The Holy Orders, or perhaps more precisely the Inner Sanctum, have conducted the affairs of the Mountain up here, far removed from the concerns of everyday life.'

'You surely don't question the existence of the Keep itself, do you?' asked Holthim.

'I question the way it has been used. You are so removed that you no longer understand the consequences of your decisions in real life. Tens of thousands of Maelir have been killed because of decisions you've made: sons have lost their fathers and fathers their sons. Homes, villages, towns and cities have been destroyed, and people have burned, bled and starved to death because of you.'

'Because of the Faemir,' said a Liche.

'Not just the Faemir. Because of *you*. You have had the power all along to end it and you have chosen not to end it. Perhaps you are right – the Faemir are cold, vicious killers … but so are you. You kill with the words you speak in the Circle. You never see the blood on your hands because you are so far removed, but you are all cold, vicious killers. All of you.'

The collective cry of outrage was deafening. The Holy Men shouted at him in one tumultuous outburst, faces flushed and angry. Only Micah sat calmly, and he and Atreu exchanged a glance as Leyvin called the Circle to order.

Lythos' voice finally rose above the others. 'I demand Ascender Atreu be dismissed now. He has no place addressing the Circle.'

Leyvin raised his hand and waited for silence to again take hold. 'I have heard all that I want to hear. I hereby dismiss Ascender Atreu from this judgement.'

Micah's voice sounded clear and distinct. 'I haven't heard all that I want to hear. I challenge the First Speaker's decision.'

Atreu watched Leyvin closely. The First Speaker sat motionless, the only visible sign of what he was thinking was the red flush on both his cheeks. Atreu knew Micah had little to lose. Since he had only entered the Circle, he had nine lives still available to him, while Leyvin's position as First Speaker was at stake.

Leyvin went to stand up and then slumped into his chair and looked away. 'I withdraw my call for dismissal,' he said flatly.

There was a stunned silence.

Atreu filled the void. 'You have had the chance to end the killing all along, but you have never even considered it. You have steadfastly claimed all the power for yourselves. You claim that through you the Maelir control the Mountain. That is a lie you have spread. The Holy Orders control the Mountain and the sixty faces I see around me control the Holy Orders. And why has there been so much death and destruction? Because all of you are desperate to cling onto the power that those chairs you are sitting on give.'

There was some uneasy shifting.

'You vote, you have rules and regulations to ensure fairness, but you keep the power to yourself. The windriders claim places in the Circle – they have a burning desire to have the Order of the Wynde consecrated – yet you stall them and block their progress because you don't want to share power. You are playing a waiting game because you know the food in the Keep will last a good while and because you believe the Keep is safe from direct attack. The defences the windriders once provided you with are not essential.'

The tall Liche interrupted. 'But you were talking about the Faemir.'

'Yes,' said Atreu, 'and I still am. The cause of the problem is the same. You shut the windriders out just as you have always shut the Faemir out. It can't go on. My truth lies in words all of you have spoken before but have never understood fully. The twins of life must be brought together, as partners. And what we create between us is something entirely new, something different to what we have created separately. A third way. Perhaps the new Order of the Wynde can achieve that. Between the rock and the light is the wind. That is the only Order I wish to enter.'

He fell silent, expecting an explosion of voices around him but nothing came.

'The Book,' said Leyvin, his voice low and husky. 'We cannot make any judgement about your truth unless you show us the power of your Talisman.'

Atreu held up his Book. 'This ... this is my story. Everything I have learned is in here.' He turned to one of the last pages. 'Listen to this – these were words I spoke to Teyth after my final Zenith:

*

Micah was right – all the Holy Men were – but they just didn't take it that one step further. The opposites had to be brought together: the rock and the light, the Mountain and the Sun, the Felsen and the Liche. But they forgot the most important pair: Maelir and Faemir.'

*

He held the Book above his head. 'None of you will be able to read those words, but I want to bring the clarity of my truth to you. I want peace between our two people.'

'So you have no proof?' said Lythos.

'As I said, none of you will see the words I have just read in here. And even if you could, what proof would that be? Since when does a judgement depend on proof? Praether spoke last time of an apotheosis – a term I only half understand. If it depends on the clarity of my truth, then an apotheosis is what has occurred in me or through me or however it happens.'

'An apotheosis depends on the permanence of your truth, not your perceived clarity,' said Leyvin. 'Has your understanding held firm in your mind since Zenith?'

Atreu struggled with the question, rolling it over and over as he tried to formulate an answer. Finally, he said, 'My understanding has deepened since Zenith. I see more and I see more clearly. There are two more twins that I see must now be brought together – the power of Zenith and the balance of Equinox. Zenith without Equinox will ultimately lead to self-destruction, and Equinox without Zenith is stagnation.'

'Fine words,' said Leyvin. 'Fine words indeed, but I must now move the motion that no apotheosis has occurred. Whether we accept Atreu's truth or not, no permanence has been achieved. We have heard the evidence from the Ascender's own mouth – his perception of his truth is still changing.' He looked at Micah, almost willing him to challenge, but the Holy Man sat motionless.

'That no apotheosis has occurred,' repeated Leyvin and every hand in the Circle went up.

Atreu had a sinking feeling that he had somehow walked into a trap. He was unsure what to do next so he simply stood there, chewing his bottom lip.

Leyvin regarded him closely as the silence lengthened. Finally, he said, 'We are waiting for you to continue. Surely you have more to tell us.'

The subtle implication of Leyvin's words didn't escape Atreu. He knew he was implying what he had said so far in his address wasn't enough. Ideas rolled around in Atreu's head, but none of them formed into sentences.

'We can finish your address now,' said Leyvin, 'if you so wish.'

'We need your proof,' said Micah. 'Why are you convinced of your truth?'

'I ... I just know,' said Atreu. 'I feel it.'

'We all have felt our truths,' said Leyvin. 'Even those who are eventually judged as failures feel their truths. We need more than your conviction.'

'I ...' he trailed off, unable to finish.

The silence was filled by a low rumbling noise in the distance.

Atreu's thoughts suddenly cleared. 'You want proof?' he said.

'You just heard some proof. What has been happening over the last year? Instability all over the Mountain has increased, and its most destructive manifestations have been moving further and further upslope.'

'You have an explanation for this?' said Holthim.

'The first words of the Book of Maelur give us the answer. Most of you would have committed it to memory. First Speaker Leyvin, perhaps you could tell me what the first two sentences are.'

Leyvin was taken aback.

'Are you not familiar with them?' asked Atreu.

'Of course. Of course ... *I write this for the generations of Maelir to come so that they may learn of the great Mountain which is the axis of the universe, its spirit the heart of the world ...*'

'Please, go on,' said Atreu.

'I can't see the point of this but ... *And as with any heart, when it is broken it cries in pain for what has been lost, and when it is mended it cries in joy for what has been regained* ... do you want more or have we had enough of this farce?' He looked around at the other members of the Circle.

'You've said enough,' said Atreu. 'The proof you want is in the Book of Maelur. The opening reads, *I write this for the generations to come*. There is no mention of the word Maelir.'

'You're lying,' said Lythos. 'We all know the words.'

'It used to have the word Maelir there,' said Atreu, 'but no longer.'

'This is an outrageous and stupid lie,' said Lythos. 'Ascender Atreu is obviously clutching at anything to save his judgement.'

'He speaks the truth,' said Micah calmly. 'I have the Book of Maelur here, thanks to arch-librer Praether.' He pulled the Book out from under his robes and opened it to the first page before he passed it to the Felsen monk next to him. 'Please, all of you, read the first words before you pass it on.'

Each Holy Man studied it carefully before he handed it to the next one. By the time it reached Leyvin, the First Speaker was livid. He looked at the words, almost like he wanted to tear them off the page with his eyes. He examined the cover and flicked through the remainder of the Book as if questioning its authenticity.

'You'll notice,' said Micah, 'that the word has not been erased or covered up. It is as if the word was never written there in the first place.'

'It must be a forgery,' said Lythos, who had been in the part of the Circle which had not been passed the Book. 'Let me have a look.'

Leyvin ran his fingers over the intricate leatherwork embossed on the front and back covers. 'This is no forgery,' he said simply, as he passed it on for the remainder of the Circle to examine.

'The proof is there,' said Atreu. 'Maelur himself sees the future of the Mountain belonging to Maelir and Faemir.'

'That is one interpretation,' said Leyvin.

'The heart that cries in pain is the instability we have around us,' said Atreu. 'As war grew, so did the instability. The Mountain has been speaking to us all along, and no-one has been listening. It has been crying in pain for all the Maelir and Faemir who have died and who continue to die. We have been tearing the Mountain apart with our discord. Can't you see? And now the instability has come to the Keep. You all know this has always been the most stable place on the Mountain. And now we feel regular tremors and the glorious towers you have built are crashing to the ground.'

'As I said, that is one interpretation,' said Leyvin, 'and you have certainly given us something to consider.'

'Consider this, First Speaker Leyvin.' Atreu's eyes locked onto his and refused to let go. 'The Nazir are at the Summit. Both Teyth and I have seen them in the tunnels under the Hold. Other evidence is the Dusk creatures that have been attacking Maelir and Faemir alike in increasing numbers over the last year. You want another interpretation: the Nazir have been burrowing their tunnels through the heart of the Mountain ever since the Maelir banished them from its slopes. Silently, secretly, they have been laying their plans for an onslaught. Perhaps they have ripped the heart out of the Mountain, and its slopes will become so unstable that everything will collapse in on itself and there will be nothing left to fight over.'

A barrage of shouts erupted through the room.

Leyvin tried to make himself heard above the furore, but in the end, the Circle only fell silent when Atreu started to speak again.

'Judge what I've said. Ultimately you have no proof but that which your own hearts accept. Just remember, if you accept my truth then you must realise your position and that of the Maelir is far more dire than your worst imaginings. The Maelir and Faemir must unite against the Nazir, or else Dusk will inherit the Mountain. Or worse still, there will be no Mountain left at all.'

There was a knock from outside the arched doors, and all eyes watched the Felsen monk get up from his chair. His head disappeared through the opening for a moment. There was a brief exchange which Atreu couldn't hear, and the Felsen then returned to his seat.

'What news do you have, Felsen Fystaff?' said Leyvin, who seemed relieved that something had broken the impact of Atreu's words.

'First Speaker Leyvin, I wish to report that the baresark Faemir has escaped.'

Chapter Twenty-four

Rhea scanned the horizon in a desperate search for the breaking dawn. There was no sign of the darkness retreating, though she knew morning must be close. She looked across at the surviving Faemir warriors – even in the pre-dawn light she could see they were streaked with sweat and blood. And all around them the stench of grale merged with the subtle pungency of the newly dead.

The injured and the dying lay protected in the centre of the permanent battle formation. Again and again the grale had attacked through the night, always regrouping at some unseen point downslope, adding more beasts to their number and attacking from a new direction. Although the intelligence of the beasts was obviously not great, Rhea soon realised these were no random forages. The beasts had been trained and were being controlled in some way.

The expressions on the faces around her were grim. No Faemir battalion had ever been under siege this way before, and their natural fighting style was attack and not defence. No-one had faltered. Any warrior still standing did so with a sword in her hand. They would fight to the last Faemir, but with each grale wave their numbers fell and their collective strength weakened.

'Can't we move some of the dead ones?' asked Meirith. 'The smell is unbearable.'

'We're going to have to bear it a little longer,' said Rhea. 'The bodies are at least blocking the path of some of the beasts.'

'Where have they all come from?' said Meirith. 'Here, look at this one.' She ran the blade of her sword along the sparse hair growth on the hide of one of the dead grale. 'They aren't creatures who live in snow normally.'

'Who knows in what caves the Maelir have been keeping them. I only know that I will make those damn men pay for what they are doing to us. We talk peace and look what happens.'

'You really think Valkyra has betrayed us?'

'Either deliberately or through her stupidity – it makes no difference in the end. Yes, she has betrayed her people.'

'Here they come again.' The cry from the Watcher sent a chill of fear through Rhea.

Rhea steeled herself as if she was waiting for a blow. Through the pre-dawn air she saw the grale coming towards them again, hundreds this time, as if they had all massed for the final kill, red-eyed, slavering, their grunts and growls growing louder as they approached.

And then they charged. The beasts' numbers had swelled to such a point that the Faemir could no longer fan out effectively against them, so Rhea ordered the warriors to remain in the tight formation.

Howls and shrieks pierced the air as sword met flesh, and the blood flowed again as if an old wound had just been prised open. Screams merged with the bestial shrieks as tooth punctured flesh and one Faemir after another felt the savagery of the Dusk beasts. But the formation held – despite degenerating at times into a wild manic flurry of swords and arms, the formation held.

Only this time, when the bodies of the grale started to pile up, the beasts didn't flee. They kept coming, somehow sensing that the Faemir were weakening.

'Stand firm,' cried Rhea. 'It's nearly dawn.'

She rammed her sword through the throat of a grale and quickly withdrew it to fend off another attacker bearing down on her.

The ground started trembling and several of the Faemir lost their footing. Suddenly the formation was vulnerable. Several of the grale burst through the Faemir defences and now the warriors had to watch their backs as well.

A blood-chilling scream raked the air, and Rhea could see Meirith had been lifted from the ground by one of the beasts. The Faemir was struggling wildly as the grale shook her from side to side. Rhea broke the formation to race towards her, but as she pushed her sword into the animal's soft, yielding flesh, Meirith's scream stopped dead. Rhea looked up as the grale tottered in a death spasm and saw she had been too late. Meirith had been bitten in two.

In a howl of rage she ran out past the tightly bunched Faemir into the middle of the attacking grale. She thrust, sliced and hacked as they bore down on her, until she slowly disappeared under a mountain of quivering, foul-smelling flesh.

And then dawn broke.

The grale bellowed and shrieked wildly as the light hit their eyes, and they began careering into each other in a desperate panic.

'Stay in formation,' called Rhea, as the beasts ran in all directions around her. A few of the Faemir who had started to chase them now held back.

More light filtered across the Mountain side and the grale's disorientation increased. Finally, as if ruled by some blind instinct, the beasts found the right direction to retreat, and they charged downslope and out of sight.

Rhea returned to view the carnage. Mutilated Faemir bodies

lay across the blanket of white. Her stomach churned at the sight of Meirith's severed torso.

'Bury them in the snow,' she said, her voice shaking with rage and sadness. 'Bury them all, and let's get away from this place.'

As the morning sun rose, the Mountain glowed red.

*

'They won't live through another night like that,' said Atreu, after Verlinden finished reading to him. He reached over and put his arm around her as they lay next to each other on his bed.

'We have to do something,' she said, her voice quivering slightly. 'My sisters are dying.'

'The Circle makes its decisions in its own good time,' said Atreu. 'After it received the news that Valkyra had escaped, they weren't in the mood for listening to much more of anything I said.'

'But you told them I wanted to address the Circle.'

'Yes, I said more than that. I told them that they should judge the truth of your Ascent along with the other Ascenders.'

'And will they?'

'They are considering it. Like I said, it's hard to rush a Circle decision, even though they have time pressure on them now. Equinox is tomorrow so your address has to be today.'

'How can they judge my truth anyway?'

'The same way they are judging mine. Look, if they accept what Praether and I have been saying about the Books then you have a chance. You're the only one who can read what you've just read to me. They can't dismiss that easily.'

'But what if I lose the ability? Both you and Praether have said the Books are elusive.'

'I think we at least have a chance for peace now, Verlinden.'

'And you're just letting the Circle decide?'

'What else can I do?'

'And what about my sisters who are dying down there?'

'There's nothing I can do. We have to wait for the Circle to go through its process.'

'In its own good time, right? We can't rush it.'

'Yes,' said Atreu.

Verlinden suddenly got out of bed.

'What's the matter?' said Atreu.

'Don't you ever *do* anything?'

'Teyth used to say that to me. What can I do? I'm only an Ascender. I've addressed the Circle the best way I could, and hopefully they will act on it.'

Verlinden glared at him. 'Why don't *you* act on it?'

'I can't, I may know what should be done, but I have no power.'

'Of course you have power, Atreu.'

'Ideas and beliefs only have power if someone acts on them. That's what I'm hoping the Circle will do.'

'You *hope*? My sisters are dying and you're talking about hope and ideas and beliefs. Atreu, you can do a lot more than just sit here and wait for sixty Holy Men to decide how many more die.'

'What can I do?'

'Haven't you learnt anything? You've given me the answer yourself. The windriders are the key. If you control them, you control the Keep. Go to them. They'll listen to you. You want them to have their Order, you want to become part of the Order. Go to them. Take charge. They'll follow you.'

Atreu swallowed. 'You don't think I should wait for the Circle?'

'If you have the power to stop deaths and you don't, then it's the same as bloodying your own hands.'

Atreu nodded. 'I said the same thing in my address. You're right.' He got up from the bed. 'I could be waiting forever. The Order of the Wynde is the key.'

He got up, tied the cord on his broadcloth and said, half smiling, 'Excuse me, Verlinden, there's something I have to do.'

*

By the time the dead had been buried and the wounded and unconscious had been loaded onto makeshift stretchers, it was almost noon. The sun hung wanly in the sky, casting a baleful light on the mottled snowscape.

Rhea threaded her way through the maze of grale bodies, stopping occasionally to thrust her sword deep into the heart of any body which showed signs of being half alive.

Fires were still being quenched and packs loaded when she arrived back at the camp. She walked to the stretcher where Ahrai lay, still unconscious from the tremor which had destroyed the Hold.

Rhea knelt down next to her and looked at the deathly pallor of her face. She reached down to touch her hand. It was cold, but not yet fully devoid of life. She turned Ahrai's hand around to see the deep scar in her palm.

'I'm sorry for this, Ahrai,' she said softly.

She felt the rays of the sun on her face and arched back to catch more of the warmth. It had shone so rarely since they had reached the Summit. And now it was well into autumn, and the sun would soon disappear altogether behind bank after bank of snow clouds.

A chill ran through her. Since they had arrived at the Summit, the days were growing shorter and the nights longer. How long would it be before the creatures of the Dusk gained ascendancy? She had experienced grale attacks before, but nothing like the ones last night. Perhaps their numbers would grow as the darkness in which they thrived grew. She knew one thing: she had to get the Faemir away from this place.

'What ... is that smell?' said a familiar voice.

Rhea looked down to see Ahrai had regained consciousness and was blinking in the pale sunlight.

'It's night beasts,' said Rhea, 'but don't worry, they're dead.' To her surprise, she realised she was still holding Ahrai's hand. She went to pull away but then changed her mind.

*

'I'm not sure if I can convince the others,' said Riell.

'They'll listen to you,' said Atreu. 'If the windriders want a new Order, they're going to have to force the issue. They need to take charge and show a new direction.'

Riell was busy examining the struts of his wings for any sign of stress damage. 'To tell you the truth, I don't know if I'm convinced of the course of action you're suggesting, Atreu. It's one thing to refuse to fight the Faemir, but it's a different matter to bring a whole battalion up here.'

'You'll be rescuing them, Riell. Do you think they would turn around and attack you after you've saved their lives?'

Riell ran his fingers along the material of the wings, testing its tension. 'You've never fought them, Atreu. Once they were up here, there would be no stopping them. They could take the Keep. We have the advantage when we can come at them from the air and they're on open ground, but in the dense cluster of buildings up here, we wouldn't stand a chance.'

'Riell, you're not listening to me.' He pulled the windrider's arm away from his wings.

'Atreu, you can't be serious.'

'I am.'

'You want us to bring the surviving Faemir to the Keep? Do you expect them to surrender their swords, like prisoners? If you think they'll do that, then you don't know them very well.'

'Let them keep their swords.'

'So they can kill us the moment we land?'

'I thought you really wanted the Order of the Wynde?'

'I want the Wynde consecrated,' said Riell, 'but I don't want to wipe out the Felsen and the Liche in the process.'

'Can't you see you'll need to force the Orders' hand? They've given the windriders nothing for thousands of years because you've never been in a position to demand it. Now you are – and you have to make decisions that show that you are willing and able to exercise the power you have.'

Riell looked Atreu in the eye. 'Look, Atreu, one of the Felsen Circle members was expelled last night after your address. Micah has nominated me for the vacant seat, and he tells me I have a very good chance.'

'Perhaps, but Micah's is only one voice in sixty. And even if you win the seat in the Circle, it doesn't guarantee the Wynde will be consecrated. Far from it.'

'But it's a step in the right direction.'

'Yes, but it's too slow, and people are still dying.'

'Faemir are dying.'

'Yes, but downslope the war is continuing. Maelir are still dying in droves as well – you know that better than I do.'

'I have to do what's best for the windriders.'

'Peace is what's best for all of us – and bringing the Faemir up here would be the single most important step we can take to achieve it.'

'Look, Atreu, I can't realistically expect a squadron of riders to rescue Faemir who have sworn to kill every last one of us.'

Atreu felt a wave of anger. 'You're just like the rest of them, you know. You don't have a third way. It's really the same direction. You're only interested in your own power, Riell. It doesn't matter about anyone else.'

He turned to go.

'Wait,' said Riell, and Atreu swung back to face the windrider. 'I can't promise you anything, but I'll speak to the other riders.' His expression softened. 'Micah told me what you said during your address about the Wynde. We owe you our support.'

'Thank you, Riell, but if you really believe you can't convince them – '

'Look, Atreu, I'll do what I can. Perhaps some of us can go down and fire arrows at the grale from a safe distance – that may help. Perhaps we can aid the Faemir without jeopardising the Keep. Something may be possible.'

Atreu placed his hand on the windrider's shoulder. 'Thank you, Riell.'

The windrider nodded and Atreu left.

*

The afternoon sun had disappeared behind dense, grey clouds as the Faemir trudged downslope. The winds which had been blowing the stench of grale down towards them from the Summit had now eased. Rhea was grateful at first, although now the eerie stillness plagued her as it had a number of times since she had gained consciousness.

She had counted just over a hundred able-bodied Faemir remaining. If they lost too many more, even an effective defensive formation would be difficult to hold under another onslaught. She was unsure in which category to place Ahrai. The battalion leader had insisted on walking, despite the fact that she obviously felt weak. Rhea strode beside her and reached out to support her when she looked like she was about to collapse.

As they made their way through a jumble of ice and rocks, Rhea felt the cold beginning to seep into her bones again. She thought for a moment of making camp here, partly protected by the boulders of ice, but decided she wanted to move as far downslope as possible before dark. She glanced at the horizon and saw through the blanket of cloud that the sun was already dipping dangerously close to the horizon.

Ahrai's voice broke through her thoughts. 'Do you realise that I don't ever remember retreating from anywhere?'

'No – Faemir don't retreat,' said Rhea.

'Then what are we doing now?'

'You didn't see how many beasts there were. They kept regrouping and coming at us again and again. That's what we've got to do now: regroup and come at the Summit again. We'll return though – I can feel it.'

'I can't.'

'I'm not surprised. You look so pale you probably can't feel anything. You should have let us carry you.'

They trudged through the snow in silence for a moment.

Ahrai finally spoke. 'You're leader again, Rhea. What does it feel like?'

Rhea shrugged her shoulders. 'I don't feel like leader of anything at the moment.'

'We're almost down to the size of our old coveyn. Have you noticed that?' asked Ahrai.

Rhea nodded slowly to herself.

The battalion halted. Below them was a steep cliff face. Rhea pointed to a ridge to their right.

'There,' she said. 'We can make our way down along there, and then set up our camp with the cliff protecting our backs.'

She knew she was taking a calculated risk. The vertical face would enable them to concentrate their defences and use a more effective battle formation, but it would also mean that they had no place to retreat to if the grale broke through.

The temperature was dropping rapidly as the light started to fade, and Rhea moved her fingers quickly to try to keep the blood flowing. 'My hands are numb,' she said. 'How are yours?'

Ahrai lifted her hand palm up to show her. 'The scar's still there, Rhea. The scar's still there.'

Rhea couldn't bear to look so she turned away.

*

Atreu found Praether slumped face down on the table in his librum chambers. He shook him but he seemed strangely lifeless.

'Praether,' he said, shaking him harder.

The arch-librer finally opened his eyes.

Atreu laughed nervously. 'I thought for a moment you wouldn't wake up.'

Praether blinked and his eyes watered.

'You should go to bed,' said Atreu.

Praether started coughing, and Atreu stood helplessly as the old man's body shook and convulsed.

Finally the spasm eased and he tried to straighten up.

'Atreu,' he said, 'I used to be able to forget my age, but it's becoming more and more difficult for me.'

'Don't speak like that, Praether. You're just tired. You should be asleep in a bed, not lying here.'

'Do you know I haven't moved from here since we examined the two Books. Micah and Riell came to see me, even Leyvin came, again pretending he didn't want my advice.'

'We all need you.'

'No,' said Praether. 'That's just it. I didn't feel I had anything to say to them. It's almost as if I've said all I could possibly say in my lifetime. I'm not sure I have anything more to contribute.'

'You're not planning to die on us, are you?'

Praether didn't answer.

'Are you?' repeated Atreu.

'I'm so very tired, Atreu.'

'Come on, let me help you to bed.' Atreu went to help the arch-librer up.

'No, just leave me. I'm all right.'

'Well I for one need your help.'

'I'm not sure if I'm of use to anyone anymore,' said Praether, shaking his head.

'Verlinden read in my Book that the Faemir are retreating from the Summit.'

'Did she? So, she can do what I can no longer do. See, I was right – I no longer have a role to play.'

'Don't be absurd. I can't read it either, nor can anyone else on the Mountain. Just listen to me: the Faemir are being attacked by grale and I've asked Riell to – '

'You do what is right, Atreu. Please don't ask me for my advice. I have given you all my answers. You are the one who must bring the three Books together. I will not live long enough to see it happen.'

'Don't say that.'

'Atreu, you must face the reality with me. The Talismans have already been given to those twins who will make their Ascents over the next nine years. None of those Talismans are Books. Even if the Circle decides on another Book for the next Ascent, I'm not going to live the ten years it's going to take to see it come to fruition. The way I feel at the moment, I'm going to be struggling to make the one day till Equinox.'

'Does it have to be three Books?' asked Atreu. 'How can you be so certain two won't give us the power and wisdom we need?'

'So even you doubt me now, Atreu?'

'No, Praether, no.'

'It is my truth. Think about how firmly you hold your own, and then you can begin to feel how firmly I hold mine.'

'Three books then.'

Praether shook his head. 'I have had my chance, so I have no cause for complaint. As I told you, there have been other Book Talismans.'

'And the Ascenders all failed?'

Praether fell silent for a moment. 'I had such high hopes for your father,' he said finally. 'I know he held to his truth with such conviction. But, as you've learnt, conviction is not enough.'

'What was in his Book?'

'That was his problem – he didn't know. Perhaps you'll get a chance to ask him one day. He may have found more of his truth since.'

'And the others?'

'There were three others, but they were all consumed by the power of their Talisman before final Zenith. Books are not easy to master.'

'And Father didn't succumb?'

'No, Tyr was stronger than the others. I remember he fed from his Book and gained strength, just as you did. There are many similarities between you and your father.'

'And still his Ascent was judged a failure.'

'Yes, Atreu, it was – and the vote was unanimous.'

'You voted against him?'

'I had to.'

'And the other three didn't even make it to Equinox?'

'No.'

'So Father was closer than all the others?'

Praether hung his head and began to weep onto his hands.

'Praether, what's wrong?' Atreu put his arm around his shoulder.

'This could have been my final triumph, Atreu. The fulfilment of my truth.' The arch-librer was weeping uncontrollably now.

'Praether, please, stop.'

Praether wiped his eyes and looked at Atreu. 'I'm sorry. I don't know what the matter is with me today.'

Atreu looked the arch-librer in the eye. 'Your truth will be fulfilled,' he said softly.

'But, Atreu, you don't know how close I've been all my life, how close I could have been right now.'

'If only Father had succeeded.'

'No, Atreu, you don't understand. There was another Ascender with a Book Talisman who did succeed.' The tears started welling up again.

Atreu frowned in confusion. 'But if this Ascender succeeded, then – '

'Yes, he should be here in the Keep, and we should have his Book with us right now. You don't have to tell me, Atreu. I know what should be. We should have the three Books here right now and my truth should be fulfilled.'

'Where is the Book?'

'It was a long time ago, Atreu. The Ascender was the most powerful the Circle had ever seen. His command of his Talisman and his truth was so complete there was talk of an apotheosis. He was voted *into* the Circle soon after his induction into the Felsen.'

'What happened?'

Praether swallowed. 'He ... his understanding grew too clear, I think. He saw through too many people ... he saw through all the Rituals and conventions we had built. He wanted to dismantle them all and return to a simple, basic system, one where the Circle and the Orders lost power.'

'That wouldn't have won him too many friends.'

'No – it made him many enemies, and they plotted to bring him down at every turn.'

'And they succeeded?'

'No, Atreu, they didn't. He was too clever for them. He anticipated everything they tried and blocked every move against him.'

'So what happened to him? Where's his Book?'

Praether looked at the lines on his hands. 'He just left one day. The only Holy Man who has ever done it. He grew sick of the machinations against him, the empty arguments, the pointless Rituals and faulty reasoning, and he took his Book and left the Keep never to return.'

'And no-one knows where he is?'

'No, Atreu, no-one has seen him since the day he left.'

'Did you know him well, Praether?'

Praether looked up and Atreu could see his lip was trembling. 'He was my brother.'

Atreu suddenly became aware of his breathing. As he exhaled, he saw a wisp of vapour escape his lips.

'Metheus,' he said.

Praether sat up, startled. 'How did you know his name?'

'I've spoken to him. I know where he is.'

'What? Why didn't you tell me before? We're identical twins, Atreu. You must have known.'

Atreu nodded. 'The first time I saw you. It's just ... I don't know ... I had a sense you didn't want to speak about your brother.'

'I haven't heard his name spoken since the day he left, Atreu. The only Holy Man ever to leave the Circle, his name was banned and he was struck from our records as if he never existed. And now ... now you are telling me he is alive and you've spoken to him?'

'Yes, he saved my life.'

'Metheus.' Praether said the name slowly. 'I'd placed him in a dark corner of my memory, yet he is the reason I have devoted my life to books. My obsession grew the day he left, almost ... almost as if it was a substitute for him being here.'

The arch-librer's eyes filled again, but this time a look of pure joy crossed his face.

Atreu said, 'He's on Vygird, in the Caves of Arach. He's been there many, many years.'

'The Caves of Arach? The Lower Reaches?' He grabbed Atreu's sleeve. 'You must return to him. Take the other two Books with you. Here, the Book of Maelur is yours now.' He pushed it towards him. 'The three must be brought together. Only you can do it.'

'I can't leave the Keep now.'

'Go – I'm telling you, Atreu.' His eyes shone as they had never done before, and a deep rich red colour rose in his lined cheeks. 'The final veil just fell for me. There was always something I just couldn't see, my whole life, no matter how hard I looked and how much I tried to pretend to myself that my vision was perfectly clear. But now I see it all. Go, Atreu, go to the Plains of Vygird. My truth will be fulfilled there.'

'And what about *my* truth, Praether?'

'They're one and the same, Atreu. You will learn as I have learned. All the truths become one in the end.'

Praether went to get up but he was suddenly racked by another coughing fit. And this time it didn't stop. He coughed until it sounded to Atreu like he was tearing into his lungs.

He put his arms around the arch-librer to try to calm him. At first it had no effect and Praether continued to convulse, but then, finally, the convulsions eased.

Atreu continued to hold him long into the silence after the fit had stopped. It took him a while to realise the arch-librer was growing cold. He pulled away and saw that the life-light had left Praether's eyes.

He felt the tears starting to well up but he blinked them away and smiled. The look on Praether's face was one of sheer joy.

'I will find your brother Metheus,' said Atreu softly. 'I will promise you that.'

Chapter Twenty-five

As darkness consumed the Mountain side, they came again: grotesque, misshapen, eyes blood-red and teeth bared. Rhea and those Faemir who could still stand had their swords drawn and stood tensed in battle formation.

This time the grale didn't charge, they simply kept walking on their twisted legs with the same awkward, shuffling gait. They came closer with every step, as if they instinctively knew they would finish the Faemir this time.

Through the still night air, the rancid smell of burning dung reached Rhea's nostrils. She watched the hundreds of pairs of red pinpricks as they approached. They've learnt from our previous night's encounters, she thought. They are in no hurry. They know we won't attack them or try to run away, and that we'll just wait for their onslaught. Well, at least this time there was a surprise in store for the grale.

Rhea glanced across at the faces around her. The warriors were all resolutely focused on the approaching beasts as if mesmerised by them. Ahrai stood, sword in hand, to her right.

Rhea waited, counting her breaths, feeling the beast's odour enter her body. Although she didn't look around, she pictured the injured Faemir lying behind the thin wall of warriors that she and the others formed. And behind them was the white vertical slope of the cliff face, the one advantage they had.

Then she gave the command.

The battle wail filled the air as the Faemir warriors fanned out in a wide arc and hit the grale with a wild fury, hacking and slashing at them with deft yet powerful strokes. At first the beasts were in total confusion, bellowing, roaring, unable to decide which way to run. One after another, they were stunned as blades hit their vital organs. They froze for a moment, then tottered and fell in death shudders.

But soon the tide turned. The grale kept coming, ignoring their fallen brethren and bearing down on the Faemir warriors. Once the element of surprise had been lost, the battle became a grim one. Each Faemir was now surrounded by beasts intent on tearing into human flesh with sharp teeth and ravenous mouths.

'Formation,' cried Rhea, and the warriors all turned, charged through a maze of grale bodies and resumed their initial positions with their backs to the cliff wall.

There was an awkward shuffling amongst the grale for a moment, as if they were unsure where their prey had gone, and then they focused on the re-formed battle cluster in front of them and they charged at it.

Screams tore the air as Faemir were gored, but the warriors stood their ground, tightening their formation each time one of their number fell. And the grale died in far greater numbers, until the bodies of their dead and half-dead blocked the way of the others. Fewer and fewer came through the obstacles until, finally, the attack ceased.

Rhea looked up from her bloodied sword and saw the remaining grale disappear into the darkness downslope.

A cheer rose up among the Faemir, but Rhea didn't join in.

She knew the battle was far from over and the night still stretched in front of them like a long, black road.

*

'Where is that damn brother of yours?' said Micah, his voice strained as he, Atreu and Verlinden stood out the front of the doors to the Areol.

'He knows he's meant to be here,' said Atreu.

'I have to go back in,' said Micah. 'The Circle isn't going to wait forever. Once dawn breaks and Equinox arrives, we must begin the judgement process.'

'Can't his address be heard tomorrow?' asked Verlinden.

'You don't know the way the Circle works,' said Micah. 'This is the only time Teyth has.'

'I'll see if I can find him,' said Atreu.

'Damn that brother of yours,' said Micah. 'Doesn't he know how much trouble we've all gone to so that he would have another chance and his Ascent could be judged?'

'He knows, Micah, he knows,' said Atreu.

Micah shook his head. 'I've done so much for him. The two of you risked your lives. And Praether ... Praether ...' He looked away, unable to finish.

'Uncle, you're upset. I know that. Just go back in and try to gain us a little more time. I'll go find Teyth.'

'All right, Atreu. I'd better go back – I'm not even supposed to be out here.'

Atreu began walking down the corridor. When he heard the doors to the Areol creak shut again, he turned to Verlinden and nodded as if to say, you know what to do, then kept walking.

Verlinden pressed Atreu's Book, which she was carrying under her tunic, closer to her chest.

*

Atreu returned to his room where Teyth was sitting at the table with his battle-axe propped up against it, waiting for him.

'You really think it will work?' asked Teyth.

'I think Verlinden has a chance of making it work,' said Atreu. 'She's right, we can't wait for the Circle to go through all its processes in full. We'll be waiting for ever. We have to force some issues.'

'These Faemir are good at forcing things.'

Atreu looked at his brother curiously. 'You know, there have been no sightings of Valkyra since she disappeared from the Halls of Healing. You would think that from all the reports we've heard about her in the past, she would be running amok.'

'You would think so,' said Teyth, looking through the window at the lights of the Keep. 'It seems to me that the instability is doing all the damage out there. Another spire toppled earlier this evening.'

'I want to thank you again, Teyth, for what you're letting us do.'

'You know there has never been any need for thankyous between us, little brother. I gave up my Zenith for Verlinden – it was easy for me to give up my chance of being judged at Equinox as well.'

'The Circle probably won't give you another chance.'

'To tell you the truth, Atreu, I'm not sure that I care very much for being judged by the Circle. From what you've told me it's all talk, and I think I've grown more used to action since my Ascent began. I'm not sure if I want to stand in a circle of sixty Holy Men and argue a case.'

'It's sharpened our differences, hasn't it?' said Atreu.

'What has?'

'Zenith, our Ascents. I used to think we were so similar. The differences were there but they seemed so minor.'

'Not anymore, little brother, not anymore.'

A silence lengthened between them.

'You've never met Valkyra, have you?' said Teyth finally.

'No,' said Atreu. 'Although I saw a painting of her once in Peleusar, and I thought it was Verlinden. And I read about her in the Book of Maelur, so I feel I almost know her.'

'But you've never spoken to her, never laid eyes on her, have you – although you've had the chance since you came back from the Hold.'

'No, I haven't. That's right.'

'Why?'

'I ... I don't know, Teyth.'

'Does she frighten you, little brother?'

'She's been paralysed for most of the time since I returned. How could I be frightened of someone who is bedridden?'

'You tell me.'

Atreu chewed his bottom lip. 'Yes, she frightens me.'

Teyth looked into his brother's eyes. 'I think I know her as well as any Maelir could ever know her. I understand her because in many ways she's a lot like me.' His eyes burned through Atreu's. 'And you know what, little brother? She frightens me.'

*

The grale came at them again and again as the night wore on, each time more frenzied and determined than the time before. The Faemir casualties grew with each attack, but they stood firm. Even during the lulls between the onslaughts, Rhea gave no-one time to worry about how long it was before dawn. She urged the Faemir to stack the dead grale bodies to form walls which hindered the charges.

'Why not close the gaps?' said Ahrai, as she and Rhea dragged another beast into position. 'Then none of them would be able to get through.'

'I've learnt that it's never sound battle strategy to lock yourself in. These gaps in the wall may be making it easier for the beasts to get to us, but with this cliff at our backs, I want to keep some escape routes open.'

Ahrai felt suddenly dizzy and sat down.

Rhea rushed to her, but Ahrai pushed her away. 'I'm all right. I just need to sit down for a little while.'

'Lie down with the others,' said Rhea. 'Rest. We can do without you for the next attack.'

'No,' said Ahrai. 'Everyone needs rest – we don't have the time.'

She got up again and helped Rhea with another grale. 'You're determined to win this battle, aren't you, Rhea?'

'Of course – would I be determined to lose it?'

'You know what I mean. This is your chance, isn't it, to make up for the poor leadership you showed in that village all those years ago.'

Rhea grunted as they heaved another grale.

Ahrai rubbed her scarred palm. 'You want to make amends, don't you?'

*

When the doors of the Areol opened again, Verlinden seized her chance. She pushed past the two Holy Men who stood outside and the Felsen monk who had opened the door from the inside.

Once in the room, she walked towards the centre of the Circle without hesitation. Atreu had warned her about the slight curve in the floor so her strides were firm and sure.

All eyes were upon her as she took her position in the centre, but there were no words of protest – the Circle sat in stunned silence. She stood under the star-filled dome, legs shoulder width apart, her arms by her side as she surveyed the faces around her. Her gaze only locked onto Micah's for a brief moment, enough for her to register the mixture of confusion, surprise and exhilaration on his face.

'Felsen Fystaff, could you please ask the guards to come in and remove the unbidden entrant?'

Verlinden turned to the Liche who had spoken. 'You must be First Speaker Leyvin.'

'Felsen Fystaff, where are those guards?'

'I would recommend the guards don't try to remove me,' said Verlinden. 'And I would also recommend that ignoring me won't make me go away.'

'You dare to bring a weapon into the Circle?' asked Leyvin.

'I don't need a weapon. I suggest you tell your guards to wait outside.'

Leyvin hesitated and then signalled for the two Liche Holy Men to leave. 'Micah, you will pay for this.'

'He knows nothing. I am here because I wish to speak to you and you have the time.'

'What have you done with Teyth?' demanded Leyvin.

'Nothing. I returned to the Keep with the intention of negotiating peace between the Faemir and the Maelir. You are all aware that I required to speak to you, yet you have not even indicated when this might be.'

'We have many things to discuss.'

'Yes, I know, there is a war on.'

'Is this how you reward the hospitality of the Holy Orders?' said Leyvin. 'We released you from imprisonment and have allowed you limited freedoms within the Keep.'

'Yes, very civilised of you. I know how civilised you are and what barbarians my people are. I also know civilisation is only possible when there is peace. Because we've been too weak and scattered for thousands of years, you've had your peace, while we've had war. You've been able to build your civilisation while we've been the savages. That has all changed now.'

'What do you want?' asked Leyvin.

'I took part in Zenith. I know it was only the final day, but you obviously have no strict requirement of taking part in all nine days. I want you to hear my truth and judge it. I want to be given the same chance as every other Ascender.'

'An Ascender must be Maelir,' said one of the Liche.

'Why?' asked Verlinden, turning to him.

'The Mountain, the Orders, the Keep and Zenith all belong to the Maelir,' said a Felsen monk.

Verlinden turned to him. 'Why?'

'The Maelir have created a great civilisation on the Mountain,' said another Felsen. 'We have built cities, made great works of art.'

'Have the Maelir control of the Mountain because they have created a great civilisation, or have they created a great civilisation because they have control of the Mountain?'

'An interesting point,' said Leyvin, 'which we could debate for hours if we had the time.'

'To you it may just be a point for discussion,' said Verlinden, swinging back to face the First Speaker, 'but it is the basis of my truth. Of course we behave like barbarians – you have given us no choice. Who knows what we could have achieved if we had been in control of Zenith all these years.'

'So you don't deny that you and your people still want Zenith?' said Lythos.

'My people want Zenith, and I want Zenith for my people. I have always claimed that. What I want for the Faemir is to share Zenith with the Maelir.'

'Why should we give up what we have?' asked Lythos.

'Because you know it is best for both our peoples, because it is best for the Mountain ... and because you have no choice.'

'We always have choice,' said Leyvin. 'That's what the function of the Circle is – to make decisions based on the choices we have.'

'Or to avoid making decisions,' said Verlinden.

'Ascender Verlinden, please tell us your truth.' She turned to Micah's familiar voice, grateful that he had bestowed on her the honour of the title Ascender.

'I understand you – all of you,' she said. 'I lived the first nine years of my life in a village in the Lower Reaches as one of those whom we call Faelen. I lived the next nine years as part of a Faemir coveyn so I understand their ways. Now I am not fully Faemir or Faelen but a mixture of the two. At first, one side sought to overwhelm the other and my Faemir side won the battle, banishing the Faelen to the furthest corner of my mind.'

She drew a breath as if reliving the contest inside her, then she continued. 'But since Zenith, the warring opponents have found peace. Neither has been victorious, but I have found strength and clarity in the merging of my two warring sides.'

'And you claim, Ascender Verlinden,' said Micah, 'that Maelir and Faemir will find similar strength and clarity if they merge?'

'Yes,' said Verlinden, 'but I don't put my truth to you as an option for you to consider. The way of peace is the only choice you have. If my warring sides had not made peace, I would have gone mad. If the Maelir and Faemir don't make peace, we will all be destroyed.'

She nodded in the direction of the empty seat not far from Leyvin. 'I see you have a vacancy.'

'Nominations have been taken,' said Leyvin. 'That is another in a long line of decisions we will be making tonight.'

'I believe one of your candidates is the windrider, Riell. You are obviously open-minded enough to consider changes to rules and conventions that have been in place for a long time.' She reached up and pressed Atreu's Book against her breast. 'The next vacancy that occurs I will nominate for.'

There were cries of outrage, but Verlinden silenced them by pulling out Atreu's Book and holding it high for all of them to see.

'And I claim this Book to be partly mine. This is my Talisman as well as Atreu's. It now belongs to both of us.'

'You cannot claim a Talisman,' said Leyvin.

'Not unless the Talisman claims you first,' she said. 'I can read things in here that Atreu cannot read. The Book of Atreu has become partly mine just as the Book of Maelur became partly Praether's.'

'What can you read in Atreu's Book?' asked Micah.

'I can read what is happening to the Mountain side below us. The grale are claiming the Summit as their own, and although the remaining Faemir are making a stand, I don't believe they will live to see Crosanct.'

'Why should that concern us?' asked Lythos.

'Because once the grale and the other creatures of the dusk claim the Summit, you will never get it back.'

'We have heard Ascender Atreu's beliefs regarding the Nazir,' said Leyvin.

'Maelir forces at Crosanct and Faemir forces at the Summit have all been decimated by the forces of dusk, and neither of our peoples have spilt even the smallest drop of Nazir blood. The Dusk People are the real enemy we should have been fighting all along. I just hope we haven't weakened ourselves so much that our combined armies won't be able to stand up when their real attack begins.'

'What are you suggesting we do?' asked Holthim.

'Do? I don't believe you have the power to do anything anymore,' said Verlinden. 'You have no choice. Either you give your support to working towards peace or your decision will become irrelevant.'

'That's outrageous,' cried Lythos. 'We have listened to your rantings and all you do is insult us.'

'The windriders are already out of your control. You have no way of receiving information about the state of the Mountain or of giving orders without them. What sort of power does that leave you? If you don't give in to the windriders' demands, the Order of the Wynde will soon realise they don't need you. You can then make all the decisions you want – it won't make any difference.'

Lythos stood up. 'How can we all just sit here and listen to this from a Faemir who has burst into the Circle and deigns to tell us what we should do.'

Micah said, 'I demand that Liche Lythos be asked to sit down.'

'Liche Lythos, please sit down,' said Leyvin.

Lythos glared at his brother. 'Now, suddenly, we have strict adherence to convention. I'll sit down when you order the Faemir to be thrown out.'

'Liche Lythos, please sit down. I will be forced to name you if you don't sit down.'

'Name me, you weakling,' said Lythos. 'You may be happy about a Faemir lecturing to the Circle, mocking and insulting us, but I'm not. Name me and we'll see who wins. I'm sick of your arrogant talk of subtleties and clever arguments. The choice is clear.' He looked at the other Holy Men in a sweep of the Circle. 'First Speaker Leyvin has to go. He allows Faemir to burst in on our judgements. He is so weak we will soon have windriders and Faemir occupying seats that have always been occupied by Holy Men of the Liche and Felsen. Which one of you will be thrown out to make room? I certainly won't move.'

'Liche Lythos, I have no option but to name you.'

Lythos folded his arms across his chest. 'And I have no option but to challenge the naming. I just hope all of you here know what the decision you're about to make means.'

'I request,' said Holthim, 'that First Speaker Leyvin, Liche Lythos and Ascender Verlinden leave the Areol so that we may make a judgment on the challenge.'

Leyvin stood up and glared at his brother.

The silence was broken by Verlinden's voice. 'I haven't finished,' she said.

'Our conventions state that you must now leave,' said Holthim. 'We will call you back once our decision has been made.'

'I am not going to wait for you to enact your conventions. One thing I learnt with the Faemir was to adapt to changing circumstances, and adapt quickly. I see no adaptation here. Don't you see the sense of urgency? People are dying as we speak – Maelir and Faemir – and you continue with games of naming and challenges. I don't care if you think it has worked for you in the past. It's not working for you now.'

She looked at Holthim. 'If I were you, I'd call on the two of them to resume their seats.'

'You don't understand –'

'I understand more than I want to understand.' She drew a series of deep breaths and glanced from one face to another. 'Perhaps I'm wasting my time here. It's pointless negotiating with people who have no power. Decide whatever you want – it won't matter. Atreu has asked the windriders to rescue those of my people who are still alive after the grale have finished with them. I don't yet know whether or not he has been successful, but whatever happens, you will not be consulted.'

Verlinden put the Book back under her tunic, and staring straight ahead, she walked out of the room.

*

Rhea could hear the growls from past the wall of dead grale. The smell burned her nostrils as she stood, battle-tense, waiting for the next attack.

'Why aren't they coming?' asked Ahrai.

'I don't know,' said Rhea. 'They seem to be holding back for some reason.'

The ground started rumbling and then shaking around them.

There was a shout and Rhea looked up to see a sheet of white coming down towards them from the cliff top. The next thing she knew, she was buried waist-deep in snow.

It was at that moment that the grale attacked again.

*

'What was that?' Atreu sat bolt upright.

'A small tremor,' said Teyth. 'We've been getting them all night.'

'No, there was something else.' Atreu grabbed his ears in a desperate attempt to try to fight off the stab of pain that he suddenly felt.

'What's wrong?' asked Teyth, getting up from his chair.

'Can't you hear them?'

'What? Hear what?'

'The voices. I don't know how many. They're screaming. Can't you hear them?'

'No, Atreu, I can't hear anything.'

Atreu clutched his ears more tightly as the voices grew louder. Under the impact, he fell off his chair and rolled on the ground.

Teyth got up from the bed. 'Atreu.'

Atreu rolled away as Teyth tried to approach him. 'Leave me,' he cried. 'Leave me.'

Then, just as quickly as the voices had risen from the silence inside his head, they stopped. He was left with an aching void, a wound that would never heal.

Slowly he stood up, fighting to make sense of what had just happened.

'Are you all right, little brother?'

'No, Teyth. No, I'm not all right.' He cocked his head towards the door as if listening for an echo he expected to hear. 'Come with me,' he said. 'I don't think I want to face this alone.'

Teyth slung his battle-axe behind his back and they walked out.

*

Rhea felt the sting of grale teeth on her flesh for the first time as one of the great beasts tore away part of her upper arm. Swallowing the scream that raced to escape her lips, she shook herself free of the snow that had fallen and rammed her sword into one of the blood-red eyes that glared at her through the gloom.

The grale bellowed and reared back, exposing its soft underbelly, and Rhea hacked at if furiously. Two other swords flashed from somewhere and the beast teetered and then died.

Rhea cleared out more snow so that she could move more easily. Out of the corner of her vision, she could see many of the other warriors had also freed themselves and were no longer trapped.

The grale were retreating again, but she knew the darkness had not ended. She looked at the wound in her arm and watched as the blood started to seep out into the frozen night air.

*

Teyth followed Atreu as they made their way along the narrow, cobbled streets of the Felsen monasts. He had given up asking his brother where they were going, because Atreu's face contorted into the most unspeakable expressions of horror every time he asked the question.

They stopped before a building and Atreu looked at the blackness of the open doorway.

'This is it,' he said flatly.

They entered the Felsen darkness, Teyth still following Atreu through the twisting corridors.

Teyth nearly gagged. The familiar smell of death reached his nostrils, and he reached back for his battle-axe.

They turned a corner and the full stench hit him. It was as if the smell was a blow which almost knocked him from his feet. Battle fetor was nothing new to him, but he had never experienced such a concentration in an enclosed space.

He opened his eyes and saw Atreu on his knees weeping. In front of him were dozens of Ascenders sitting cross-legged in a formation of concentric squares.

They were all dead.

*

Valkyra looked at the bloodstains on her hands as she tightened the straps of the wing harness. She was fascinated by the pattern, stopping now and then to examine a part of her hand more closely.

When she had finished with the straps, she shot a glance at the two dead windriders who lay on the ground to her right.

How strange it felt to kill again after being helpless for so long. Not good, not bad – just a little strange. She would get used to it again.

Without looking back at the darkness of the monasts behind her, she ran towards the edge of the cliff and felt the updraughts fill her wings as the ground disappeared.

Chapter Twenty-six

The Mountain bucked and heaved under Rhea's feet as if she was perched precariously on the back of a giant beast. Thick sheets of snow rained down from the cliff top above them. This time a thick whiteness invaded the dark until she could see nothing else.

And then she realised she could no longer breathe.

She began to push frantically at the snow in front of her face. Her lungs screamed for air, but all she could see was white on white. The cold stung her arms and face as her movements became wilder.

Until, finally, the black of night appeared again.

She blinked the snow from her eyelids and looked around. The other warriors were freeing themselves from their icy tombs. Above them she could see dark patches on the side and at the top of the cliff where the Mountain had shaken off its snow cloak and now lay exposed to the air.

Rhea climbed out of the snow and peered downslope, praying that the grale weren't massing for another attack. There appeared to be no sign of them. She clambered across the piles of snow to help Ahrai and the others dig out the injured Faemir who still lay buried near the cliff wall. Fortunately, because of the slope of the overhang, the snow here wasn't nearly as deep as where she had been standing.

After a moment, Rhea and Ahrai exposed Saretha's face to the air. Ahrai bent down and placed her ear next to the battalion leader's chest.

'Is she still alive?' asked Rhea.

'Barely,' said Ahrai, pressing down on Saretha's chest with both her hands.

'She still hasn't gained consciousness from the collapse of the Summit,' said Rhea.

'Perhaps it would have been better if none of us had survived it.'

'Don't be a fool, Ahrai. You're a Faemir – don't forget that.'

Ahrai nodded slowly to herself as she continued to massage Saretha's chest and noted that some colour was returning to her cheeks.

There was a rustling noise above them.

Ahrai looked up, but all she could see was the cliff face standing out like a reverse silhouette against the night sky. And at the top of the cliff, dark patches of rock fought through the whiteness as if night itself was trying to eat into the snow. She stared at the dark outcrops as if mesmerised.

Then she realised they were moving.

'Dusk-rats,' she had wanted to cry, but the first one had already dropped down onto her face.

*

Verlinden felt her stomach turning and placed her hand over the words in Atreu's Book, unable to keep reading. She looked around Atreu's room. Where had he and Teyth disappeared to? Her sisters weren't going to survive the night. Something had to be done now.

She had to find Riell. The windriders had to make the decision to help the Faemir now. She closed the Book, tucked it under her arm, and got up.

The ground was trembling by the time she got to the door.

*

The dark rain fell all around them as thousands of Dusk-rats dropped from the cliff face above the Faemir.

Rhea had lost her footing at first, screaming in agony as the razor-sharp teeth pierced her skin. All she could feel was pain, a hundred points in her flesh crying out. Instinctively her sword cut and thrust at the rats, and as quickly as they had pierced her skin, they withdrew lifeless, falling to the ground.

Rhea fought her way back to an upright position, swinging her sword in a full circle above her head to protect herself from the still falling Dusk-rats.

'This way,' she cried to the others, so that they would mimic her technique.

The others, those who were still on their feet, copied her and the night air was alive with the whirring of swords and the death-screams of the rats.

But many still fell to the ground unharmed, and the onslaught was now from two directions as the Dusk-rats attacked the exposed legs of the Faemir from below.

Rhea thrust at the beasts around her legs, only to feel the claws of another which had dropped onto her hair. She tore it away with her free hand before it could bite her scalp, but it took a clump of her hair with it.

The Mountain side started to shake again and Rhea barely managed to retain her footing. She saw several of the other Faemir hadn't and the rats now swarmed over them. She felt her own strength ebbing, her legs buckling under her.

Then a battle cry rang from the sky.

The wail first shuddered through her and then lifted her upwards. She saw a lone windrider swooping down towards them.

Rhea didn't need see the face to know it was Valkyra.

The others had recognised the battle cry too. Their spirits lifted and they fought with renewed vigour.

'Valkyra!' The cry rose up from the warriors' lungs.

Some of the Faemir climbed from the ground where they had fallen, shook off the Dusk-rats and stared fighting again with renewed strength.

Valkyra, the entire length of her body blood-streaked, landed in the middle of the melee, tore off the harness and threw herself into battle. The rats ran towards her at first as if the Maelir blood that had dried on her was a magnet, but she fought them furiously.

The balance had suddenly changed. The Dusk-rats had stopped falling from the cliff top and were now all on the ground. With so many bearing down on Valkyra, the other warriors had less to contend with.

Rhea swept a path through the frenzied beasts towards her leader.

Valkyra waved her back. 'These are mine,' she cried, her eyes wild with the fury of the baresark.

Then, just as quickly as the attack had begun, it ended. As if responding to some unheard command, the rats collected again into what looked like the clusters of dark, moving rocks and raced downslope past the Faemir and disappeared into the distance.

'So,' said Rhea, 'once again, Valkyra, you relieve me of my command.'

Valkyra smiled, baring her teeth in a horrific grimace as she sheathed her sword.

*

'If you are lying to me, Leyvin, you will pay.' Riell ran his fingers along the material of his wings as he eyed the First Speaker carefully.

'Don't you ever accuse me of lying, Riell,' said Leyvin. 'You have broken your covenant, remember, and you're going to have to live with that.'

'And your offer has the backing of the Circle?'

'The time has come for action, Riell. The Keep has been desecrated. Ascenders are dead. We have to get things moving. That's why I'm here. That's why I persuaded the Circle that we had no choice. We've acted and we've acted quickly.'

'*You* persuaded them?'

'This is not the way I would have it under perfect circumstances, Riell. You know that. I'm not going to pretend otherwise. But these are far from perfect circumstances. The offer is a firm one.'

'I am now in the Circle?'

'Yes.'

'And I have ultimate control over the use of the windriders in battle?'

'Yes.'

'But I didn't ask for that.'

'Perhaps you should have, Riell. The Circle decided you were right. We have been ordering too many windriders to their deaths. Now they're your responsibility.'

'But ... but what if I don't want it?'

'You can't have it both ways, Riell. We have come to the conclusion that our decision making in battle situations is too slow. We've often taken your advice – now you're officially in charge.'

'That's a big difference, Leyvin.'

'Yes, it is.'

'And what do you want in return?'

'I request nothing,' said Leyvin. 'I'll let your conscience decide what you think you owe me.'

They became aware of a figure in the doorway. It was Verlinden. She ignored Leyvin and spoke to Riell. 'Have you decided yet?'

'On what?' asked Riell, suddenly feeling as if a heavy burden had been placed on his shoulders.

'On whether or not you're going to leave my sisters to die tonight?'

*

Atreu and Teyth stood in silence next to the bodies of the two windriders Valkyra had strangled. They had followed the trail of the dead Felsen lying in crumpled heaps on the cobblestoned streets and alleys of the monasts.

'She cannot remain alive,' said Teyth, finally breaking the silence.

'How many Faemir have you killed, Teyth?'

Teyth shook his head. 'Don't bring that up, Atreu. These two windriders may have been carrying swords, but the Felsen monks and the Ascenders were totally defenceless.' He looked his brother in the eyes. 'How could she kill Ascenders who were meditating?'

'It's a war, Teyth.'

'I can't believe you are defending her actions.'

'I'm not defending anyone's actions. You can't defend anyone's actions in war.'

'Valkyra has to die – she'll never end the war. Perhaps the others will – Verlinden seems convinced of it – but Valkyra will never stop fighting. Believe me. I know.'

Atreu nodded slowly. 'We need peace more than ever now – but I still don't know if killing her is the answer.' He looked down at the motionless windriders.

'Come on,' said Teyth, 'don't look at them anymore. We need to see Riell.'

*

'Are we Faemir or Faelen?' asked Valkyra as she viewed the scene in front of her with disgust.

'My strategy was working until the rats came,' said Rhea.

'The smell is making me ill.' Valkyra raised her voice so that the others could hear her command. 'Break camp. We're not going to stay here like cowards. What's happened to all of you?'

'You haven't seen how many night beasts there were,' said Rhea, drawing Valkyra aside.

'Rhea, you've had another chance at command, and you've failed again. Is this all that remains of our victorious fighting force which reached the Summit?'

'The Summit collapsed after you left, Valkyra. It was fortunate any of us survived. We've been defending ourselves against the rats and night beasts ever since.'

'Good or bad fortune has nothing to do with war,' said Valkyra. 'Only weaklings believe in fortune. You either live or die – and if you live, you continue the fight.'

'Valkyra, I recommend we wait until dawn before we move. We have so few warriors left that an attacking formation is impossible out in the open.'

Valkyra waved her away dismissively.

Rhea sighed. 'Where to, Valkyra?'

'Downslope,' she said. 'We're going to hunt night beasts.'

Rhea glared at her, open-mouthed. 'You're insane. You want us to seek them out?'

'Since when have Faemir run from anything? Never when I've been in command. Attack, always attack. Never wait. Look at the pitiful state they're in, cowering with their backs to the wall, surrounded by stinking carcasses.' She glared back at Rhea. 'Either give my commands or die by my sword. They're the only two choices you've ever had.'

'We barely have enough able-bodied warriors to carry all the injured.'

'Leave them,' said Valkyra.

'What?'

'You heard what I said. We can't fight effectively if we're burdened by so many of the injured.'

'Some of them may recover.'

'And many more warriors will die trying to protect them when they should be free to do battle.'

Rhea and Valkyra faced each other as another tremor shook the ground. Rhea thought about reaching for her sword and then turned away.

'Leave the injured,' Rhea commanded, her voice sounding hollow. 'We're moving downslope before dawn.'

*

Lythos banged the table with his fist repeatedly, making the candle jump.

'What are you doing? Have you taken total leave of your senses?' he said. 'Do you realise what that Faemir baresark has done?'

'Just calm down,' said Leyvin.

'How can I calm down? Our Ascenders have been wiped out by that Faemir baresark and you've just handed over control of the windriders to Riell. What possessed you to argue for that? How ... how ...' The words strangled in Lythos' throat, unable to come out.

'Lythos, I said just calm yourself. What should I have done? Ordered the windriders to attack the Faemir and wipe them out?'

'Yes,' spluttered Lythos, 'that's what you should have argued for.'

'And if you were in my place that's what you would have done?'

'Yes, Leyvin, of course. There's no other option.'

'If you believe that then you're the fool, brother. Just calm down and listen to me. Atreu and Teyth have been exhorting Riell to take his windriders down to rescue the surviving Faemir.'

Lythos shook his head. 'How can we even think of rescuing murderers?'

'Listen to me, Lythos. There's nothing more pointless than giving commands no-one will take. Even if I could have persuaded the Circle to vote to send the windriders down to attack the Faemir, which I doubt, the riders would simply have refused to go.' He moved closer to the candle flame and Lythos could see the shadows play on his face. 'Can't you see what I've done?'

'You've given away all control.'

'That's why you'll never be First Speaker, Lythos. You have no subtle understanding. Riell won't know what to do. He has the power now, but he won't be able to cope. He will be responsible for the deaths of his own windriders now. Their actions in healing the baresark have already resulted in many deaths in the Keep. He will be feeling the weight of that decision.'

Lythos lowered his voice. 'So what do you think will happen?'

'He won't want the responsibility. Can't you see that? He will voluntarily return it to us. That's better than anything else we could have done. He will be eternally grateful when he hands it back to us. You must be able to see the exquisite beauty of my course of action. I've given him something I never really had to give him, and he will give back real power to us in return.'

'I don't know, Leyvin. I hope you haven't been so clever it will backfire on all of us.'

'Trust me, Lythos. I understand power. Riell will try to make a decision, but in the end, he will be paralysed. He is not detached from his windriders. He will be unable to place them in jeopardy, yet he knows people will continue to die if he does nothing.'

'How do you know he won't bring more Faemir to the Keep – that's what he's being urged to do.'

'After what the baresark has done? Not a chance. Mark my words: before the night is over, Riell will be in here begging me to relieve him of command of the windriders.'

'I hope you're right, Leyvin. I hope for all of our sakes that you are right.'

*

The Faemir warriors moved swiftly downslope following the grale and Dusk-rat tracks. The ground continued to tremble and small pillars of rock erupted from the snow as they marched on, but Rhea noted a renewed vigour and determination in the Faemir despite their depleted numbers.

Valkyra had always had that effect on the others. They would blindly follow her over a cliff face if that's what she required.

Rhea herself felt the renewed surge of energy and purpose, and she resented the effect that Valkyra was having on her. She looked at her leader as they strode through the nightscaped Mountain side together. Valkyra had made no attempt to wash any of the blood from her body, and she cut a terrifying figure against the white slope.

The battalion stopped when a huge chasm yawned in front of them. The prints they had been following seemed to lead straight into it.

Valkyra signalled the others to resume their battle formations as she and Rhea walked up to the edge of the chasm and looked in.

'This is where they're coming from,' said Rhea. 'Look at the slope. It's steep but the beasts would be able to climb it easily.'

Valkyra didn't acknowledge Rhea's words and instead took a step closer to the chasm.

'We're here!' she cried into the pale blue depths and an echo resounded below them.

Rhea grabbed Valkyra by the arm. 'What are you doing?'

Valkyra shook her off. 'We've always defeated our enemy by showing no fear. Either those beasts come out or we're going in there after them.'

'You've taken leave of your senses, Valkyra. The beasts are not in our way now. Let's just walk around and head downslope.'

Just as Rhea finished the sentence, she felt Valkyra's blade at her throat.

'Your cowardice has infected the others,' said Valkyra. 'Tell me why I shouldn't cut out the infection.'

The slope shook violently and they both fell to the ground.

Rhea ran her hand along her throat and then looked at the blood on her fingers.

'Get up,' said Valkyra. 'The wound is only a small one. The time has come to redeem yourself.'

As Rhea got to her feet, she saw hundreds of red eyes staring at her from deep within the cavern. With a start, she realised they were growing larger. The grale were emerging from their hiding place.

The two of them raced back to the others and completed the battle wedge with Valkyra at the head. As the grale climbed over the lip of the chasm, the wedge moved forward and met them full on.

At first the grale didn't know what hit them, and many tumbled back down into the chasm's depths. But soon the weight of numbers told and the grale pushed the Faemir back.

Valkyra hacked at the beasts with a fury none of the others could match – but it wasn't enough. As the formation was pushed back further, more and more grale climbed out, roaring and bellowing, onto the Mountain's slope. Soon the wedge was surrounded and the beasts mauled into the trapped Faemir.

Valkyra gave the signal to fan out into an attacking manoeuvre, but none of them could move. The grale bore down on them from all sides and Faemir after Faemir fell.

'This way!' cried Valkyra, pointing in front of her.

She had managed to hack a path through the advancing beasts and the others followed her.

The wedge which had started to fall apart now re-formed, pointing in the direction Valkyra was moving. Grale after grale fell under her baresark fury and the warriors fed from her strength.

And even when the Dusk-rats joined the fray, Valkyra continued through the army of night beasts, relentlessly cutting a path through the hordes that emerged shrieking, chattering, bellowing and roaring from the depths.

Rhea felt Valkyra's power course through her as in no other

battle. No matter how many of the beasts she killed, her arms didn't grow tired. In fact, she grew stronger, her swords flashed faster, instinctively knowing where to thrust. How could she have doubted Valkyra? They were invincible as long as they kept attacking.

And then the Mountain shook as it had never shaken before, and the entire Faemir battalion was knocked from its feet.

Rhea felt the darkness swarm above her. She felt the weight of the night beasts pressing into her, pushing her further and further towards oblivion. She felt the smell overwhelming her. She felt the points of pain as sharp teeth embedded themselves into her flesh, even though she knew she would suffocate before the rats found her vital organs. She felt the warmth of the seething mass and slowly, almost gently, she closed her eyes.

Then the warmth disappeared and the cold night air of the Upper Reaches hit her again.

She looked up and saw the beasts fleeing the Mountain side for the cold blueness of the open chasm. She pushed back a pile of dead Dusk-rats which still lay on top of her. To her surprise, they all had arrows embedded in their bodies.

Rhea stood upright. Other Faemir were also shaking themselves free of the dead rats. All around were the quivering bodies of grale, many with arrows protruding from their eye sockets. She looked up, and there, to her amazement, she saw what must have been over two hundred windriders hovering not far above ground.

'Formation!' Valkyra's voice called the Faemir to renew the battle.

'No formation.' The voice was almost identical in tone and pitch, but it came from the sky.

Three windriders, each carrying someone, landed not far from the Faemir warriors. Verlinden, Atreu and Teyth unstrapped themselves and stepped forward to allow the windriders to re-join the others in the safety of mid-air.

'The war is over,' said Verlinden.

'Formation!' cried Valkyra again.

'No formation!' cried Verlinden, walking forward to face her sister.

The Faemir warriors, still stunned by the turn of events, stood around in confusion, unable to decide what to do.

'The war between Faemir and Maelir is over,' said Verlinden. 'We all have a new enemy, or at least an old enemy which has returned – the Nazir.'

'What are you talking about?' said Rhea.

'These beasts that you've been fighting – they are Dusk-spawn. The Nazir are the real enemy of both our peoples.'

'Liar,' screamed Valkyra. 'Don't listen to her. I am your leader.'

Atreu started walking towards the Faemir. 'The windriders are here to take you to the safety of the Keep,' he said.

'Don't listen to him,' said Valkyra, 'They will imprison us.'

'She's wrong,' said Atreu, walking closer towards Valkyra and fighting the wave of fear that threatened to engulf him. 'We need all of you. It will take our combined armies to defeat the Nazir. You've only had a taste of what they can do.'

'Formation!' cried Valkyra again, as Atreu approached.

None of the Faemir moved.

Atreu stood a few paces away from Valkyra and looked her in the eyes. 'We can't let you return after what you did.'

Valkyra laughed. 'I'll return when I choose to return. And next time I'll bring the entire Faemir army with me.'

Atreu still kept his gaze fixed on her but he addressed the remaining Faemir warriors. 'You won't be prisoners,' he said. 'You can keep your swords. We believe you have left your injured ups-lope. We have great Healers in the Keep – just ask your leader here. We'll take all those you abandoned with us as well.'

An all-embracing silence weighed down on the Faemir.

Rhea finally sheathed her sword and started walking towards Verlinden and Teyth.

The others wavered, but one by one they sheathed their bloodied swords.

'Formation!' cried Valkyra, her voice ringing across the Mountain. Again and again she screamed the word until her voice cracked, but the Faemir ignored her and began walking behind Rhea.

Valkyra glared at Atreu with venom in her eyes. 'You think this is over,' she said to him in a low voice. 'I see there are two Ascenders who I must have overlooked.'

She lunged at him with her sword, but was thrown off-balance by another tremor. Atreu stayed on his feet and continued to stare at her.

Before she had regained her footing, Teyth had run the distance between them and now stood next to his brother, brandishing his battle-axe.

'So, Teyth, you think you can best me this time?'

Teyth felt the baresark fury grow within him. He knew Valkyra threatened his life this time.

He pushed his brother away. 'If you attack me now,' he said, 'I will kill you.' He clenched his teeth.

Then Valkyra lunged at him and sword met axe with a noise that rang around the Mountain. Again, she came at him – no finesse, no skilful manoeuvres, just raw fury. Teyth's axe met her every thrust, blocking and parrying.

Time and again, the Mountain shook under their feet and they fell sprawled to the ground, only to jump back up and resume the battle.

And as sword clashed with axe, Atreu could see the darkness massing again deep in the chasm. And all around more chasms were appearing.

'Quickly,' he cried. 'They're coming.'

The windriders flew towards the Faemir. There was a moment of hesitation, as they hovered just above their heads, but then they landed and began strapping the Faemir into their harnesses.

Riell landed next to Atreu. 'Come on – let's go.'

'What about Teyth?'

'We'll try to get him, Atreu, but unless he defeats Valkyra, I don't think it will be possible.'

Atreu and Verlinden were the last two to be airborne. The Mountain still heaved below them and Valkyra and Teyth were locked in combat.

Atreu saw them as they stood toe-to-toe, weapons clashing furiously. The ground was still convulsing and they fell continuously, only to get up again and resume the fight, not wearying – if anything, each growing stronger as the battle continued.

And then the Dusk-spawn re-emerged from the chasm. The dark horde focused in on the last remaining living things before them. If Valkyra and Teyth noticed the grale and Dusk-rats bearing down on them, they gave no indication. Their battle continued.

As Atreu watched, he saw one of the windriders swoop down so that he hovered just behind Teyth. For a moment he thought Teyth would choose not to be rescued from the approaching horde. Then Teyth reached up with his free hand and allowed himself to be taken up.

Just as he left the ground, Valkyra lunged forward and grabbed his legs, and the three now flew just above the heads of the oncoming grale. Atreu could see the windrider was losing the little altitude he had gained – all three were in danger of falling into the seething mass of Dusk creatures. Then the windrider steered towards the main chasm from which the beasts were emerging and he caught a strong updraught. He quickly gained altitude and was now soaring high above the chasm.

But the battle was not over. Teyth and Valkyra rained blows on each other with their free hands. Several of the windrider archers started to fly in their direction.

Then it happened.

For Atreu it was unreal, like watching someone underwater. His night vision gave him a better view than anyone else, and he cursed the clarity of his sight. He saw Teyth simply let go of the windrider, just as they were above the middle of the chasm. Teyth and Valkyra were still locked in a bizarre embrace as they disappeared into the Mountain.

Atreu tried to catch Verlinden's eye, but she was looking away. As Riell tilted and turned in mid-air to join the others, Atreu shot one last glance down below.

A chill like no other chill he had ever known swept through the length and breadth of his body. The Mountain lay below him, pitted and scarred by chasm after dark chasm. And from the scars they now emerged, pushing their way past their Dusk minions, a purposefulness in their movements distinguishing them from the grale and rats they had sent to pave the way. Sharp-boned and angular, with twisted limbs and pale lidless eyes, they came. There were no shrieks, no cries, no screams, no howls, no clamour.

Silently, the Nazir claimed the Summit.

Epilogue

The Reader lingered over the final words for a moment, then slowly, reverently, closed the book.

'So, my young friend,' he said, without turning around, 'you have decided to join me again.'

'How did you know I was here?' said the voice behind him.

The old man lifted the book which now lay flat on his open palm. 'This told me.'

'And all these other books, what do they tell you?'

'Everything, my young friend, I learn everything from them.'

He took another book from the shelf with his free hand and held it the same way he was holding the first book. Turning in the direction of the voice, he said, 'Do you see how I've learnt balance from these two books?'

'Equinox.'

'Yes, my young friend, the balance of Equinox.'

'Have they learned, though, those who I have left behind?'

The Reader shook his head slowly. 'We can never be sure until the next book tells us, but the uncertainty, the expectation, that is the joy of it, is it not?'

'Yes, that is the joy. But, tell me, where am I?'

The old man laughed. 'A *where* question. It has been a long time since someone has asked me that. You are within the tale, of course, as we all are.'

'I see ... and who am I?'

The old man stopped laughing and turned back towards the shelf. 'You are now a Reader, like me.'

'But I once had a name, didn't I?'

'Yes, my young friend, you were given a name, but I think you can work out what it was without my help.'

The old man placed the two books back on the shelf. He ran his fingers across their spines until he came to the next one.

'Ah, the third one,' he said.

Dear Reader

Thank you for reading *Equinox* and continuing the journey with Atreu, Verlinden and the others. Sorry we had to leave them at such a cliff-hanger, but The Books of Ascension trilogy is a single continuous story, so I hope you're keen to see how the final mysteries are uncovered. I've done everything I can to make sure there are no cliff-hangers or loose threads at the end of the final book, and if you want to find out what happens to some of the characters from *Zenith* that didn't appear in *Equinox*, you won't be disappointed with *Eclipse*.

A special thanks to those of you who take the time to review my books for other readers. Whether you've written a review or not, if you enjoyed *Zenith* and *Equinox*, I'd love to hear from you. I reply to everyone who drops in and leaves a comment. I like hear from readers, so please do. The easiest way to leave a comment or question is through the Contact Dirk form on my website (www.dirkstrasser.com/contact-dirk.html).

Looking forward to hearing from you.
Dirk Strasser

Eclipse: The Lost Book of Ascension

Dirk Strasser

Eclipse

What happens if the days keep getting shorter?
And shorter?
Until there is an eternal night?

Eclipse

What happens as the darkness grows?
And the creatures of dusk take control of the Mountain?
And the quest for the lost Book is the only hope?

Can you see the story breathing?

Stories of the Sand

Dirk Strasser

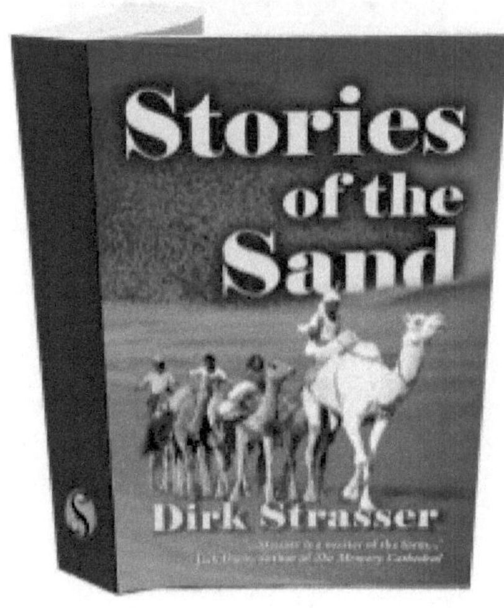

Watch as the sands take shape...

A desert wind whispers of memory and regret
An army marches high in the golden skies
A traveller grows tired of seeing the end of the world
A man no longer wants to be human
A people run eternally from the rising sun

'Dirk Strasser is a master practitioner of... the short story. This complex and intelligent collection... leaves an indelible after-image in the mind's eye.'
    –Isobelle Carmody, author of *The Obernewtyn Chronicles*

About Dirk Strasser

Dirk Strasser has won multiple Australian Publisher Association Awards and a Ditmar for Best Professional Achievement. His short story, 'The Doppelgänger Effect', appeared in the World Fantasy Award-winning anthology, *Dreaming Down Under*. His short fiction has been translated into a number of languages, and his acclaimed fantasy trilogy, The Books of Ascension – *Zenith*, *Equinox* and *Eclipse* – has also been published in German. His fantasy and science fiction short stories have been collected in *Stories of the Sand*. He founded the Aurealis Awards and has co-published and co-edited *Aurealis* magazine for over 25 years.

www.dirkstrasser.com

Twitter: @DirkStrasser

Join the conversation about The Books of Ascension with #booksofascension

Glossary

Ascenders – those twins who, in their eighteenth year, make the Ascent to the Summit of the Mountain in order to gain entry into one of the Holy Orders

Ascent – the Ritual, formalised by the Holy Orders, of making the journey to the Summit of the Mountain for Zenith

Coveyn – a band of Faemir warriors

Crosanct – the monastery located at one of the few gaps in the continuous wall of cliffs that separate the Mid-Reaches from the Upper Reaches

Dusk People (Nazir) – the people who long ago had been banished from the Mountain by the Maelir to live on the Steppes, forever in the Mountain's shadow

Dusk-rat – a small, dangerous, light-sensitive rodent of the Steppes

Equinox – the time of year when day and night are in perfect balance and when Ascenders are judged

Faelen – an insulting term used by Faemir to describe women who live with the Maelir

Faemir – the race of women who seek to destroy Maelir culture and civilisation

Felsen – the Holy Order of the Rock, characterised by austerity and powers of meditation

Grale – ferocious, light-sensitive beasts from the Steppes

Liche – the Holy Order of the Light, characterised by their use of astute arguments and clever word play

Lower Reacher – a Maelir from the Lower Reaches

Lower Reaches – the lower, sparsely populated region of the Mountain bordering on the Steppes

Maelir – the race of males who control and dominate all aspects of life on the Mountain

Maelstrom – the giant river which flows down the Mountain

Maelur – the leader who brought the Maelir to the Mountain and made the first Ascent

Mid-Reacher – a Maelir from the Mid-Reaches

Mid-Reaches – the densely populated middle region of the Mountain, separated from the Lower Reaches by the Rimforest

Nazir – the Dusk People

Order of the Light – the Liche Holy Order

Order of the Rock – the Felsen Holy Order

R'angkur – a meditative technique taught by the Felsen at Crosanct which allows people to spontaneously generate body heat and withstand extreme cold

Rimforest – the ring of forest which encircles the Mountain, separating the Lower Reaches from the Mid-Reaches

Rituals – practices and techniques used by the Holy Orders as part of the Ascent

R'lung – the herb used by Liche Holy Men to enable them to travel long distances without rest

Sage – the title given to the Holy Man appointed to oversee an Ascent

Steppes – the flat region at the base of the Mountain which always lies in its shadow

Talisman – the object given to an Ascender by his sage which will determine the nature of his Ascent

Upper Reaches – the frozen upper region of the Mountain separated from the Mid-Reaches by a ring of cliffs

Watcher – a Faemir whose task is to secretly observe Maelir in order to gain advantage in future battles

Windriders – the former Ascenders who ride the winds of the Upper Reaches with constructed wings and whose function is to aid and protect the Holy Orders

Zenith – the phenomenon which occurs during nine days in midsummer where the sun passes directly over the highest point of the Mountain, the ultimate mystic power of which is experienced by twins at the Summit